MW00623010

CHECKMATE CHARLIE

THE DRAGON MAGE BOOK 9

SCOTT BARON

Copyright © 2019 by Scott Baron

All rights reserved.

Print Edition ISBN 978-1-945996-31-3

No part of this book may be reproduced in any form or by any electronic or mechanical means, including information storage and retrieval systems, without written permission from the author, except for the use of brief quotations in a book review.

"The solar system consists of Jupiter, plus debris."
– Isaac Asimov

CHAPTER ONE

Some of the bodies strewn across the grounds of the Tslavar base were still intact, a few even seemed as if they might be sleeping, if not for the unnatural angles of their necks and limbs, that is. The rest, however, had clearly not been so fortunate.

The facility was located on a small planet in the heart of a piece of territory quietly controlled by Visla Dominus, yet it had somehow been kept out of public awareness, mostly via a concerted effort at anonymity. Yet, it had been found. Anything could be found, if you wanted it badly enough.

Charlie walked through the carnage, stepping over disembodied limbs and slick pools of Tslavar blood. His defenses were up, spells ready to be cast if needed, but he knew none of that was necessary. The killing had been not only violent, but also very, very thorough.

Behind him a small team of rebel pirates, as well as one very perplexed, sword-bearing woman, were fanning out through the facility, seeing if there were any weapons, supplies, or intelligence that could be recovered. In a facility like this, there was bound to be at least something of use. But that was not of interest to the bringer of death.

Dozens upon dozens had been slain. Skilled fighters and casters among them. Even some of Visla Dominus's elite mercenary shock troops lay among the dead, their many years of training unable to save them.

To the layman, it would appear that a fighting force of extraordinary magnitude had hit the facility with a well-coordinated attack, overwhelming the occupants with sheer numbers and violence. But Charlie and the others knew better. It wasn't a hit team they were looking for. Not by a long shot.

This wasn't the work of a death squad. This was the work of one *very* angry man.

"Found him," Charlie said, when he spotted the pale form of his dear friend sitting atop a ruined structure, the limbs of those crushed as it crumbled atop them jutting from beneath the rubble. "You all stay back here. I've got this."

Charlie stepped over bodies and rubble as he drew closer to his blood-covered friend. The carnage didn't faze him. This was not the first such scene of death they'd come across in the past several days. Charlie just hoped he might be able to make it the last. At least until they had some semblance of a plan. For now, however, simply retrieving the Geist was his priority.

The Wampeh was staring out at nothing, his gaze unfocused as he fiddled absentmindedly with the incredibly dangerous wand in his hands. He'd let loose with it, quite obviously not even attempting to rein in the powerful weapon's highly volatile magic. The result was a level of indiscriminate slaughter most unusual for one of his skill.

But Bawb wasn't himself. Not since the capture of his love by their foe. An enemy who had hectored them across both time and space. And now, Visla Malalia Maktan, aka Visla Dominus, had his Ootaki love in her grasp, and he'd been utterly powerless to stop her.

And worst of all, it was his own friend's Magus stone that had made her capture possible.

Leila. Charlie's queen. His and Hunze's friend. And it was her stone, her power, that had brought this about. An ancient, immense magic capable of overwhelming even his Ootaki love. And Bawb had run away.

It was eating at him, consuming him like an angry fire burning in his gut, though he knew full well that he had not done so out of cowardice, but rather, a logical calculus. It was a decision made in an instant. A realization that he simply could not hope to overcome the magic coming his way. And if he were to fall on that day, there would be no hope of rescuing Hunze later.

So run he did. Something utterly foreign to the master assassin. But survival was key, and, thus, he acted immediately and without a second thought.

"Hey, man," Charlie said, reaching out to him through their silent, magical bond.

They were friends. Comrades. Brothers. But even so, in his current state of despair, it would be a very bad idea to sneak up on the Geist––as if you could actually *sneak* up on him, that is.

Charlie stepped over a toppled chunk of the building and sat down beside the silent Wampeh. "Hey, Bob."

"Charlie," the assassin replied, quietly.

"Been busy, I see," he noted.

Bawb nodded, but remained silent, his anguish palpable.

Charlie simply sat quietly beside him a long moment. The energy crackling off of his friend was still dangerous, but he seemed to have calmed, at least somewhat, getting it under control in his presence. That it was Hunze's Ootaki hair he wore that gave him such magic was definitely *not* helping the situation.

"Listen, man. A lot has gone down in the last couple of days. There's a lot we need to catch you up on. We really should get back to the fleet. We have more ships now, and some new allies as well. And news from Earth, even," Charlie said, rising to his feet. "Come on. Let's get back and get you cleaned up. Once you're a bit less gore covered, you and I can grab something to eat and talk about it. If you want, I mean."

Bawb turned his head and flashed a bloody, sharp-fanged smile. "I'm not hungry," he said in a way that actually frightened Charlie a little.

Charlie maintained a neutral expression, and he managed to keep his adrenaline from spiking, thanks to Ser Baruud's extensive training. But the realization that his friend had been feeding, and on non-powered victims, at that, was horrifying.

This was not good. This was *very* not good. Bawb had gone off the rails, and Charlie really, *really*, needed to get him to the other Wampeh Ghalian. They'd know how best to help him, because in matters like this, despite their friendship and bond, Charlie was way out of his depth.

Bawb and his kind simply didn't feed off of non-powered beings. There was no reason to. No need. For him to have done so in his rage illustrated the true depths of his despair. The longer he went without finding Hunze, the more unhinged he'd become.

The prior slaughters they'd come across were at least straightforward scenes of carnage and torture. But if these had signs of Wampeh Ghalian feeding, they'd need to be even more thorough in their cleansing of the site than previously.

"We'll find her, man. But we've gotta go," Charlie said, gingerly resting his hand on his friend's shoulder.

Bawb looked at Charlie's hand, then back to his face. There was a hint of fear in his friend's eyes, and in that moment of realization, Bawb's mind cleared, at least a bit.

"Right. We should get back," the Wampeh muttered, then rose to his feet and walked through the ranks of their search party and back to the waiting ships.

"Freya, you read me?" Charlie asked over comms.

"Yep, what's up?"

"This place is a mess, and it might compromise us. We need it cleansed. I'm talking scorched earth, here. Could you use your plasma cannons to torch the place top to bottom?"

"Of course she can," Daisy said softly at his side.

"Damn, you're a quiet one," he said of her stealthy arrival.

"When I want to be. But yeah, don't worry about this place. We'll burn it all," she said with a little grin. "And we'll even hit it with some pulse blasts, just to fuck with 'em. They won't know what the hell happened here."

Charlie smiled. Daisy was not one to mess around, and once she got going, she was definitely a force of nature. And her knack for asymmetrical warfare tactics was proving to be a boon already.

"I like it," Charlie said. "Leave them wondering what they're up against."

"Precisely. From what I hear, they don't really understand tech, so we can stage this place to look all kinds of confusing to them. Keep 'em on their heels."

"Cool. Thanks, Daisy."

She looked over at his blood-soaked friend and felt a pang of sympathy. "You got it. Now, go take care of your friend. He looks like he needs someone to talk to. Like, *really* needs it."

"He's not exactly the chatty type on the best of days."

"Maybe not, but he can't keep going on like this."

"I know," Charlie said, wondering if anything he might say could possibly help. "I know."

CHAPTER TWO

Bawb settled down quietly aboard Freya, avoiding Leila's sidelong glance from her seat, quickly noting all aspects of the unusual ship that he could, as was his assassin way. The insanely advanced tech, however, proved to be a bit difficult to intuit, even after his time on Earth.

Freya was her own thing. Her build design, though initially created by AI and human minds, had been birthed in a most unconventional manner. And since that day, every aspect of her development had been very, *very*, outside of parameters. For pretty much everyone she met, she was the most cutting-edge craft they'd ever seen, but they had no idea how any of her systems really worked.

Daisy did, of course. But after nearly two decades with her AI offspring, the two had grown not only close, as might be expected of mother and daughter, but also tight as battle buddies who had gone through the deepest of shit and come out the other side in one piece. Daisy knew every inch of the ship, and in that, she was alone.

Of course, Freya could shift the nanites coursing throughout her structure to make her inner functioning more apparent for visitors, but at the moment she was focused on other things. Several, to be exact.

Bawb had quietly trailed Charlie into the AI ship rather than the other available vessels when they prepped for liftoff. Charlie had thought his Wampeh friend would opt for one of the magically powered craft that had been part of their search team, but Bawb simply followed him aboard the Earth ship and took a seat.

Leila had come along on the search for their Wampeh friend, but had stayed aboard Freya, protected by the deadly craft while remaining close to Charlie as they surveyed yet another site of carnage. After her capture by Malalia, Charlie wasn't about to let her out of his sight again.

But Bawb's choice of craft now put them both in an uncomfortable position. Charlie had recovered his love, but the Wampeh had lost his. Not to mention that Hunze had been lost because of Leila, in her own, entirely unintentional, way.

Bawb ignored her and sat silently in his ergonomic seat, staring ahead even as Freya torched the scene of his wrath, cleansing all signs of his unleashed violence, disposing of any identifying traces that might hint at Ghalian involvement. He didn't even bother watching the destruction on her internal monitors.

Daisy swiveled in her seat to face her guests. "So. We should talk. This guy's not okay in the head. What exactly do we do with him?" she quietly asked Charlie and Leila.

"We take him back to the others. Get him cleaned up. After that, I'm really not sure," Charlie replied. "I'm hoping the Ghalian have some secret trick up their sleeves for situations like this. Just get us back to the rally point and we'll go from there."

"I feel horrible," Leila said in a hush, her fingers

absentmindedly touching the Magus stone hanging around her neck.

Her stone, her power, had nearly killed him. And that might have almost been a better outcome in her ailing friend's mind. Because her stone had been what caused Hunze to be captured in the first place. And getting her back would be a challenge unlike any they'd ever faced.

The Malalia they were facing now was a whole lot more dangerous than the one they'd defeated on ancient Earth all those years ago.

"It wasn't your fault," Charlie soothed. "You didn't do it. Malalia did. You were used for your connection to that Magus stone, and quite creatively at that. It wasn't your fault. Bawb knows it, Leila. He may be hurting, but he's a very logical man."

"But he won't even look at me. He can't. Every time he does, you can see the anger in his eyes. He blames me."

"He's distraught, and this'll take time. But eventually he'll come around. We've been through too much together." Charlie turned to look at his Wampeh friend seated across the cabin. *"Hey, you want to join us and talk about this?"* Charlie asked him with their silent connection.

Bawb said nothing.

"He still won't answer me," Charlie said. "I think for now we'll need to let the Wampeh handle him when we land."

"He didn't say anything, Daze. What does he mean, 'won't answer him'?" Sarah asked inside Daisy's head.

The guy's talking to himself, Daisy silently replied. *I hope Charlie hasn't lost it too.*

"Well, to be fair, you talk to yourself all the time too."

But you're in there, so it's different.

"No telling what he's got going on in his head either," Sarah replied. *"Maybe he's got some secret friend living in there too."*

"Won't answer you?" Daisy asked casually.

Charlie realized his new friend hadn't ever seen him with

Ara or Bawb. "Oh, yeah, that. Sorry, I forgot you didn't know. We share a bond with our Zomoki friend. It's kind of like a silent link between us."

"*Ha!*"

Shut up, Sis.

"But I don't think he's in the mood to talk at the moment. Are we almost there?" Charlie asked.

"Three minutes," Freya replied.

It was a little odd, the way the ship was always listening, but Charlie was getting used to the ever-present AI minds of modern times. He just didn't usually fly with one. But since he and Ara had been separated, it had become a necessity. And finding his Zomoki friend was very high on his list of priorities. It was a strange feeling, not sensing her anywhere nearby. Even when she had been trapped on Earth, he still *felt* her. But this? There was no trace.

Wherever she was, it was nowhere nearby.

Freya dropped out of warp and passed through the pirate fleet, then landed a few minutes later among the few ships that had come down to the surface of the rebel force's new rally point world. Given what had happened at their prior safe harbor, most opted to stay aloft.

Freya did a quick scan, tapping into the small, stealthy micro-satellites she'd dropped in orbit. No sign of anything out of the ordinary. They were safe, for now. She opened her airlock doors, and Bawb silently rose, then wandered off on his own, without a word.

"He hates me," Leila said when he left.

"He doesn't hate you. He just misses her, and he's worried. And knowing it wasn't your fault won't stop the hurt, no matter what his rational mind tells him, so just let it go for now," Charlie replied. "We'll get her back. And once we do, he'll be better."

He truly hoped they could pull that off, because Charlie had

9

no idea what the other Wampeh Ghalian would do if one of
their own went *truly* off the rails, no matter how valuable a
member of the order he was.

CHAPTER THREE

Once her guests had disembarked, Daisy stepped out of her ship and crossed the landing area toward the grounded form of Marty's bulk. He was surrounded by a mishmash of pirate vessels, the crews of each of them enjoying some downtime on the surface, while they also casually made sure the AI ship and his teenage friends didn't get any wise ideas and fly off anywhere.

Like a group of protective big brothers, the pirates were keeping a watchful eye on Arlo, Kara, and Vee. Like a group of dangerous, gregarious, and heavily armed big brothers, that is.

Daisy could see the teens sulking from a hundred meters away, so obvious was their misery at being stuck there like that. But it was necessary, and despite understanding their reasoning for doing what they'd done, nevertheless, Daisy was not amused at being forced to chase her kid and his friends across a freaking galaxy to save their asses from Arlo's poorly thought out attempt to impress a girl.

That they'd actually pulled off not only the warp to the brink of the portal so flawlessly, but also managed to then utilize a warp in the magical realm piggybacking with Kara's growing power once they had crossed over, was not lost on Daisy. And, despite her anger, she was secretly quite pleased to see they'd managed not one but two feats of rather impressive navigation. And while combining warp tech and magic, no less.

Freya herself had said few AIs could have managed that. Of course, Marty was her and Joshua's kid, so she was bound to be a little biased. But her point was valid. What they'd done was more than many of the more seasoned AIs in the fleet could have pulled off, and they did it without the benefit of extensive combat experience.

Like it or not, both Daisy and Freya had to accept the reality that their kids were growing up, and pretty soon they'd be doing whatever they wanted, whenever they wanted, regardless of what their parents said. They weren't quite there yet, however, and the two were damn sure the kids would be as prepared as possible when that time finally arrived.

Unexpected, however, was the impromptu addition of two new teens to the equation. Ripley, Daisy could handle. She was her niece, after all, and Sarah had been training her up right pretty much since birth. Unfortunately, she was back in Earth's galaxy.

Kara and Vee, on the other hand, had been raised to be proper females of power users' families. A retinue of guards would keep them safe, so all they needed to focus on were social skills and the other things expected of young women of their stature in that realm. Fighting was simply not on their agendas.

Until now.

"If I'm the one watching over them, then you can be damn sure they're gonna learn how to fight," Daisy had decided when she realized she was now going to be Mama Bear to a pair of new cubs.

"You think they'll take to it?" Sarah asked.

"I hope so. Arlo's got skills, despite the stupid shit his brain convinces him to do."

"Teen brain," Sarah chuckled.

"Whatever the excuse, he was still way out of line this time. I mean, what the hell was he thinking? Jumping across galaxies like that?"

"He wasn't thinking, Daze. There's a girl involved. You know how teenage boys can be."

"Don't remind me. Anyway, whatever brought it all about, I've gotta get these kids at least a little bit prepared for whatever may come."

"But you grounded them. Quite literally, in Marty's case," Sarah noted.

"Yeah, but fighting is coming, Sis. This is war, so their real punishment will have to wait until we're safe."

"Seems kind of funny, training the kids to fight and be a part of all this when you're just going to ground them again when it's all over."

"Necessity makes for unusual circumstances, I guess. Now, which of these pirate fellas do you reckon wants to be a demonstration partner?"

Kara and Vee watched Arlo's mom run through a laundry list of fighting styles that would be most effective for combatants of their size and strength. Techniques that relied more on leverage and speed than brute strength.

Daisy could get away with those as well, of course. Her genetically enhanced muscles and bones were more than capable of it. But the teens from another world would need more specialized training. Interestingly enough, Daisy found as they got into the nitty gritty of it, that Kara was stronger than she looked. And with her father being weak and in danger, the teenager actually *wanted* to fight.

But Daisy was also well aware that it was when you'd learned the basics of a combat technique that you were most dangerous, to yourself. The overconfidence of getting an initial handle on a new skill made many take unnecessary risks, so she was very careful to drill that tidbit into the teens' heads.

"You're new to this. Don't get cocky. Cocky gets you captured or killed. You got it?"

"Jeez, Mom. Dramatic much?" Arlo grumbled.

"Hey, mister. You've trained with me long enough to know it's true."

"Yeah, I guess," the teen reluctantly agreed. "But I think Kara's got a little more going for her than I ever did."

"He's not wrong about that," Sarah noted.

It was true, Kara's powers were growing exponentially now that she had been afforded a solid period of time without Malalia siphoning off her energy. And her concern for her weakened father was only strengthening her resolve and driving her to try harder.

Revenge wasn't the best of reasons to enter into combat, but it certainly did tend to drive one to train all that much harder in preparation for it, and that was good enough for Daisy.

And if Kara could actually learn to wield her magic *while* she was fighting, *then* the girl could really become a valuable asset. But until that happened, Daisy was going to train her to defend herself as best she could without relying on any of that hocus-pocus crap. A punch in the balls could drop an opponent just as well as any spell could. Better, even, Daisy suspected. And that would have to suffice for now.

"Arlo, run them through the form again," Daisy said, then stepped back to watch her son push aside his jovial teenager mask and get serious once again.

He may have been a goof, but he was a goof she and Vince had been training since he was a wee boy, and despite his silliness, Arlo was one hell of a fighter when he put his mind to it. And as a peer, having him train the girls made the unusual activity a bit more palatable for them. And as an added bonus, it afforded his mother a chance to step back and really observe.

"You know, Daze, I think these two might be okay," Sarah said as Kara and Vee moved through the lesson.

Yeah, they're picking it up quickly, Daisy agreed. *But practice is different than combat. Let's just hope we never wind up in a position where we need to actually test their skills.*

CHAPTER FOUR

Leila had sought out the group of master assassins who were currently embedded with the rebel pirate fleet shortly after they landed. While several had departed after the fiasco with Visla Dominus's ships attacking their prior rally point, a few had opted to remain with their new allies. At least for a bit longer. Plans had to be made, and there was still much to discuss.

To that end, Malalia Maktan's former captive had quite a lot to talk with them about when she went seeking an audience.

"You're Charlie's woman," Farmatta said with a warm, grandmotherly smile.

Leila had already been informed of the true nature of the woman, as well as the other master assassins of the order who were now part of their cause.

"Yes," she replied. "Charlie and I are together."

"Glad to see it. He seems like a nice young man," the old woman said, inhabiting her sweet old lady persona by pure second nature.

"That he is. But I've come to speak with you about more pressing matters. Matters that will be of direct interest to the Wampeh Ghalian."

Farmatta's smile didn't waver a millimeter, but the tiniest flash of interest sparked in her eyes. "Oh? And what would you wish to discuss with us?" she asked.

Leila noted that two other Wampeh had silently arrived. One particularly large man, hunched over his crutch—the one called Leif, she'd been told. The other was a tall, slender woman with a sword strapped to her back. Zilara, the de facto leader of the bunch.

Apparently, they were *always* aware of the goings-on around them, their eyes and ears picking out tidbits of interest. And though they'd been deep in conversations with the nearby pirate rebels, Leila's words had caught their attention.

Kort and Wagyah were out gathering intelligence first-hand, and Pimbrak was still away. The only other Wampeh Ghalian master present on this world was Bawb, and he'd gone off to be with his thoughts. Charlie had headed out to find him, hoping to perhaps talk him down, at least a little.

But there was no time to think about what he was doing at the moment. That was his task. This one was Leila's.

"You already know that the woman known as Mareh is not what she seemed," Leila began.

"Indeed. It seems Visla Palmarian's wife is quite the master of infiltration and disguise," Leif noted.

"It's not just that she embedded herself in their lives," Leila continued. "It's that she has been stealing power from Visla Palmarian and his daughter for years upon years. And before that, she was doing the same to countless other power users. I know, not only because she told me as much, but because I've known her since childhood. Mareh Palmarian is not just Visla Dominus. That's bad enough, but she is also Malalia Maktan."

The Wampeh did not react with even a modicum of surprise.

"Yes, we've heard," Farmatta said. "And a disturbing bit of information, that is. The Maktans were a blight, even before that one went mad and destroyed Tolemac. Though we should thank her, really. Her overstep helped trigger the downfall of the Council of Twenty."

"But she steals Wampeh blood to maintain her youth and give her the ability to take another's power."

That did cause a slight stir.

"It is a most unusual trait that she possesses," Zilara noted. "It shouldn't be possible. A one-in-millions occurrence. But it's just our luck that this Maktan woman should be the one who has this ability."

"She used it to gain a huge amount of power several thousand years ago, when we fought her last."

"We've heard of this battle. As well as the outcome. Though, it would seem she was not as vanquished as you had originally believed," Farmatta said. "And if she has been stealing Wampeh blood from members of our order, I think we can now gather at whose hands many of our missing members may have fallen."

"She doesn't simply drain them, though. She keeps them alive, I think."

Now Leila had the others' attention.

"What do you mean by that, dear?" Farmatta asked, the old woman's kind eyes hard behind the sweet façade.

"When I was taken back to the tower on Slafara as a prisoner, the captain of the ship I was on mentioned he had one more package to pick up and deliver. When we arrived at the Palmarian estate the next day, there was a Wampeh in chains, being led into the cells. He was hooded, but with the complexion, it was impossible to mistake him for anything else."

"Did he have a name?" Zilara asked.

"None was mentioned, and I couldn't see his face. I'm sorry."

"It's not your fault. They were careless enough in merely allowing you to catch sight of him at all," the slender woman replied. She turned to her fellow assassins. "You know what this means."

They nodded.

"Excuse me? What does it mean?" Leila asked.

Zilara allowed herself a rare sigh. "It means that things are a great deal more complicated than we had originally anticipated. And, given the true nature of our enemy, it is safe to assume that our spies in the Palmarian estate have been compromised."

"You had spies there? I didn't see any."

"And *you* wouldn't. But one of Dominus's power could. And it has been some time since we've received any word from Pimbrak."

"Isn't he one of the six masters?" Leila asked.

"He is. And unrivaled at the use of shimmer cloaks and disguises. But he has gone silent. And right around the time of your escape. If what you say is true, and with the amount of upheaval in that estate at that time, he would have returned with this news well before now."

"But the fleet jumped away when we were attacked."

"Yes, but we Ghalian have ways to keep in touch. And, given what we've seen, we should have heard from him by now. In the absence of such contact, we must assume him dead. Or worse."

"Worse?"

"As you've just informed us," Zilara said, "it seems death would be the easy way out. He may very well have become a meal for his captor. And if she is as powerful as you say, she is undoubtedly hard at work breaking his mind. He's a strong one, and unlikely to give up information without a fight, but this would explain how our training facility's location was compromised. As well as the fleet."

"So what you're saying is, anything he knew of our plans might now be compromised?" Leila realized.

"I fear so," Zilara replied with a sad look in her eye. "In which case, I can only hope he finds a way to end himself before any further damage is done." She turned to the large cripple. "Leif, have our operatives send word to all facilities, safe houses, and allies. They need to enact the compromise protocols. Tell them to follow option nineteen."

"What's option nineteen?" Leila asked.

"For us to know and you not to," Zilara replied. "We have seventy such emergency protocols, but which we use is only decided at the last instant, as you've just seen. Even the number spoken aloud refers to a different procedure entirely. This way, whoever may have been compromised cannot be forced to give information they do not know. And for an enemy to go through all seventy options would give us more than enough time to not only note them, but counter as well."

"I'll be back shortly," Leif said, then turned to walk away, vanishing in his shimmer cloak in an instant.

"There's something else," Leila reluctantly said, touching her Magus stone.

"Oh?"

"It's about Bawb. I'm worried."

CHAPTER FIVE

"You sure you don't want to join me? I'm feeling pretty peckish after all of that space travel," Charlie said silently to his ailing friend.

Bawb still wasn't speaking much, but at least he did shake his head slightly this time, which was a marked improvement from his stony-faced demeanor of earlier that day. And he had cleaned off all of the Tslavar blood, so there was that. Not many things were quite as disconcerting as having your best friend casually chilling out while soaked in blood as if it was nothing. Even if he was an assassin.

Hell, Charlie was a gladiator and had slain a fair share in his time, but that didn't mean he wanted to have a layer of gore on him for any longer than the battle itself. Bawb, however, was in a different frame of mind. And it wasn't a good one.

"Listen, man. You've gotta eat something. I mean a real something. Food, you know? You're gonna wear yourself thin. Much as I know your limits are far greater than mine, or anyone I know, for that matter, we're still in some really dangerous waters here and can't afford to have you at diminished capacity. Hello? Earth to Bob?"

The Wampeh turned to Charlie slowly and fixed him with a tranquil gaze. *"I appreciate your concern, Charlie. I will be certain to acquire something from one of the many ships' galleys shortly,"* he said, then turned and walked away.

Yeah, sure, Bob. Nice try. I am totally not buying that for a minute, Charlie thought as he watched his friend drift off from the parked ships. It was terrible to see, though Charlie had witnessed a similar occurrence when Hunze had been frozen in stasis not that long ago.

She may have been taken from him, in a way, when that had happened, but it was different then. She wasn't in harm's way. She'd been trapped in stasis, but at least she was home and safe when that had happened. But now? She was not only in danger, but was in Malalia's clutches as well. And her hair was so incredibly powerful, that woman would stop at nothing to possess its magic.

Compared to before, it was about as bad a situation as could be. And Charlie was pretty sure it would only get worse before it got better. And with someone as dangerous as the Geist in play, *anything* could happen.

"Looks like he's not exactly a happy camper," Daisy said, walking over from the little patch of open ground, where she'd been drilling fighting techniques into not only Arlo and the girls, but some of the pirates who'd been observing and wanted to join in as well.

"Yeah, you could say that. His headspace is pretty damn far from clear, that's for sure," Charlie replied. "I saw your little practice session, by the way. The boy, he's got some skills. You train him up?"

"Arlo? Yeah, I've been teaching him since he was little. All of us have, though I don't think anyone expected him to need to put any of that stuff to actual use. We won the war, after all. This was all supposed to be done with. And yet, here we are. In another conflict. And now he's sparring with space-faring pirates and raiders," she said, shaking her head. "It's not a mother's first choice for their kid, ya know?"

"I can imagine. But he was holding his own pretty well. I know how these pirates can be. They wouldn't give him an easy pass just because he's young. In their world, it's perfectly fine to pummel a teen if it helps him learn faster." He glanced at the sword strapped to Daisy's back. "Though I think in his case they might refrain, given who his mom is."

Daisy chuckled. "Wise choice. And after what he just did, I'm definitely going to be the one whooping his ass. Just as soon as we get home." She paused a moment. "And after he's done being grounded, that is."

"I can imagine. Running away to another galaxy? Oof, I can imagine how well that went over when you heard. So, how long you thinking?"

"Until he's twenty," she replied with a laugh.

"I saw that violet-skinned girl is still throwing some pretty serious stink-eye your way. Kara, the visla's daughter. Leila spent some time with her and the other one. Says they're good kids, though both seem to have grown up living pretty sheltered lives."

"They're sure as hell not sheltered anymore," Daisy said. "At least they're learning to defend themselves now. It's a crash course, but there's just no avoiding it."

"Not with what we're all up against," Charlie agreed.

"I feel bad for them, though. Especially Kara. I can imagine what she's going through. But just because you're worried about someone doesn't mean you can go rushing in with no plan. That's how people get killed."

"Or in her case, captured and drained of her power," Charlie noted. "I can sense it on her now. It's getting stronger. That kid's gonna pack one helluva wallop when she gets older."

Daisy looked at Charlie with a curious expression. "About that. How exactly does that work with you? Sensing magic and stuff. I mean, I get it that some of these magic people have skills and whatnot, but you're from Earth. You're human, like me."

23

"Well, to be fair, you're only *mostly* human, apparently," he replied. "And what a mindfuck that has to be. To be related to Malalia Maktan, of all people. The high queen bitch of the galaxy. I mean, damn, that's a surprise if ever there was one."

"He's got a point, Daze. Our great to the umpteenth power grandma is an alien wizard from another galaxy," Sarah silently noted.

Yeah, and a totally evil one at that, Daisy replied. *Just our luck, right?*

"But you said you're bonded with your pale buddy via *magic*? And with a space dragon, no less? How does that work? I mean, how is that even possible?"

"Long story short, we blood bonded by accident. The dragon and me, that is. Thing is, it was the sort of thing that kills pretty much everyone, but being from a different galaxy, my body reacted differently. And since then, things have kind of compounded."

"And your girlfriend? It looks like there's some tension between her and your buddy. Love triangle or something? If you don't mind my asking, that is."

"Wow. Smooth, Sis."

Bite me, Sarah.

"Ha, no. Nothing of the sort. In fact, Bawb is quite happily bonded with his own girlfriend."

"So why the drama?"

"Because Leila accidentally got her caught by Malalia. It wasn't her fault, and Malalia totally used her, but it's created some drama regardless."

"Oh, shit. Well, I guess I can understand that," Daisy replied. "But I'd hope he'd understand if it wasn't exactly her doing."

"He knows, and I know he doesn't really hold it against her. But he's distraught, and all I can do for now is just be the best friend possible. That, and try to get Hunze back."

Daisy felt a tingle on her back. Stabby was agitated.

A tall, pale woman appeared out of nowhere a moment later.

"Holy shit!" Daisy said, her now-magical sword instantly in her hand, her power whip crackling to life from her wrist.

"It's okay, she's one of ours," Charlie said.

"I know. But damn, you shouldn't sneak up on people like that."

Zilara merely smiled, but Charlie laughed heartily.

"Oh, if she was actually sneaking up on you, you'd be dead already. She's what's known as a Wampeh Ghalian."

"A what, now?"

"An assassin," Zilara said calmly as Daisy lowered her sword, her power whip falling silent. "I thought it would be helpful for you to see firsthand the functioning of shimmer cloaks and how their invisibility can be detected, on occasion. As I suspected, that unusual blade of yours is sensitive to power, though I've never seen anything like it. May I?"

"Sure," Daisy said, handing the bone sword over grip first.

"It appears to be quite dull, yet I sense tremendous potential," Zilara said as she ran her finger along Stabby's edge. "Bonded to his wielder, I take it?"

Daisy was impressed. "No one ever gets that."

"I am not no one."

"Obviously," Daisy replied with a grin. *I like this one.*

"Me too," Sarah agreed.

Zilara studied her a moment, the pale woman's calm gaze piercing deep. "You carry another within you," she finally said. "A great benefit in combat, I would think."

"How the hell did she know that?" Sarah exclaimed.

Zilara smiled. "Fear not. I was informed of this Sarah by your son while speaking with your ship. An amazing mind, that one, and a talented boy as well. He fights with great skill for his age, I might add, though he could benefit from a bit more discipline."

"Tell me about it," Daisy sighed.

"I'm sure you are very aware," the Wampeh joked. "But I

have come to speak with you about another topic. A *very* interesting one that could be of great use to us in the coming battle. Apparently, you possess the unique ability to defend against our enemy. Dominus, Malalia, call her what you will."

Daisy shifted uneasily. "Well, yeah. There's a reason for that. Apparently, we're related."

"You are related?" Zilara gasped. To shock a Wampeh Ghalian, the news was apparently an even bigger deal than she'd originally realized.

"Yeah. She was on my planet a few thousand years ago, and, apparently, she's my great-great-great-great––"

"I think she gets the idea," Charlie said.

Zilara seemed energized by the revelation. "This must be kept secret at all costs. If you truly possess a familial immunity to some of her spells, this could be an edge in combat that could turn the tide."

"If I knew how it worked," Daisy griped.

"That her spells were not working against you will already have her doubting her abilities. And that doubt might cause her to hesitate. And hesitation means defeat. I shall consult with the others."

"Before you do, there's one more thing I'd like to discuss, if you have a minute," Charlie said.

The look in Zilara's eyes told him she'd been expecting this. Expecting, but waiting for *him* to broach the subject. And now that he had, the conversation could finally be had.

CHAPTER SIX

"I will be fine," Bawb said without a trace of emotion in his voice.

The gathered Wampeh Ghalian masters studied him with calm eyes and blank expressions. In fact, to any observers, the conversation was as benign and relaxed as could be. The underlying tension, invisible to all but fellow members of the order, was anything but.

"This is why it is not done, Geist," Zilara said. "The life of a Wampeh Ghalian is a solitary one."

Bawb held her gaze but said nothing. Bonding with another was simply something Wampeh Ghalian did not do. In fact, only twice in the recorded history of the Wampeh Ghalian had a master done so. And in each instance, the choice had met with a poor outcome. One bad enough as to require the intervention of the other masters.

And that was what was being determined now. The others had come to assess him. To judge his level of damage. Whether or not he was still the man they trusted with their lives. For despite his infamy, if a Wampeh Ghalian––*any* Wampeh Ghalian––truly went off the rails and descended into madness, they would be culled by the others with brutal precision. A dangerous cancer in their order excised before it could spread and cause more damage.

Bawb knew this, of course. In fact, in his time, he had been called upon for just such an incident, rare as it may be.

"I am in control," he finally said.

"We've seen the images of the slaughter," Leif said, casually leaning on his magically charged crutch. "It was excessive. And––"

"And thorough," Bawb cut him off. "None were left to speak of it. And my interrogations were quite detailed."

A silence once again hung in the air. This time, Farmatta was the one to break it, the old woman cracking her knuckles and rolling her shoulders like a fighter readying for a match.

"It was, at that," she agreed. "And you fed. On the unpowered."

Bawb didn't blush, but his carefully maintained façade slipped for just an instant. "I did," he admitted. In that regard, he had gone overboard in his grief. The others had seen. There was no use trying to deny it.

Farmatta nodded once. "What's done is done. I assume you'll not do it again?"

"I shall not."

Farmatta shared a glance with the other Wampeh. Zilara locked gazes with her a moment before speaking at last. "Very well. We shall speak of this no further."

Bawb nodded, his jaw muscles twitching at the conflicting emotions still welling within him. He was safe from the Ghalian judgment, but he was not consoled, nor was he comforted. For now, that would have to suffice.

"I have a suggestion," Farmatta said as the invisible tension between them dissipated. "We've been faced with a few unpleasant surprises from our enemy of late. Let us take this opportunity to see about utilizing one of our own, shall we?"

. . .

The Wampeh Ghalian masters had quietly taken their leave of the other planet-bound rebels, heading across the globe to the opposite side entirely. They weren't completely sure what might happen, and a bit of distance would be the safest thing.

Of course, they had informed the captains of their plans. One wouldn't want to cause unnecessary panic among the fleet, after all.

"Oh, aren't you lovely," Farmatta said, the old woman's smile growing as she removed one of the five Bakana rods from its newly stitched carrying pouch.

She caressed the length of metal, reaching out carefully, seeing what she might sense from it. The rod in and of itself was nothing worth note. In fact, it seemed to have no power at all in its solitary state. But when its brothers came into play, *that* was when things got interesting. And with several additional rods present, it was getting *very* interesting indeed.

Farmatta's preferred combatives were all magical, due to her advanced age as much as her proficiency with spellcasting. The opportunity to utilize the Bakana rods excited her more than anything in recent memory.

To be able to share the power of those holding the other rods was an intoxicating prospect. And, as very skilled users, they all knew full well the dangers of the rods and would ensure they did not draw too much power from the others. For as a Bakana rod could enable one to cast with another's power, it could also drain all connected to dangerously low levels.

For that reason, Bakana rods had always been kept under close guard and only utilized in the most dire of circumstances. Until they were all thought to be destroyed, that is. Lost to the ages in one final, horrific battle.

But with Bawb's shocking surprise of not just a pair, but *five* of them, the prospect of actually utilizing one of the legendary weapons had aroused in Farmatta an enthusiasm she'd not felt in a great many years.

Zilara, Leif, and Bawb would wield three of the other rods, while Farmatta drew a bit of power from each of them, channeling it into a work of greater magic. It was for that reason that they had relocated to the other side of the planet. With the power she would be tapping into, there was always the possibility that things might get a bit out of hand. Unlikely, but possible. But with the fleet's safety in mind, it was far better to be safe rather than sorry.

As each took hold of their Bakana rod, the otherwise powerless lengths of metal suddenly emitted a trace of something else. Something new. A strange, indescribable essence of power. Intangible, yet present.

"I believe we should start relatively small," Zilara suggested as she casually twirled the meter-long rod in her hands.

"Of course," Farmatta replied. The old woman then cast a simple force spell, directing the magic toward a small hill nearby.

Her intent was to see if she could cause one of the trees dotting the hillside to perhaps sway, or maybe even topple, but without the usual draw on her power that casting with that much energy from that distance would require.

Farmatta didn't feel the others' power, nor did they feel her drawing from it, but when she cast, the trees on the hill were not the only things disrupted by the magical surge. In fact, the entire hill itself exploded in a shower of dirt and rock as the force spell plowed right through it.

All of the Wampeh Ghalian masters were topped off on power from recent feedings, but even so, each felt their legs briefly weaken from the unexpected and overly-rapid siphoning of the magic from their bodies.

"My gods, the power," Farmatta gasped.

"You were to start *small*," Zilara grumbled.

"That *was* small," the old woman replied. "Oh, these are far more powerful than I'd ever imagined. And so very dangerous. We will have to be exceptionally cautious in their use."

"Agreed," Leif said, casting a little whirlwind spell, pulling power from the others as easily as they had from him. "Only a fraction of my usual expenditure of power was used to cast," he noted. "Each of us contributed a portion of our power to that spell."

It was as they'd always heard in legend but had never experienced first-hand. The effortless sharing of power among a group of casters. They had an amazing new tool in their arsenal. And even Bawb was smiling.

He'd stored the rods for a long, long time, but had never had the pleasure of utilizing them. Not until now. And these were proving to be an even more fortuitous item to have recovered than he'd originally anticipated when he and Hunze had retrieved them.

Bawb wasn't all right. Not by a long shot. But he did feel a glimmer of good spirit, and it showed. His fellow Ghalian masters sincerely hoped it would linger.

CHAPTER SEVEN

In a holding position orbiting Dark Side moon base, Zed's massive AI command ship was playing host to the sort of guest he and Admiral Harkaway had never thought they'd have within their walls. In addition to Korbin's newly modified and exceedingly deadly war vessel, as well as the admiral's husband's ship, the *Váli*, they now had another craft in Zed's spacious hangar deck.

A Ra'az ship.

For the AI network, processing the words and actions of their former enemy was a rapid and easy enough thing to do. They were supercomputer minds, after all, and when they weren't slowing things down to converse with the meat brains, discussions, arguments, points, and counterpoints, could all occur in milliseconds.

They'd reviewed all of the footage of Grundsch's behavior since his arrival, both on Earth's surface, as well as his flight into battle against the invading forces. What the Ra'az warrior hadn't known was that every Ra'az ship mothballed and in storage had also had a small monitoring system installed.

The devices were put in place in the event that a craft was

stolen by some rogue element. But with an actual Ra'az pilot aboard and fighting on their side, the transmitted images were of a far different variety than the system's installers had originally intended it for.

The odds of any Ra'az actually making it back to Earth to steal the commandeered craft and use them against its inhabitants were slim to none. After the Great War had ended, not only with the destruction of the Ra'az homeworld and their queen, but their orbiting forces around Earth and the Chithiid world of Taangaar had also been obliterated.

But that wasn't enough. There was still a massive Ra'az conquering fleet spreading out into the systems, gathering resources for their queen and her hive. But the people of Earth now had something the Ra'az were lacking. They had a fully functional warp system, and one that would allow for far, far greater distances to be covered in a fraction of the time required by the Ra'az fleet.

What would take the Ra'az a decade of travel, the resistance fighters could achieve in a day. And it was all thanks to Freya and Joshua's retooling of the captured Ra'az warp orb technology. They'd worked hard after the war on Earth, and they had succeeded in turning that tech into a tool of great power. The combined human and Chithiid forces then set out to hunt down and destroy the last of the Ra'az, no matter how long it took.

It hadn't taken long. The invaders were sloppy and overconfident in their movements, sure the reinforcements from their hive back on their homeworld would keep replenishing their ranks. They had no way of knowing that world was no more. And when the last of the Ra'az Hok fleet had finally been captured, it seemed the brutal alien threat had finally been eradicated.

There were few prisoners. The Ra'az weren't ones for surrender. And so it came to pass that the most aggressive species in the galaxy was no more. At least, not until a lone survivor was dragged across a magical space portal and back to Earth. And, amazingly, he had proven himself to be an ally rather than a foe, and in a most unexpected way, at that.

Grundsch had rushed into battle back on Slafara when they'd come under attack, putting himself in harm's way for a race other than his own. He'd done so for Kara Palmarian, protecting her and being gravely wounded in the process. That unexpected act of entirely un-Ra'az selflessness had earned him a reprieve from the executioner.

And now he'd risked himself again, but this time for his new home. A planet his kind had formerly invaded. A place he now called his own. And the secret surveillance footage of his stay thus far had shown no sign of deceit. In fact, he seemed to legitimately struggle with his situation, as would be expected, rather than fall into the pattern of a carefully planned act.

Grundsch was one of Earth's people now, and he'd fought bravely in its defense. It was time, the leadership agreed, to reward his newfound allegiance.

Bahnjoh and Baloo sat on either side of the massive Ra'az as he waited for the rest of the attendees to arrive. The canines were on their best behavior, somehow seeming to sense the importance of the moment.

"Hey," Korbin said, quietly. "I was thinking. I might have a way to help these two be better hunters."

"Oh?" Grundsch replied.

"Yeah. I'll swing around your place when we arrive back on Earth to give it a try, if you're okay with that."

"If it will help Bahnjoh and his friend, I am most certainly okay with the idea, though I am curious as to the specifics."

Admiral Harkaway strode into the meeting space, followed by several of the fleet's captains, as well as a dark-haired Asian man with flashes of gray at his temples. His name was Chu, and he was one of the original crew of Dark Side base, having helped the infamous Daisy with all manner of technological advances, including the repurposing of stolen alien tech.

"A pleasure to meet you in person," Admiral Celeste Harkaway said, striding fearlessly up to the enormous alien whose kind had very nearly brought humanity to extinction.

"Admiral. It is an honor," Grundsch replied. He had no queen. Not anymore. But this woman was the closest he'd come in his new life.

"The captains and I wanted to thank you personally for what you did out there, fighting the enemy fleet."

"I did what needed to be done," the alien replied.

"Yes, but I'm sure you appreciate the significance of precisely those actions. You defended Earth, Grundsch. You put aside your historical hatred of our kind and joined forces with those you had formerly fought against. Not because you were forced to, but because you wanted to."

"Earth is my home now," he said. "And I will do all that I can to protect it."

He scanned the faces of those around him. Humans. Chithiid. Urok. Even a few Kathiri were present. These were his hivemates now, however unlikely.

"And to protect its people," he added.

Admiral Harkaway nodded appreciatively. "I'm glad you've committed to this new family, Grundsch. Because in this day and age, that's what we all are. Not a hive, as was the way of your kind, but close enough, I think."

Grundsch allowed himself a little smile. "You are worthy hivemates, I think," he said.

And there it was. Without the need for a control collar, he was a part of Earth's people of his own free will, however unlikely that may have been. Celeste nodded to Chu.

"Hey, so Zed asked me to fix a little something up for you, now that you're part of the team and all," Chu said. "It was a little tough to get working at first, since I didn't have an actual

Ra'az to help me test it out, but we're pretty sure this should be up and running now."

"What should be?" the Ra'az asked.

"Just give it to him already," Zed interrupted. "My God, you all love beating around the bush."

For a superpowered AI who pretty much ran the fleet, Zed certainly did not mince words.

"Ah, right," Chu said, hastily handing a box to Grundsch. "Hope ya like it."

The huge alien opened the lid and smiled wide when he saw the contents. A Ra'az power whip, like the one that was destroyed during the fighting on Slafara. But this one looked a little different. Modified. Excited, he slid it onto his wrist.

It fit perfectly.

With just the tiniest bit of concentration, he connected his will with the device. It immediately shot out a twenty-meter beam of thick power, the length crackling where it fell to the deck. He grinned broadly as the power whip retracted into the device.

"Thank you. This is a most wonderful surprise."

"We wanted you to be properly armed for not only aerial combat, but ground fighting as well," Zed informed him. "We saw what you did with your ship in the battle, so it just seemed fitting someone of your abilities should have one of these. They are Ra'az tech, after all."

Grundsch knew the device had been stripped from one of his dead hivemates in the war, but whatever discomfort that thought may have caused was quickly pushed down. That was a different time. And this was a different life. One where a Ra'az warrior had become an unlikely defender of those he'd once sought to destroy.

CHAPTER EIGHT

The meeting aboard Zed's ship had wrapped up, and the captains had returned to their various vessels. Korbin, however, remained behind a moment longer. There were some things he wanted to know. *Needed* to know. And this was the group that could give him the answers.

Zed had directed him to one of the more modest conference rooms, rather than the expansive space they'd utilized when bringing their new Ra'az ally officially into the fold. It was a comfortable space, and several AI minds were already tapped into the chamber's systems when he arrived.

On the display screens flush-mounted within one of the walls were a collection of images taken from just a few days prior. Things Korbin wanted very much to get all the details about that he could.

But he knew patience was required, though he'd already been quite patient, since his niece went missing. Nevertheless, the meeting wouldn't begin until Admiral Harkaway joined them.

The door slid open and a somewhat unexpected group of guests were ushered in and joined him, nodding their greeting.

He knew them all, having met many of them at the family dinner at Ripley's parents' house.

"Finn. Sarah," he greeted the teen's parents.

"Korbin," Finn said. "Good to see you, though I wish it wasn't under these circumstances."

"You and me both," the visla agreed. "Rika," he said, turning to another arrival. "Marban. Thanks for coming."

"Wouldn't miss it," the pirate said.

"Don't worry. We'll get 'em back," Tamara added as she strode in, her metal arm sporting a new design, he noticed. A more combat-friendly color scheme. Her nephew was missing, and *someone* was gearing up to kick names and take ass.

"Thanks," Korbin said, then made his way around the others, thanking them for coming. Shelly and Omar were there, their cybernetic replacement limbs tuned to perfection in anticipation of whatever might come. So was Fatima, the almond-eyed woman's silver hair pulled into a braided spray of a ponytail.

Vince walked in a minute later with Captain Harkaway and his wife, the admiral.

"The others couldn't make it, but we're going to beam them a link to the discussion," Vince said, then took a seat with the others.

"You ready to go, Joshua?" Captain Harkaway asked the air.

"Yes, Captain. Cal, Sid, Mal, and Zed are all present as well, and we've been discussing our situation while we awaited all of your arrival. We've got a few ideas."

"Excellent," he said, turning to the admiral. "In that case, dearest?"

"Right," Celeste said. "So, let's not beat around the bush, shall we? Korbin, I know you've been anxious for information about your niece's impromptu trip to the other side. Now, as you can see on the screens, the portal crossing itself wasn't anything out of the ordinary, aside from the way in which they managed to accomplish it."

"Yeah, and rest assured, that kid is so damn grounded when he gets back," Vince noted.

"Yours and mine both," Joshua agreed, though he was impressed with how well Marty had calculated the warp. One could be angry but still proud, after all. Of course, he wouldn't mention that to the assembled group.

Korbin watched the images a long moment. "What I fail to understand is how they were able to overcome the security arrangements. If these timings were so regimented, how did a couple of kids manage to do this? I understand Kara's motivation. Hell, I'm worried about her father as well, but this is beyond her capabilities."

"Ah, that would be our fault," Zed replied. "You see, since the enemy captured an Urok ship, which does not communicate using our particular technological methods, we AIs still share data freely amongst ourselves, though we do partition it to those working in specific areas. Such as those guarding the portal."

"But Marty got that information," Sarah growled, her nanite arm rippling slightly with her annoyance. "Jesus, Zed. How could you let *that* pair get their hands on the timing?"

"What are you saying, Sarah?" Vince asked, slightly defensive. "That's my kid."

"You know what I'm saying, Vince. And it's not like Ripley isn't just as bad. Our kids are smart. Like, *really* smart. But they both do some really dumb shit sometimes, and we have to keep an eye on them."

Vince knew that Ripley had been seriously hurt just days prior. And though the teen was now fine, thanks to not only the nanites living in her body, but also the dose of the healing Balamar waters that had flooded her system, he thought it best to go easy on the girl for Sarah's sake.

"Yeah, you're right," he admitted. "But they'll be all right.

Your sister and Freya crossed over after them—without even telling me, I might add."

"I'm sorry, Vince, but time was of the essence, and you know how Daisy can be," Zed chimed in.

"So we go too," Korbin replied. "My vessel is modified with your weapons now. And I've seen what these others are capable of."

"I'm sorry, Korbin, but that's simply not an option at the moment," Cal interjected. *"The timing is compromised, and, while we can open it from our end for brief moments, until we verify the newly encoded schedule is received on the other side, we can't risk opening the portal long enough for a ship to pass through. We're still tracking down several of the enemy's craft that snuck across and jumped away as it is."*

"But it would only take a second," Korbin protested.

"And in a second they can force more of their cloaked ships through," Zed replied. "No, Cal's right. We just can't do it right now. Not for any longer than it takes for a tiny drone to pop through. They're up to something, and we don't know what it is, but it can't be good."

"What exactly do you mean?" Vince inquired. "Has this invading force shifted their tactics somehow?"

"We aren't sure," Admiral Harkaway replied. "Zed, would you please put the images up?"

The shots of the portal were replaced by a frozen frame clearly taken from the other galaxy, the mass of enemy ships right up on the drone taking the picture made that abundantly clear.

"They got the drone," Zed said, "but it did manage to transmit this to the satellite, which then relayed it to the next drone that successfully returned to us. Tell me, Korbin, what do you see?"

He didn't need to squint or enhance the image to make out

the distinctive shape. He knew damn well what it was. What was unclear was exactly what it meant.

"That's a new portal," Korbin replied. "A tiny, little portal."

"Precisely. And we have no idea where it leads or why Dominus even created it. And for that reason, as well as all the others, we need to pause and assess," Zed said. "Believe me, I'd love to go charging in there guns a-blazing, but there's something new afoot, and we need to find out what it is."

"So send me across to do just that," Korbin replied. "I'm a powerful visla, and my ship is more than capable of––"

"It's not happening," Cal cut him off. *"I'm sorry, Korbin, I truly am. But this must wait. There's more at stake than just your niece."*

"If the children are with Daisy, I'm sure they'll be safe," Vince said. "So there's that."

"And if they have liaised with Charlie, then they are likewise in good hands. I trust him with my life and know he'd stop at nothing to protect them," Marban added, but Korbin noted a slight hesitation in his voice.

The group discussed other elements at play in the other galaxy. Those they knew about, at least. Then the meeting adjourned and the assembled humans headed for their ships.

As they walked, Marban leaned in and whispered to Korbin in passing as he and Rika made their way to the *Fujin*.

"We'll help you get them back. Come talk with us when we're back on Earth."

He and the tattooed pilot then peeled off toward her ship, leaving Korbin wondering exactly what his friends might have in mind.

CHAPTER NINE

Korbin had every intention of heading over to have that little chat with Rika and Marban, but an unexpected visitor delayed that plan, though he wasn't exactly unexpected. Grundsch had been requested, after all. It was just that Korbin hadn't expected him to come so soon after their arrival back on Earth.

With him were the two enormous canines, one on either side. Since neither Leila nor any of his other family were present, Baloo had taken to following Bahnjoh and Grundsch wherever they went. He was a pack animal at heart, and with his main family unit absent, he had found another that would suffice.

The slender, golden bands around each of their necks were not only intact, but appeared fully charged with magic, just as Korbin had left them. The plan had been to provide the animals with some degree of protection against magical attacks should they encounter Tslavar invaders again. Bahnjoh had already been frozen once, and Korbin feared he might not be so lucky next time.

"I've come, as you requested. And I brought the animals," Grundsch said, stating the obvious.

"Thanks, Grundsch," Korbin replied.

"If I may, what is it exactly is it that you wish to do with them?"

"Ah, yes," Korbin said, a hint of a smile growing on his lips. "I had an interesting idea, and I wanted to test it out on them."

"You wish to make them test subjects?" the Ra'az asked, a little defensively.

"Not like that. Nothing bad will befall them. Actually, this could be quite beneficial to them. To all of us, really."

"Hmm. Go on," Grundsch said, not entirely convinced.

"Come here, you two," Korbin said, then reached down and rested his hands on the two animals' collars as they sat at his feet. "So, the idea is to utilize the konus collars they are already wearing to aid them in their hunts," the visla said, then began casting, concentrating on forcing the very specific power into their collars on top of the magic already stored within them.

It was a relatively minor thing. No more than a simple, magical push and pull, really. But if Korbin's plan worked as he hoped it might, then they would be able to utilize the scanning technology of this galaxy in concert with the magical powers of his own.

"Okay, that should just about do it," he said, removing his hands from the golden metal.

"You did nothing to them," Grundsch noted, a bit perplexed.

"Ah, but I did. It's a very subtle series of spells, but they took to the konuses quite well. Now, let's go see if it worked."

"Go? Go where?"

"To my ship," Korbin replied.

"Bahnjoh. Baloo. Come."

"No, no. Leave them here," Korbin corrected his Ra'az friend. "You'll see why in a minute."

"Stay here," Grundsch directed the animals, then followed the visla across the landing area to his waiting craft.

The pulse cannons and rail guns were seamlessly mounted

to the vessel now, retracted into protective housing that served the dual purpose of also camouflaging the weapons' presence from prying eyes.

The two stepped inside and settled into their seats. Grundsch was overflowing the sides of his, the seating arrangement having never been designed to accommodate the bulk of a Ra'az Hok.

"Maybe we should have taken yours," Korbin joked as he lifted off into the air.

The two of them rose high in the sky, finally coming to a hover at just under two thousand feet. Korbin then activated the fascinating scanning device Cal had gifted him, pulling up images from the ground, greatly magnified without the need of using precious magic to generate them.

"Do you see them?" he asked his passenger.

"The two quadrupeds. Yes, I see them," Grundsch replied. "But I fail to see how––"

Korbin flipped a switch, and the display changed to infrared. The canines remained where they were on screen, but all sorts of other heat signatures were now visible, hiding in the brush.

"Ah, a heat detection device," Grundsch said approvingly. "I've used them often in the past. They are most helpful in hunting down..." He let the rest of that thought go as he realized that was a different life, and hunting a planet's populace was most certainly frowned upon. "Now, what is it you are attempting to do with Bahnjoh and Baloo?"

Korbin pointed to the screen. "Scan for a target. A deer. One they couldn't possible see or smell. Downwind and hidden. Can you find me one?"

Grundsch chuckled as he leaned in closer to the screen. "Can I find one, he asks. I'll have you know, I possess a particularly keen pair of eyes. In fact, once, I––there's one," he abruptly cut himself off, pointing to an almost invisible heat signature out among the trees and shrubs.

"Are you certain? It's a bit hard to make out."

"I am certain," the Ra'az replied. "You asked for a difficult target, and I found you one."

Korbin couldn't help but enjoy his friend's newly rediscovered sense of humor and renewed confidence. It seemed that being a part of society as more than a slave had done wonders for the man's psyche.

"All right, so here's how the spell works," Korbin began. "I planted a subliminal guiding directive into their konus collars. Now, if it functions properly, they will feel the urge to head in the direction I send to them."

Grundsch nodded approvingly as he realized what this meant. "You can then steer them toward an enemy who is hidden in battle. How wonderful. You can guide them straight in for the kill."

"Yeah, that's the plan," Korbin said as he urged the animals toward the hidden prey.

The two men watched on the screen as Bahnjoh and Baloo raced ahead, drawing closer and closer to the hidden deer until it was flushed from cover. It had been well hidden, disguised by the chaparral around it and downwind of the beasts. But when they were almost upon it, the animal sprang to its feet and took off at a run. Then the chase was on, and no collar guidance was needed.

"Well done!" Grundsch cheered as the animals took down their target. "With this, we will be able to direct them into the most difficult of situations," he said appreciatively.

"That, or guide them away from it if needed."

"Away?"

"It's not cowardly to flee unwinnable odds, you know. Sometimes you simply can't win, but you can survive to fight another day. It's a calculus that men of action such as you and I understand, but instinctive creatures like Bahnjoh and Baloo aren't aware of. But we can help them.

Grundsch nodded his massive head. He was a Ra'az Hok, and his kind were not accustomed to backing down. But his species had also been driven extinct by precisely that sort of thinking, and he would do well to recognize that and adapt accordingly.

"What's up?" Korbin asked. "You just got really quiet."

"I was thinking about my hivemates."

"Ah, that. You're the last of the last, I hear."

"I am."

"But why can't there be more?"

"Our queen is dead, and the Ra'az Hok need a progenitor of her genetic line to carry on. Without her and the stasis-frozen princesses, the remaining Ra'az would have died off anyway, regardless of their being hunted down in the final years of the war or not. And while there may be a few in cryo stasis floating around somewhere deep in space, we are a dead race, and for all intents and purposes, I am the last."

Korbin sat quietly a moment, then patted his companion on the knee. "Well, then. We'd better do our best to keep you alive, eh?"

Grundsch allowed himself a little smile. "It would be appreciated," he said with a low chuckle.

"Well, that's the plan. And it's a good one, because I think we're going to need you when things get really hairy," Korbin said. "And I fear that may come sooner than later."

CHAPTER TEN

The powerful casters hard at work many billions of light years away in a distant galaxy were straining both their magical powers as well as their mental acuity as they struggled to create a new portal for their demanding visla.

They'd successfully managed to superpower the limited amount of Ootaki hair they possessed. The discovery of the properties of the power emitted by the strange sun spewing deadly plasma through the portal previously created by their leader had been an amazing one. A sun that acted in a manner far exceeding any documented in their own realm. It could deliver an almost endless supply of massive power.

But it would only charge Ootaki hair.

It was an unusual wrinkle, and Visla Dominus had previously used all of the Ootaki hair in her possession creating the portal itself. They had the perfect tool to power their next steps, but their resources that would have benefited from it were all lost in its creation. The irony was not lost on them.

But the visla had acted quickly and decisively as soon as she'd learned of the sun's true power. Her minions were at this very moment scouring every inch of the galaxy to bring what little Ootaki hair they could scavenge back to the research arm of her fleet.

That their hair grew so slowly was the biggest issue. There were plenty of Ootaki to be found, the vast majority kept as slaves by the major power users in the systems. But only a few still had any hair worth shearing. Dominus had used them up when she confiscated their locks to power the first portal, totally unaware that a fraction of the amount she used could have sufficed, given the way it reacted to the target system's sun.

The rest of the hair had been shorn and sold and traded across many worlds in small quantities. Yes, there was Ootaki hair to be found, but they'd have to collect it on a nearly strand-by-strand basis. Not the most effective way to gather the amount they needed.

But then a windfall landed in their laps. An Ootaki with not only a great length of hair, but *first growth* hair, never cut in all her years. It was somewhat of a loss that the hair on the sides had been shorn at some point recently, but the hair that remained was nevertheless a potent source of magic, brimming over with stored energy.

That she was Visla Dominus's enemy was an added bonus.

Visla Malalia Maktan, aka Visla Dominus, had been assisting her casters personally, adding her considerable powers to help them slowly chip away at the unconscious woman's natural defenses.

It was amazing and unheard of, but this Ootaki actually controlled her own power. If they simply took her hair, the magic dissipated immediately, returning to her body. So they needed to find a way to use her with her hair still attached. But the power she possessed meant keeping her locked in a deep sleep spell. A stasis to keep her from breaking free.

Malalia felt confident she could handle the woman's power, now that she'd had a bit more time to properly study her, but it could be close, and she had no intention of using that much power on a hypothetical.

Also, the Ootaki woman was getting stronger by the minute.

When the team of casters had successfully used the hair Dominus had managed to obtain to create a much smaller portal to a somewhat remote system, they had unlocked the key to their victory.

They could now harvest the energy flowing through the far larger portal via the new one, and its diminutive size prevented ships of any real size from crossing over to disrupt their work. Meanwhile, the sun's power flowed steadily through, and Hunze, the slumbering Ootaki, was positioned in a prime location to absorb all of it.

"We're getting closer, Visla," an excited caster reported when she took another measurement of the gathered mass of Ootaki hair's power. The shorn locks were glowing with potential, and Hunze's more than any of the collected lengths combined.

"Her hair is gaining in power at an amazing rate. It's even more powerful than we'd hoped."

"Yes," Malalia agreed. "The power is growing steadily. But we are still a long way off from being able to open our new portal. And this one is the key."

"Indeed. If we can gain control of her power––"

"*When*," Malalia corrected.

"Ah, yes. When we gain control of her power, we will be able to open a portal nearly as large as the original."

"We can scale it down a little," her visla noted. "Just large enough for our vessels to pass through. Now that we know we can continue to power the portal from both sides, there is no need to waste energy. It would be far wiser to conserve it, ready to deploy it in greater amount if need be."

"Of course, Visla. As always, you are wise in your decisions."

Malalia didn't mind the woman's ass kissing. In fact, she'd found that a healthy dose of fear and ambition could lead most to achieve far more than they'd normally believe themselves capable of. All they needed was a little push and a pat on the head from time to time.

"You've done good work," Malalia said. "Keep this up and there will be room for your advancement."

"Oh, thank you, Visla!"

"*But*, you must also be very careful to keep this one in stasis. As her power grows, so do her own natural defenses. And those are already straining to snap her from our spells."

"We will add additional castings to the containment spells, Visla. We will not allow her to wake."

Malalia certainly hoped not. The woman was definitely a power suck. The number of high-level casters who had to continually rotate in and out of the facility to recharge their own power while their colleagues took over to keep her asleep was worrisome.

"Carry on. And summon me if there is any notable progress."

Malalia then departed the vessel, leaving her workers to continue magically prying away the slumbering Ootaki's defenses. She'd have stayed herself, but there was other work to be done. Work she couldn't leave to others.

The visla's transport craft landed aboard her large command vessel in short order. When she reached the navigation center, all of the images and intelligence their craft had managed to bring back from the other galaxy was displayed on magical projectors.

A handful of her craft were still in the target system, safely hidden away and far from the sun, Earth, and its moon. All three of those were swarming with all manner of craft. Apparently, there was a cooperative allegiance of races guarding the portal. But that was no matter. She'd conquer them all soon enough.

"Our ships will gather here, Visla," her captain said,

zooming in on the image of a half dozen of their craft floating in a cloud.

"This location is the key to our victory. And as such, its very existence is of the utmost secrecy. The clouds will hide our fleet from prying eyes, allowing us to––"

Malalia turned her head ever so slightly as the door opened. The briefing paused. One of the crew hurried in carrying a tray of refreshments for the visla and her team and placed them on the nearby console.

"Thank you, that will be all," the captain said, dismissing the crewman.

The door sealed as he hurried out, and the briefing continued. "As I was saying," Malalia said with a little smile. "This is the key to our victory. And only those in this room know its *true* location."

As the meeting continued, the Tslavar crewman hurried away from the locked-down chamber. The Wampeh Ghalian's well-paid spy had been in place for some time now, embedded within the fleet and moving ever further up through the ranks, until he was aboard the command vessel itself. It was risky, but it appeared to have finally paid off. It had cost a small fortune, but Tslavar mercenaries were more loyal to coin than any leader, no matter how powerful.

Though the spy had only caught a glimpse of it, the facts were plain to see. Visla Dominus was amassing a substantial part of her fleet on a cloudy world. It was crucial information to get back to the others. The Tslavar quickly made his way to a shuttle, gaining transport to a supply craft under the pretense of acquiring something for their ship at the request of the higher-ups.

He was already aboard the command vessel, so no one questioned his statement. Once you had that sort of clearance, you had free rein to come and go as needed.

The disguised Wampeh Ghalian spy who had paid him was

embedded in the supply ship. His Tslavar appearance was unlikely to be probed there, as power users rarely visited those menial workers, yet it was a key position in the fleet. As a hub, a great many crew of other ships visited his craft, allowing for the dissemination of intel. And this bit was of the highest priority.

"Fascinating information," he said when he'd received the news. "A cloudy world? There are many."

"Yes," his agent said. "But to hide a fleet it needs to be of decent size. And to have the ability to continue supplying them, it can only be in a relatively small number of systems, should they wish to remain anonymous and resupply from within."

"Agreed. But that is for the others to determine," the spy said. "Remain safe, my friend, and keep your eyes and ears open for any further information."

The spies then parted ways, the crucial intel soon to be on its way to the Ghalian masters.

Meanwhile, safe on her command ship, Malalia Maktan's smile had grown wide as she looked at the images her lackeys had presented. They'd managed to secure a perfect location for her fleet to prepare itself. Only, it was not where any would think to look for it.

All she needed was control of Hunze's hair and she would begin. Then, billions of light years away, within the periphery of the gas and ice clouds of the fifth planet from Earth's sun, her forces would arrive.

Hidden by the planet called Jupiter's gasses, the portal would open, yet still draw from that system's sun. *Then*, her invasion would begin in earnest.

CHAPTER ELEVEN

"I'm just worried about her, is all," Charlie said as he sat quietly as Leila reclined in the comfort of his arms.

They were sitting near their new friend Daisy's ship, where a group of people had gathered together, watching as the sun set lower in the sky. It had been a much-needed decompression for his queen. Her confinement in Malalia's clutches had truly tested her mettle, just as the loss and eventual recovery of her Magus stone had.

Things had worked out for her and Charlie, but now Bawb was suffering for it, and Ara was missing. But at least they could be confident the dragon wouldn't do anything crazy. Bawb, on the other hand, was still on edge enough that there was no telling if he might cross the line again if pushed too far.

Leila tilted her head and looked up at him a moment. "Charlie, Ara's a Zomoki. A wise and powerful one at that. I'm sure she's fine."

"But she's still not back. I thought she'd regroup with the others by now. She should be here."

"You are concerned as to the whereabouts of your Zomoki friend?" Rovnik asked. The pirate captain was taking a leisurely walk, out to stretch his legs on the planet's surface, while his men enjoyed some fresh air before what promised to be a lengthy time in space once again.

"Yeah, I don't know why she's been gone so long," Charlie replied.

"When you didn't return after things went all sideways during Dominus's ambush, she was pretty distraught. After all, from what I heard, you were basically blown off her back in the fighting and left drifting in space," the pirate captain noted.

"Pretty accurate description," Charlie said with a wry grin.

"And when the fighting was over, and everyone had regrouped and been accounted for, she jumped back to the edges of that system to see if she could reach you."

"Only, I wasn't there," Charlie realized.

"Precisely."

"Shit. I boarded a Tslavar ship and commandeered it, and the Drooks helped me make an escape to another system. I was nowhere near when she came back."

"I heard about that and wanted to ask you personally. Is it true? You actually took an entire ship single-handed?"

"Trust me, Rovnik, it wasn't as impressive as it sounds. There were only about twenty or thirty crew, and since they were busy kicking our people's asses, they weren't thinking about being boarded."

"But you managed to not only survive in space, but then somehow guided yourself to the ship, landed upon its back without being detected, entered it, sealed the breach, took down over two dozen highly trained crew, and freed most of the Drooks while making an escape. Is that about right?"

Charlie scratched his head. "Jeez, when you say it like that, it sounds a lot more impressive."

"Brother, you have no idea. There's been a lot of talk about it among the men. Marban told stories, of course, but only a few of us had any real experience fighting at your side. This? This story will serve us well and bring a great many daring men to our side."

"And women," Leila interjected.

"Naturally," Rovnik replied. "That goes without saying. It was just a figure of speech."

Leila chuckled. "I know. I'm just giving you a hard time. But back to the issue at hand, where do you think Ara might be?"

"My best guess? Seeing as she thought you were captured by Dominus's ships––"

"Which I was, just not at that particular moment," Charlie noted.

"Yeah. Given that, I'd think she'd have followed up on the chatter we've been hearing about all the mischief going on back at Slafara. That's where you were, right?"

"Yeah, but we escaped."

"She doesn't know that," the pirate noted. "And it's where I'd go if I were her."

"But it's dangerous there. Like, *really* dangerous. And they almost certainly spotted her when we were last there."

"You don't have to convince me. I'm just telling you where I *think* she probably went."

A violet-skinned girl rose to her feet and hurried over to them. "You're going to Slafara?"

"I didn't say––" Charlie began.

"Take me with you! My father is there, and he needs me!"

"Not if Malalia is still running that place, kid."

"But––"

"No way. If we do wind up going there, I promise I'll see what I can find out. But there's no way I'm dragging you with us into harm's way."

"But––"

"No buts. It's too dangerous, and we'll have a hard enough time looking out for ourselves as it is, let alone keeping you safe."

"I can take care of myself. My magic is getting stronger."

"So I've heard. But you don't really know how to control it yet. And Malalia's one bad apple."

"I've known her my whole life."

"Which is why it's even more important you stay here," Charlie said with an understanding sigh. "Look, I get it. You've got all kinds of emotions tied up in this, and it makes sense. But the fact of the matter is, the woman you thought you knew is one of the most dark, evil, plotting bitches I've ever come across, and she wouldn't hesitate to hurt you or anyone else who got in her way. And hell, if she could, I wouldn't put it past her to use your father to get to you as well."

"But—"

"So, no buts. It sucks, I get it, but you know it's the right thing."

Anger burbled through the teen, her emotions in a jumbled mess. "It's not fair!" Kara said, then stalked off.

Arlo, quietly watching from nearby, peeled off to follow her.

"You sound like a father. You realize that?" Leila asked.

Charlie tightened his arms around her and kissed her head. "Maybe one day. After all of this madness finally ends." He loosened his grip and slowly rose to his feet, dusting off his pants. "So," he said, helping Leila up, "are you up to heading out to see what's really going on back on Slafara while we look for Ara?"

"Of course. Should we get Daisy?"

"Nah. I was thinking we want to go in all stealth-like, and her ship may be stealthy back home, but here, she sticks out like a sore thumb. But that's okay, I know just the guy for the job."

"Oh, you don't actually mean—?"

"Yep. He's a weird dude, but Tym's one helluva pilot. And the shimmer ship should be good to keep us from prying eyes better than any other asset we have."

"But Malalia can still spot us," Leila pointed out.

"If we're close enough, sure. But Ara and I don't need to be *that* close to connect. All I need is to reach her with our bond. If she's actually there, of course. And if she is, I'll get her this place's location and we'll all bug out of there ASAP."

"You've planned it all out, haven't you?" Leila asked.

"Sort of. But you know what they say about the best laid plans of mice and men."

"No, I don't. And what are mice?"

Charlie pulled his queen closer, enjoying the soothing comfort of her warmth pressed against him. "I'll tell you on the way."

CHAPTER TWELVE

Bawb sat quietly in his seat aboard the shimmer ship. He hadn't said so much as a word since they'd made their first jump toward Slafara. Now that they were nearly there, it at least seemed logical he'd speak up before they landed.

Or so Charlie thought.

He was wrong.

When the Wampeh invited himself along on the mission to seek out Ara on the dangerous planet of Slafara, he did so not because he felt he could be of service in tracking down their Zomoki friend any better than Charlie could, but because it was *Slafara* they were visiting. Malalia's planet. Visla Dominus's home.

If Hunze was anywhere, this was as good a place as any to find her. Wearing his vest of her hair, he would feel her power call to him if she was nearby. Even without the hair, they were bonded now, and he could very likely sense her regardless. She was his woman, as he was her man, and if Malalia had taken her into her towers, nothing would stop him from getting her back or going down trying.

It was a problem, and not a small one, either. Charlie felt a little odd talking with the other Wampeh behind his friend's back, but Bawb's head was not in a good place, and, much as he hated to admit it, it seemed like the right thing to do.

"You are a smart man, Charlie," Farmatta said as the others boarded Tym's craft. "And you are correct in your fears. The Geist is not well. But he is one of us. One of the legendary of our order, at that. I have hopes he will rein in his anger and be of use to you yet on this mission."

"And if something goes wrong?"

Farmatta sighed at the thought. "Then we will have to revisit this when you return. For now, go. Find your friend, and come back to us safe."

He thanked her for her time and counsel, then boarded the shimmer ship and took a seat beside Leila. Fortunately, the craft was quite spacious, and there was no reason for them all to share the same crowded area during the flight. It wouldn't be a long one, but given how Bawb still hadn't spoken to her, the separate accommodations would reduce the stress levels, at least a little.

Of course, Tym was ever the chatterbox as they flew, and when the Drooks paused to take a little recharge break, the oddball pilot was pleased to find he was within long-distance skree range of his old friend Olo. Normally, he'd not have expended the magic just to say hi, but he was a wealthy man now, and due to his blue-skinned friend, no less, so why not give him a call.

"What are you doing back?" were the first words out of Olo's mouth when he heard Tym's voice.

"Is that how you greet the greatest pilot in the galaxy?"

"*Second* greatest. And you didn't answer my question. You were to fly the ship through the portal. Hell, you were paid quite handsomely to do it."

"And I did."

"But, you're back."

"As always, my friend, your grasp of the obvious is amazing!" Tym teased. "Oh, you should have seen it, Olo. It was glorious. I made the run for the portal just as planned, the ship humming at top speed as magic attacked me from all sides. It was even worse than that time at Horkus. You remember that?"

"How could I forget?" Olo replied, and Tym could almost picture his friend subconsciously rubbing the scar on his thigh.

"Well, I made it. And the planet on the other side? It was beautiful! Not so much in the way of women, though. Not the kind I prefer, anyway. Too symmetrical for my taste."

"You fly to another galaxy and all you are concerned with are the women?" Olo said with a chuckle. "You never cease to both amaze me and live down to my expectations, Tym. But none of that explains how you're back."

"I figure, what good are riches if I can't spend them, right? So when an opportunity to be of service presented itself, I jumped at the chance. The first man from our galaxy to cross that portal. And *twice*! I even have a new ship."

"It's not *your* ship, Tym," Charlie called out from the other end of the command center.

"Is that Charlie? Tell him I say hello."

"Olo says hello."

"Hi back to Olo," Charlie replied. "And it's still not your ship."

"Right. So the vessel is actually a captured Tslavar shimmer attack ship. And get this. It's powered by *free* Drooks! Just like your favorite craft. Isn't that amazing?"

"You're in a *shimmer* ship?" Olo asked. For just a moment, Tym almost thought he heard a note of jealousy in his friend's voice.

"Maybe we'll meet up after this current mission. I'm sure you'd love to see it. If you can," he added with a laugh.

"Because, a shimmer ship. Yes, I get it. Ha-ha, Tym. You're so clever."

"I know, right? Anyway, listen, I have to go. The Drooks are ready to jump again. But I'll skree you when we're all done here."

"Fine. Maybe I'll come swing by the staging area when you are."

"Oh, that was compromised. We're at a new one now. I'll have to send you the location later, though. Gotta go. Talk to you soon!"

Tym disconnected the skree and settled back into pilot mode. "Okay, to Slafara we go!"

Two more jumps and they finally arrived in distant orbit over their destination. Though it used a fair amount of magical power to do so, they stayed shimmer-cloaked through the jump so they would arrive invisible. Even though it would just take a moment to activate the spell, Charlie didn't want to take any chances.

Not if Malalia might be around. She could pierce a shimmer if she wanted, but her minions would not be so powerful.

Of course, with the maddening jumble of magic swarming around the planet, it was damn near impossible to tell who was there or not. And given Visla Dominus's powers, she could undoubtedly mask her location even more than the current jumble was already accomplishing.

"Take us in, Tym. But stay well clear of the towers in Palmar City. If Malalia––I mean, Visla Dominus––is on the planet, that's where she'd most likely be, and we do not want any part of that crazy bitch."

"Copy that," Tym said, echoing a bit of Earth slang he'd taken a shine to while spending time with the cyborg pilots at a local watering hole.

"Ara, can you hear me?" Charlie reached out as they entered

the atmosphere and began the descent toward the city. *"If you're here, answer me."*

Silence.

"Bawb, the ambient magical buzz might be creating a filter of sorts. Would you try reaching out with me? Maybe our combined call can cut through the obstruction."

A long silence hung in the air.

"Very well," Bawb finally agreed.

The two men called out to Ara simultaneously, sharing their link as they tried to reach their Zomoki friend. But as before, there was no reply, but a faint twinge at the edge of their combined senses made them both take note.

"The magical interference is ramped up. Can you feel it?" Charlie asked.

"Malalia has increased it since your escape," Bawb noted, then resumed his silence.

Charlie turned to Leila. "Babe, do you feel anything?"

The Magus stone was warm on her chest from the sheer pressure of all the magic scattershot around them, but it was not flaring up. This was all merely an annoyance, but not dangerous.

"Sorry, there's nothing out of the ordinary. Besides the jumble of magic, I mean."

It was interesting, feeling the Magus stone's power now that she had regained possession of it. It seemed that ever since she had connected with it when it had been stolen and was still hanging around Malalia's neck, something had shifted on a fundamental level. As if overcoming the evil woman's power had finally made the Magus stone recognize her in a deeper way. As more than just its owner, but a rightful blood-bonded wielder of its strength.

Sure, Leila hadn't figured out how to do any of that stuff with it yet, but something was different for sure. And she had reason to believe her control of the stone would only strengthen from here on out. And landing in hostile territory like this, she feared she might need it.

"Okay," Charlie said as the ship invisibly touched down in a relatively secluded and open part of the city. "Let's search and get some answers."

CHAPTER THIRTEEN

There had been something in the air, but what it was remained unexplained as Charlie and his friends exited the shimmer-cloaked ship from its relatively hidden landing spot. They had selected the location not only for the cover it provided them when stepping out of the invisible ship—avoiding the odd appearing-out-of-thin-air-in-a-crowd issue—but also for its clear egress route.

If shit went bad, Charlie and Tym were of the same mind on the necessity of a very accessible escape path.

"Hang here with the ship, and keep your comms on," Charlie told the pilot. "They might be able to tap into a skree, but these should hopefully still be secure. Or at least secure enough, unless they've figured out our comms as well as the satellite relay."

"Wait, they can tap into skrees?" Tym asked. "I thought that was impossible."

"Ask Bob about that one. It seems like that little glitch in their magic is a feature more than a bug. At least to the few who know how to exploit it. Isn't that right, Bob?"

The Wampeh merely nodded once, silently. He was in

disguise, but today he would not be walking the streets of Slafara as Binsala the jovial trader. In all his years he had always slipped into that persona as easily as changing a pair of gloves. But now, in his distressed mental state, putting on that cheerful face simply wasn't an option.

"Okay, guys. This is gonna be super casual. Just gather a little information and see if anyone's seen a giant, red Zomoki around here anywhere. She's kinda hard to miss."

Leila stayed right at Charlie's side, holding his hand as they walked, looking like no more than a happy couple out for a stroll. And, despite their current mission, that was the truth, to a large extent.

Being forcibly separated the way they had was something it would take time to fully deal with, but one of the results was their affections were stronger than ever. Absence really did make the heart grow fonder, it seemed. And they could only imagine what Bawb was feeling.

For a Wampeh Ghalian to not only take interest in a partner, but to then bond with one? From what the other masters had said, it was incredibly rare. And for one such as the Geist, even more so.

"Hey, those look like Dominus's ships," Charlie noted as they drew closer to the central area of town.

The craft weren't hovering near the gardens atop the Palmarian estate, so that was a good sign. Malalia wouldn't park at ground level and sneak around, now that she'd taken over the place. At least, they hoped not. But that meant her goons were there. Somewhere.

"We're still a fair distance away from the towers, and I know this neighborhood from my time with the girls," Leila said. "There's something we should do while we're here."

They turned down a side street and made their way casually along the winding route, pausing to purchase a snack, look at trinkets, and casually ask if anyone else had noticed that strange red thing in the sky the other day, while Bawb trailed far behind, questioning in his own way.

None, it seemed, had any news of anything out of the ordinary. At least, not in the shape of a giant Zomoki flying through their city. There had been a disturbance at the Palmarian estate, but Charlie and Leila already knew all about that particular incident.

They played their parts, chatting pleasantly, then headed off down the street.

"This way," Leila said, guiding them to an ornate, yet relatively modest building.

She strode to the doors and keyed the magical chimes. A servant appeared a moment later.

"Yes? How can I--Oh, it's you."

"I've come to speak with Visanya's parents."

"Of course. Please, step inside."

Charlie and Leila followed them into the foyer, where mere seconds passed before the Ootaki girl's adoptive parents rushed in to greet them.

"Where's our daughter? What has happened to her?" the teen's mother asked in a panicked tone.

"Please, darling. Calm yourself," her husband said, quietly. "I'm sure her friend here will tell us all she knows."

"That's why I'm here," Leila said. "Vee--Visanya wanted to come herself, but it was simply too dangerous for her to do so. I hope you understand, that as she is so close with Kara, that makes her a target as well."

"A target? But why? Who would want to hurt our daughter?" her father asked.

"This will come as a shock, I'm sure, but the Palmarians are not who they seem."

"What do you mean? Karasalia and our daughter have been friends since they were toddlers."

"Yes, and they will remain that way, I'm sure. But there has been a deception in the Palmarian estate. One that threatens not only Kara, but anyone associated with her as well. You've seen the craft docking at the tower, I assume."

"We have," Vee's mother replied.

"Then you've also noted they are not ordinary vessels. In fact, they are part of a growing war fleet belonging to a visla going by the name of Dominus."

At that name, Vee's father blanched.

"What do you know of this person? That is a name known only to very few of us."

"I'm sure. And we know there's been a resistance forming quietly," Charlie chimed in. "But the thing is, this Visla Dominus is actually someone you know."

"Nikora Palmarian is *not* Visla Dominus, I assure you."

"Oh, we know he isn't," Leila replied. "It's Mareh. And his wife is not only a powerful visla, but she possesses a rare Wampeh magic. She's been draining Visla Palmarian for years."

Vee's parents went pale at the realization of just what that meant. The sheer power that woman must possess.

"So, you understand why it was imperative we keep Vee and Kara as far away from here as possible," Charlie stated. "To bring her back to you would only put her at risk."

"But she's just a girl," her mother said, tears welling in her eyes.

"And an Ootaki," Leila added. "Before you protest, we know what she is, and she is safe. But if the charade is over, then there's no way Mareh would let her go on living a free life. Not when Vee possesses a power that she wants."

The teen's parents looked at one another, unsure what to do. They wanted to protect their child, but also knew Leila was right to keep her as far from this place as possible.

"I think you should go on a vacation," Leila suggested. "You know your daughter is safe, and I'll gladly relay a message back to her from you as well, letting her know you are okay. But it's going to get much more dangerous around here, and you'd be better off somewhere else."

"My sister," the woman muttered. "We can go to my sister's home. It shouldn't raise any suspicion, and she's a long flight from here. Many systems away."

"Then I suggest you do that," Leila said. "I'm not sure how long this will last, but you have my word, we will do all we can to keep your daughter safe and get her back to you when this all ends. But for now, get *yourselves* to safety so she has parents to return to when the time comes."

Visanya's parents were not happy. Not by a long shot. But at least they knew their girl was alive and safe. And Leila was right. They had to be there for her when they were eventually reunited.

Leila and Charlie stepped back out to the street. The meeting hadn't lasted *too* long. It had been an unplanned detour for certain, but one well worth the time.

"Uh, Leila?" Charlie said with a concerned tone as he scanned the throngs meandering the roadways.

"Yeah?"

"Where's Bob?"

They both looked around. The Wampeh was nowhere to be seen.

"Maybe he just went to take a look at—"

A shrill alarm warning rang out from not too far away. Charlie and Leila both realized a moment later that it was emanating from the Palmarian estate, to be precise.

Charlie felt his adrenaline surge. "Oh, shit."

CHAPTER FOURTEEN

"Bob, where the hell are you?" Charlie silently sent out to his friend. *"Shit's going haywire, dude. Alarms and people freaking the fuck out. Where are you?"*

The Wampeh assassin's absence from the area was more than a little disconcerting. In concert with the obvious trouble at Visla Palmarian's estate, it quickly graduated to downright alarming.

"Meet me back at the ship," Bawb finally replied, but said nothing more.

"Sonofa—Okay, listen. We've got to get back to the ship," Charlie informed Leila.

"But we haven't finished what we came here to—"

"Bob just replied. *Finally*. And he said meet him at the ship."

"Do you think all of that commotion is his doing?" Leila asked.

"Do you have any doubts?" Charlie replied. "Come on, we need to hustle. We can't look like we're running, but we can at least take the most direct route possible."

Leila didn't hesitate, falling in step with him as they picked up their pace, walking at a quick clip, but more the pace of people who weren't in the mood for a leisurely stroll than a pair of fleeing accomplices. Looking back, she noted several new ships had swooped in to hover above the visla's tower. None had the look of a command craft, fortunately, but there was simply no telling who might be aboard.

"Tym, we're coming back to you hot," Charlie said over their comms. "I hope to hell they didn't compromise these things," he muttered.

A moment later their pilot's voice crackled over the device. "It's not that warm out, Charlie. I mean, compared to––"

"No. We're coming in *hot*. As in, get the damn ship ready for immediate dust-off and a jump as soon as we're back aboard."

"Oh. *Oh*. I see. Right. I'm on it. Did something go wrong?"

"I honestly don't know, but I'd wager money on it," Charlie replied.

"Okay. I'll be ready. What's your ETA?"

"Probably ten minutes. Maybe less, depending on how many pedestrians are in the way. We'll see you soon," he said, then clipped the comms device back to his waistband.

The couple made good time through the streets of Palmar City. Apparently, the commotion at the visla's estate was drawing a fair amount of the usual foot and conveyance traffic toward the center of town, leaving their route somewhat more open. Casualty vampires looking for a fix were inadvertently providing them a clear means of escape, it seemed.

"Is he back yet?" Charlie called out when he and Leila finally barreled into the waiting shimmer-cloaked vessel.

"Bawb? Nah, you're the first. Why? Isn't he with you?"

"No, he went off on his own."

"But I thought the plan was––"

"We know what the plan was, but, apparently, he had a plan of his own he didn't fill us in on," Charlie grumbled.

He looked outside at the increasing number of Dominus's

craft now hovering at the visla's estate. This was most definitely not good.

A pale man abruptly appeared in front of him, discarding his shimmer cloak as he boarded the craft.

"Get us airborne, Tym," Charlie called out, then turned his attention back to his Wampeh friend. "Care to explain what that was all about?"

Bawb turned to Charlie but said nothing.

"Is that blood on your lips?" Charlie asked. "What did you do?"

Bawb cocked his head slightly. "She is not in the tower."

"Hunze?"

Bawb nodded once.

"What did they say to you? Could they have been hiding her?"

"She is not there. Of this I am *quite* certain."

"What the hell did you do, Bob? This wasn't the plan!"

"Plans change," was his simple reply.

Charlie shared a bond with his friend, and he could feel a new power radiating off of him. A substantial one at that.

"Oh, hell. You drank from someone? You actually not only broke into Malalia's tower, but you attacked her guards and even fed on one?"

"He was a power user. And a rather strong one at that," Bawb replied matter-of-factly. "They are taking no chances in that building," he said of the upgraded security detail.

Bawb didn't mention the massive slaughter that had occurred both coming in and going out of the estate, but Charlie figured his estimates of the blood spilled at his friend's hands were pretty accurate. Given the freakout he'd previously witnessed, it was pretty much expected.

"We've got company!" Tym shouted out to his passengers. "Better get yourselves seated, and fast. I'm gonna have to use some evasive maneuvers!"

Charlie and his friends managed to get themselves into seats just as Tym spun into a barrel roll, dodging a barrage of magic flung at them by what appeared to be nearly a dozen pursuing ships.

"We're a shimmer ship, Tym. Why are they able to see us?" Charlie asked with a pained grunt as he was flung into his seat even harder.

"We're in one of Dominus's shimmer ships. Even with its magic altered by Korbin, there's still enough of their original stuff in here to key in on now that they know we're here."

"But how do they even know that? We were invisible!"

"Obviously. But whatever happened at the tower seems to have set them all off on the highest of alerts. Even if we'd stayed perfectly still, with the amount of magic they were throwing around, there's no way we wouldn't have been spotted."

Charlie shot an angry look at Bawb, and for just a moment, the distraught assassin almost looked apologetic.

Almost.

"Can you get us into open space?" Charlie asked.

"I think so."

"Then do it. If we get clear enough of the obstacles down here, I may be able to throw out a few diversionary spells that might shake them up enough to let us jump."

"If they stop blocking us," Tym added.

"They're in front, too?"

"Afraid so. And more are––"

Tym abruptly went quiet as wave after wave of magical flames washed over the pursuing ships. The ferocity of the attack made them peel off immediately and run for cover while they regrouped, lest they be destroyed outright. The craft in front of them, now lacking proper support to continue their blocking maneuver, spun away as well.

Apparently, the sight of a giant, fire-breathing Zomoki was enough to make them place their survival above all else, and that visceral run-away response provided the escaping ship with the window it needed.

"Ara!" Charlie exclaimed with overflowing joy.

"I'm locking on to your ship's jump signature," Ara informed Tym. "We are jumping immediately. Follow my lead!"

And just like that, the Zomoki and her shimmer-cloaked friends vanished from the sky, leaving burning ships, slaughtered guards, and a whole lot of explaining to be done in their wake.

CHAPTER FIFTEEN

"Fascinating. Look at this bit here, Cresh," Visla Malalia Maktan said as she pried open the housing on a basic pulse pistol. "It seems to connect to some sort of power contained in this part of the device, and, yet, there is absolutely no magic to be sensed."

She touched the trigger gently, discharging a pulse round that slammed harmlessly into the far wall of the chamber, diffusing in the magical catch-field as many before it had done.

"Yes, Visla. It is a most unusual bit of work, this alien 'technology' device," Visla Cresh said, leaning in to better see the particular mechanism that was being pointed out.

She had taken leave from her previous position breaking down the overall mechanics of the Urok vessel and was now working side by side with Visla Dominus herself. It was an unprecedented honor for her, and she strove to impress her visla every chance she could.

Vislas Hoomra and Galvash had both remained aboard the Urok ship with the members of its captive crew who had "seen the light" and come to be most helpful in understanding the workings of the craft. The officers, however, would rather die.

And several had, before their underlings began to feel their resolve falter.

Of course, they had no intention of slaughtering anyone of actual value. Not if they could avoid it. But a few carefully performed executions, well within eye and earshot of the victim's subordinates, could work wonders when it came to loosening tongues.

While they'd made very commendable progress with both the prisoners and the ship itself, it was Cresh who seemed to possess the most intuitive knack for the unusual designs. It was all still foreign gibberish to her, of course, but more than the others, she at least, seemed to be making some actual sense of it.

For that reason, Visla Dominus had her transferred aboard her own craft. And it was there that the *really* interesting things were being studied.

More than just the Urok ship had been recovered, it turned out. There were also small, seemingly autonomous craft that had been periodically sent through the portal, though their function was still somewhat of a mystery. They'd appear, send out some sort of non-magical pulse, then fall silent.

Only when the portal re-opened did they re-activate and power up their drive systems. Apparently, they were designed to surreptitiously carry information back and forth from galaxy to galaxy. At least, that's what the prisoners had said during one of the more productive torture sessions.

That was an issue with the whole torture thing. The Uroks were a very rank-conscious species, and as a result, they tended to hyper-compartmentalize information to just those whose rank and position warranted it. While some militaries would utilize similar protocols to ensure secrecy of plans and data, the Uroks appeared to do so entirely due to their rather unusual social system.

It was only by blind luck that the man who happened to

break and give them information also possessed a position that afforded him at least a modicum of knowledge that was of use to the visla.

Malalia may have been from a magical galaxy, but she'd been to Earth once before, and she had witnessed firsthand the mechanical weaponry its people devised, even thousands of years in the past. She knew them. How their minds worked. And, though she was hell-bent on conquering every last one of them, she couldn't help but admire their perseverance and ingenuity.

If she'd been born into a world with no magic, would she have had the impetus to devise all of these unusual, mechanical devices to do the work of a simple spell? Malalia couldn't say for certain, but, regardless, she would do all that was in her considerable power to better understand her enemy in every way possible.

It had been lucky for Earth's forces that no AIs had been caught on this side of the portal. While they could endure any torture and simply shut themselves off if need be, if Malalia had her hands on that level of computing genius, she might begin developing weapons-grade spells specifically targeting them.

As it was, she was unaware of that unusual aspect of her enemy's forces. And while many of the Uroks being questioned knew of the AIs, they were seen as simply names and positions within the enemy forces and nothing worth noting. Not unless specifically questioned, anyway. And that was how the existence of artificial intelligence skated past Malalia's interrogators. Not by subterfuge and wit, but because they simply didn't know what to ask.

The other devices, however, she was rapidly developing an understanding of. Even a rudimentary grasp of how warp travel functioned, though she was also made very aware of the dangers of using it in this galaxy.

"Excellent," she'd said. "Our enemy is crippled and unable to flee."

"They have fled, though, Visla," Cresh noted. "Though we do not know how efficiently."

"From what we've gleaned, they fly blind, like children, only reaching the general area of their intended destination on occasion, and even then, mostly by sheer luck," Malalia replied.

She continued to deconstruct the system. Working it backwards, deciphering the technology as best she could. And not just the warp, but everything. It was the first time in ages she'd felt so engaged in a project.

Usually she could simply call upon her formidable magic to handle any task, but this? This was different. This forced her to use more than the power of her magic. It made her flex the muscle of her mind. And she was reveling in it.

"It's interesting, don't you think, Cresh? The way there is a logic to the illogic of these devices."

"It is, Visla," Cresh replied. "It just takes thinking like the enemy. As if we were ignorant of the ways of power."

"Yes, precisely," Malalia agreed.

"By approaching these with the naiveté of a child, we find ourselves able to look past our ingrained prejudices and preconceived notions of how things should work. And you're absolutely right. In that case, there really is a logic to the illogic of it all."

Malalia smiled warmly at her underling. She'd chosen wisely, bringing this one under her wing. Visla Cresh may have been a rather powerful visla in her own right, but she was proving time and again to be worth far more than just what her power was capable of. The woman had an impressive mind, and one that was up for the challenges her visla was presenting her.

"Visla Dominus?" Captain Darus said as he entered the testing chamber.

"What is it, Captain? You know how I loathe being interrupted while in the middle of my experiments."

"Yes, Visla, I am aware. However, we just received a long-range skree from one of our vessels. They jumped as quickly as they could to get into range to pass along the message."

"Jumped into range? Where was this craft originating from?"

"Slafara, Visla," he replied.

Malalia's power crackled around her as her attention quickly shifted focus to the man standing before her. "What happened, Darus?"

"An attack on the estate, Visla. A great many casualties, including Visla Sima and Emmik Thorsin."

"They dared attack the Palmarian estate? How many were there? How many vessels in the attack?"

"That's the unusual thing, Visla," Darus began. "There were no ships. Not that participated in the attack, anyway. It was a ground assault."

"A group charged the gates? A daring and audacious move."

"Yes, Visla," he said, pausing a moment, realizing how mad what he was about to say would sound. "The thing is, it wasn't a group of attackers. It was only one."

"*One*? How could a lone attacker do the damage you're describing?" Malalia asked, but the answer was already dawning on her. The one she'd failed to capture at the fall of the Ghalian training facility. It had to be.

Captain Darus confirmed her suspicions. "It was a Wampeh, Visla. A Wampeh Ghalian. And he made quick work of our men."

Malalia smiled as she pondered the situation. It was an unexpected sight that made Captain Darus even more uncomfortable than he already was.

"Visla?" he quietly inquired.

Malalia stood silently a long moment. The Ootaki woman

was safe with her, a long, long way away. But her other assets were not.

"Did he recover my Wampeh?" she finally asked.

"No, Visla. He is still intact and secure in the tower."

"Good," she said, her grin spreading. "But my, how they are getting so daring. Daring and confident. And very soon, it may well be their undoing."

CHAPTER SIXTEEN

Being reunited with Ara, even after a relatively short separation, was a welcome comfort for Charlie. Their bond reached farther than he had originally realized, and her total absence had made him note it even more acutely.

Bawb was also bonded with her, in his own way, but not by blood. He was bonded by the sharing of power. It was still a strong connection, but not nearly as robust as what he and Hunze shared. And she was still missing. Captured and held somewhere far away. Far enough that he sensed no trace of her whatsoever.

For a Wampeh Ghalian to feel such deep emotions was unusual. Dangerous. And if it continued to cause erratic behavior from him, it could become something the other masters would eventually need to handle, however they might deem necessary.

Charlie and Ara discussed the situation when they arrived back at the rally point. Bawb had gone to sit alone again once they'd landed on the planet's surface, and his friends had left him to his thoughts.

"It is not something the Wampeh Ghalian are known to allow,"

Ara said. *"There is a reason they have remained in the shadows so successfully for so long."*

"I know. But he's a legend to them, Ara."

"Even so, if their legend jeopardizes the institution as a whole, even he may become a liability."

"What are you saying? They'll kill him?"

"I honestly do not know. It would seem a likely option. But given who he is, and the value he has for them, perhaps they'd resort to somewhat less drastic options."

"So they'd imprison him, basically?"

"It would not be ideal. But yes, it could happen."

"Better than death for most, but not for Bob."

"I know, Charlie. But perhaps I can help, at least a little," Ara said, then fell silent. She then dipped her massive head slightly and closed her great, golden eyes in concentration.

Charlie felt her reaching out over her connection. Reaching past him, all the way to their Wampeh friend. But she wasn't speaking to him. Nor was she attempting to cast with him as they'd done in battle. Ara was pulling from him. Taking a portion of his pain and grief, while feeding him a little of her power to cauterize the magically bleeding psychic wound.

It didn't change the man much, at least not that Charlie could sense. But it did take the edge off of his grief, and along with that reduction came a sense of clarity of mind and improved judgment that his friend had been lacking of late.

Ara released the tenuous connection and opened her eyes, all without their friend being any the wiser as to what she'd done.

"I didn't know you could do that," Charlie quietly said. *"I could feel you reaching out to him through our bond. But you didn't exactly heal him. What was that?"*

"Something I have only done twice before, and then, only in the most dire of times," Ara replied. *"But I felt the Geist's pain. And, given*

the circumstances, believed it was warranted. He is hurting terribly, Charlie."

"Trust me, I know."

"I am sure you do. I hope this will help right his mind and bring him back from the precipice. To lose him would be a great blow to our cause. Not to mention—"

"Not to mention, he's our friend," Charlie said, finishing her thought.

Ara nodded.

"The Wampeh Ghalian will keep a close eye on him, so we'd be wise to keep him from running off on his own again. As best we can, at least. I believe that once we are engaged in a productive action and seeing results, Bawb will return to his senses even more."

"He'd better," Charlie said, noting one of the assassin masters walking their way.

It was Zilara, the tall, slender Wampeh master. "One of our spies managed to work through the ranks since our insertion and is now deeply embedded within Dominus's fleet," she said. "And they've sent news. Come, we are going to brief the others."

Charlie followed her to the nearby clearing, where the captains and other Wampeh had gathered. They had considerately selected an area clear enough of trees as to make a comfortable space for Ara to join them without difficulty. Say what you would about the Wampeh Ghalian, but they were considerate hosts.

Leila was already there and moved seats to join Charlie. Daisy and her youthful entourage were there as well. The lone Chithiid in the galaxy sat perched atop a rock, his AI friend surely listening in over his open comms line. And, of course, Tym and the pirate leaders were also present.

"Let us begin, shall we?" Zilara said. It was a rhetorical question. "We have received information from one of our most valuable assets," she began. "This person is deep within the enemy's fleet—"

"Close enough to slay Dominus?" one of the captains interrupted.

Zilara let the rudeness slide. "Close enough? Perhaps. But, given what we know of Dominus's power, that would be a fool's errand if attempted single-handed. So, to answer your question, they are not making any such attempts. Instead, they are silently gathering information and observing, but taking no other action."

Charlie glanced over at Bawb and was pleased to see the steely stare of concentration had returned to his friend's eyes. Sharp. Taking in every detail. For the moment, at least, it appeared the Geist was back with them. Mostly, anyway.

"Our spy has been privy to many fragments of information, but none so useful as what I'm sharing with you now. For the first time, we have actionable intel. Visla Dominus is preparing a second assembly point, from which she will be launching her next attacks. Somewhere other than the portal's location. They've only just begun to gather, from what our spy could tell, so if we are able to preemptively strike that smaller group of vessels while they're separated from her main fleet, we may be able to disrupt her plans greatly."

"That's excellent," Rovnik said, his fellow pirate captains nodding their agreement. "When do we attack?"

"That is the issue we have gathered to discuss," Zilara replied. "All our spy saw were images. Images of a group of ships surrounded by clouds."

"So we go to those places," Daisy said. "Seems simple enough."

"There are a great many, Daisy," Zilara said.

A rumble of murmurs passed through the pirates.

"We know of cloud worlds. We've used them to hide ourselves on occasion," Rovnik noted. "And Zilara is correct. There are dozens of them in inhabited systems. And far more if you count the uncharted ones."

"Indeed. But from what our spy heard, this clouded planet is just a few worlds away from a rich, populated one. So that narrows our search considerably. But the search will be difficult, as many of you know. The enemy will be shielded by clouds, mist, ice, and storms. And many of these worlds wreak havoc on magical probes at a distance, so we will have to get relatively close to locate our prey."

"And if we find them? Then what?" Dukaan asked. "We have had our staging area attacked once already, and were woefully unprepared."

The others weren't happy to admit it, but the Chithiid was right. They'd been overrun and driven to flee despite their swelling ranks. Dominus's numbers were simply too great.

Bawb stepped forward, a calm but somewhat scary look in his eyes.

"The first step in any battle is knowing your enemy. Learning their strengths and weaknesses," he said. "And I know this enemy well. She is arrogant. Overconfident. Comes from a life of privilege. But she is also smart. We must separate her from the body of vessels we wish to attack. Lure her away. And when we do, we strike hard and fast."

"Bawb is correct," Zilara said, she and the other Wampeh Ghalian clearly pleased the Geist had finally joined them again, and in more than just body. "So for now we split up to search. We move fast and quietly. Locate them and assess only. Once we've determined their staging location, we shall meet back here and plan our response. If we are successful at staging an ambush in their own clouds, they won't know what hit them until it is too late."

"The Ghalian way," a pirate captain noted.

At that little crack, all of the masters smiled in unison. "Indeed," Zilara replied with a pointy-toothed grin.

CHAPTER SEVENTEEN

The rebel fleet divided itself into several groups before the scouting parties headed out. The newcomer ships were still being retrofitted to prepare for the upcoming fight, and more were arriving. They trickled in slower than before, however, as new multiple-jump location precautions enacted to protect this new rally point were slowing the lesser-powered craft significantly.

But it was all in the name of safety for their burgeoning fleet, and, thus far, it seemed the tactic was working. And more than just ships were arriving. Supplies and materials to help upgrade them were now pouring in as well, a great portion of them arriving in a steady stream, guided by a stocky man with colorful braids in his hair.

It seemed that Quintz, once separated from the constraints of his role as Mandoog's henchman in his underworld domain, had taken a shine to the whole rebel thing. And he and the pirates were getting along famously.

What had begun as a reluctant bit of assistance from a man fearing for his life, had become an actual enthusiasm for the cause. And with it, the secret supplies and resources Mandoog was attempting to withhold—even under threat of Wampeh Ghalian retribution, no less—were being slowly ferried out to help expand and reinforce the growing fleet.

But not all of the craft were in need of upgrades. In fact, the vast majority were fairly robust, and the dozen-plus captured Tslavar warships were a formidable defensive ring should any attempt to surprise the others as they were engaged in improvements and repairs.

The pirate-crewed craft were also too large to sneak into the clouded worlds unnoted. For this mission, the smaller to mid-sized craft were far more capable, and of those, they had many.

Ara, of course, was not a ship. But she was Charlie's ride once more, and more than capable of carrying out their task. Bawb was also coming along, as Charlie and Ara both wanted to keep an eye on him, hoping their invisible bond would key them in to the need for any intervention before things got out of hand again.

Bawb, however, would be flying aboard Kip with Dukaan, their warp linked to Ara's magical jumps once again. Leila was joining in on this mission, and she was sitting atop Ara with her king ,while their friend rode the AI craft.

Charlie had explained that he thought it best if his Wampeh friend flew with them, given the circumstances. He'd put it to his friend tactfully, suggesting that Kip might need a bit of assistance with the jumps, and Bawb's powered presence could greatly help the little AI ship.

Whether he knew it was a ploy to keep him and Leila from an uncomfortable flight together was never stated, but, as his spirits and clarity of mind were returning, Charlie was pretty sure his friend knew the score, and was glad he went along with the plan willingly.

Their target world was quite far away, and was an unusual one at that. The mists and clouds covered a planet that was almost entirely water, with only a few small islands dotting the vast oceans. But there was supposedly a society there. A hidden one. And for that reason, it was a very likely location for one such as Malalia to use for her machinations.

Daisy and Freya, on the other hand, were tasked with surveying the handful of floating cities of Annabit. Each of the cities was magically suspended high above the core of the gas giant, the magical properties of the mists tapped into and utilized in the castings that were keeping them aloft.

It had become something of a power loop, the city's spells pulling from the ambient power over so many years that the magic had come to require only a handful of casters to adjust it and keep it flowing. And the main city of Raxama was reported to be a shining beacon of civilization on the gaseous world, though one not terribly fond of outsiders, if rumors were correct.

That particular world had not been frequented by any of their pirate brethren, nor anyone else in the rebel fleet, for that matter. So, although Tym and his shimmer craft would be accompanying her, it looked like Daisy would be flying in blind.

"Better you than me," Charlie joked when he heard the description of Daisy's destination.

"Oh? Why's that?"

"Let's just say I have no desire to have any run-ins with bounty hunters in cloud cities," Charlie replied with a mischievous chuckle.

"Not a fan of carbonite, eh?" Daisy joked.

Charlie was caught off guard. She raised an amused eyebrow. "I'm from Earth, dude. That's a classic, even in my time."

"Oh, yeah. Mom has a massive entertainment collection," Arlo chimed in. "Like, we're talking, *extensive*." The teen turned to the girls. "If you want, I can show you when we get back home."

Kara's pale violet cheeks blushed slightly.

"Oh, Rip showed us some," Vee jumped in, saving her friend from the embarrassing attention.

"But we'd love to see more of them," Kara added. "*If* we go back, that is."

It was something of a sticking point with the girl. She was finally in her own galaxy, and her father was in dire need of help, yet she couldn't do a thing about it. She'd tried, and nearly gotten herself, as well as Arlo and Vee caught for their troubles.

But this was war, and, despite his overly impulsive acts, Arlo was a good kid and a great pilot. Additionally, he and Marty were a valuable part of the team now that they'd found a way to make the warp drive work in this galaxy, thanks largely to Kara's help.

"You're going to one of the safer worlds," Daisy informed him.

"I get to go?"

"Yeah, and you're taking the girls with you. It seems they can help Marty steer his warp better, somehow, so it would be foolish not to use that. But you get a chaperone."

Farmatta waved and smiled at the teens, her old woman act embarrassing him, even though he knew she was far more than what she appeared.

"Moooomm," he groaned. "Why?"

"Because you screwed up, kid, and I want eyes on you. And trust me, I'll find out if you try anything stupid again. Believe me, you don't want to cross that one," Daisy said, nodding to the old Wampeh. "Now, you'll be flying to a pretty quiet planet. There are only a few inhabited cities there, and they are all located on the tops of mountains. The rest of the surface is covered by clouds. You're only there to see if there's anything out of the ordinary, you hear?"

"Yes, ma'am," the teen sighed.

"Okay. Because as confident as you may be, you and Marty aren't ready to take on a bunch of enemy ships. Are we clear?"

"Yeah," he grumbled.

"Good. Now give your mom a hug."

"Moooomm."

"No lip, mister," Daisy said, pulling her son in tight. "Now, you be careful out there, and listen to Farmatta. She's been around a long time and knows more about this sort of thing than you'll ever hope to. So be polite, and try to learn from her."

"Okay."

Daisy ruffled his hair. "Good. Now, get going. And be safe. We'll see you back here shortly."

Arlo and the girls walked toward the waiting AI ship. Marty had already prepped for the trip, having been listening in over Arlo's comms the entire time. Farmatta fell into step beside them.

"An adventure. How fun!" she said, appearing for all intents and purposes to be a sweet old lady.

A sweet old lady who could kill a dozen men and dispose of their bodies before they hit the floor.

"Yeah, at least we get to do *something*," Arlo said.

Kara, however, had other plans. "We need to make a stop on the way," she said.

"You heard the directives. We are to go straight to our destination and perform a survey, then return back here with our findings. Nothing more," Farmatta reminded her.

"But there's someone I need to speak with. It'll be quick."

"No. You know the plan."

"But she's a healer," the teen protested. "And she might be able to help your friend."

Farmatta paused a moment. "A healer, you say?"

"A powerful one," Kara added.

"Hmm. Well, if it's on the way, I suppose we could make a little detour," the old woman conceded.

"Fantastic! Thank you!"

"Don't thank me yet. Now, where is it this healer lives?"

Karasalia told her, and the Wampeh nodded her approval. "Not far out of our way at all. Very well. Let's be off, then."

Farmatta stepped into her shimmer ship and immediately vanished. They knew she was still right there with them, but the woman's power was extensive, and there wasn't a trace.

"Uh, where exactly is it we're going?" Arlo asked as they stepped aboard Marty.

"We're going to find a friend," Kara replied. "Her name is Amazara."

CHAPTER EIGHTEEN

The warp-jump Marty made—with a bit of help from Kara—went perfectly. Farmatta had jumped along with them, but had merely linked her magic to that of the AI ship's course, opting to go wherever fate would take them rather than guide them herself. It was important for the youngsters to make their way without her help, and she was perfectly content to sit back as silent, invisible support should they need it.

Fortunately, her intervention was not required, and Marty and Kara successfully steered his ship to roughly the place they'd intended to arrive.

Give or take a few thousand miles.

"Hey, now that was pretty good, right?" Marty blurted enthusiastically.

"Yeah, dude. Not bad," Arlo agreed. "Thanks, Kara."

"I'm glad to help," she said, looking out the ship's forward windows.

From their vantage point, the planet seemed just a ball of colors floating in the black. But soon they would descend into the atmosphere, and all of that blue and green would expand into oceans and forests. It was a beautiful world, both from space and on its surface, and Kara found herself viscerally moved at her return.

"Amazara's place is just down——"

"I've got it," Marty said, flashing images of the woman's hilltop home onto the screens. "Just like you said. I'll set down behind the hill so we don't freak out the locals."

"It's appreciated," Kara replied. "The hike up the hill isn't too far."

"A hike actually sounds nice," Arlo said. "It'll feel great to get out and stretch our legs a bit."

Kara thought back to the last time she'd come to this place. So weak, unable to even make the trek afoot, relying on her uncle Korbin's conveyance instead. But this time she felt good. Better than good, even. She was stronger than ever, and the trek to the hilltop would be a piece of cake.

Marty took a roundabout approach, just skimming the treetops before dropping to the ground at the base of the hill. He'd kept his unusual ship out of sight. There was no sense giving away their presence if they didn't need to, even if Visla Dominus didn't have a presence here. Safe and unobserved was the order of the day.

The teens stepped out into the fresh air, breathing deeply and enjoying the smell of lush forest and clean skies.

"The trail's just over here," Kara said, then started walking, a spring in her step.

It would be good to see Amazara again. The two had connected when she was last here, she thought. If only her uncle was with them as well, she had a feeling he and Amazara had some unfinished business they needed to hash out, even if neither would admit it.

The trek to the top went quickly, the teens' agile legs easily carrying them over the rocks and stumps that littered the way. The light filtered through the trees just right, illuminating the path, while shading them from the midday sun. All in all, it made for a very refreshing hike, and in no time, they arrived at the summit of the hill.

Arlo nearly tripped when he saw the tall, pale-blue-haired woman with silver eyes watching their approach from her porch. He could see why Kara's uncle had a thing for her. The woman radiated both femininity and strength to the Nth degree.

"Amazara!" Kara called out, gleefully running to hug the healer.

"Oh, how much better you look, Kara. Your color has returned. And your energy, I see." Amazara reached out with her empath's touch and felt the teen's magic.

Her eyes tightened slightly. This wasn't just a bit of an improvement. This was a massive shift. That meant her suspicions had been correct. Someone had been intentionally stealing power from the girl. But now she was on the mend and coming back into her own power. And from what Amazara could tell, it would be quite substantial.

"I'm sorry. My manners," Kara said, stepping back. "This is Vee."

"Ah, yes. The Ootaki girl Korbin mentioned. I'm so pleased to meet you."

Vee blushed at the woman's pure warmth. Her hair had been unable to hold color for some time now, and it was nice to get out and talk to people again. People who didn't want to make her a slave, that is. But the readiness with which her true nature was revealed was, nevertheless, a needed reminder, lest she forget and get careless when among less friendly company.

Kara gestured casually to the young pilot standing quietly by.

"And that's Arlo."

"Hi."

Amazara noticed the slight blush that briefly flashed to Kara's cheeks when she introduced the boy, just as she caught the reciprocal shifting in his posture at the attention. Teens, she mused. It was cute.

"I'm delighted to meet you. *All* of you. Would your friend like to join us? Perhaps a pot of tea?"

Kara and the others looked to where Amazara was gazing, just in time to see Farmatta shed her shimmer cloak.

"Farmatta? I didn't see you land with us," Arlo said.

"Nor would you, boy," she replied with a chuckle. "It's a pleasure to make your acquaintance, Amazara," the assassin said. "I've heard a lot about you."

Amazara knew full well what the old woman truly was and wasn't fooled by her act for an instant. But she was also not afraid. Not in the slightest. Farmatta noted the woman's pulse and temperature hadn't shifted one bit. And she'd known a shimmer was being used. Indeed, this woman was gifted. And more than that, she'd passed the Wampeh's little test.

The two women clasped hands in greeting, sensing one another's power as they did. If there was to be a fight, Farmatta almost always resorted to her magic, and Amazara could feel the woman's strength. But this was more akin to how Baloo and Bahnjoh were when they first met. Sniffing around one another before becoming fast friends.

The assassin wasn't one for making friends, per se, and especially not at a time like this. But, nonetheless, she took a shine to the healer, which was saying something. And from what she could sense, the feeling was mutual.

"Yes, some tea would be delightful," the older woman said with a warm smile.

Amazara showed her guests into the kitchen and prepared a pot, then the five of them took a seat out on the porch, resting in the shade and appreciating the cool breeze.

"I'm glad to see you, Kara, but I must admit, I'm a bit surprised you are here. And where's your uncle? I haven't heard from him since your last visit."

"Uncle Korbin is gone," Kara said, immediately regretting the choice of words when she saw Amazara stiffen and catch her breath. "I mean, he's fine. But he's not here," she quickly added. "We kind of had a problem. Well, a fight, actually. And because of that, we wound up crossing a portal into another galaxy."

Now *that* news really got Amazara's attention. "Korbin is in another *galaxy*? But how is that even possible? And how did you manage to return? And why without him?"

It was a lot of questions, and Kara knew she'd have to answer a lot more, but that could be done aboard Marty as they flew to their destination. For now, the short and sweet version would have to suffice.

"Arlo was taking me back across the portal to find my father. That's how I returned."

"But without your uncle? I know how protective he is of you."

"Yeah, he's not going to be happy about this, I know," Kara sighed. "But we're on a really important mission now. We're flying to a cloud planet to try to see if there's any trace of Visla Dominus's ships."

"You're kids, and yet they send you into battle?"

"Not battle. Just recon," Arlo interjected. "And believe me, Farmatta won't let us get into any trouble. My mom made sure of that."

The old Wampeh merely smiled politely in her deceptively sweet manner.

"But Dominus is dangerous. And powerful."

"Don't I know it," Kara groaned.

"What is it, Kara?" Amazara asked, sensing the girl's dread.

"The thing is, we finally know who Visla Dominus really is."

"His true identity? That's fantastic!" Amazara replied.

"Yes and no," Arlo noted.

"What does he mean?"

"Remember my stepmom, Mareh?"

"Yes."

"Well, *she* is Visla Dominus."

Amazara gasped. "No! That's impossible. But, how? We should have sensed her."

"Oh, that's where it gets even worse. Apparently, she's actually someone named Malalia Maktan."

At that, Amazara nearly dropped her teacup.

"I know it sounds crazy, but it looks like she's been stealing Wampeh blood and using it to gain their abilities for hundreds of years, getting stronger and staying young. With their blood in her, she's been taking people's power. My father's power. And mine as well. She's been draining us for years. Since I was just a little girl, in fact."

"That would explain your weakness, and the sudden surge in power now that you've not been home. But how did no one notice?"

"It's a simple trick," Farmatta noted, joining the discussion. "The wounds only require the slightest of healing spells, and the whole process only takes a minute, and is easily wiped with a little memory block spell."

The implications of what she'd just heard landed on Amazara as if an elephant had jumped on her back. It was impossible. But if Malalia Maktan was truly alive, then the greatest of the Council of Twenty threats ever known was back, and she was leading a new fleet even more dangerous than her former one.

Amazara and Korbin had fought together against the remnants of the Council in the past. It was how they first met, in fact, and they'd done all they could to keep that group from regaining a foothold in any of the civilized systems. But now, if what Kara was saying was true, a far greater threat was already upon them, and they hadn't even seen it coming.

"I'm coming with you," she said, rising to her feet to clear the dishes.

"But you don't even know what—" Arlo began.

"It doesn't matter. Malalia was an integral part of the Council in the past, and Dominus has been amassing power in the present. That they're one and the same? The implications are staggering."

"Well, I was hoping you'd want to come," Kara said. "And we definitely need your help. We've got a sort of damaged Wampeh of our own, and he could really use your healing skills."

Amazara flashed a look to Farmatta. "Dominus?"

"Not directly," the old Wampeh replied. "But she took his woman. An Ootaki he'd bonded with."

"He is a *bonded* Wampeh Ghalian?"

"I know. It is something of an anomaly, and we do not bond for a very good reason. And now, as a result of this, he is not himself. And for one as skilled as the Geist, that is very, *very* dangerous."

"Did you say the *Geist*? But he died hundreds of years ago. The battle of Tolemac—"

"We believed so as well," Farmatta replied. "And you know your history, I see. Even that rather obscure piece of lore. But you'll be interested to find that a great many details of that event are not quite as we assumed."

Dishes rattled noisily as Amazara quickly washed them by hand. Normally, the act was a soothing bit of meditation for her, cleaning manually rather than with magic. But her emotions were rising, despite her training.

"This could get messy," she said, as she placed the last dish on the rack to dry. "We're leaving. For a while, it would seem. I need to get a few of my things."

Amazara walked from the kitchen without another word, lost in her thoughts, leaving her guests to their own devices for the time being.

"So, she's coming with," Arlo mused. "Cool."

"I like her," Vee said. "I can see why Korbin does too."

"Shh. Not so loud," Kara replied. "That's their business."

As if to punctuate the sentence, Amazara reappeared silently. They had not even heard her coming. Even Farmatta was impressed by the woman's stealth, though *she* had noted her approach. But, then, she was a Wampeh Ghalian master.

Amazara dropped a few bags onto the counter and opened one, pulling some containers of healing herbs and teas from the shelves.

"Is that a slaap?" Kara gasped as she glanced inside the bag.

"One of them," Amazara replied matter-of-factly.

"May I?" Farmatta inquired, gesturing to the other bags.

"Be my guest."

The assassin opened the nearest bag and looked inside. A smile of true delight spread across her lips. There were harnesses loaded with enchanted blades, several konuses, and a few more obscure weapons and restraints.

In the other bags were garments that, while practical, were also fashionable. More importantly, they each possessed more than a few hidden pockets, as well as a few threads of Ootaki hair woven into them. This was a kit worthy of any warrior, and even up to the standards of a few assassins.

"More than just a healer, I see," Farmatta said with a grin.

Amazara flashed an amused look. "I *am* a healer," she replied. "Let's just say, I have something of a colorful past." She sealed up the bags and slid them over her shoulders. "Now, where is this cloud-covered world you spoke of?"

CHAPTER NINETEEN

At first glance, it appeared as if little specks of chocolate were dotting the foam of an enormous cappuccino, the dark spots barely visible in the vast sea of white. Then Marty and Farmatta's ships closed in on the cloudy world and the focus shifted.

The dots were actually mountaintops, though only a few on the entire planet were inhabited. Most were just low enough that they spent most of their days beneath the dense mists of the cloud layer. And people, just like most plants, tended to gravitate toward the sun.

"We should fly a grid," Farmatta sent to the others over the comms unit Marty and Arlo had provided her for her craft. "Once we have the locations of the inhabited cities mapped out we can more effectively plan our next steps."

"Makes sense," Marty replied, already scanning the cloudy world below. "For a simple survey, we should be able to pinpoint the inhabited ones pretty quickly. Doesn't look like there are too many actual cities down there."

"There aren't," Farmatta noted.

The old woman had warmly offered to take Amazara on her

ship when they'd departed for their cloudy destination, and the healer had gladly taken her up on the offer. Kara was a little put out—she had been hoping to catch up further with her during the flight—but there would be time for that later.

And Amazara had seen the little look Farmatta gave her when she made the offer. The woman wanted to discuss something. Something kept private from the others.

"How much experience do you have with my kind?" the assassin asked as they ran their search pattern.

"Wampeh? A bit," Amazara replied. "If you mean Wampeh *Ghalian*, then I'm afraid none at all."

Farmatta nodded once. "As I expected, but you never know. From time to time my brothers and sisters find themselves in need of a healer, so the possibility, however slim, still existed."

"This is about your friend, the Geist. Tell me, how can I be of help?"

It was unusual for the assassin to be at a loss for words. She'd seen and done so much in her long life, nothing really fased her anymore. But this? This was a truly unusual situation.

"He is not a normal man. And I mean that in terms of not only Wampeh Ghalian, but magic users in general. You see, he possesses an unusual connection with his woman."

"The Ootaki, yes, you said."

"What I didn't say was that this Ootaki is special. Very special, in fact."

"How special are we talking, here?"

"She is in full control of the power contained within her hair, and the process that gifted her such potential also bound her even more tightly to the Geist. They're symbiotic, in a way. Drawing from one another. You must keep this to yourself, which I trust you will, but they gifted the hair to each other, and apparently freely, and out of love."

Amazara wasn't an expert in Ootaki power usage and magical transfers, but even she knew the basics of their unusual hair and how its power increased exponentially based on the way it was harvested. Freely given was rare. Given out of love was unheard of for the enslaved race.

Farmatta watched the realization dawn on the woman. "Ah, yes. You see the problem."

"He could be incredibly dangerous."

"And if he becomes so, we will have no choice but to put him down, though we are loath to do so. And thus, we come to your task, if you are able. We need you to heal his mental wounds. To put him as much at ease as is possible. There's no way to shed him of this bond, but if it can be muted somewhat, I am hopeful he may return to his normal self. At least, enough to no longer be a threat."

It was a lot the assassin master was asking of her, but Amazara had seen far more than any would believe in the early days of her freedom fighting with Korbin and their colleagues. It would be a challenge, but it was one she was willing to attempt.

"I'll do what I can," she said.

"I know you will. I just wanted to be sure you knew what you were in for. And if memory serves me, and the rumors were true, our stopping at this world may be a fortuitous coincidence."

"How so?"

Farmatta smiled. "We'll both see soon enough."

It was at the fifth, and largest, city they visited that something of interest was mentioned. All of the prior stops had been uneventful, though poor Vee had to stay aboard the ship the entire time. With intense sunshine on the summits, and no cloud-cover above, her Ootaki hair would catch far too much light and undoubtedly draw a lot of unwanted attention.

Now that coloring would no longer stay in her hair, she was hopeful Amazara might know a way to magically dull its golden shine. Otherwise, her daily life would always be one presenting some degree of risk.

At least, on this world the question of danger increasingly appeared to likely be just local issues at play. There had been no reports of Tslavar warships hiding in the mist. In fact, so far, there were no signs of dangerous visitors of any sort worth noting.

But then, at last, they had something.

"It's terrifying," the local herb vendor said when Amazara inquired about any unusual things in the area.

"Oh? How so?" she asked.

"In the mist. There's been a disturbance."

"What sort of disturbance? I'm sure plenty of things live in the clouds."

"Not like this. Whatever it is, some people don't come back when they head down. Why, my own supplies are growing dangerously low," she said, gesturing to her small baskets of dried plants.

Amazara chatted with her a little while longer before joining back with the others. "I'll be going down into the mists. To the base of the mountain," she informed her companions.

"You're gonna do *what*?" Arlo blurted. "But, why? I don't know if you've been listening, but people are saying there's something messed up down there. Probably a Tslavar staging area. You can't go down there. It's dangerous."

"I know," Amazara said, adjusting her clothing to allow better access to her weapons. "But when I was speaking with the herbalist, I noticed a very unusual plant in her wares. She only had a tiny bit left, but she told me it grows at the foot of this mountain."

"You can't go down there just for some stupid plant," Kara blurted.

"Unless it explains a Tslavar presence," Amazara replied.

"Why would it do that? It's just a plant," Arlo griped.

"Because it's a very unique species. I've only heard stories of it, so I don't know if the tales are actually true, but it is reputed to grant rather substantial restorative powers to Wampeh."

"Which is what Bawb needs," Arlo realized.

"Precisely. But it is also something Dominus would covet. If she's truly been taking Wampeh power all this time, it could be a great boon to her if she discovered it was more than just a story."

"And if there are Tslavars here..."

"Precisely. So, our needs are two-fold. This plant might be able to help your friend, and we must procure some. And if the Tslavars are gathering it as well, we need to tag their ships with trackers to see where they're going," Amazara said.

"Or we destroy the Tslavars before they leave the surface," Farmatta said, matter-of-factly.

"We can't just take out an unknown number of mercenaries," Arlo objected.

"*You* can't," the assassin replied with a smile.

"We're getting ahead of ourselves. First and foremost, we need to gather what we can and find out what's actually down there. It shouldn't take me long."

"Why you?" Kara asked.

"Because I'm not afraid. And because I know what the magical power signature of the plant is. The little sample that woman had left was enough for me to now be able to identify it by the feel of its power. One of my gifts," Amazara said.

"We must remain unnoted," Farmatta pointed out.

"Oh, believe me, I have no intentions of engaging them at all."

"Intentions and reality are often not the same thing."

"Farmatta's right," Kara added. "If it's Mareh––Dominus's men, they'll be looking out."

"Which is why I'll make my approach using a natural camouflage," the healer replied, walking toward a pen containing several domesticated Malooki.

The horse-like creatures walked right up to her, sensing her energy. Their mood-colored manes shifted to cheerful, warm tones. Amazara paid the owner for the use of the animal, then slid atop its back, sans saddle, so it appeared as if it were a wild animal. She then began the descent into the mist.

CHAPTER TWENTY

Amazara rode swiftly down the trail, descending into the murky twilight of the mist surrounding the mountain and covering the planet's surface. The swirling vapor possessed an unexpected and almost imperceptible sweet aroma, unlike normal clouds. It did, however, grow colder as she traveled lower, and it pressed heavier upon her with every step of her descent.

The trail, likewise, grew more treacherous as she proceeded, as if it was a tangible, terrestrial reflection of the mood carried in the air. Despite all of this, the Malooki remained surprisingly calm, though its mane did occasionally shift as movements in the mists spooked it.

"It's just winds," Amazara quietly soothed the beast, stroking its neck as she sat perched atop its back. "We'll be down soon, and then we'll head right back up to the sunlight. Just as soon as I've gathered what I'm looking for."

She had been hopeful that maybe she'd have the good fortune to come across some of the plant she sought on the way down, but none were anywhere near enough for her to sense as she reached out with her power. It was looking like they would indeed have to go all the way down.

The Malooki was sure-footed, she noted. To be this comfortable on the trail, and in the mist, Amazara wondered if the animal had been tamed as an adult, after many years running free in the area. She'd have to remember to ask when they returned to the stables up above.

The vapor in the air had an eerie way of muting sound, and even the footfalls of the animal directly beneath her were muffled by the time they reached her ears. And there were other sounds out there. Strange ones she couldn't quite make out. For all she knew, they could be very loud, yet relatively far away, or they could be far quieter and nearby. It was simply impossible to gauge.

She strained her ears, listening for the distinctive sound of mercenaries milling about. Their gear always had that particular clang to it. Those who hadn't been drilled in the necessity of stowing one's shit and locking their gear down tight, that is. They were often the first to fall in combat, never given the opportunity to correct their sloppy ways.

For Amazara, riding bareback atop the Malooki not only afforded her the benefit of being able to slide to the side and conceal herself, making it appear as though the animal was wild and alone, but it also kept her from any unwanted noises from riding gear.

The weapons she wore on her body were snugly fitted into their respective sheaths and holsters, all concealed in her otherwise normal-looking attire.

Something tickled the edges of her senses. Just a hint of it, but the sought-after plant was nearby.

"Come on. We're heading over that way," she said, gently nudging the animal with both her knees and her mind.

The two trotted quietly for several minutes as she zeroed in on the energy signature.

"There you are," Amazara said, sliding from the Malooki's back.

She pulled an empty sack free from where it had been secured at her waist and drew the longer of her blades. She could have simply taken cuttings, but seeing as they were going to war, and with Wampeh Ghalian on their side, if she could successfully transplant one of the shrubs, it could prove a most valuable healing tool for her deadly allies.

Amazara started to crouch but froze, the hair on the back of her neck abruptly drawing tight against her goose-bumped skin. She glanced at the Malooki. Its mane was shifting to a disturbing shade of gray. It was trying to blend into the mist, she realized. And that could only mean––

The beast moved silently, lunging through the air without making a sound. A silent predator of the mist about to make another kill. But this prey wasn't so easy a target.

Amazara dove to the side, rolling to her feet, now empty-handed, her blade still buried in the creature's thickly muscled chest. It was a good thing she'd chosen that one to dig with. Her shorter knives would likely not have had the reach required to pierce the beast's heart.

She couldn't stop and ponder that, though, as another shape leapt from the mist. Amazara forewent drawing her blades, instead pulling magic from the konuses worn on each wrist. Heavy, ornate, and brimming with power, they had been a gift from Korbin many years ago, and had served her very well in more than a few times of crisis.

The magic surged through her, the killing spell breaking the attacking creature's body despite its dense bone structure. It fell to the ground, sliding to a stop at her feet. Despite it wanting to kill and eat her, Amazara nevertheless felt a pang of sympathy for the ruined animal as it whimpered in agony. She was a healer first, a killer second.

Without hesitation, she drew a blade and drove it through the creature's skull with a magical boost adding to her strength, ending its suffering instantly. She then pulled her blade free and retrieved the other from the beast's accomplice. Or was it its mate? There was no time to investigate that hypothesis. There were likely others out there, and she needed to gather her booty with haste and get back to the safety above.

Amazara made quick work of a pair of the plants, prying them from the moist soil, their root balls intact. Those, she carefully tied into pouches, casting nourishing spells, ensuring the roots stayed viable. She then turned to the other plants and began cutting away as much as she could fit in the remaining bag.

Amazara very nearly threw her knife when the old Wampeh materialized in front of her from within her shimmer cloak. "Funny. I didn't sense you this time," she said, forcing her heart rate back to normal.

"Because this time I didn't wish you to," Farmatta said with a grin.

She had already taken a liking to the unusual healer, which was rather novel for her in and of itself. But after that little display of martial prowess and situational awareness, her presumption of Amazara's true nature and hidden skills appeared to have proven more accurate than she'd even hoped. There was indeed far more to the healer than met the eye.

"Come, there are more nearby. You would do well to gather what you need and get back before it gets more... *interesting*."

Amazara didn't need to be told twice, and within a minute she'd filled her bag to capacity. She turned to mount the Malooki and noted that Farmatta was already gone. She smiled to herself. The wily assassin was undoubtedly nearby, watching. And rather than creep her out, it gave her a little warm feeling in her stomach. The woman could kill her with a snap of her fingers, most likely, but despite that, Amazara couldn't help feel a fondness toward her.

And the feeling was mutual.

CHAPTER TWENTY-ONE

"Maybe he'll drop by and join us for a drink," Tym said over the comms system Cal had installed in the captured shimmer ship. "I mean, the offer's out there. I did score something of a windfall with that last job he sent my way, and Olo's always game if the drinks are on someone else's tab."

Daisy sighed. *Drinks with smugglers in a floating city? What could possibly go wrong?*

"*Yeah, I know. That doesn't bode well. Not for us, anyway,*" Sarah replied.

Tell me about it. Though if he gets drunk enough, maybe he'll shut up for a minute, Daisy mused with a chuckle.

It had been a tedious several jumps with the chatterbox pilot. As he was in a Drook-powered craft, Freya had to dial down her warps to not overextend the poor casters powering the ship. It was the one time tech from back home had a bit of an advantage, even if that wasn't the case for most of the ships that crossed over. They simply didn't have Freya's magic-imbued nanites to guide them.

Warp tech could cover vast distances in an instant, similar to how magical jumps worked, she supposed. But when comparing them side by side, warping had a clear advantage in both range and frequency. And so, Freya slowed her roll to allow the talkative pilot to keep up as they made their way to scout the very distant and very secluded cloud-covered planet.

They didn't know much about the world of floating cities in the sky, but Daisy was anxious to check it out. An actual floating city? It was just too cool, and she'd been the lucky one to get to investigate it.

The inhabitants were rather reclusive, apparently, and pretty much no one ever ventured there but cutthroats and miscreant scum. But that was what made it kind of perfect for Visla Dominus if she wanted to set up shop there. Cities not tethered to land? Ideal for docking her ships not only around them, but above and below as well.

Add to that a particularly antisocial population with a penchant for violence, and who were highly unlikely to be speaking to anyone from outside their system, and you had a prime staging point for an invasion force.

Now they simply had to determine if such a force was gathering there. Given the visibility issues with the strange nature of the planet's magical clouds, simply scanning from space wouldn't cut it. Not this time, anyway, and it was up to Daisy and Tym to tag-team around the cities to see what they could find.

Of course, Tym had his shimmer cloak, which was of exceptional quality, so unless he was specifically targeted by Dominus's ships, he should be able to sneak by quite easily. And as for Freya, she possessed a form of active camouflage that, while not perfect in flight, would nevertheless hide her quite well in the swirling clouds. The shifting mists, she realized, would blend in with the quirks of in-flight camouflage perfectly.

"Okay, Tym. We're gonna go on in," Daisy notified their counterpart. "You ready to rumble, Freya?"

"You betcha. I'll just have my nanites do their visual shifting thing, and we should be good to go."

"Great. Whenever you're ready, kiddo."

"Heading in," she replied, descending into the layer of clouds below. "It's worse than we expected," Freya said a few minutes later. "I can't see shit down here. My scans are all kinds of messed up. How's it looking on your end, Tym? You picking anything up with your magic stuff?"

"Nah, all the ambient power in the clouds is wreaking havoc with my probes as well. We're going to have to rely mostly on visual. I mean, I can *sort of* pick things up, but not enough to be terribly efficient."

"I hear ya. Okay, then, swing around to my right and we'll begin."

"Already there," Tym replied.

"I call bullshit," Freya retorted. "You do realize I can see the clouds moving around you despite your shimmer, right?"

"Oh," was all Tym managed to come up with.

"Wow, Freya. You actually made him go quiet. We should celebrate or something," Daisy said with a laugh.

"You know, this cloud tracking thing might be useful with the enemy," Sarah noted.

I was thinking the same thing, Sis. The clouds don't lie, but what if there was some way to rig them to? If the magic folks can figure out a way to do that, maybe it'll serve as a good diversion for our forces.

"A weakness that cuts both ways? I like it," Sarah replied.

Daisy squinted at the monitors. "Oh, shit."

"What is it?" Tym asked.

There it was, a magically suspended city, connected by floating skyways, green spaces, residential, and commercial sections, all of them held aloft by magic.

"I can see the city. And it's really freakin' cool."

"So what's the problem?"

"Freya, zoom that in, will ya?" Daisy asked.

The image enhanced, confirming her concerns.

"There's a blockade around it," she informed him. "Though, from what I can tell, they don't seem to be Dominus's ships."

Tym focused his magic on the armada lying ahead of them. "You're right. They're not Dominus's. They're pirates."

"Good pirates or bad pirates?" Daisy asked, amused that she was even posing that question.

"One way to find out," Tym replied. "I'll skree them and see if they are interested in making some coin. Or fighting the good fight for a cause. And if that doesn't work, maybe they know Marban and his men. Gimme a minute."

Tym did his thing, while Freya counted the ships with her scanner as best she could. The magical clouds were concealing some of them, though, making her math questionable at best.

"I'd estimate at least twenty, if not more," Freya finally announced.

"Just wonderful. Well, hopefully they know Marban," Daisy replied.

The pirates received Tym's skree message, but they didn't reply. Not verbally, at least. Instead, they launched into a full-press assault.

"What happened, Tym?" Daisy asked as Freya dove into the clouds, dodging magical attacks.

"It seems like they most likely *do* know Marban. But, judging by their reaction, I don't think they like him very much."

"Just our luck," Daisy grumbled as Freya spiraled up into the sky, firing her cannons in her wake.

"This shooting behind you thing is really messing with magic people's heads, Daisy," she noted as the pursuing craft quickly scattered and regrouped.

There were definitely at least twenty craft—that they'd been able to see, that is. But as they'd worried, the clouds concealed many more than that, and all were swarming after the two nosy ships. Freya engaged them, with her nanites shielding against possible stun attacks, while Tym fired his own salvos at the pursuing pirates. Unfortunately for him, every time he did, they were able to get a fix on his shimmer ship's location.

He had few options, and the choices were getting worse.

"What should we do, Daisy? They're all small ships, and it's impossible to target them all effectively," Freya said, concerned at the sheer quantity of attackers pursuing them.

"Just keep it together until we can get clear—"

A magical blast shook the ship, but Freya's shields held.

"Tym, we need to do something," Daisy transmitted.

"I agree. Though I've never been one for suicide runs, this could be pretty glorious."

"This guy. I swear, he wants *to die."*

If I didn't know better, I'd agree. Now hurry up and find us a—

A dazzling flurry of magically hurled debris combined with a scattershot peppering of powerful spells disrupted the pursuing ships, outright destroying one and sending at least three others spiraling back into the clouds.

"Woo hoo!" a voice belted out over the skree on Tym's ship. The open comms link picked it up and transmitted it to Freya in real time. "You're all clear! Now why don't you sit back and let a *real* pilot show you how it's done."

Olo had come after all, and these pirates were standing between him and his drink. And any who knew him, knew that was not a wise idea.

"Sit back?" Tym shot back. "I just flew to another galaxy, Olo. Another *galaxy*. Sit back? Ha! Not a chance," he said, then dove into the fray once again.

"I've still got a higher count than you, I'll remind you," Olo shot back as he too plunged back into the swarm of confused pirate craft.

It was impressive watching the two master pilots drive each other to greater feats of daring and skill. They were taking it up a notch in their desire to one-up the other, making their already talented flying even more so.

"Oh, you're bringing up the count again, are you? Fine. It is *so* on!" Tym said with a madman's laugh. "Daisy, you and Freya go do what you need to do. Olo and me? We've got this."

Freya activated her active camouflage as she dove into the clouds. But she'd calculated the trajectory of the craft on her tail and quickly shifted aside just a little, then came to an abrupt stop, hovering in place, mostly invisible, unless you knew what to look for.

The pursuers didn't.

They shot right past, scouring for the fleeing ship at high speeds. Freya, meanwhile, slowly made her way through the clouds toward the city, making sure to do her best not to create a trackable wake as she flew.

"We'll touch down and do a quick survey. Given the reaction of these guys, I think if there's no sign of Dominus in this city, it's a fair bet there won't be at any of the others."

"Yeah, they're not fond of visitors, it seems," Olo noted as his ship corkscrewed around a trio of pursuers. "You take your time, though. I'll be up here, teaching my friend a few tricks." A ship burst apart in his wake, Tym clearing the pursuer for his friend.

"That's another for me," the yammering pilot claimed with glee.

"They're actually racking up points, Daze. This is ridiculous."

Ridiculous or not, it's buying us some time, so we'd better not waste it, Daisy replied as Freya moved in to land. *But damn, Sis, look at 'em go. They really are some of the best pilots in the system,* she marveled.

Daisy was right. For all their bluster and bravado, the two men could walk the walk as well as talk the talk, and it was a sight to see.

Freya set down in a little clear space that seemed

infrequently trafficked. "This is about as good as I can manage, Daisy," she said. "I hope it's close enough for your needs."

"Should do just fine, kiddo," Daisy replied, grabbing a pulse rifle and picking up her sword.

She'd just begun strapping Stabby to her back when she felt him reach out with a magical, visceral *want*. The sword *wanted* violence. He wanted to feed.

"No, Stabby. We're not randomly killing someone just so you can have a snack," Daisy chided. "Sarah, you felt that, right?"

"Yeah. And it's more than a little creepy."

"Let's hope that's the extent of it," Daisy replied. "We don't have much time, and the last thing we want out there is trouble."

CHAPTER TWENTY-TWO

"We're in trouble, Daze."

No shit, Sarah, Daisy grumbled at the ride-along in her head. *I think we are very much not welcome here.*

It wasn't a feat of intuition that told her as much, it was the angry stares of the rather disgusting local inhabitants. The planet appeared to be inhabited almost entirely by a race of tall, multi-limbed creatures who walked on a rippling bundle of thick, almost tentacle-looking appendages that seemed to lack bones, judging by the wave-like way they moved.

And rather than arms, they had what seemed to be similar limbs, though they also possessed clusters of smaller growths that functioned much as fingers did. Or so Daisy and Sarah assumed. The locals didn't seem to be very keen on conversing, and a *hand*shake was out of the question.

She had made a quick pass of as much of the city as she had been able, but with every step, Daisy fell under more and more scrutiny.

We're definitely the minority here, she noted.

"That's an understatement. It looks like we're just about the only

bipeds in the whole place," Sarah added. *"And the few others that are here don't look like the most savory of types."*

Which would go along with the pirate ships that attacked us.

"Yep."

I'm sticking out like a sore thumb, Sis. I think we can pretty safely say that given the utter absence of any Tslavars whatsoever, along with these pretty damn obvious glares of way more than just a normal distrust of outsiders, the odds of an entire fleet of intruders going unnoted seems pretty damn unlikely.

"Agreed. You need to get out of here before things get ugly."

Yeah. There's no trace of Dominus, and we're definitely not welcome here.

"I totally agree, and I'm sensing that—on your left!" Sarah abruptly yelled inside Daisy's head.

Her sister knew by now to trust her ride-along's warnings implicitly. Sarah shared her eyes and ears, but she could focus on different sights and sounds than what Daisy was preoccupied with. It made her the perfect wingman and had saved both their asses more than once.

Daisy spun away from the attack, her sword flashing free of its scabbard as she turned, slicing the ugly, spiked club that had been flying right at her head cleanly in half. The chopped-off segment landed on the ground with a heavy thud.

Sword held at the ready, Daisy slid into a casual fighting stance. She could feel the bone sword's energy connecting with her. Stabby was lusting for blood.

"Freakin' psychopath," she grumbled to herself.

The onlookers observed with minimal interest, and those who were passersby paid no heed to the attack. Apparently, the attempted murder of an off-worlder wasn't all that noteworthy.

Daisy sized up her attacker. It appeared to be a male, judging by his size and attire, though with an entirely novel species, she couldn't be entirely sure.

The creature waved the sliced-off end of its club menacingly, yelling in some unintelligible jabber she couldn't understand.

That stupid translation spell Korbin put on me was supposed to handle this, dammit. What the fuck?

"It might be that they've never encountered this race."

They'd never encountered humans, either, but it works with us.

"Well, I don't know what the problem is, but whatever it is, we can't understand him."

No shit, Sarah.

"Say something. Maybe he'll understand you."

Daisy figured it was worth a try. "Hey, do you understand me? I'm just passing through. I don't want to fight you."

The creature threw away the chopped handle and laughed, then pulled a slaap from a pouch worn around his waist.

"It's one of those slaap thingies," Sarah exclaimed.

Shit. He understood me, Sis. It's a one-way problem.

"The magic in the clouds. I bet that's it. And locals would have had to learn to compensate for it, while Korbin's spell doesn't."

Whatever it is, this guy's armed, and I—

Daisy felt Stabby's grip grow warm in her hands. The sword was humming with anticipation. Anticipation of violence.

Looks like you might get to play after all, Daisy mused as she watched the tentacled man slide the weapon onto his appendage, readying for an attack. *I guess it's time to show off your magical defenses again, because from what I've been told, those slaap things are seriously dangerous.*

The onlookers leaned in a bit. This was the good part. It seemed the fun bit of the fight was about to begin.

The man moved to attack, his posture shifting as he prepared to send his deadly magic her way. But rather than absorb or deflect the onslaught, Stabby did something utterly unexpected. Her living bone sword was full of stolen magic, and he was ready for action. And action was far more than playing defense.

The sword suddenly pulled free from her grip and flew through the air in a magic-powered blur, impaling itself in the aggressor's chest. The small group of onlookers gasped. Now *this* was something different. Something even this tough crowd had never seen before. And it was actually a bit disconcerting.

That feeling quickly increased to outright panic when Stabby went one step further, sucking the man dry, leaving an empty husk before flying back to Daisy. She caught the sword with ease, the grip landing square in her hand, as if it knew precisely where it was going. And that it did. Daisy shared his DNA. They were a part of one another. And they were not having any more of this bullshit.

There were more of them, and there was magic at play. But it seemed she had more magic on her side than she'd originally thought. And it had been a while since she'd *really* had a fight.

Well, well. This could get interesting, Daisy mused, then turned to the crowd and flashed a wicked smile.

The onlookers' eyes went wide, whether in a face or on stalks, and they scattered. The armed friends of her attacker were suddenly left exposed as the people they were hiding behind fled. They took a look at the sword, pulsing with power, then their desiccated friend, and glanced questioningly at one another. A split second later they turned and ran. Whatever trouble this woman and her sword were, they wanted no part of either of them.

The sword tugged at her hand, wanting to chase and stab and kill.

"No, Stabby. We're leaving," Daisy grunted, forcing Stabby to hold back and not pursue.

Chided, the sword obediently ceased his pulling.

"Jeez, I'd worry about you becoming an *actual* psychopath if it wasn't for the fact they were trying to hurt us first. But seriously, you need to keep that in check."

"Daze, enough talking to the sword. We gotta go!" Sarah warned loudly in her head.

Shit, you're right. Got carried away for a second. Daisy activated her comms. "Freya, we're gonna need to dust off, and quick."

"Problem?" the AI asked.

"Yeah, but it's handled. I don't know for how much longer, though. How are the boys doing up top?"

"Having a blast, from what I can tell," Freya replied. "You know, they're actually really good pilots. Both of them."

"For once, men living up to their braggadocio. How refreshing," Daisy replied with a chuckle as she raced for her waiting ship.

They'd have to cut the competing pilots' fun short and get back to the rally point to plan their next steps. This planet was not only a wash, it was a total clusterfuck.

"Hey, you two. We're leaving."

"But I'm still one behind," Tym whined.

"I couldn't give two shits about your dick-measuring contest," Daisy gruffly replied. "We need to go. Now."

"Dick-measuring contest?" Olo's voice chimed in over the comms. "*Again*? But we did that years ago. And I won, by the way."

"It was cold out!" Tym objected.

Daisy sighed and shook her head. "Oh, for crying out loud," she grumbled, cradling her head in her hands. "Look, you can argue later. Just break off and jump back to the others. We're chalking this planet up as a no-go. Dominus definitely isn't here."

Freya powered up her warp and vanished in a crackling blue flash. Moments later, and somewhat reluctantly, the two pilots followed, jumping in tandem, Tym leading his friend to the new rally point.

"You're still down one," Olo gloated as they left.

"Yeah, yeah. Just you wait," Tym shot back. "It ain't over yet."

CHAPTER TWENTY-THREE

In the desert on the outskirts of Los Angeles, Marban watched from a safe distance as Korbin and Rika teamed up, pooling their magic along with Earth's weaponry to devise new ways to penetrate magical shielding.

The pirate was pleased to see the tattooed woman back to herself, all healed up and ready for a fight. She had fire in her, and far beyond any put there by Malalia or the Kalamani shaman. Rika's drive was all her own.

As for Korbin, the man was an utterly devastating spellcaster. In fact, Marban had never personally met a visla of his power. Having him on their side was an enormous boon to their cause. Fortunately, though nothing had been consummated or really discussed yet, seeing Rika's unguarded emotions when he saved her from the Tslavar invaders had effectively extinguished any jealousy the pirate may have had toward the handsome and charming spellcaster.

Rika liked the jovial pirate. A lot, from what he could tell, and Jo had hesitantly confirmed as much.

"Don't worry, man. You're in there. It's just, she's kind of a tough nut to crack. Plus, there's a lot on everyone's plate at the moment."

Jo was right about that. The time hadn't been right to push the issue—there was simply too much at stake and too much in the works at the moment—but he was at ease knowing it would come eventually. Marban was a patient man, and for the likes of a woman such as her, he could most definitely wait.

In the meantime, he took pleasure in watching the befuddling magic she wielded. That odd combination of power from both their galaxies. Rika's power, it seemed, could quite easily disrupt their enemy's spells. Whether or not it was something Visla Dominus could adapt to and eventually counter was unknown, but for now, it was an advantage.

She could only imbue a few items with traces of her power, though. If she wasn't physically present, it seemed her magic didn't like sticking to weapons systems. But when she *was* there, the railgun sabots tinged with her power pierced even Korbin's toughest shields.

Joshua had a tiny sample he'd set a small swarm of Freya's nanites to work on, but it was a totally different kind of magic than they'd dealt with before, and for some reason they were having a hard time breaking down that unusual amalgam of power. So, in the meantime, they'd use the original batch Freya had produced.

"You might find this interesting," Cal informed his magical associates as a small squad of cyborgs, led by Sergeant George Franklin, hauled out a smaller-sized rail gun, designed to be able to function with not only the larger craft, but also ideally afford the ships traditionally too small to house one the ability to possess at least some version of the hypersonic projectile technology.

"I see Cal and Zed have you on gun schlepping duty," Rika said to her cyborg friend.

"It's good to stay active," George replied. "Besides, if I help them with this, I also get to watch all the testing of the fun new toys."

"So, this one meets your approval?"

"Oh, yeah. You'll see," he said with a laugh. "Hey, Marban! What's up, buddy?"

The pirate strolled over and shook the cybernetic soldier's outstretched hand. "Good to see you, George. You look well."

The square-jawed soldier's smile widened. "I'm a cyborg, dude. I *always* look good."

"Sergeant Franklin," Korbin greeted the new arrival. "What have you brought us this time?"

"You'll love this. You want to tell them, Zed?"

The orbiting AI had been key in the device's design and was quite proud of the result.

"Thank you, Sergeant. I'd be glad to. As you can see, Korbin, this is a smaller version of the standard ship-mounted railgun system. Kind of like what was retrofitted onto your ship, but more compact, and not quite as advanced. But here's the interesting bit. It can scale to fire not just its own standard railgun sabot, but can also accommodate the larger ones the big boys use."

"Nice, Zed," Rika said, appreciatively. "Makes it far more versatile."

"Exactly. And it also just so happens to be equipped with a test version of our latest sabot. Cal and I wanted to see just what it could do against your strongest shielding spell, Korbin."

"You want me to cast too?" Rika asked.

"Not this time, but thanks. You won't always be around to help ensure our weapons can penetrate, so we really do need to refine a system that will give us an edge. And to that end, we've got a little something from Joshua and Freya in play."

"Oh?" Rika asked. "Dare I ask?"

"Joshua has been able to stabilize the magically charged nanites Freya originally devised," Cal said. *"It is our belief that if two rounds are fired in close succession, the nanites of the first will weaken the shielding enough for the second to pierce it."*

"Ah. And you need a robust shield spell to test against," Korbin realized. "Okay, I've got you covered."

The visla hopped in a waiting transport that then drove him the mile to where the foot-thick ceramisteel plate was awaiting his magical reinforcement. The testing had been constant, and the destruction of drones was now only called for once in a long while. They had plenty, but at the rate they were going, that could change quickly enough.

Surveying the thick metal, Korbin called upon his power and laid it around the target, securing as robust a shielding spell as he could manage to put in place on short notice.

He then hopped back into the vehicle and was quickly carried back to the staging area. The target was displayed on several screens, the visual apparatus ready to slow the image and show it frame by frame for better analysis.

The railgun was pushed into position, then the AIs took over, powering up the device and locking its targeting systems on the distant objective.

"First a regular sabot," Zed stated, then fired off a round.

The image showed a flash of heat as the hypersonic round impacted the shielding, but there was no damage to the plate.

"Slow-mo replay," Zed said as the image rewound and played again. "You can see the magic's power crumple the sabot and reduce the entire thing to molten slag. Nice spell, Korbin."

"Thank you, Zed."

"Now, let's try again. But this time with a round coated in a molecule-thin layer of those special nanites Freya cooked up on its tip. We theorize it might not penetrate, but should at least weaken the shield."

The weapon hummed to life and fired off its round. The

sabot was destroyed by the shield once again, but this time it looked different, and a smattering of the melted metal actually splashed harmlessly on the target.

"And the replay," Zed said. "Ah, yes. See here? How the tip actually pierced the shielding before the rest of the sabot was liquified by the shield? This means our theory was correct. And if we can place a follow-up round on the same target point, it should be able to penetrate. Korbin, how long does the shield take to adjust and repair itself?"

"Twenty seconds, tops," he replied. "Though mine tend to do so much faster. Perhaps five seconds."

Marban raised an eyebrow.

"What can I say? I'm good," Korbin said with a little laugh.

"I believe it's time to try out the newest water round. Would you agree, Zed?" Cal asked.

"Yeah, I agree. It's time," the AI replied. "Just so you know, we're using regular old tap water for the moment. No way we're wasting our limited Balamar waters for this. Now, if this goes as expected, the first round will weaken the shielding and create the beginning of an opening. And with that, the second *should* be able to penetrate clean, allowing it to do its thing on the target. Once through the target ship's hull, the sabot will disperse the water mist. In theory, anyway. Only one way to find out."

"But how do you target the same place so accurately?" Marban asked. "These will not be stationary targets. They will be warships, and in combat, no less."

"A very good question," Cal replied. *"But we've developed a rapid-fire mechanism allowing for near-tandem projectiles to be launched. The second will follow milliseconds behind the first, thus capitalizing on the primary round's impact."*

"You can do that? That's some impressive accuracy," Marban noted.

"We're AIs. Math is our strong suit," George said with a laugh. "Come on, I wanna see this."

All eyes turned to the monitors as the rail gun prepared to fire its two rounds. With a blast of electromagnetic power, the device launched both sabots in quick succession, the metal flying on target at several times the speed of sound.

The result was a flash of flying metal and mist.

"Replaying," Zed said as he cued up the slow-mo images.

The first round impacted as expected, the tip piercing the shield but the body being destroyed. The second, however, arrived almost immediately after it, and *that* sabot passed through the shield cleanly, striking the metal plate with enough kinetic energy to make the thick material ripple from the impact.

The sabot remained intact, for the most part, as it passed though the ceramisteel. It was then that the remainder of the outer shell peeled away and an explosive burst of water vapor sprayed out in a mist.

"Yes!" George exclaimed. "Now we're talking!"

Korbin was quite impressed. It would still be difficult accurately targeting a craft in the heat of battle, but the system seemed likely to succeed if they could just get a shot on Visla Dominus's command ship. There was just one problem.

"The same issue still remains," Korbin stated. "If the visla is not present, the ship will not fall. And more importantly, the healing properties of these waters will strengthen any who are not a Wampeh. The risk is great."

"It's a chance we have to take, Korbin," Rika said, her tattoos briefly flaring with her emotions. "It's not like we have any other options."

Marban observed the exchange quietly, his brain mulling over something he'd chatted about with Jo earlier in the day, when they discussed the previous time Rika had been injured. The time Jo stood watch over her.

Marban had posed a question. A random thought. Something that seemed to make sense, but the idea was a somewhat crazy one. Jo thought it was crazy too, but she liked it even more because of that aspect.

"Guys," the pirate said to his friends, "I have an idea. But we'll need to take a little trip. All of us."

CHAPTER TWENTY-FOUR

The two ships, one powered by magic and aliens, the other a warp craft flown by a human and her artificially intelligent co-pilot, made their way in tandem to the distant system containing the most unusual of races. But they weren't a technologically advanced culture, nor were they a powerful military ally. In fact, these were a people hidden and protected by the few who knew of their existence. And even fewer knew their location.

But Rika had history with the Kalamani people. The tribe's shaman had not only saved her life when she was mortally wounded while defending their village from Tslavar mercenaries, but had also given her something else in the process. Something that made her more than human. Something that gave her extraordinary power.

The swirling, nearly translucent white tattoos, their magical pigment inked into her skin. Her source of power. It had made her a new woman, and one facet of that existence was as a protector of the Kalamani.

Jo had been there before, but Marban, Korbin, and George, had never set foot on Kalamani lands. But as friends of Rika, they'd be greeted as guests, not invaders. At least, Rika hoped so. With the spirited tribe, one never could be entirely certain.

"Okay, now, you guys need to be on your best behavior," Rika said after they'd landed their ships in the clearing near the village. "Last time we were here, Ripley kind of ticked off the elders."

"You doubt our manners?" Korbin asked.

"I'm not worried about your manners. It's just, these are primitive people, so a lot of what might seem like normal and even polite behavior could seem rude to them. Look, I trust you guys. Just, I don't know, follow their lead, I guess."

"How cute. She's nervous," Marban joked as he gently nudged her.

"They made me what I am, Marban. It's important to me I don't disappoint them."

"I know. Don't worry about us. We won't embarrass you," the pirate said. "Now, relax. We have work to do."

"I know. And it starts now," she replied, holding her hand up in greeting as a group of warriors armed only with spears and arrows approached from the tree line.

The Kalamani were skilled in stealth. It was only the familiar sight of Rika and Jo's ship that led them to so brazenly approach in the open. And even so, with the three strangers walking beside them, she was certain arrows were nocked and ready to fly from the shadowy tree line if need be.

"Varahash, it is good to see you," Rika called out to the approaching warrior leader.

"Rika. Jo. It is pleasing to see you both once more. But who are these newcomers?" he asked, gesturing to the men with his spear.

"Friends. And enemies of the Tslavars and their leader," Rika replied, spitting on the ground for emphasis.

The warrior nodded his approval. "I am Varahash," he said, approaching the men.

"George," the cyborg replied. "An honor to meet you, sir."

"You are like Jo, are you not?"

"I am," George replied. "How did you——"

Varahash merely tapped the tattoos swirling around his eyes. It was then that Rika noticed a few new, faintly pulsing lines added to the design. Blue ink blended into the black. The shaman had upgraded his hunter's vision, it seemed.

"My name is Korbin. I come in peace from a distant realm, seeking your assistance with a matter of great importance."

"A politician," Varahash snorted with a chuckle. "The Elders will speak with you soon enough." He turned to Marban, studying the man's lengthy scar that ran from the crown of his head to his collar. A man of action, obviously. Varahash nodded his approval and smiled. "An admirable scar. Warrior?"

"Of a sort," the pirate replied. "My name is Marban, and I thank you for your hospitality, Varahash."

The response met with approval. Varahash had a good feeling about this one, and judging by the way Rika kept glancing over at him, it was apparent she did as well.

"Come," Varahash said, then turned and began walking toward the village.

It was pretty much as Rika and Jo had described it. The one thing that was a bit different from their expectations, however, was the warm welcome Rika received when the inhabitants saw her.

"Rika!" a little girl shouted, running up to her and wrapping her leg in a hug. The other children came streaming out of their tents, likewise swarming the normally intimidating woman.

Rika was all smiles, as were the parents of the throng of cheerful kids. It was a straight-up love fest, and the often-surly pilot was the center of attention.

"I wouldn't believe it if I didn't see it with my own eyes," Korbin marveled.

"Seriously," Marban agreed. "Jo, what's up with all of this?"

"Remember when I told you how Rika got her tattoos here?" Jo asked.

"Yeah."

"Well, the reason she was inked like that was because it was the only way to save her life. She was terribly wounded protecting the villagers. That kid there, in particular," she said, noting the laughing child hanging from Rika's arm. "She proved herself a protector of the Kalamani that day. And because of what she did, they saved her life. And in the process, the shaman went a little bit farther than just healing her."

"The power tattoos," Marban realized.

"Yep. After she was stabilized, she was then made something more. But none of it would have been possible if not for their shaman's frankly remarkable healing skills."

A shadow flashed across Korbin's face for a moment. "I know a great healer, back in my realm. She would be of great use to us in the coming conflict."

"What is it?" Marban asked, noting the shift in the power user's spirits.

"Nothing. I just find myself missing her, is all."

"She someone special?"

Korbin stood quietly a moment. "Once. But that was a long time ago," he replied, pulling himself out of the momentary funk.

Marban patted him on the back in the firm, jovial way only a pirate could manage without seeming patronizing. "It will work out, my friend. You're too likable a fellow for it not to."

Korbin couldn't help but chuckle, and the cloud lifted from above his head.

"Marban, come here! I want you to meet some people," Rika called out.

"Duty calls," the pirate said to his companions, then trotted over to join the laughing tattooed woman.

"Unusual," Korbin noted.

"Yup. Never thought I'd see that one smile like that," George agreed. "Seems there's quite a bit more to her than meets the eye," he said, flashing Jo a quick, knowing wink.

The visitors were quickly made at home in the village, the locals eager to meet the new friends. And they were friends, that much Rika had made abundantly clear. And with her seal of approval, the air of the whole affair shifted from slightly cautious to openly festive.

One man, however, merely stood quietly and watched. Observing how Rika behaved, but also how her spirits seemed to brighten when she interacted with the scarred man. There was something beneath that gruff façade. Something noble. A history. The shaman whispered to his young apprentice, and the youth nodded once before taking off running to fetch what was requested.

The elders were gathered together, greeting the newcomers far more warmly than the previous group of visitors who had stumbled upon their world. But a lot had changed since then, and they were now on the side of Rika's Earth, whether they wanted to be or not. The only other option was the horrible green men, and that would not do.

"Korbin is a power user from another galaxy," Rika informed them. "An ally. And a powerful one at that."

"We have power on our world as well," one of the elders said. "And we are not weak, as you well know, Protector."

"Yes, but even with my enhanced magic, Korbin is far stronger." She turned to the visla. "Show 'em what you've got. That tree off at the far end of the field. It's not anything sacred or important, I already asked."

"Are you sure that's a good idea?"

"They need to see exactly what we're up against."

Korbin nodded. Actions did speak louder than words. And *this* action far louder than most. Calling up his magic, he cast a simple, yet powerful, force spell. Though no visible attack occurred, the tree shattered, splintering into tiny pieces.

Even for a culture that wielded forms of magic in their daily lives, the Kalamani had never seen magic used like this before. It was incredible. It was also terrifying.

"This is what we are up against. What I'm trying to keep you safe from. We have a plan to stop the leader of the enemy, but we'll need potent magic from this world."

"What could we possess that might stop magic of that magnitude?" another elder asked.

"It was something Marban thought of," Rika said, flashing a proud little smile. "A very clever idea at that."

"The thing about it is, there are materials from your world that are poison to those from mine," Marban said. "If we add those to our weapons, then it will have the effect of disabling our enemies without requiring direct contact or a killing blow."

"There are a few types of plants here. If you would help us find and gather samples, we will bring them back to our world to prepare for battle with the enemy. And hopefully, to keep them from discovering yours, and other, worlds in our realm."

The elders talked amongst themselves a moment, while the shaman quietly looked on, still impressed with Korbin's innate magic. Finally, they came to an agreement.

"We will help you for the sake of this battle," the eldest said. "But, Rika. We are concerned for your welfare. You are a part of the Kalamani now, and we protect our own."

Rika smiled and focused her power. "That's okay," she said as she began glowing not white, but purple, and levitating off of the ground, rising up into the air, then stopping a few meters high. "I've learned a few new tricks. I'll be fine."

The shaman laughed aloud. A joyful, amused sound. He waved to a few of the tribesmen to go help gather whatever his levitating friend needed. Rika nodded her thanks to him and returned to the ground.

"Show off much?" Marban joked.

"Hey, I was just making a point."

"Come with us," one of the young tribal gatherers said. "We will help you gather what you need."

Rika, Jo, and Korbin followed, but Marban stayed in place, the shaman's apprentice stopping him with a hand on his chest.

"Not you."

Rika looked back, curious.

"It's okay. I'll catch up," Marban called after her.

The shaman gave Rika a little nod. Whatever he had in mind, Marban was in good hands.

"This way," the pirate was told as the apprentice led him past the waiting shaman and toward his private tent.

"Ow! What the hell?" Marban said as the ancient man poked him with a tiny stick dipped in some organic substance.

A welt immediately formed.

"Hmm," the shaman muttered, then poked him with another, different stick.

"Hey!"

The welt rose as quickly, but this one was smaller.

"Hmm," the shaman mused, gears turning in his mind.

The process repeated several more times as they covered the distance to his tent, and by the time they arrived, Marban was a mess of itchy welts, some small, some large. Unfortunately, the old man was just getting started.

CHAPTER TWENTY-FIVE

It had been a relatively long series of jump-warps, and Ara and Kip were fine-tuning their linked transit. It was the one thing allowing the magical creature to travel even farther than she could on her own. But it was still a long way to the watery world.

Of course, there was also the brief detour when Ara sensed something. She wasn't sure exactly what it was, but Charlie picked up a hint of it as well. An odd flavor of magic, and one that could very well be related to their quarry. They searched every world within the system they'd detected it, but came up empty.

That was the problem with magic. It was possible to sense something but never discern exactly where it had come from. Space was *huge*, and there was a massive amount of random out there.

You could go your whole life and never come across it, or you might stumble upon it over and over. It was just one of those things. And with so much nothing between worlds and systems, there was a lot of room to miss.

Ultimately, the scent faded, and they gave up the hunt and continued on with their journey.

The planet looked beautiful from a distance. Different from most of the worlds they'd visited in the past. The blue-white clouds gave it the impression of a swirling ball of mist, like a fortune teller's magic crystal ball. It was the surface that gave the orb not only its color, but its all-encompassing cloud cover.

Over ninety-nine percent of the globe was covered with water. The limited land that did exist dotted the endless oceans in a few spots, no more than an island here and there, but nothing remotely resembling anything larger.

It was the very nature of this world that led them to believe perhaps this might be a prime staging area for Visla Dominus's assembling assault fleet. The reports had said the spy had seen clouds, and this type of planet was perfect for their needs. And it wasn't too far from populous worlds, though this one seemed relatively deserted.

Not only would the global cloud cover provide protective camouflage for an endless number of vessels, but with small islands spread out periodically, the crews of those ships could still make landfall if needed. And, though unusual in their nature, there was plant life and abundant oceanic creatures with which to feed a large fighting force.

"We should start with the largest islands," Charlie suggested over their comms. "If they were going to be using this place as a staging point, that's where they'd go."

"And if we run into them?" Kip asked.

"We kill them before they report us," Bawb replied.

Dukaan shifted uncomfortably in his seat. "And if we are compromised?"

The Wampeh smiled. "Then we slaughter as many as possible before making our escape."

Something in the bloodthirsty way he said it made Dukaan shudder despite his certainty that he was not on the Wampeh's menu.

"Let's try to avoid the whole 'mass slaughter' thing, if we can, okay?" Charlie said. "All right, Ara. Let's do our thing."

The mighty Zomoki dove down through the clouds, descending toward the water far below. They were flying blind, but the temperature change, as well as shift in moisture in the air, made it abundantly clear when they drew near. In addition, the smell of water in the air cued her in to their proximity.

"We should be upon the surface momentarily," Ara announced over her comm unit. "I would recommend slowing your rate of descent, Kip. Water can be quite hard when contacted at speed."

"Oh, I have no desire to demonstrate that firsthand," the AI replied with a chuckle. "Slowing my roll. Copy that."

A moment later they popped through the lower layer of the mist into a slender band of relatively clear air just above the surface. The air current was gently pushing the clouds up ever so slightly, allowing for a bit of unobstructed visibility.

It was water as far as the eye could see.

"I had some thermal readings on the way in," Kip informed them. "I'll guide us to the land masses. They showed up fairly clearly, and I've got a bead on 'em from here."

"Excellent. Thank you, Kip. We will follow your lead," Ara said, falling in behind the little ship.

They flew at a high rate of speed, as there were no land obstructions to worry about, and in a relatively short time, they happened upon a small, uninhabited island. Or, at least it *seemed* uninhabited.

"Ara, you feel that?"

"Yes, Charlie, I do. Most odd."

Ara flew a quick loop around the island, dropping in low to survey the terrain.

"What's she doing?" Kip asked.

"There's something," Charlie replied.

"Uh, no, there isn't."

"Yes, there is. Ara and I both sense it. There's a population down there, only, we can't see it."

"Charlie, there's nothing down there at all. No signs of people. No signs of Dominus's fleet. Nothing."

"Just trust us, Kip."

They looped around the island twice more, the faint hints of civilization tickling both the Zomoki and her rider's senses, but Kip was right. There was nothing to find.

"Odd. Let's try another," Charlie suggested.

The Zomoki and warp ship sped away to the next dot on Kip's land map, and once again sensed civilization. And once again, they found nothing.

"Most strange," Ara mused.

"Seriously. Hey, Kip. Steer us to a big one next. There's gotta be something to what we're sensing," Charlie said.

"Will do," the AI replied, shifting course. "We're coming up on a really big one," Kip notified them an hour later.

It would have been far faster to pop up into a ballistic arc out of the atmosphere, but that would negate the point of their low-level survey. But they did pull slightly higher, skimming the underside of the clouds as they flew, gathering information about the world's strange mists.

"Ara, what's that?" Charlie blurted.

"Did you guys see that?" Kip chimed in over comms.

"Something in the clouds," Leila noted. "There, then gone."

Ara abruptly spewed a burst of flames, clearing the water mist from the area.

A small—and quite startled—craft was suddenly revealed. The ship apparently had no idea there was anyone else there and panicked, abruptly veering, nearly clipping Kip as it did, just before diving beneath the waves.

"Oops. Sorry, dude," Charlie joked over comms. "Looks like we scared the shit out of that poor guy."

"Talk about a brown trousers moment," Kip agreed.

"You do realize that the pilot instinctively dove *beneath* the water when faced with a potential threat," Bawb noted.

"And *that* would explain why we keep sensing people but can't find any of them," Charlie said. "They're not *on* the islands. They're underwater."

"Yes, Charlie," Ara replied. "It would seem so. But where?"

Bawb smiled an amused grin. "I have an idea. But you are not going to like it."

CHAPTER TWENTY-SIX

Kip was the first to dive beneath the blue waters surrounding the island. While he was designed for flight in the vacuum of space, his frame was robust enough to withstand the pressures of the ocean to a degree. He couldn't go excessively deep—he'd been a toaster in his former life, after all, not a submarine—but his capacity was more than enough for what Bawb had in mind.

In addition to being water-tight, Kip was also able to submerge without requiring the use of specialized magic. Underwater travel was a rather unique bit of magic that few possessed, though the most basic versions could be used by laypeople for short immersions.

Ara could protect herself fairly well, and that magic would extend to Charlie and Leila atop her back. But should they need to spend any significant time submerged, her passengers would need to transition, riding within the small AI ship instead of atop their Zomoki friend.

"You think they'll find anything?" Charlie asked, as their friends dove into the ocean.

"I don't know," Leila replied, resting up against his welcome bulk.

Her Magus stone was silent around her neck, but the connection she'd begun to form with it was now a constant. And it seemed to be growing stronger, even if she didn't quite know how to control it. At least she could feel it, and that was a start.

Kip had only been submerged for a short time when he abruptly popped back to the surface.

"Hey, guys! Bawb was right, the island is hollow."

"You're certain?" Ara asked.

"Oh, yeah. The entrance is plenty clear once you're underwater. And it's *big*," Kip replied. "And I can't wait to see what's inside."

"You ready?" Charlie asked his dragon friend.

"Of course."

"Then let's go see what we've discovered."

Ara cast her protective spell and submerged beneath the surface. It wasn't a bubble. At least, not in the traditional sense of the word. More of a magical skin that covered her and her passengers in a thin layer of air, keeping them dry as they traveled beneath the water.

Kip was waiting for them, his exterior lights turned to low settings. The ambient light was more than enough to see where they were going, though, and the entrance to whatever lay ahead was not so far beneath the surface as to cause too significant a visual impairment.

The opening appeared to be a magically produced one, smooth rock creating a large, oval-shaped access point. From what they could tell, it was more than big enough to allow a fairly good-sized craft to enter, unnoticed from the surface.

"Okay, guys. Keep your eyes open and your heads on a swivel," Charlie commed the team. "No telling what we might find in there, so be ready."

"Copy that. Weapons are hot," Dukaan replied. "We're good to go, as Kip is so fond of saying."

"It sounds cool, Dookie," the AI replied. "And anyway, we *are* good to go."

"All right, then. Let's do it. Take us in, Ara."

They'd decided the Zomoki would go first simply because she possessed powerful magic, and should they encounter any of Dominus's mercenary force, she and Charlie were far better prepared to deal with them than Kip, despite his weapons array.

The dragon and her spaceship remora quietly glided in through the opening. The tunnel was short, the walls of it not just smooth, like the entrance, but also possessing a faint luminescence. The additional illumination was not required, though, as a mere hundred meters in, the tunnel opened up into a vast space. One with more than ample light streaming in from above.

Ara surfaced slowly, her head breaking the water's surface with the smallest of disruptions. Kip, likewise, rose from below. What they had discovered was unlike anything any of them had even seen.

"Whoa," Charlie gasped. "Now *that* is impressive."

The others couldn't agree more. High above them, a crystalline dome reflected a gleaming magical light, highlighted by the periodic stalactites gleaming brightly, formed by thousands of years of dripping sea water.

Below the vast cavern's roof was a massive city of smooth-hewn rock, the seams nearly invisible with their precision fitting. The pool they'd surfaced in appeared to be the end of a crescent bay that led to the shoreline of the city. Farther back, they caught glimpses of what appeared to be magically illuminated garden plots, the light nurturing the vegetation to optimum health.

In the water itself, areas were partitioned off to make a form of sea plant grow house. Beside them were narrow-slatted pens where large fish swirled in schools. Off along the shoreline, row after row of craft ranging from small to quite large were lined up. With the lack of swell or waves, they sat quietly in place, a floating fleet of sorts.

"It seems we've found our missing inhabitants," Bawb mused.

"And there are a lot of them," Kip added. "Heat signatures moving in."

"We see them," Ara replied. "They are moving at a leisurely pace and do not appear armed."

"They have konuses," Dukaan pointed out.

"Everyone has a konus," Leila replied. "Remember, they're tools more often than weapons."

"Well, I guess let's go meet the locals, then," Charlie suggested.

Ara and Kip both lifted into the air, skimming along just above the water, then landing softly on the pristine sands of the open beach section of the shoreline.

Interestingly, the locals seemed to have no fear of the Zomoki, leading Charlie to wonder if perhaps they'd seen her kind before. Kip, however, was something of a novelty. A ship from another galaxy would be, though the sight of a Wampeh disembarking as its doors opened did not faze anyone. Dukaan's four arms, however, seemed to draw a bit of attention.

A muscular man approached them, ambulating between his single leg and two arms as he walked. Charlie couldn't be certain, but it appeared as if these people had perhaps evolved from some sort of aquatic creature, their tails becoming a single load-bearing leg and their forward fins growing into arms. He didn't see any sign of gills, though, so he couldn't be sure, and it was far too soon to ask what might be seen as a rude question.

Their hair was a bit opalescent, almost as if it had evolved from scales at one point. For all he knew, it had. In any case, the look on the fellow's face was pleasant. Not threatening in the slightest, and without that underlying sense of something not quite right he always seemed to find. And *that* was a nice change.

"Hello," he called out to the visitors. "I am Flothbar, constable for this quarter. I must inquire, what is your business on Valoom? We so rarely get visitors here."

So that's what it's called, Charlie mused. *And damn, this guy is seriously easygoing for a lawman.* "We're searching your planet for signs of a terrible threat. A visla going by the name Dominus."

"Dominus?"

"A woman. Powerful. Evil. Preparing a huge fleet of warships and massing them at a cloudy world."

"Oh, we'd have heard if something like that was happening here," Flothbar said pleasantly. "All of the cities are in close contact, and there haven't been any reports or any sort of fleet, let alone warships."

"Be glad," Bawb said. "They are a formidable enemy."

"Well, there's been no sign of anything like that," Flothbar said, the crowd around them slowly filling in with curious, utterly unthreatening faces. "But then, we're so far from most other systems that people almost never visit us." He turned toward a woman in more regal attire ambulating toward them. "Emmik Tamal! Wonderful to see you. I was just greeting our new guests. They've come looking for a Visla Dominus. Apparently, there's some sort of drama unfolding in the other systems."

"Oh?" the woman said. "What sort of drama?"

"A war is brewing, Emmik. And it threatens *all* systems," Ara said.

"I see," the emmik replied. "And who might you be? It is so rare to have a Zomoki visitor to our realm."

"You've seen my kind before, then?"

"Once in a very long while. But among our people, Zomoki have always been considered a sign of good fortune. And one of the elders? Am I correct in my assumption?"

"You are."

"I thought as much," Emmik Tamal said. "So few of your noble race speak, after all."

"Indeed. A wise observation, Emmik," Ara replied, politely.

The emmik turned to the gathered residents, all of whom had quietly observed the discussion. "My people, this is a fortuitous event. Prepare a feast for our new guests. This is a cause for celebration!"

The crowd cheered merrily. Apparently, feasts were a part of their societal life, and this promised to be a good one.

"Constable, if you'd please show our new friends the way to the feasting grounds, we will show them what hospitality means on Valoom!" The emmik turned back to Ara. "The area might be a bit tight for you, my new Zomoki friend, but we will clear a space to accommodate your impressive size. Do you have a preference in foods? We have a wide variety, and I think you'll find the unique flavor the volcanic ovens impart to them to be a welcome change from magical roasting, and most enjoyable."

"My thanks, Emmik Tamal. I am an omnivore, and not a fussy eater. I will gladly sample whatever you wish to prepare," Ara replied.

The emmik smiled broadly. A *talking* Zomoki as guest of honor in her city? They'd speak of this across the globe for years. "Wonderful!" she said. "And a glorious feast it shall be!"

It wasn't what they'd been expecting, but the promise of festivities brightened the spirits of the travelers. All but one pale visitor, that is.

CHAPTER TWENTY-SEVEN

Magically restrained and held in a state of slumbering stasis, Hunze lay motionless but for the rhythmic rise and fall of her chest as she was trapped in a dreamless sleep. The warm glow cascading onto her through the large forward window was feeding a steady stream of magical power into her hair, which was now brimming with even more power than before.

The constructing of a small portal to redirect the plasma wave of Earth's sun flowing through the portal had been an inspired idea. A method had actually been found to allow Malalia's forces to utilize that power without the need of being anywhere near that larger portal itself.

If their enemy pulled it clear from the sun and sent ships through, they'd already stored enough power in the limited quantity of Ootaki hair they'd managed to source to keep their smaller cousin open. The collection of the golden locks now powering that portal could do so almost indefinitely.

Anything as large as a ship would be unable to pass through it. But the little window between systems was more than enough to allow them to harvest power, safe from disruption.

The difficult part of the whole project was going to be

breaking through their captive's innate defenses. It was something Malalia and her top vislas had been hard at work at since the Ootaki's capture. She was the most extraordinarily powerful of her race any of them had ever seen. And her hair would not function at all without her attached to it.

It was a dilemma, but Malalia was slowly figuring out ways to pick at the protective layers of magic blocking her from using the slumbering woman's power. And once she did that, once she gained control of that power, then the *real* portal would open. The new one that would allow her invasion to begin in earnest.

The planet her forces had located for her was perfect. Close to their primary objective, yet far enough away to make casual discovery nearly impossible. The gas giant was enormous. By far the largest planet in the solar system.

They were preparing to take up a position in the outermost layers of the swirling bands of clouds and gasses, allowing them to harvest power from the system's sun while remaining hidden. And though a gas giant, the planet itself possessed incredible mass.

In fact, the world their adversary called Jupiter was so dense at its center that it was nearly a sun itself. But as it possessed a gravity well that was simply not quite strong enough, it was unable to ignite. And it was around this failed sun they would be staging for their attack.

Interestingly, despite the heat its mass threw off, it was apparently generating no power that would be of any use to Malalia and her forces whatsoever. Same solar system as the sun, yet a drastically different power output. She did hope, however, that perhaps once they'd crossed her fleet over they'd possibly discover different uses for it.

But that wasn't Malalia's main concern at the moment. Breaking Hunze's defenses was.

"Any progress on your end, Cresh?" she asked her powerful aide.

"Almost none, Visla. Whatever it is fueling her defenses, it is seemingly entirely autonomous. She has no control over it whatsoever. Her power is essentially protecting itself, and her in the process."

Most would fear Malalia's wrath, and Cresh did, to an extent. But she had also worked alongside her visla for some time now, and the two had established something of a shorthand in that time. Along with that came a welcome familiarity that included the acknowledgment of Cresh's considerable talents. If she couldn't make it work, it was not for lack of effort.

"Let me see what I can pry from her," Malalia said, gently reaching out with her magic.

As with every prior attempt, Hunze's power defended itself immediately.

"Frustrating, to say the least," Malalia grumbled, releasing her magical probe.

She paced the chamber, mulling over what options she hadn't yet attempted. There had to be something, some way, to work around the hair's annoyingly effective protections.

"What is this?" Malalia asked, noting a small box taken from the Urok craft. "What have you been trying to do with the aliens' tech?"

"Oh, it's not tech, Visla. I was merely experimenting with the properties of the unusual material they constructed the container with," Cresh said, opening the container. Inside were some strands of Ootaki hair. "It is a small quantity, and only some short ends with very little power, but it seems that the power emitted by the sun's rays is capable of penetrating this far easier than our own substances."

"Fascinating," Malalia said, removing a strand from the box and wrapping it around her finger. It was old, and short, no longer than five inches or so, but it did have the feeling of new power. The sun's power. "Hmm. I wonder."

She turned her attentions back to her slumbering captive,

then slowly raised her hand, pointing the finger with the hair around it at Hunze's motionless form. Malalia closed her eyes and felt for the power gently pulsing against her own, the little piece of hair that was now under her control, ready to do her bidding.

It wasn't much, and its power was limited, but that wasn't the idea. Instead of an assault, this time she focused, not on chipping away Hunze's defenses, but on embracing her power, reaching out with the Ootaki power under her control.

Again, Hunze's hair shut her down. It had been fast, and firm, and even Cresh felt it, despite not casting. But this time something was different.

Despite the failure, Malalia smiled. Before she was shut out, she felt Hunze's power respond. It had only been for a split second, but the handshake between Ootaki powers had been there. It was nothing she could use. Not at the moment, at least, but she was on the right track.

"Visla, you realize what this could mean!"

"Do not get ahead of yourself, Cresh," Malalia replied. "There is potential, yes. But we must move methodically. Patiently. I've learned what problems impatience can bring upon us."

"Of course, Visla."

"Now, what of the new portal?"

"We will have to stage toward the outermost edge of the cloud band due to the heat and density deeper in. But our vessels should arrive under cloud cover, as planned, and the Ootaki hair link on the other side will begin drawing power from the sun immediately."

A happy smile grew on Malalia's face. "And *then* there will be no way to stop us."

CHAPTER TWENTY-EIGHT

The new drone was ready to go, all prepped and loaded with its delivery package for the satellite waiting for it on the other side of the portal. The unit was already reconfigured to send a multiple-layered signal––one readable by normal units, one limited to AI.

The combined AI and fleet leaders were relatively certain that the captured Urok ship's crew had been compromised by now, given the cross-portal attack that had occurred. There was simply no other way the enemy could have known the timing of the portal. So, a misdirect was devised. One signal the enemy could read, and one the few AI minds on the other side could extract from the message. If they were close enough to receive it, that is.

Daisy and Kip could be anywhere for all they knew, and the modified signal could very well be reaching no one. And with no responses coming back through, there really wasn't any way to tell.

"The drones simply aren't coming back across," Admiral Harkaway said.

The assembled captains of the fleet muttered amongst

themselves. This was a problem.

"What assurance do we have that the satellite on the other side is even still intact?" one of them asked. "For all we know, these messages aren't even being received."

"It's a problem, we know," Harkaway replied. "But Joshua has a little something he's been working on that may help us ascertain whether or not the satellite is still up and running. But in the meantime, we send the drone through as planned. It will only take it a few seconds to send its payload, and this is a scheduled, but extremely brief opening, so the likelihood of it being intercepted before it can send is minimal."

"And they won't have the space and time to send any of their ships through. Nothing of any size, anyway," Zed noted.

"Even if they could, I think they'll likely play possum in hopes that we haven't realized they know the timing now. Waiting for a longer window to strike. It would be foolish to give up that tactical advantage over a mere drone," Joshua added.

"Agreed. Now, I've had the drone add a false data packet that identified a weakness in their magical shielding. It instructs our forces to shift their attacks to exploit that vulnerability," Zed said. "Just as Korbin identified."

"And while it is an actual weakness, it is minimal, and of no real value to us," Korbin pointed out. "But they don't know you have me working with you, so it seems likely they'll perceive this as a legitimate tactical plan."

"And when they adjust their shielding spells to compensate for our supposed new attack parameters, we will be preparing to utilize the vulnerability their shift will create," Korbin said.

"A rather inspired plan, Korbin," Admiral Harkaway said. "And while it will be a short-lived advantage that this gives our fleet, those precious extra seconds will hopefully let us disrupt their forces enough to shift the tide of battle, when the engagement finally occurs."

"Is the revised shielding phase for our ships loaded in there too?" a Chithiid captain asked. "That is also of concern."

"Thank you for bringing that up," Admiral Harkaway said. "The answer is yes, and no. Yes, we will also be instructing our forces on the other side of a new defensive phasing for our shields. But no, that will not be the actual setting. We'll transmit the true parameters via the AI read-only layer hidden within the message."

"Ah, I see," the Chithiid replied. "So, they will be focusing their attacks based on one set of assumed defenses, but we will be utilizing a different set. Correct?"

"Yes, that pretty much sums it up," Korbin said. "I've worked with Cal and Zed fairly extensively to test how attacks and defenses will react to a variety of magic, and we think we've come up with something that should be fairly effective. *That* information will be shared with the fleet, and it is quite different than that which the enemy will be allowed to intercept."

"And we have adapted the railgun sabots to better pierce the enemy's magical defenses," Cal added. *"With the help of Joshua's nanites, Rika's unusual magic, and the Balamar waters, we should be able to effectively strike their ships with at least a few rounds. But in order for the liquid payload to deploy properly, you will all need to adjust your firing systems to deliver the rounds at a lower velocity than you are accustomed to."*

"Why's that, exactly?" one of the human captains asked. "Faster should be better able to get through their shielding."

"Yes and no," Cal replied. *"Yes, it might get through the shielding easier, but no, it would still require a magically tipped round to weaken them first. And the second round is the one carrying the payload. And if that second sabot travels too fast, it won't achieve maximum dispersion of the waters, but may very well pass entirely through the craft without a chance to deliver the payload."*

Korbin turned to the captain. "And, you see, the entire point is to have the waters vaporize *within* the craft. For the mist to go airborne. If Visla Dominus is aboard, we will only have one chance at taking him out with the waters, so we have to make it count."

"So we send through a message that we have weapons ready that *seem* to be able to work against our magical enemies. But I said it before, what good is it sending messages if we have no idea whether or not our people on the other side are even receiving them?" the human captain griped. "We could be walking into a slaughter for all we know."

"I'm handling the communications issue," Joshua said, hoping to soothe the man and alleviate his concerns. "I've been working on a new system, based largely on some of the more unique elements of my new ship's design."

"What, it's going to break into a billion pieces at the first sign of trouble?" the man joked.

"Essentially, yes. Though not a billion. More like seventy-three. Seventy-three tiny relay drones, each disguised as debris. None are known to the Urok prisoners. In fact, no one outside this room has the slightest idea they exist."

"So, how do these little drones work? If they're tiny, how much good can they be?"

"Individually, not much at all," Joshua conceded. "But working together, they will form a loose network for our communications. They will burst transmit the signal to the satellite on one end of their chain, and the other end closest to the portal will pass back through to update us, while the others remain in place."

"Huh. That's actually quite clever," the man admitted. "Nice one, Joshua."

"I can't take all the credit for it. The initial idea was Freya's."

All gathered for the meeting knew of her and Daisy's unscheduled crossover, just as they were aware they had not returned to their own galaxy. Joshua was stoic. He was a former military AI, so it only made sense. But he was also her partner, and digital or not, the two were as tight a couple as could be found among their flesh-and-blood counterparts.

"We'll get her back soon," the human said. "We'll all do everything we can to make sure of it."

"I know you will," the great AI replied. "For now, prepare your ships and ready your crews. We will be sending through our message shortly. Once we hear back that they know our new weapons appear to be ready and are ready, we'll schedule our attack. And, hopefully, we'll end this conflict once and for all."

CHAPTER TWENTY-NINE

The assembled fleet surrounding the portal's blazing hiding place within Earth's sun was in preparation mode. Just returned from her impromptu flight to a distant system, Rika would summon the portal, as scheduled, and they would push through their new drone updates for the satellite on the other side. Every ship would be on high alert, ready for their enemy should another attempt at incursion be made.

Rika and Jo took up their position alongside Korbin's craft, his modified weapons systems all fired up and ready to rock, if need be. Hopefully, this would be a relatively simple attempt. Just a quick open and close. Not even anything long or large enough to allow for more than their intended package. Dominus's fleet wouldn't have more than a split second to make an attempt, and they were on high alert, prepared to stop anything.

But it was not a threat from the other side they needed to worry about.

"Okay, I'm going to open the portal in one minute," Rika transmitted to the waiting fleet. "Jo, start the countdown."

"You bet," her cybernetic co-pilot replied.

"Korbin, you ready?"

"Finger on the trigger," he joked, enjoying that particular bit of Earth slang. Magical weapons didn't have triggers, after all, but with a full array of pulse, plasma, rail weapons installed, his magical ship was now something of an anomaly.

Marban had also come up to watch the proceedings, though he was confident Rika wouldn't need his assistance. It was a simple one this time. And quick. What could go wrong?

He should have known better than to ask.

"Forty-five seconds," Jo announced.

"Contact!" an Urok captain called out over open comms. "Incoming craft!"

All eyes were on the sun and the ultimate location of the portal once it pulled clear. No one expected a single Tslavar ship to make a charge at them from behind. But that's exactly what seemed to be happening.

"How many?" Zed asked. "I'm only seeing the one." But he knew with the possibility of shimmer ships, there could always be more.

Not this time, it seemed.

"Just one, Zed," the captain replied. "It's not opening fire. It looks like it's making a run for the sun itself."

"It's trying for the portal," the AI realized. "It knows the timing and is attempting to cross back over. Probably to provide details on our fleet to Dominus's fleet. Korbin, Rika, can you two stun it? If we can box it in and prevent it from crossing over, it could provide a useful bit of intel."

"It's flying pretty straight," Korbin noted. "Yes, I think so. Funnel it toward us, and we'll take it down."

"Twenty seconds," Jo intoned.

"Should I stop, Zed?" Rika asked.

"No. Keep the count going. We can't afford for them to know we're on to them. If they realize that, our satellite misinformation will be pointless."

"Copy that. Fifteen seconds," Rika replied.

"Cover her, Marban," Korbin said as he peeled away, leaving Rika to handle the portal, while he attempted to stun the craft into submission.

"How did it sneak in? Didn't we tag them all?" Sid asked from his observation position on the moon.

"Some slipped through. This must be one of 'em," Zed replied.

"Ten seconds."

Korbin and the ship were on a collision course. The only way the Tslavar craft had any hope of making the short window of opportunity was to come barreling in as fast as it could. The pilot wasn't terribly skilled, but at least he understood the timing aspect of what he was attempting. Now all the visla in his way had to do was disrupt his Drooks and deflect the ship harmlessly away from the portal.

If he could.

"Five seconds," Jo transmitted.

"Come on, you," Korbin growled as he focused all of his stun magic in one intense attack. He followed it with a power spell strong enough to bounce the ship to the side and off course, but not enough to damage the craft. If the stun spell flew true, that is.

Fortunately, it did.

"Portal opening," Rika announced just as the approaching ship veered off from its trajectory and spun away from the portal.

The drone and Joshua's new toy blasted through in an instant. "Portal closing," Rika announced, dropping it back into the sun as fast as she was able. A moment later, it was once again deep within the sun's burning plasma.

Nothing had attempted to cross over. Or if it had, it was melted to slag before ever making an appearance. They were safe, and the delivery was a success.

"Reel that ship in," Zed commanded. "Then bring it over to me. I want to have some words with their captain."

"I'll grab it," Marban offered. The pirate was an old hand at snagging ships from space, and though this one was now tumbling end over end, it was small enough to be relatively easy to grab with a few choice spells.

Ten minutes later, the captured Tslavar ship was safely resting on Zed's hangar deck, its unconscious crew transferred to holding cells and its Drook casters freed of their collars and placed in a recovery room until they came around from the stun spell.

The ship's captain was strapped into an uncomfortable metal chair in a room not specifically designed for interrogation, but one that was imposing enough to serve the purpose just fine. The thermostat was turned down as well, making the room even more uncomfortable. Precisely what they wanted as they tried to pry information from the Tslavar captain.

They needn't have worried. The man was not nearly as tough a nut to crack as the majority of Tslavar mercenaries they'd previously dealt with. In fact, the mere threat of "enhanced" techniques was enough to get him talking. And once that dam had broken, details came spilling out almost faster than Zed could record them.

"What do you think?" Zed asked Admiral Harkaway an hour later as he replayed the recording for her. "My sensors indicate this guy wasn't lying. He was scared shitless, and, frankly, I don't know how someone of his weak composition even made it to captain."

"It was in his details," Harkaway replied. "He said they were amassing as many ships as possible. An utterly enormous fleet. If their side is anything like ours, there are only so many top-notch captains available. Beyond that, they have to make do with what they can get."

"And this is what they could get? Maybe this won't be as difficult as we expected," Zed joked.

"Unfortunately, his other bit of information leads me to believe otherwise," the admiral replied. "If what he says is true, Visla Dominus is preparing for not just another probe of our defenses, but an all-out attack. They just need time to get the pieces in place. All of the ships they're modifying for the attack, gathering at the staging point to launch a blistering assault."

"The numbers do sound rather unlikely, though," Zed noted.

"Perhaps. But if they've been planning this as long as I fear they have, then it's quite possible he's not exaggerating. And you heard him. Despite his fear, he was cocky. At least, as much as he could manage in his current position. He said the fleet would be unstoppable. That we wouldn't stand a chance against their combined strength. And he believed every word he said."

"I know," Zed replied. "His vitals didn't spike at all when he said that. Are you thinking what I'm thinking?"

"If you're thinking we need to accelerate our plans and strike first, and with everything we've got, then yes, I am," she replied. "We have intel that finally gives us a little advantage. When's the next portal opening?"

"It was randomly generated. Next one's in just a few hours."

"Then it works to our advantage. We can update the information hidden on the AI-only wavelength. Tell the others that we're moving up the timeline. We don't have a choice. If we want to capitalize on this intel, we've got to strike soon."

"Agreed," Zed replied. "The clock is moved forward. The battle is coming sooner than later."

CHAPTER THIRTY

The undersea denizens of Valoom had arranged quite a spread for their guests, and from what they could make of the enthused chatter from their gracious hosts, Ara's presence was like having the leprechaun at the end of the rainbow stick around to have dinner with you. Not only was it good fortune to merely *see* a Zomoki, but to have one of them spend time in your presence was considered a most auspicious sign.

On top of that, Ara *spoke*. She was one of the old ones of lore. The good tidings her presence would bring to everyone in the city couldn't be measured. Charlie joked that there would be a lot of good luck babies born in about nine months––if that was how long this race's gestation period was, that is.

Given the sheer joy, not to mention bragging rights, that their presence was bringing the locals, the visitors felt no guilt at the festivities being put on in their honor. After a tour of the city's finer sights, Charlie and his friends were then led to the large plaza toward the central avenue that led to the water.

"Come, we've prepared the seats of honor for you," Flothbar informed the newcomers.

Indeed, it was a special place just for the guests. An expansive area had been cleared for Ara's considerable bulk, and a long table capable of supporting the sheer weight of the quantity of food a Zomoki her size could eat had been carefully placed for her convenience. It simply would not do to have their guest of honor eat from trays on the ground.

The others were led to a raised platform upon which a long table had been loaded with delicacies from the undersea realm. Fish, and plankton, and sea greens, and protein from the sea. Even breads, though they were unsure what they were baked from, were piled in steaming platters.

"Please, allow me to seat you," a young girl said.

She bore a striking resemblance to the emmik, Leila noted. Most likely a close relative, if not her own child.

The youth ushered them to their seats, and once they'd taken their places, the uncomfortable realization of their arrangement became clear. Not knowing the tension between Leila and Bawb, their hosts had seated them directly beside one another.

Being aware of the importance of the event, Leila and Bawb merely smiled politely and thanked their hosts as they took their seats. Charlie wished there was something he could do, but decorum was the order of the day.

Charlie, seated on the other side of his queen, leaned over and whispered in Leila's ear, "You gonna be okay, babe?"

She squeezed his leg under the table. "I'm fine," she replied, though she was anything but.

The murmuring crowd politely quieted as the emmik took to the platform with their guests and made a brief, but heartfelt speech, at the conclusion of which, their guest of honor was presented with an impressive spread of volcanic-roasted delights.

Ara bowed her head and expressed her deepest thanks,

which utterly delighted the crowd. Then she flung one of the roasted sea creatures into the air, catching it in her mouth as it fell, much to the delight of the onlookers.

"Overdo it much?" Charlie silently joked.

"I thought it would be nice to give them what they want," she replied. *"And apparently, I'm quite a hit, from what I can tell,"* she added with a chuckle.

The Zomoki had signaled the beginning of the festivities, and everyone dug in, the chattering diminishing rapidly, replaced with the sounds of happy chewing. Bawb ate without pleasure, though he put on a good show of it. But his friends knew it was just that. A show.

He also drank, not using his spells to displace the alcohol for a change. But Charlie was at least pleased to note that his friend wasn't being *too* excessive in his liquid comfort. Nevertheless, he was worried about the Wampeh.

Leila also tried to put on a happy face, but sitting there with Bawb like that was just too uncomfortable. Finally, she simply couldn't take it anymore.

"Look," she said, leaning toward her Wampeh friend, "I know you know I didn't mean for any of this to happen. And I know you know just how bad I feel about it. But I think you need to hear it from my mouth one more time."

"You do not need to––"

"Yes, I do," she interrupted, careful to speak quietly and keep the smile on her face for the sake of any who might be observing them. "It was *my* stone that caused Hunze to be captured, and it tears me up inside every time I feel its power, knowing she is in Malalia's grasp because of it. But I couldn't control it, Bawb. Malalia found a loophole. A way to use my stone against my own friends. And even though I'm finally beginning to connect with my Magus stone, I still have no idea how to control it. Do you know how terrible that feels?"

He sat quietly a moment. "Are you done?"

Leila sighed. "I suppose so."

Bawb turned to her and looked her in the eye. *Truly* looked in her eyes for the first time since Hunze's loss.

"I *know* it is not your fault. And I know there was nothing you could do in that situation. I am, however, having a rather difficult time with this, I am ashamed to admit. But that is not your fault either."

Leila and Bawb stared at one another a long moment, then turned back to their meals. What had needed to be said––for now, at least––finally had been. And, *hopefully*, they could begin to heal.

Hours later, their bellies full and their spirits high, Leila and Charlie took a little stroll after the feast, safe and content in this undersea bubble of grace. For the moment, at least, they were perfectly safe and not facing a single imminent threat. Not in their immediate vicinity, anyway.

The post-meal meander not only helped their food settle and digest, but also allowed them a little quiet time to just *be* with one another.

"The crystals in the dome, they look almost like stars when the lights are dimmed like this," Leila noted. "It's quite beautiful, really."

"Admiring the sights?" an older woman asked. She was sitting quietly on a low wall, enjoying the calm of night.

"I'm sorry. We didn't see you there," Leila apologized.

"Not to worry. There's plenty of beauty to go around," she replied, eyeing the couple with a warm smile. "But you're new here, and the timing of your visit is most fortuitous. The Wamble is strong this week."

"The Wamble?" Charlie asked.

"Our name for it. A healing glow that swims along the

underbelly of the surface clouds. Some say soaking in its light brings long life and great happiness."

"And you've seen it, I assume?" he asked.

"I am very old, and very happy," she replied with a wink. "Of course, there are those who will say it is just the ionization of the clouds reacting with the magnetic shifts of the poles and the humidity levels of the oceanic shift. But I think the original interpretation is much nicer, don't you?"

"I do," Leila replied. "It sounds lovely. But our friends will be resting now, and I'd hate to wake them."

The woman smiled. "There's more than one way to the surface, dear. If you follow this walkway past that taller building then turn left, there is a small path between homes that will take you right to the dome's wall. Look for a dark patch in the glow and you'll find the tunnel to the surface. You're young and strong and sure of foot, I assume. You should have no trouble with the climb. And I think you'll find it most worthwhile. Here, take this, it'll be a little chilly this time of night," she said, offering the woven blanket folded beside her. "Just leave it here when you're done. I'll retrieve it in the morning."

"Thank you," Leila said.

"Yeah, that's really kind of you," Charlie added.

"You are our guests, and I wish for you to love our home as much as we do."

"I'm sure we will," Leila replied. "Come on, Charlie."

She took his hand and headed off, following the woman's directions. The tunnel was right where she'd said, and the climb was, indeed, not a difficult one. Fifteen minutes later, they felt the cool breeze of fresh air waft across their faces.

Interestingly, Leila also felt a different sensation as they stepped out into the open air. Her Magus stone, tugging at her senses. She was finally connecting with it in a way that seemed to make sense, though she had no idea how or why.

"The lights, Charlie," she said, staring at the swirling glow in the clouds above them as he spread the blanket and pulled her down to join him.

"I see, babe. They're beautiful."

Leila lay back into the comfort of his arms, and the two of them let go of their thoughts and worries, reveling in the magical beauty of the Wamble. It was everything the woman had said it was.

They stayed up there for a long time, not talking, but just being. Finally, they descended back into the cavern and left the woman's blanket where she'd been. They didn't worry about anyone taking it, this place didn't seem to suffer from any sort of crime, least of all theft of a blanket.

"Ah, there you are," Bawb said when Charlie and Leila arrived at the lodgings they'd been provided.

"What are you doing out here?" Charlie asked. "It's late, Bob."

"I have been thinking," the Wampeh replied. "And I have come to believe that the Magus stone may be the key to saving Hunze." He turned to Leila. "I've come to help you learn to harness its power."

"I thought you couldn't do that," she replied.

"Normally, no. But this stone is different. It is reaching out to you, and you to it. And, though I am by no means experienced with this sort of magic, I believe I can help you solidify your connection. And if that happens, then, perhaps, you can use it to undo what it has done."

Leila flashed Charlie a look, to which he responded with a little nod.

"Okay," she said. "When do you want to practice?"

"Now," he replied.

Neither Leila nor Charlie commented on the late hour. Leila simply nodded and followed him to a nearby clearing that appeared to be some sort of playground or sporting field.

The ice between the Wampeh and Charlie's queen seemed

to be melting faster than originally anticipated, and Charlie, for one, felt a huge weight beginning to lift from his shoulders. Whether the damage would mend fully, he didn't know, but this was certainly a good start.

He then turned and stepped inside, leaving them to discuss, and practice, and begin to repair their friendship.

CHAPTER THIRTY-ONE

Freya exited her warp with Olo and Tym following close in her wake, their jump magic tied in to her warp drive signature. But there was a problem.

At one stop on the way back to rendezvous with the others, they'd actually encountered a pair of Dominus's ships, quite by accident. The warships were large enough to carry a sizable contingent of smaller craft within, and, upon seeing the strange tech-magic ship they had launched an assault.

Freya and Daisy discussed their options. Yes, they could most likely handle the smaller ships, but the large ones could be a problem. Olo and Tym, though ready for a fight, reluctantly agreed with the human and her AI's plan. They would jump away. There was simply too much at stake to waste time fighting unnecessary skirmishes when a war was coming.

And they'd done precisely that. Five times, to be exact, yet the enemy ships continued to follow them through warp. With more time, they could have adjusted to perhaps pull the magically jumping ships farther and faster, shaking their tail, but for now, that wasn't an option.

"We're screwed, Daze. They're still with us," Sarah warned.

"I know. Freya, you have any thoughts?"

"Not about this magic stuff. Olo and Tym both said there's no way they tapped into their jump spells," Freya replied.

"Well, that's just fucking great," Daisy grumbled. "These bastards have figured out a way to follow a warp signature."

"Seems that way," Sarah agreed. *"And they're jumping farther than normal, riding our wake somehow."*

"And if we warp back to the fleet, we'll give away their position," Freya added. "But we can't keep warping indefinitely."

"I know, kiddo. Even if we tire out the main ship's Drooks, they'll just launch the smaller ones for backup. But how the hell did they manage to learn how to do that, anyway?"

"I'm not sure, but maybe it's the captured Urok ship. If they figured out how their warp works, then perhaps they were able to extrapolate and use that knowledge to track our warp tech as well."

"But even *we* can't track warps."

"No, but then, we don't use magic," Freya said as she slid into evasive maneuvers yet again.

"So, we don't seem to have much of a choice, then, do we?"

"I don't like it, Daze, but I'm afraid not," Sarah said.

"I agree," Freya chimed in. "It's the only way."

"Fine. I'll tell the others." Daisy fired up the comms and reached out to the two pilots flying with her. "Guys, we're unable to shake them, so it looks like you're gonna get your wish after all. We need to destroy all of those ships before we return to the others. If we don't, we'll be leading them right to our people."

"Yes!" Tym blurted.

"Yes?" Daisy asked.

"I'm still one down. Now I can finally take back the crown," Tym said with a laugh as he spun away from the others, engaging his shimmer and opening magical fire on the enemy ships pouring out of the Tslavar battleships' hangars.

"You're still going on about that?" Daisy groaned.

"No way you'll top me," Olo called out with a hoot, then dove into the mix himself.

"These two have a death wish."

"They're just reveling in their skills," Freya said. "And I get it. I mean, I could outdo them, but as an AI, well, I have something of an unfair advantage."

"In your dreams, machine!" Tym retorted over their open comms.

"In my dreams?"

"You heard me," the crazed pilot replied with a laugh.

"Uh, Daisy?" the AI said.

Daisy thought about it a moment. "Yeah. Go for it, Freya," she finally said. "No one talks to my girl like that."

"Awesome!" the AI replied with a happy yelp, then spun into battle. "Okay, I count twenty-six of them," Freya announced. "Since I'm starting at a handicap, I suppose I'll need to take out at least three to even up."

An attacking ship flashed from the impact of her plasma cannons and railguns.

"Make that two."

"Nice shooting, machine. But it'll take more than that to catch up to me!" Tym said, his cloaked ship taking down a pair of enemy craft. "Two down. I'm up one. And you know what, Olo? When I've reclaimed my title, I'll bet the women on Earth will trip over themselves for a night with Tym. But maybe I'll throw my leftovers your way," he said, sassing his friend.

"In your dreams," Olo shot back, taking out a Tslavar ship, then spiraling away from its companions' return fire. "And you said they were too symmetrical. One down. Even."

"Not for long, my friend. And I can make do with symmetry for a time. But don't worry, even though they're not blue, like you prefer, the women there are still pleasing to the eye, for the most part."

"Hey, watch it, buddy," Daisy chimed in just as Freya took out another ship.

"That's two. I'm catching up!" the AI exclaimed.

"Oh dear Lord. She's got the competition bug now, too," Sarah sighed in Daisy's head.

"Pay attention, all of you. We've still got that pair of warships, as well as these damn attack craft, so stay focused," Daisy chided them all.

"Two more!" Tym exclaimed, another pair of Tslavar ships falling prey to his invisible attack just as his shimmer ship was abruptly rocked by a fierce magical attack.

The warship's relative silence had apparently been a ploy. They were more than ready for a fight, but they'd sent out their attack craft as a lure. A decoy meant to trap the invisible enemy. And every time Tym's cloaked ship landed a spell, they tracked its trajectory.

It wasn't a guarantee by any means. They could just as easily have missed every attempt. But once that first volley of spells hit the cloaked ship, disrupting its camouflage, its ultimate demise was all but a given.

"Tym's hit!" Daisy called out, Freya spinning immediately and racing to his aid.

"I'm coming!" Olo shouted.

Tym's damaged craft bucked and rolled as it was buffeted by more spells, its shielding barely holding. The swarming attack ships pulled back, allowing the larger warship a clear line of attack, but Freya took advantage of their sudden shift and knocked down five of them in quick succession with a blistering volley from all of her weapons at once as they foolishly pulled away into a predictable perimeter.

They were blocking the shimmer craft from escaping the warship's spells, but in so doing, they had positioned themselves like so many targets, all lined up and ready to be shot down. Freya was more than happy to oblige.

Olo, on the other hand, had seen the writing on the wall and shifted his attention away from his friend's damaged craft. If he flew to his aid, they would both be killed, so, instead, he was making an all-out attack on the warships, preventing them from delivering the coup de grace on his friend.

"Holy hell, that guy's good," Sarah marveled as the blue-skinned pilot went utterly ham on any of the smaller ships that attempted to block his charge at their larger base craft.

Daisy glanced from her own fight for a moment. Sarah was right. Olo was unleashing sheer carnage on the enemy, plowing right through their defensive perimeter with no concern for his own safety. His flying wasn't that of a jovial competition anymore. This was an enraged man out for revenge. And he was living up to his boast of being the best non-AI pilot in the combined systems.

The nearest warship hadn't expected a single craft to be so ballsy as to charge them head-on, and Olo was able to use that surprise to his advantage, landing a series of expertly placed spells on crucial areas of the vessel. The smuggler knew the weak spots of a good many types of craft, and this just happened to be one of them.

The structurally weak section just behind the command center cracked under the ferocity of the pinpoint attack, and the warship abruptly fell silent. Olo then turned his attentions to the other of the large vessels.

He'd managed to purge their bridge of air, likely killing the command crew within moments, while leaving the sealed-off Drook chamber intact. They'd save them later if they survived, but for now, he had a dangerous opponent in his sights. And this one was ready for him.

Olo guided his ship into a corkscrew attack, avoiding the flurry of defensive and offensive spells heading his way. But his counterattacks were deflected by the enemy's more powerful shielding. The pilot didn't seem to care, barreling straight toward them regardless.

"He's going to Kamikaze them," Daisy realized. "Freya, can you--"

The stealth ship's rail guns swiveled and let off a burst of supersonic death. The warship was a long distance away, and swarming attack craft were still in the way, but she was one of the greatest AI minds ever to live, and her rounds flew true in the vacuum of space. With no resistance, they had no problem covering the distance in an instant.

A few of the rounds Freya launched were likely to encounter one of the smaller ships en route, so she even dialed up the velocity of those particular rounds, ensuring they'd pass right through those ships if they did happen to make contact. And a few of them actually did, punching through the smaller craft like pieces of paper as they sped toward their ultimate target.

The small craft didn't tear apart, but a few appeared to have been positioned just right--or wrong, depending on your point of view--the sabots turning their flight crew to a bloody mist before exiting the other side of the ship and carrying on their way.

Olo was closing in fast, heading right for the defensive shielding of the Tslavar craft. Just as he was about to find out whose shields were stronger, the magic wall in front of him rippled, then fell as Freya's stream of nanite-coated rail gun sabots weakened, then tore through the magical barricade.

The blue man grinned, his heart focused on death and vengeance as he unleashed everything he had on the warship, his spells redirected not to their original targets, but rather, locking onto the many holes Freya's weapons had provided him. Holes through which his spells could enter and do the utmost damage to the sections of defenseless ship.

Unlike the other craft, this one did not simply fall silent. Apparently, Olo hadn't held back at all, and the resulting wave of deadly magic had caused the craft to burst from the inside out. Olo swerved clear of the flying debris and quickly rejoined Freya as she picked off the remaining ships that were suddenly in disarray when their commanders ceased to be.

It was a slaughter, and Olo was fine with that.

"Is that all of them, Freya?" Daisy asked.

"Yeah. I tracked all of the launched ships, and none escaped."

"So, they shouldn't be able to follow us when we warp now."

"Nope. Though we need to try one or two to be sure."

"We will. Good job kiddo. Now, get us over to Tym's ship and give me a soft seal," Daisy said, sliding into her snug EVA suit.

It was a nice thing about living when she did. In old times, spacesuits were bulky things that restricted movement and could snag on debris. But with the passage of time came advances in tech, and now their suits were form-fitting and thin.

The material was lightweight, but it insulated and protected far better than the old designs. And they were shock resistant as well. An impact would harden the material instantly, adapting and diverting the force, while remaining structurally intact. Only the helmet bore any resemblance to the old-school ones, and that was just a comfort factor that wearers had preferred as new iterations were designed.

Freya latched onto Tym's damaged ship and attached the umbilical as best she could, using her maneuvering jets to stabilize the larger ship. Daisy passed through Freya's airlock doors and scrambled into the flickering shimmer ship.

"Pretty torn up in here," she said. "Making my way to the command area."

"Copy that. Olo is coming in hot. He'll be with you in a minute," Freya noted.

"Aww, shit," Daisy said as she rounded the corner to what was left of the pilot's nest.

"Not good, Daze."

I know, Sis. I know.

Tym was there. What was left of him, anyway.

The damage to the ship had apparently sent a sharp wall of debris right into the man. Even with what seemed to be a hastily cast protective spell to keep him from suffocating in the void, his injuries within it were severe.

The blood had pooled inside the magical shell around him, making him look like a macabre lava lamp as he floated now that the magical gravity had been negated.

"Freya, prep your stasis pod, stat!" Daisy said as she grabbed the floating man as best she could. The magical encasement was tough to get a handle on, but she'd be damned if she'd let something as ridiculous as magic stop her.

"You think it'll work on his physiology?" Sarah asked. *"It's designed for humans, and this guy is anything but."*

We have to try.

Daisy was racing down the corridor to Freya's umbilical when Olo descended through another hole, protected not by a space suit, but by a magical shell. One look at his injured friend and he turned a deeper shade of blue.

"Give him to me."

"Olo, I have a device on my ship. One that might be able to save him. But you have to get out of my way. Now!"

Olo hesitated a moment. He could see his friend's injuries were almost certainly fatal, and there was no healer close enough to help him. They'd have to make several test jumps before returning to the rally point to make sure they still weren't being followed, so it seemed Daisy's option was the only one they had.

He stepped aside, allowing her to pass. "I'll take care of the Drooks," he said, doing his best to hide the emotions racing through him. "They should be safe in their chamber. If so, I'll link them to my ship so they can jump with me. This craft is salvageable, in the right hands."

Daisy nodded once and hurried past him. She knew he was hurting, but there was no time to waste. It seemed to be a recurring theme in her life.

CHAPTER THIRTY-TWO

Marty and Farmatta made the joint warp-jump back to rejoin the fleet with not only a new member of the resistance, but a potentially game-changing little shrub as well. Farmatta was most intrigued by the plant, and she had even taken a small piece of one of the leaves and placed it in her cheek.

Amazara had first tested the plant for toxicity, of course, and had found it utterly benign. Not that any other result would have stopped the old Wampeh from doing what she wanted anyway. There was a credible rumor that this unusual plant she'd previously never even heard of might be of healing benefit to her kind. There was simply no way she wouldn't try it on herself.

Confidence in her own magic was high——it was her primary weapon, after all, and had been used so often as to become purely instinctive at this point. As a result, she was quite certain she could overcome any ill effects the plant might produce. But none had arisen. In fact, she felt quite good, though Amazara was of the belief that a bit of magical processing would make an extract of the plant far more potent. In any case, it seemed the plant was the real deal. And they'd discovered it before Dominus.

Unfortunately, however, that was the only good news on that particular front, as they had obtained no new information on Dominus's fleet, which had been their actual reason for their visit to that particular world. That aspect of their trip to the cloudy planet had been a wash.

Arlo had Marty come in for a landing beside the other craft that were already waiting on the surface. It seemed a good many of the ships tasked with surveying other clouded worlds had come back, and likely empty-handed as well, since they were back so soon.

The teen was both glad to once again be in the secure embrace of an actual fleet, but at the same time, he was also a bit bummed out that his time with Kara was ending. Sure, they'd been with the others, and busy on a mission, but it had been nice, the two of them getting to spend the time together.

For her part, Kara was glad to be back on solid ground after the long flight. And, much as she was enjoying Arlo's company, she was also very anxious to speak at length with Amazara about her rapidly growing powers. She'd actually vaporized a man not so long ago, and without a konus, no less. Things were changing rapidly, and in ways she had no control over. Her power was growing in ways she couldn't quite grasp, and she needed guidance. Without her uncle Korbin around, Amazara was her best bet.

Farmatta set her ship down beside Marty and exited, immediately handing several carefully packaged samples of the healing plant to one of the younger Wampeh Ghalian awaiting her return. They would then be immediately distributed to the other masters, who were not present at the moment. Secrecy and speed were of the utmost importance, as was keeping the discovery from Dominus's awareness.

The young Wampeh knew what that meant. Should he be in

jeopardy of capture, he would destroy the samples, along with himself. It was a protocol only used in the most dire of circumstances, but this was just such a time. Too much was at stake to take any chances.

"When do you think you will be able to formulate an extract?" Farmatta asked Amazara as they walked to join the assembled captains who had already returned from their expeditions to other clouded worlds.

"It seems fairly straightforward," the pale-blue-haired woman replied. "Getting it perfectly dialed in may take some doing, but I think I can likely achieve an acceptable refinement within a few hours. Of course, it will get better as I have practice, as well as real world results to adjust by."

"Naturally," Farmatta said. "I am very interested in seeing if this plant will help our ailing brother. Hopefully, you will have a sample to try on him when he returns."

"I'll do what I can. But in the meantime, I have prepared the most basic of tinctures."

"Already? When did you manage to do this?"

"I had some time in transit. It's not my finest work, but the extract should have a fairly decent potency."

Farmatta looked at the little vial held out in Amazara's hand. "May I?"

"Of course."

The Wampeh opened the vial, took a single drop, and placed it on her tongue. "Oh, this is quite nice," she said, as a slight shiver raced through her body. "I cannot wait to see what the refined version is like."

Zilara waved in greeting as the two women joined the pow-wow already in session. It wasn't a formal meeting, but rather, a casual comparison of findings from the assembled captains' trips. Even Quintz, Mandoog's former muscle, was there, though he had returned empty-handed as well.

"It seems none of us have had any luck thus far," Rovnik

said, scratching his head.

"Nah. It's been nothing but a wild Farminga chase," Quintz agreed with the pirate.

"Not entirely pointless, though," Amazara said. "We've been doing far more than just searching for Dominus, you realize. In fact, we now have a rather useful map of potential rallying points for our forces, should we need to take cover to regroup."

Quintz looked at the lithe woman questioningly. "Uh, who's this one, again?"

"*This one* is Amazara," Farmatta replied.

"Again, *who*?" Quintz repeated. "And what does this *woman* know of military strategy?"

The mildly annoyed Wampeh was about to reply when Amazara gently put a hand on her shoulder in a way that said, "I've got this."

"Do you remember the battle of Axengial?" Amazara asked.

"When the Council of Twenty's resurgence was crushed and their hidden stronghold taken? Of course. We all know about that. A great battle, though a fair number of years ago," Quintz replied.

"Yes, it was."

"You were there?"

Amazara allowed herself a tiny smile. "There? Oh, yes. In fact, I was the one who planned it. Along with my dear friend Korbin, that is. So, *that's* who this *woman* is, to answer your question."

Farmatta's face remained neutral, but Amazara could have sworn she *felt* the Wampeh laughing, though she uttered no such noise. Farmatta turned to Zilara. "You see?" the old woman said. "I told you, she's more than meets the eye."

"Indeed," Zilara said with a pleased grin. "We are honored to have you with us, Amazara."

"Thank you," she replied. "It's my great pleasure."

"Welcome to the resistance."

CHAPTER THIRTY-THREE

Not long after the massive Zomoki and her AI ship companion returned to the waiting rebel fleet, a damaged shimmer ship joined them. The craft continuously flickered in and out of visibility, towed by a pair of ships, one of technological origin, and one magical, as it made its descent to the hastily cleared area where the other rebel vessels were parked.

The landing was not pretty.

It was pretty clear to all on the ground watching its approach that the ship was going to require a lot of work to become spaceworthy again. It had taken a beating, and more than a little TLC would be needed to get it up and running.

The same could be said for its pilot. If he somehow survived, that is.

Daisy had called ahead and notified the others of their status as soon as she and Olo had exited their warp-jump. She and the blue-skinned pilot had both been glad to hear that a healer was now with their motley bunch of rebels.

Tym had survived the transfer into Freya's stasis pod, and he now rested within the tech device, silently trapped at the brink of life and death. The AI ship didn't dare attempt any repairs using her onboard medical tech, however. The man was an entirely new species for her, and she had no idea what might happen. And there was simply no way she'd put a single nanite into him.

But the stasis pod was holding him in limbo. For the time being, at least. Daisy would have to get the healer aboard sooner than later, though, she mused as she stepped out of Freya's airlock, Stabby strapped to her back.

"Hey, Mom," Arlo greeted her, Kara, Vee, and a woman with pale-blue hair joining him at the landing site along with a few Wampeh and pirates who'd come to see the damaged ship up close.

"There's my boy! C'mere!" she said, pulling him into a tight hug and kissing his head repeatedly.

"Mooooom! Stop it!"

"Not a chance," she replied with a laugh.

"Not every day you get to embarrass him in front of a girl, after all," Sarah laughed.

So true, Daisy agreed. "So, is this the healer?"

Amazara stepped forward and offered her hand. "I am Amazara. It's a pleasure to––"

She abruptly stopped, her eyes widening slightly as they fixated on the white sword peeking out from its scabbard slung over Daisy's shoulder.

"What–What is that thing?"

"Hey, he's not a thing. That's Stabby," Daisy said, drawing the blade from its sheath and handing him grip-first to Amazara.

The healer was almost reluctant to touch the weapon at first, but finally wrapped her fingers around the grip. "It's not enchanted," she mused, turning Stabby over in her hands, examining the sword carefully. "But it contains power. *Great* power," she realized.

The Wampeh who'd initially come to scope out the damaged ship was suddenly very interested in the blade, as any assassin would be. He wasn't one of the masters, but Daisy doubted he'd have any trouble slaying a room full of enemies regardless.

"There is emmik power in this weapon," the Wampeh noted. "Curious."

"There's more," Amazara added. "There is visla as well. Low-level visla, but visla all the same." She carefully tested the blade's edge. "So powerful, yet so dull," she mused, handing the sword back to its owner.

Daisy chuckled. She loved this part. "Yeah, he's only dull for you," she said, taking Stabby back and casually slicing through a fallen log lying in the cleared landing area.

"You just love doing that, don't you?" Sarah joked.

Amazara's mildly perplexed expression shifted to one of utter shock. "There is another within you!" she blurted.

"Whoa. How the hell did she know that?"

"I am an empath," Amazara replied.

"Wait, can you hear me?" Sarah asked.

"I don't know exactly what you said just now, but I can *feel* the general intent you wish to communicate."

"Holy shit. Now that *is impressive. I'm glad she's on our side."*

Me too, Daisy agreed.

"You two converse?" Amazara asked. "So, this is more than an enchantment attached to you somehow."

"Long story," Daisy replied with a little sigh. "Basically, it's my dead-not-dead sister."

"Your *what*?"

"Just go with it for now, I'll explain later. Right now, we need you to see what you can do for Tym."

Olo had just stepped out of the stealth ship and was rushing over to them after checking in on his injured friend aboard Freya the moment they landed. "You're the healer? You need to come, now! You've got to help him."

"I'll see what I can do."

"This way," Olo said, then turned and raced back into Freya's airlock doors.

The healer and the woman from Earth followed close behind.

"Freya, tell Marty and Kip what we found out about their warp tracking while we see about Tym, okay?" Daisy asked as they hurried to the man in stasis.

"You've got it," Freya replied. "I'll clue in Arlo and Dukaan as well."

"Thanks, kiddo."

The three reached the sealed pod containing the injured man's unconscious form. Amazara had seen a lot in her day, but this was *bad*.

"Was he exposed to the vacuum?" she asked, trying to gauge how bad his internal injuries might be.

"So far as I can tell, he seems to have sealed himself off in that little magic bubble thingy before his lungs were damaged, if that's your concern," Freya replied.

"Ah, another speaking vessel. Fascinating," Amazara said. "And you possess a detailed knowledge of injuries. Are you a healer as well?"

"Not exactly, but I do have diagnostic tools aboard, though they're not designed for his species, whatever that may be. The stasis pod, however, should work for pretty much anyone, though I was a little concerned his magic shell would interfere with it."

"Not this one, no," Amazara replied. "It is only designed to protect from the void, nothing more. Whatever your stasis magic is, it is able to penetrate it just fine."

"Tech, not magic," Daisy said. "But that's a whole other discussion."

"How bad? What do you think?" Olo asked.

Amazara placed her hands on the clear glass and reached out with her power, feeling the dying man's essence, though it was now mingled with this strange non-magical power keeping him on this side of the bright light by force.

"He is badly, badly damaged," she finally said, removing her hands from the pod. "Honestly, under even the most ideal circumstances, I would not be able to help him."

Olo's shoulders slumped.

"*But*, this strange device has managed to do what no spell can. It is holding him just at the brink. And with its help, I–I don't know. *Maybe* I can do something, though it will take time. I make no promises, know that. Do not get your hopes up. But I will do everything in my power."

"That's all we can ask," Daisy said. "Come on, Olo. We should let her work in peace."

"Yeah, right," he said, clearly wanting to stay, but knowing Daisy was right.

"If you need anything, just ask Freya. She'll reach out and let me know."

"Thank you, Daisy," Amazara said, then turned all of her attention to the injured man.

Across the small encampment an old Wampeh woman approached a far younger man––at least by appearances, though he was much older than he appeared.

"Geist," the old woman said.

"Farmatta."

"I hear you have found a potential refuge should things go awry."

"It would appear that way."

"An undersea society. Fascinating."

"Indeed," he replied. "And your search? No sign of Malalia, I take it? Her Dominus fleet?"

"Sadly, no. And I'm sorry for that, truly. We *will* find her. It will just take time."

"Which is wasting," the Geist grumbled.

"You know as well as I, and better than most, that to rush into harm's way without first knowing its true aspect is to court death."

"One of the first lessons of the Ghalian," he replied softly.

Farmatta assessed him a long moment, then pulled a small vial from within her clothing. "Drink this. Amazara extracted it from a particularly unique plant found on the cloud-covered world we visited. It will help."

"What is it? A healing elixir? I am fine," he said.

Farmatta looked at him calmly, and with a degree of sympathy. But also with the eyes of a Wampeh Ghalian master. "It was not a request, brother."

Bawb turned and studied the deadly woman now offering him the little vial, and in that instant, he saw himself through her eyes. Realizing just how off he had been, and how it was very likely the masters had even discussed whether or not he might need to be put down.

It was not a pleasant realization, yet he knew he would have had the same conversation were he in their place.

Bawb nodded once and took the vial from her hand, uncorking it and downing the contents with a single gulp. Whether it was the mirror held up to his behavior or the healing powers of the elixir now coursing through his system, Bawb felt a little better. A little more in control.

He was still distraught, and his rage had not lessened in the slightest, but he was seeing things clearly, his faculties regained and under control. And that meant he could focus them on the task at hand: ending Malalia's efforts and recovering his love in the process. And heaven help any who got in his way.

CHAPTER THIRTY-FOUR

Enough of the scouting fleet had returned to officially call a meeting with the reconvened heads of the rebellion. It was funny, in a way, calling a bunch of pirates rebels, especially when the person they were fighting was something of an outcast herself. But Malalia Maktan had been a key part of the Council of Twenty, and her new guise of Visla Dominus was striving to reclaim that power.

Essentially, she wanted to be the Council of One, with all of its power under her thumb. And given the raw strength she possessed, there was a frighteningly real possibility she could achieve her goal. Unless, that is, someone stood up to her. Someone who would *rebel* against her.

And thus, the pirate fleet had become a rebel one. And they were in for one hell of a fight.

"Olo? What are you doing here?" Dukaan asked when he saw the cocky pilot at the gathering.

"You know me. Always looking for coin," the smuggler replied, though his heart wasn't really in the devil-may-care attitude.

"But you said you don't do rebellions."

"I do now."

The tone of his voice and the look in his eye was more than enough for Dukaan to know better than to belabor the point. "Then I, for one, am glad to have you with us," the Chithiid said with a nod.

The last of the captains filtered down from the ships in orbit and took their seats. Then the Wampeh Ghalian did their creepy appear-out-of-nowhere trick, filling in the ranks, and they were ready to begin.

"All right, let's get this started," Charlie said, taking his place beside Rovnik and Zilara. "So, from what we've had reported back, no one made contact with a single one of Visla Dominus's fleet on any of the cloud planets. We knew it was a long shot, but it was definitely worth the attempt, especially as it gave us a little bit of time to establish some new security protocols. And it's a good thing too. We've got a new vulnerability to deal with. The good part is, it only affects a few of us. The bad part is, it's the few who can communicate with the satellite. I'll let Daisy explain more," he said, nodding to her.

"Right. Well, it seems the enemy has figured out a way to track, and even ride the wake of our warp drives. I'm not sure how, but we had a pair of Tslavar warships follow us through five warps."

"Five? That means they were able to obtain a very solid connection to your warp device," Rovnik said. "How do we know this place hasn't been compromised?"

"Because we took them out. *All* of them. So there's no chance they tracked us back here. But it's a valid concern. Those fuckers can follow us through warp. I don't know if it's something they got from the Uroks they captured or what, but it's a very real problem now."

"And we still need to get to the satellite relay near the portal, not only to update our portal timing, but now to also warn the attack fleet about this new warp problem," Charlie said. "Maybe they'll be able to figure out some way to mask it before they cross over for the big fight."

"There's more to the messages now," Daisy added. "There was talk of adding a second layer to the comms that only AIs can receive. The Urok ships don't have AIs with them, so it's still a secure comms channel for us."

"Excellent. So we can leave outgoing messages with it as well."

"Yeah. And best of all, we can leave misinformation going both ways. Stuff to throw the Tslavars off. Mess up their plans, ya know?"

"Totally. But getting there to connect to the satellite is going to be an issue. Now, Ara can jump in. That's not a warp means of transit, and she's got a comms array on her harness, but it's not an AI."

"Yeah, that won't cut it," Daisy replied. "But Freya can't warp without them being able to track her. Even if she does manage to warp farther than they can jump, I worry they'll be able to follow."

"Might I make a suggestion?" Ara said from the spot she'd comfortably crouched down in, at the perimeter of the meeting.

"What're you thinking, Ara?" Charlie asked.

"Why don't we *pull* Freya with us when we jump? We know we can link to her warp drive, but what if we have a few of us tether to her, then jump? She could keep her warp entirely powered down for the trip and let us do the flying."

Daisy pondered a moment. "Freya, you hear that?"

"Yeah," the ship replied over her comms.

"What do you think?"

"Seems like a good idea. Only one way to find out for sure, though."

"Yeah, I thought you'd say that," Daisy replied. "Okay, count us in."

"Fantastic," Charlie said. "If we're lucky, they'll have made some progress with incorporating the Balamar waters into their weapons systems in our home galaxy. And if they did, then we might finally have the solution to the Malalia Maktan problem once and for all."

"Then all that would be left is to coordinate the attack on Dominus's fleet with the other side," Rovnik said. "Zilara, will your people be ready in time?"

"Oh, we have plans in motion. But ours is a silent, cautious network. That is how we've survived as long as we have. But, yes. I have the utmost confidence in our people. They will be ready."

"So, this is really it," Charlie mused. "The ships have pretty much all been upgraded, and we've grown our numbers substantially."

"They are still in greater numbers," Kort noted.

"Yes, but once our fleet pours through the portal, we'll have them caught in a classic flanking maneuver. We block them from our end and leave them nowhere to run, then slam them from the other side of the portal. They'll never know what hit 'em," Charlie said. "We just need the guys on the other side to come through and get those specialty weapons working."

"I'm confident they will," Freya noted. "If Joshua's on the case, you can consider it done."

"Glad to hear it," he replied. "All right, then. I think the first order of business is going to be connecting with that satellite and getting our message out. Once we've done that and received a reply, it'll be a matter of time. Or, timing, to be more accurate."

The meeting continued a short time, then finally broke up, leaving Ara and Rovnik to coordinate the towing of the mighty stealth ship back to the portal. Though she'd rather fly herself, Freya knew what was at stake. She'd be towed, and that was all there was to it.

Ara and Charlie prepared as Rovnik boarded his own ship and cast a magical tether around the stealth craft. Ara and Charlie then did the same. He tested the hold the spell had on Freya. It was solid.

"Okay, kiddies. Let's do this."

CHAPTER THIRTY-FIVE

"Interesting," Ara said when they exited their jump with Rovnik's ship.

Freya had come through with them absolutely perfectly, with no issues whatsoever. It was a good thing, too, because if she'd had to fire up her warp drive, there was no way she'd be able to avoid *that* many ships.

"That's a lot," Charlie agreed, as he surveyed the redeployed enemy armada. "It's a massive fleet, but do you see how they've left the area around the satellite just a bit more clearer?"

"Making it look like they don't know it's there," Daisy said over comms. "Sneaky bastards."

"Yeah, but we're sneaky too, Daisy," Freya noted. "After all, they may be trying a little misdirect, but we're layering in a misdirect of our own using *their* misdirect. Kinda beautiful, if you ask me."

"Always finding that silver lining, kiddo. Don't ever change."

"Wasn't planning on it."

"So, what do you need from us now?" Rovnik inquired. "We can get you closer if need be, but I think even an intentionally obtuse enemy will not be able to turn a blind eye if we fly in front of them."

"No, you're right," Daisy agreed. "But Freya won't have any problem reaching the satellite from here. And since they think they're intercepting secret information, we're pretty damn secure in our being left alone. They won't burn their perceived advantage if they can avoid it. Not yet, anyway." She turned her attention back to her magnificent AI offspring. "Okay, Freya. Do your thing."

"On it. Okay, done," she said a split second later.

"That's it?" Rovnik asked. "It was supposed to be a significant message."

"And it is. That's just how AI minds work," Daisy replied over their comms link. "They may speak slowly when talking with us, but for techie stuff, they're lightning-fast. Faster, actually. Lightning's got nothing on my kid."

"Aww, thanks," Freya cooed sarcastically.

"Such a ham, Daze."

Hey, she's mine, and she's awesome. Nothing wrong with a little bragging from time to time. I do it about Arlo too, sometimes.

"When he's not driving you up a wall, you mean."

Well, yeah, Daisy admitted with a little chuckle.

"So, I deciphered the message and replied with our own. It'll be sent back, along with the decoy message when they open the portal next."

"What did they say?" Rovnik asked.

"The false message they sent says that they suffered a lot of damage when the enemy snuck through last time. The fleet is weakened and vulnerable, so they'll only open the portal for extremely short windows until they can repair and regroup."

"Nice," Charlie said. "But the reality?"

"They're in great shape. In fact, better than great. Not only do the water weapons seem to be a go, but Marban had some creative addition he came up with to make them even more deadly. Even against non-Wampeh."

"Sweet! Always count on a space pirate to come up with something wonderfully violent, right?" Charlie chuckled.

"Joshua also sent through a new series of micro sats. They're purely AI tech and should be undetectable even to the captured Urok scans. It's a daisy chain for comms. We're still supposed to use the main satellite so they think we don't know it's compromised, but now there's a totally secure backup that can relay info even if the full-size drones don't make a run through the portal."

"Damn. Joshua's pretty damn clever," Charlie admired.

"Yeah, he is," Freya replied warmly. "Timing is pretty soon, actually, so that's in our favor. Joshua said they took a Tslavar captain prisoner, and it looks like Dominus is accelerating her plans. They're ready to move on the other side when we are. They're just working out the last details and upgrading what they can."

"Good. If they can get those water sabots working, Malalia's gonna be in for one helluva big surprise," Charlie said. "Are they going to dose the crews with the water?"

"Yeah. Before they cross over, all humans on key ships will receive some. And Chithiid and Uroks will get a little topical spray down," Freya replied.

"It appears as though all aspects of this plan are beginning to come together as we had hoped," Ara said.

"Be careful saying that," Charlie groaned.

"Yeah. Don't tempt Murphy," Daisy added.

"Trust the other human to know about Murphy," he laughed.

"Oh, believe me, Charlie. Murphy and me? We're *very* well acquainted."

"Then let's not press our luck. Ara, Rovnik, latch onto Freya again and prep to jump out of here. They've got our reply message waiting to go through, so we just have to wait for the portal to open as scheduled, and they'll get our transmission. Once that clears, we'll have our own secret parallel timing in place."

"A two-pronged attack, like a pincer maneuver," Freya observed.

"A pincer maneuver?" Daisy asked with a snicker. "What are you, a German tank commander now?"

"My partner is the greatest military strategist ever to live. It's only natural I'd pick up some of his quirks over time," the AI replied. "And besides, if the shoe fits."

"Says the computer without feet."

"I could build some if I wanted a pair. But I much prefer my wings."

"Oh dear Lord, would you two stop already?" Sarah lamented.

"Sorry, Sis."

"What?" Rovnik asked, not privy to the mostly silent internal banter.

"Oh, right. I'll let Charlie fill you in," Daisy said with a laugh. "Now, come on and jump us the hell out of here. We've got a weapon that can kill Dominus, but we've gotta do our part if we want it to work."

"Right. Back to the rally point," the pirate replied. "Jump in three."

"Here we go," Charlie said, then all three of them vanished, leaving the secret message in place and their enemy none the wiser.

They made several jumps, just in case, to ensure no one was following them. When it was clear that they were indeed alone, the Zomoki and pirate made the final jump back to their waiting rebel fleet.

Charlie and Leila embraced as soon as Ara touched down. "You okay?" she asked.

"It was fine," he replied. "How's Bob doing?"

"Okay," she said. "Better than okay, actually. I really think that elixir helped him turn a corner. And he's been working with me to better control my Magus stone."

"Better? Last I heard, you could feel it but not control it at all."

Leila reached out with her power and levitated a medium-sized rock, then flung it toward the treeline with her power.

"Hey, not bad!"

"It's useless unless we get in a fight with sticks and stones, but at least it's a start," she replied.

"Well, hopefully that won't be necessary. If things go as we've planned, our ships should be able to put one hell of a dent in Malalia's plans," Charlie said, then noticed movement headed his way.

A blue man was walking toward him, and he was striding with purpose.

"Olo, what can I do for you?"

"I want in," the smuggler said.

"In?"

"The battle. Give me weapons. Top off my magic. That's all I ask."

Charlie glanced at Leila, then studied the man's face. It was there in his eyes, plain to see. He wouldn't take no for an answer. And really, he was such a damn good pilot anyway, there was no way he'd have turned him down in any scenario.

"Okay, Olo. Whatever you need, you've got."

"I *need* to kill some Tslavars," he growled.

"Well, I think it's pretty safe to say you're going to get your chance. And then some."

CHAPTER THIRTY-SIX

The violet-skinned girl possessed enormous power. The Wampeh Ghalian could clearly sense it wafting off of her as she approached. But despite being Visla Palmarian's child, and Dominus being her stepmother, no less, she was not on the menu. This one was an ally, not a meal.

"What is it, child?" Zilara asked her visitor.

Karasalia sized up the lithe assassin. Zilara was pleased to note there was no fear in her eyes.

"You have people on Slafara, right?"

A pause. "Yes."

"And you have them in my home."

It was a statement, not a question.

Zilara assessed the girl with an amused gaze. "We do," she finally replied.

"Then I need you to do something for me."

"Do something for you? And I would do this, why, exactly?"

"Because my father is Nikora Palmarian. Because he's a powerful visla."

"Not at the moment, from what I've heard."

"Because he needs help."

"My dear, whatever it is you wish of me, I can assure you, we are not jeopardizing our mission in a futile attempt to rescue your father. Your stepmother is far too powerful to be successfully deceived by our means for long."

"I'm not asking you to do anything of the sort," Kara replied. "I'm asking you to simply get a message to Shozzy."

"And who is this Shozzy, person?"

"My father's head of security. Well, *former* head, anyway. He's been placed on reduced duty."

Zilara couldn't help but admire the girl's drive, but her request was a foolish one. To risk an operative's cover, especially one of their hard-won natives, was pure folly. They'd spent a great deal of time and coin getting the woman on the serving staff to be their eyes and ears inside. They'd not risk her without very good reason.

It was clear that Pimbrak was either dead or as good as, and if Malalia had detected him, then no one's disguises would hold up. He was the best of them, and knew no equal in the ways of Ghalian infiltration. That he'd gone silent told the true severity of the situation within those walls.

"Even if we could reach your Shozzy, what good would it do? One man, especially an ordinary guard, cannot have any hope of overcoming Malalia's power."

"I'm not asking for anything like that," Kara replied. "All I want is to get him a message. To tell him what is *really* going on there. If he knows things are not what they seem, he may yet be able to help my father realize what is happening within his home."

"There's no guarantee he'd even do that."

"He's always been loyal."

"Many are, for coin."

"He risked his life for me," the teen countered. "He nearly died."

"And you wish him to finish the task?" the assassin asked.

"Because you must realize, what you are requesting will very possibly result in the end of his life."

Kara flashed back to the conversation her uncle had with her in the tower not so long ago. Reminding her that she was Visla Nikora Palmarian's child, and that, no matter if she liked it or not, her life had more value than others. And sometimes people would die for it. Even those she cared for.

"If that is the price to overcome Mareh and what she's doing to my father, then so be it."

Zilara was a bit surprised at the girl's sudden show of steel in her spine. Perhaps she'd underestimated her.

"Even if it were possible to get a message to him––and I'm not saying I can, or will––how would you even be able to prove it is from you? There is much deceit afoot, and any information, especially explosive revelations such as you wish to send, will be taken with a healthy dose of skepticism."

Kara felt her spirits rise slightly. She hadn't said yes, but the Ghalian master was still talking to her. And her opinion appeared to be swaying, even if only slightly.

"I was talking with Arlo about that," she replied, pulling a small technology-magic device from the pouch on her hip. "He calls it a video recorder. Let me show you."

Kara held the small unit on her palm and pressed the button as Arlo had shown her. A foot-tall image of her and the other teens sprang to life above the device.

"Are you sure it's working?"

"Kara, trust me," Arlo's image said. "See that light right there? That means it's recording."

"I don't see anything," Vee added, scrutinizing something not shown in the image.

"No, you don't get it. *This* is the part where we record. *Then* you play it back. Hang on a sec."

The Arlo image reached for the device, then the image cut off.

"See? Like an image disc, only there's no magic. And with no magic, there's nothing for anyone to detect."

Zilara had to admit, it wasn't a terrible plan. And the girl could record a personal message for the visla himself. Perhaps one that could even bring him around as an ally in the fight against his wife.

"What if it is discovered?"

"Arlo said it can be set so the recording self-destructs after viewing."

"But then the unit will be rendered non-functional. What good will that be to your father then?"

"No, it doesn't destroy the whole thing, just the images it stores. So when Shozzy sees his message, it will destruct. And then when my father sees his, it will do the same thing."

"And if it is discovered? If it is taken?" Zilara asked, playing devil's advocate, as she'd done before so many missions.

"No one will even know what it is."

"But what if they push the button and make it play? All will be revealed."

"Ah, Arlo thought of that too," she said.

Zilara noted the slight elevation of the girl's pulse. She liked the boy.

"Do tell," the assassin said.

"It can be set to only play for a certain person. Normally, it's a genetic thing. For my father, that would work. We're blood, so only he would be able to activate his message. But Shozzy is not. But he was healed by my uncle Korbin, and he'll still have residual magic from him. So all we need to do is take a sample of his magic from the shimmer ship he helped recharge, and then set the device to play *that* message when it contacts the same power source. He didn't heal anyone else in the building, so it'll only play for Shozzy."

The Wampeh had to admit, the girl had truly thought of most things that could go wrong with her relatively simple plan.

She might make a useful ally one day yet. "And if someone else should turn it on? Should, say, one of the Urok prisoners recognize the device and tell them what it is?"

"We record a decoy message. Something totally misleading, so that way, even if the attempt fails, it still helps our cause."

Zilara thought a long moment as she looked at the girl's earnest expression. The plan, while somewhat risky, could actually have great benefit to them all if it succeeded. And best of all, it would not require a deep penetration of the visla's tower. If Shozzy had truly been demoted, all that would be required of their agent could be accomplished on the lower, far less secured levels.

"How quickly can you prepare your messages and layer the magic detection onto the device?" Zilara asked.

A broad smile spread across Kara's face. "Oh, I already have."

CHAPTER THIRTY-SEVEN

From Earth, even with the most powerful of telescopes, the flashes in the outer layer of Jupiter's atmosphere looked like nothing. Up close, they'd perhaps seem like the typical product of the many storms swirling in the gas giant's myriad bands.

Of course, with the utterly enormous size of the planet, even something the size of the moon, or even Earth itself, would be unnoticeable at a distance. That Jupiter's mass was that of 1,300 Earths meant the enormous flashes by most standards were essentially invisible given its size. They didn't call it a gas *giant* for nothing.

But those flashes, concealed and small--relative to the planet's own size--were nevertheless massive in their own respect. A ring of light and power far larger than the portal currently nestled in the sun's burning plasma.

And this new portal, while not quite functional, was getting closer to functionality.

Visla Dominus's few ships still in hiding within the upper layers of the planet's clouds watched with fascination as the new portal appeared once more.

"It looks as though the visla is making good progress,"

Captain Yintza noted from the observation deck of her small ship.

She'd been one of the handful of craft to rush through the portal and escape the blistering barrage of weapons' fire from the enemy craft camped out, waiting for them. Most of her colleagues had been killed or captured in that incident, but she had not. Nor had the few others now in orbit with her. They would sit and wait patiently, a welcoming party for their visla. And when she arrived, they would be handsomely rewarded.

"The size is ambitious," Sorsha, her right hand and second-in-command, replied. "We will be able to fly our entire fleet through in no time if the portal can maintain that size."

"Indeed. Hopefully that time will come soon. I grow weary of waiting, and long for action," Captain Yintza said.

"I am of the same mind, Captain. But it would seem that—— Look!" Sorsha exclaimed.

Something was finally happening. Something different. The portal, while unstable, appeared to be maintaining. A relatively small ship appeared just as the magical portal failed, slicing the craft in half as it sealed.

"Damn. Another one," the captain grumbled. "Send the retrieval team with Captain Jagar's ship to see if any of the crew survived."

"Immediately, Captain," Sorsha said, then hurried from the chamber.

Captain Yintza looked at the drifting remains of the craft. It was a clean cut at least; the portal's sealing had simply erased about two-thirds of the ship. The portion that was likely drifting in space, just like this section, but on the other side of the failed portal far, far away. The other destroyed ships had not fared so well, and there had been no survivors. The remains of both crew and ship were given a magical shove and sent to their rest deep in the heart of the gas giant.

It was an honor to volunteer to test the new portal for the

visla, but after the first seven ships suffered far worse fates than this one, Yintza suspected volunteers were far more reticent. Of course, if there were no volunteers of their own accord, then there would be those selected and volunteered. It was a terrible decision to face. Test the portal, or face the visla's anger. The poor souls didn't really have a choice.

But it was all for the greater glory of their cause, she rationalized. There were losses in any conflict, and this was no different in that regard. And given the condition of the destroyed ship's remains, as well as the length of time the portal stayed open, plus the condition of the unstable gateway itself, it truly did seem as if the visla was getting closer.

Whatever she was doing in that distant galaxy, it was starting to work. And soon, they would have a functional portal of their own. One not submerged in a burning sun, no less.

Yintza watched the smaller ship belonging to Captain Jagar as it pulled the destroyed ship's remains close. A minute later a team deployed in an air-tunnel spell to survey the craft for survivors. If they knew what had befallen the previous vessels, perhaps they might have had the foresight to provide their crew with some form of protection.

"Captain Yintza, I've received a skree from Captain Jagar," Sorsha said as she re-entered the observation deck.

"And? Were there survivors?"

"Three," she replied.

"Out of the whole crew, only three," Yintza said with a sigh. "So many lost. But there's nothing for it, and at least *some* survived this time. Better yet, the visla is clearly making progress. Soon the portal will sustain long enough for our vessels to pass through unscathed. And when that finally happens, victory will be at hand."

As if to punctuate the statement with a question mark, a Chithiid heavy raider abruptly punched through the clouds, nearly ramming into the captain's ship.

"We're under attack! Defense spells on full, and all casters, take that vessel out!"

Both the Chithiid craft and the Tslavar ships seemed to be surprised at the immediacy of the engagement. The alien pilot was good, avoiding most of the magical attacks and counter attacks, while shifting the phasing of their shields rapidly enough to deflect many of the incoming spells.

But the Chithiid was terribly outnumbered. They'd been tracking a single signal. A tracer round embedded on one of the invading enemy's ships when they had surged through the portal and made a run for it. One on one, they were more than ready for the fight. But this was anything but a fair engagement.

The Chithiid fired off everything in their arsenal, hoping to create enough of a gap in the magical onslaught to effect an escape to get reinforcements. This particular layer of Jupiter's clouds was wreaking havoc on their comms, and they couldn't get a signal out to their comrades.

"Stop it from fleeing!" Captain Yintza bellowed over her skree to all ships present. "Do whatever you must!"

Every caster available turned their full attention to disabling and/or destroying the ship before it could ruin their plans. It was an ugly, crude, and disorganized attack, but against just one ship, it was enough.

The first of the spells flew true, knocking the Chithiid craft into a flat spin just as a trio of powerful spells from as many other ships also landed, their impacts from multiple angles tearing the ship to pieces so violently that even had they been wearing space suits, the crew stood no chance of survival.

And just like that, as quickly as it had begun, the fight ended.

"Jagar, exit the cloud cover and look for any additional enemy ships. It appears to have been alone, but we cannot afford to risk the compromise of our location," Yintza ordered over her skree. She turned to her right hand. "Sorsha, how did they find us? This is an enormous planet, yet they pinpointed our precise location."

"I don't know, Captain. But they seemed as surprised by our presence as we were by theirs. They did not come in ready for a fight."

"So, you think it was coincidence?"

"No. But in the absence of other evidence, I do not believe this is what they expected. Perhaps the portal garnered more attention than we anticipated."

"Perhaps," Captain Yintza mused. "In any case, we will keep one craft above us at the edge of the cloud cover from this point forward. We are too close to allow anything to hamper our progress. Our visla is making headway. We mustn't fail on our end. It is simply not an option."

CHAPTER THIRTY-EIGHT

The Wampeh who had managed to find himself aboard one of Visla Dominus's research ships had been fortunate. He was not on the main vessel, but rather, one of the additional craft aiding in the study and preparation of Ootaki hair, as well as whatever other magical items they might have in their possession, to see if Earth's sun could increase their power. To date, only Ootaki hair was affected.

Had the assassin spy been aboard the main ship, he'd have personally seen Hunze in her confinement, her hair soaking up the solar energy streaming through the small portal the visla had managed to create in front of the far larger one, channeling its power to their distant system. But he'd also have seen the visla in person, and his disguise would not have withstood her gaze.

Malalia Maktan's power was simply too great, though the man was unaware of that little tidbit. It was a simple bit of good luck that had kept him near enough to learn of the captive woman's presence, while maintaining his safety. Or, *relative* safety as it was. For the life of a Wampeh Ghalian was never truly safe.

While his order normally preferred to bring messages of great importance in person, he simply could not abandon his embedded location. There was too much at stake. But a brief departure to join a resupply run allowed him to connect with a lower-tier member of the Ghalian and relay his message. And it was that woman who made her way to the distant staging ground of the pirate fleet and their allies.

The Wampeh had to pass through several different groups of Dominus craft before she was able to source a ship she could steal easily enough to avoid notice. If all went according to plan, she'd have it back before anyone noticed it. The Drooks were off helping another, larger vessel making a long run, leaving this unessential one empty. Perfect for her needs.

She recited the spell for her Drookonus and powered up the craft, then speedily departed for her rendezvous. When she finally made it to the new staging area, she quickly made the report to Zilara and the other masters, as well as the heads of the nascent fleet, not realizing just how much one of the masters present was interested in one aspect of what she had to say.

"Held in a research craft, you say?" Bawb asked.

"Yes," she replied. "It was reported that while the other craft are also engaged in experiments with harnessing various magical power and determining how the small portal of sun energy affects them, the most heavily fortified of them contains an Ootaki woman of exceptional power."

It could be only one person. Bawb felt a little flush of hope in his chest at the thought of seeing Hunze again. She was safe, and healthy, but trapped. "And she's well kept?" he asked.

"Yes. She is unharmed and being held in a powerful sleep spell."

Zilara seemed concerned by this aspect. "You say she is well-guarded. But by what means are they keeping her contained? Surely, they have other tasks to perform."

"They do, from what I've been told, but she has a dedicated team of vislas keeping her asleep. They take shifts."

Bawb almost smiled at the news. Despite her being at their mercy, Hunze was not just strong. She was so powerful as to have scared them enough to devote *several* vislas solely to her. There was more to the briefing, but he'd heard what he needed.

Bawb rose to his feet and strapped the Vespus blade Hunze had given him to his back. He paused a moment, considering his options, then strapped Hunze's own sword across his back as well.

"No sense trying to talk you into waiting until we get a little bit more intel, is there?" Charlie asked, knowing full well his friend's reply.

Bawb didn't answer, merely casting an obvious glance his way.

"Okay, then. I'm coming with."

"You do not have to."

"There's nothing about *having* to do anything. Hunze is one of us, and we're getting her back," Charlie replied.

"Very well. Your assistance is appreciated," the Geist said.

"Damn straight. Now, there's one thing we need to do before we go after her," Charlie added. "And as much as it weirds me out to say this, you'll need to feed and power up as much as you can if we're going to have any chance of pulling this off. All of you, if we're being realistic. We need to find you some emmiks. Or maybe even an unsuspecting visla, if we can swing it."

Bawb glanced at the other Ghalian masters, then flashed a little smile at Charlie. "We are way ahead of you, my friend."

"Oh?" Charlie said, a bit surprised. "Already?"

"The Wampeh Ghalian are always prepared," he replied. "There is a place with power users to spare. Not Dominus's people, but those of a variety I will not mind draining one bit."

"I'm coming too," Daisy chimed in.

"Me too," Arlo joined in.

"No, you aren't."

"Mom, I can help."

"Not on this one. You keep Kara and the others safe. I'm counting on you to protect her, okay?"

Arlo was caught between a rock and a hard place. Adventure and battle, or being the disturbingly alluring violet-skinned girl's protector. Given the firepower they'd be taking on their mission, he supposed staying back wasn't the worst option.

"Okay," he finally agreed. "But you can't always keep me out of the good stuff."

"Oh, he'll be in the good stuff soon enough," Sarah joked.

I know. Poor kid has no idea what he's in for. But we do.

"That we do, Sis. And he'll be awesome. Been waiting a long time for that day."

Ditto. But first, let's all survive today's *problems.*

Daisy picked up Stabby and turned toward Freya's waiting form in the near distance. "I'll get us ready to go. If this isn't one of Dominus's places, then we should be fine to warp without being followed. And let me tell you, my girl can rain down a world of hurt on whoever gets in our way. A little old-fashioned Earth kick-assery to go along with all that magic jazz."

"And if we *do* encounter any of Dominus's ships, we'll have Ara latch on and jump you two clear enough to warp without being followed," Charlie added.

He then turned to his Wampeh friend, ready to ride into battle at his side once again. "Okay, Bob. Where to?"

The Wampeh replied, informing him of their destination with a pointy-toothed grin.

CHAPTER THIRTY-NINE

"There? You want us to attack *there*? Are you fucking kidding me?" Charlie blurted when he saw the target Bawb and his Ghalian associates had guided them to.

"I'm with Charlie on this one," Daisy said. "Like, holy hell, dude, that place is a fortress."

"Technically, it is a resort *within* a fortress," Bawb noted. "A playground for the ultra-wealthy. For power users who have not only used their positions to advance, but have abused them for massive personal gain."

"The worst of the worst, in that regard," Zilara added. "Which is why the facility is so highly guarded. An impenetrable, ultra-safe compound for the elite of the elite to relax and frolic unfettered."

Daisy flashed an annoyed look at the assassin. "You just said it's impenetrable."

"Precisely why our targets will have their guard down," Zilara replied.

"There is a multi-segmented entry system, along with dozens of hidden wards and castings in place to defend against attack from the outside," Bawb said.

"Not to mention the hundreds of heavily armed guards all along the perimeter one would have to pass through in order to even reach those defenses," Zilara added with a chuckle. "They pay a hefty sum for the warm embrace of such security."

"I'm glad you find this so amusing," Charlie said. "But you're describing an invulnerable stronghold. No way we're muscling our way in there. And even if we could, all of the emmiks and vislas inside would be waiting for us when we finally did break through."

"Who said anything about breaking through their defenses?" Bawb asked with a wry grin reminiscent of his amused mirth before Hunze was taken. "The weak point of all of these types of security systems is people. All we need is to gain access. Once we are within, it is child's play overcoming a single, narrow line of defense. And that is all my brothers and sisters will require."

"Hang on. How the hell do you think we'll be able to do that, Bob? I mean, as I think I've pointed out once or twice, it's a freakin' fortress."

"Oh, Charlie. Have faith," Bawb said. "I will simply enter through the front gate."

Daisy shot Charlie a curious look. "I don't think your friend is right in the head," she commented.

"That's for sure," Sarah quietly added.

"I will enter using an identity that has been kept for such an occasion. A rarest of rare moment such as this," Bawb said. "It is that simple."

"Bob, I hate to break it to you, but whatever you may have had in place here at one time, you're a few hundred years too late, now."

"Oh, of course my original cover persona is long dead. But the order has infiltrated several facilities such as this over the years across the systems, always keeping a carefully crafted identity in place in each. You see, the Ghalian prepare for the worst case, and the threat posed by Malalia truly is such an event. One worthy of burning this resource."

"The Geist is correct," Zilara said. "We can do this only once. The repercussions will be immediate, and we may even lose some of our additional cover identities at other such facilities if they up their security in response when they receive word of what happened. But this is the time. We need this power, no two ways about it."

Bawb took off his swords and then began removing all of his hidden magical weapons. There were a *lot* of them.

"What are you doing, Bob?"

"A rule of entry. No magical weaponry of any kind is allowed within the facility."

"So you're going in vulnerable?" Daisy asked.

"*We* are," he replied.

"Excuse me?" Daisy shot back.

"Zilara will be my concubine, while you and Charlie will accompany me as my servants and personal security."

"Again. *Excuse me*?"

"Do not fear, Daisy. Conventional weapons for personal guards are still allowed. Your sword, while possessing great magic, should not be detectable by the average guards. They are provided with spells to detect enchanted and magical weapons. Yours is a living blade, possessing its own power. As such, it falls outside of the parameters of their magical scans. A convenient gap in their casting, I must admit. Charlie and I, however, will be reduced to regular blades."

"I've seen what you can do with those," Charlie joked. "They're so screwed."

"And your power is internal, so, once again, something overlooked. Especially as you will be entering with me. They will merely sense the power and associate it with the person they are expecting."

"But we still have to get the others in," Charlie noted.

"And we shall. Once inside, we determine the best targets and then move quickly to clear access for our comrades under cover of shimmers. And when we fight our way out of this place from the inside, the Ghalian masters will be doing so on full bellies."

The ship they took was opulent. It was also stolen. Stripped of any markings identifying its rightful owner. Ara and Freya stayed far back, observing from a safe distance as the craft gently settled down in the guarded landing zone. Charlie and Daisy were the first to step out, each with swords on their backs, eyes scanning for danger.

"It is safe, Visla," Charlie said.

Bawb and Zilara then stepped from the craft, taking in a deep breath of the fresh air in such a relaxed and carefree manner that would make any cat in a patch of sunlight jealous.

"Visla Tormal, I am Grovahr. We were thrilled to receive notice of your visit. It is an honor to have you with us, and it's been quite some time," the greeting party's head guard said as Bawb and the others departed the ship. "Please, allow my porters to help with your luggage."

Bawb snapped his fingers, and several cases floated out of the ship. It was an excessive waste of valuable magic to make such a show of power, but that was precisely the sort of thing typically expected by the resort's patrons. Only, Bawb was using stored magic, not his own, and he would have to be careful.

Fortunately, Charlie was close behind him, and his power was regenerative on its own. If need be, he could cast for Bawb surreptitiously. But if all went according to plan, they'd have no need of any such displays after the initial one.

"This way," Grovahr said, leading the guest and his entourage through the ranks of waiting guards, standing at attention on either side.

"Looks like at least fifty of them," Charlie silently noted over his and Bawb's link.

"Fifty-two, actually," Bawb noted. *"Two are shimmered on either side of the entryway to the hallway."*

"Damn. Good eyes, man. I didn't even see them."

"Years of practice, my friend," Bawb replied with a silent chuckle.

The guards fell in behind the visitors as they passed, forming a long column, allegedly for their protection, but Bawb was relatively certain it served a dual purpose.

"You look well, Visla," Grovahr said. "I remembered you being somewhat shorter, though."

Bawb merely smiled at the man as if he hadn't a care in the world. "I can assure you, I have not grown since my last visit, though that was quite some time ago. You possess a good memory, Grovahr."

"It's my job, Visla."

"And you excel at it," the Wampeh replied. "Continue your good work, and please, do tell Chef Nooria that I would love more of her Farral stew. It's been years since it last passed my lips, yet the flavors are still as bright in my mind as if it was just the other day."

"Chef Nooria retired, I'm afraid," Grovahr said. "But I will inquire of Chef Boorden. Perhaps she shared the recipe before her departure."

Bawb halted abruptly, eyeing the man with an appraising gaze. The guards following behind nearly bumped into one another at the unexpected stop.

"I knew I was right about you, Grovahr. A credit to your position," he said, tossing a hefty coin to the man. "I do sincerely hope the new chef can accommodate the request."

Grovahr seemed to have been won over by Bawb's performance, and Charlie was glad to see his friend's acting chops were once again back to their former glory. He could charm his way into just about anywhere when required, and today was a high-pressure test of his skills. One he passed with flying colors.

"I will do my best, Visla," Grovahr said. "Now, please, allow me to show you to your suites."

CHAPTER FORTY

The portal opening had occurred exactly on schedule, as planned, though the defensive fleet was on a particularly high level of readiness when it did. Keeping things appearing normal from the other side was crucial, but they had no way of knowing whether or not the enemy would be making an attempt to cross over yet again.

One of Joshua's tiny micro satellites zipped through the moment the portal was clear enough to allow it to do so without incinerating. The system, the AI was pleased to note, had functioned flawlessly, and precisely as he'd planned.

Then, somewhat to their surprise, a drone bearing a message from the satellite passed through unmolested. It was at that moment they knew the enemy would not be making a rush for it. At least, not this time. It was a waiting game. Galactic chess. And both sides of the board were attempting to fool the other.

"This is troubling," Zed said as he read the information contained on the satellite. "The unprotected message seems pretty straightforward. They're struggling, don't know what to do, etcetera. But the AI message is far more concerning."

"What does it say?" Admiral Harkaway asked, the signal being transmitted back to Cal and the others as well.

"It says they received our message and will be ready to strike when we are. But there's a problem when we cross our fleet over. It has to do with our warp drives."

"I have the same message on my micro sat," Joshua noted. "It seems the enemy has somehow learned to track our warp signatures. Freya informed me she had to effect multiple warps to gain any real distance, and they still were right on her tail. Only the destruction of the pursuing ships allowed her to escape."

"This *is* a problem," Harkaway said. "If they can track our ships, then we'll only have one shot at this."

"We assumed as much anyway," Zed noted.

"Yes, but this removes any wiggle room. If the fight spreads out beyond the space immediately surrounding the portal, we're looking at a very difficult situation."

"So we strike fast, and we strike hard. It's the only way we can maintain the element of surprise," Zed replied. "Joshua, do you agree?"

"In this circumstance, I do. And especially given what we've just learned about who our enemy truly is."

"What do you mean?" Admiral Harkaway asked.

"That's the other part of the message. There's been quite a development," Joshua said. "Apparently, Visla Dominus is someone Charlie and his friends know quite well. Her name is Malalia Maktan."

"What did you just say?" Rika's alarmed voice asked over the open comms line.

"You heard correctly, Rika. Malalia Maktan is alive and well. And *she* is Visla Dominus."

Rika felt the world spin around her, and it had nothing to do with gravity, or lack thereof, in space. "That's impossible. She should be long dead."

"Normally, perhaps. But the message was quite clear. Apparently, she has been stealing the power from a certain type of Wampeh for some time now, gathering their ability to take another's power. From what the transmission said, she was masquerading as a woman named Mareh. Kara's stepmother. She's been feeding off the girl and her father for years."

Now it was Korbin's turn to be stunned. For Mareh––Malalia, whoever she really was–– to have amassed as much power as was implied, yet still manage to remain hidden for all these years not only to him, but to Nikora as well? Her power must be incredible.

And it also explained his friend's sudden illness. If Mareh was planning on advancing her cause, it would only seem logical that she would drain him as much as she needed if her reveal was at hand. And Mareh always had many powerful friends. Friends, Korbin realized, she was likely keeping as an unwitting stable of fresh power for her to take when the time came.

Within the Palmarian estate, none would know who she truly was. Nikora and Kara were beloved by the staff, after all. And the attackers he had fought off were embedded spies who almost certainly had no idea their employer was actually in the building.

But there had to be at least one or two captains whom she favored more than the rest. And of them, one would logically have to know her true identity. Or at least be aware that she was visiting Visla Dominus's fleet.

"We should contact Grundsch," Korbin said, the flurry of plans crystallizing into a cohesive strategy. "He was present in the household. And as a collared guard, Mareh would have likely treated him as no more than decoration. And he is far more observant than any give him credit for. He will be able to tell us which of the captains she typically uses."

"But how would that help us?" Rika asked. "If Malalia is who we're fighting, what does it matter?"

"Because, if we cross into battle and she is not with her fleet, then we may be forced to hunt her down once we defeat her forces. And if that's the case, we'll need to have an idea where she may be. The captain would be able to help steer us to the systems she frequents."

"I like the idea," Zed said. "We'll have the main body of the attack fleet pass through on the first wave, engaging the enemy and wiping the road clear. Once we've hammered them into submission and taken down their larger units, then we'll bring through our second wave of smaller mop-up ships. Grundsch will cross over in that wave."

"So we go and kick everyone's ass. And end Malalia for good this time," Rika said, an intensity in her voice most had never heard before.

"Rika, I know you won't like this, but you need to stay on this side of the portal. At least until we're decisively victorious," Zed said.

"No way. I'm not missing this. I owe that bitch some major payback."

"I understand, but we'll need a magical backstop on this side of the portal standing by. You and Korbin are the only ones who are able to control it, and if the enemy tries to cross over, we need you to be there to stop them and drop the portal back into the sun."

"But that would only happen if we lose," Rika said.

Zed paused. "I know. So let's hope it doesn't come to that."

CHAPTER FORTY-ONE

The human crewmembers of the key ships prepping to lead the assault against Visla Dominus's fleet cycled through Zed's hangar bay in quick order, their shuttle craft hustling them over and back as fast as possible.

Korbin's ship was there as well, and he was the one now carefully administering the prescribed dose of Balamar waters to each of the men and women filing past him. They'd managed to retain a fairly sizable amount after loading the specialty rail gun sabots with the fluid. That in itself was a boon.

That the crews were a species that could ingest it and live was icing on the cake. Still, there were hundreds of people who were receiving oral doses, so the individual amounts would have to be relatively small. Nothing like what Charlie and Rika had taken. But it should be enough to make them hardier and tougher to kill. That would be enough.

The Chithiid and Uroks who had volunteered to be guinea pigs appeared to have no adverse reactions to oral administration, but there was still a tiny bit of doubt. As such, topical applications, though not as efficient, were chosen for their respective species. Better safe than dead or writhing in discomfort, after all, especially right before a massive military action the likes of which none had ever seen.

"Now, remember, you are not invincible," Korbin would remind each of them after receiving their dose. "I know you feel amazing, and you are indeed fortified. But we do not know exactly how long this will last, nor how much it will accelerate each of your healing processes."

Interestingly, more than one of the crewmembers was already minorly injured in one way or another, as happens in people's daily lives, and the waters began mending them immediately. Reports of the effect spread quickly and were enough to give a confidence boost the crews would need when they finally came face-to-face with the enemy's vast forces.

They'd be in for the fight of their lives, greatly outnumbered by a magical foe. There was simply no room for fear or hesitation.

There was something else in the works, but Joshua hadn't quite been able to get it dialed in just yet. Something to help against magical attacks. Something Korbin had been prepping them for as best he could.

"The Tslavars are violent and aggressive, but they are also somewhat predictable because of it. I've provided Zed with details of their most typical attack formations and counterstrike tactics. He's already transmitted that information to each of your ships, so make sure you're all familiar with them. Also, among those details, there are a number of standard magical assaults they tend to favor most. Now, you should hopefully not have to deal with them on an up-close-and-personal level, but if you should be boarded, or taken captive, there are some counter-spells you would be well off knowing."

"But we're not magic people," one of the crew replied. "How are we supposed to fight back?"

"Zed?" Korbin said.

"Right. Each of your ships that have neuro-stim units on

board will be provided with a very, very basic load of the most simple yet effective spells," Zed explained. "Crew will rotate through and download these basic commands as quickly as your machinery allows. If all goes as we hope, most of you should be able to get through it before we engage the enemy."

"But we're still not magic people. What good does knowing a bunch of words do us?"

"Joshua, would you mind?" Zed inquired.

"Of course. I've been working on a little something that *might* give you the ability to cast basic spells. I'm not going into details just yet, but you've all known me a long time and know I wouldn't make that statement lightly. So, please. Move forward with what Zed has detailed, and I promise I will do all I can to help provide you that additional layer of protection from my end."

The brilliant AI was, indeed, well known. One of the key players in the Great War, in fact. And his reputation was spotless. If Joshua asked them to have faith, then even the most agnostic of the bunch would rustle some up for him.

Back in his and Freya's Dark Side hangar and fabrication lab, Joshua had their bleeding-edge machinery working feverishly. The project was unlike any he'd ever overseen before, and were it not for the pressing nature of their predicament, he'd have found the novelty invigorating.

As it stood, time was of the essence, and he was frankly not certain he could complete the project's refinements in time to distribute the experimental devices throughout the fleet.

Freya had been working on replicating the magic-imbued nanites with decent success before she and Daisy had so abruptly crossed over to chase down her wayward son. Those nanites were useful in small amounts to help railgun sabots penetrate the enemy's magical shielding, but were otherwise of somewhat limited use.

But Joshua was a creative mind and an outside-the-box thinker as well. A *very* creative mind, and one to find military advantages others might overlook. It came with essentially running an entire nation's defense system before the Great War. And now he was focusing that expertise on a new project.

The nanites were clever little things, tweaked and refined over the years by both himself and his partner, and now he was asking them to tweak the unusual, magical addition Freya had made to them. He had new samples to work with. A different power. Something that was more compatible with this galaxy's materials. In fact, what he was working with was *from* this very galaxy.

The dark, matte-gray material was flexible, not rigid, and its ends would seal with one another, forming an unbroken loop when placed on a wrist or ankle. It was also imbued with the strange power Rika had learned to harness after her time with the Kalamani.

If he was correct, these would be the first ever konuses created in this galaxy, and powered entirely with homegrown magic. So he hoped, anyway.

There were only a few dozen of the initial test versions of the nanite konuses produced, and those were being worn by cyborg test subjects. Joshua had recruited some of Marban's pirates at first, but he very quickly learned that even with the magic embedded within the nanites themselves and not openly exposed on the surface of the device, the men from the other galaxy nevertheless experienced a burning reaction to them.

While it was at first seen as something of an initial setback, Joshua quickly realized the unexpected benefit of the sometimes-violent reaction people from the other realm had. If the konuses *were* perfected and distributed to their forces, it was almost inevitable that some might fall into the hands of their enemy at some point. But the power within the devices was apparently unusable by their enemy, while their own forces could utilize konuses from the other galaxy.

It wasn't a huge advantage by any stretch of the imagination, but at least it was something. And so far, the newly crafted konuses had only been tested in *this* galaxy. There was simply no telling how they would work once in the other one, if at all.

Sergeant George Franklin and his men down on the planet's surface were the first of Earth's forces to receive the konuses. While mature AIs seemed to lack the necessary flexibility of mind to make the other side's magical devices work, this new iteration appeared to lack so stringent of an intent requirement.

Rika and Korbin had come to the moon facility at Joshua's request earlier that day and helped test the first completed nanite konus. Cautiously to start, then with more confidence.

"Remarkable," Rika said, feeling the power pull from the nanite band.

"It seems to function much like a konus from my realm," Korbin noted. "But we'll have to train your people in the ways of casting in order for them to work."

"I've got an idea on that," Rika said. "Something we saw with Ripley. If we use the neuro-stim, we should be able to load a few spells in short order without requiring months of training."

"You think it will work?"

"Yeah. But there's only one way to find out for sure," Rika replied.

It was an odd concept for Korbin to wrap his head around. That these mechanical minds could not only learn and store spells from his world, but also discover and devise new ones from this galaxy as well. It was a process that had taken millennia where he had come from. Lifetimes of trial and error.

But here, with these mechanical minds that were capable of so much, they could figure out spells in a fraction of that time with their combined processing power. It was as if they had the knowledge of entire civilizations at their disposal. And they were sure as hell going to use it.

Another benefit of using the cyborgs as test subjects—beyond their ability to download and store any spell instantly, faster than any neuro-stim—was the fact that cyborgs, if captured, could be a silent force waiting for activation. They were flesh on the outside, but their mechanical cores meant almost none of the stunning spells would actually work on them. They'd register the attempt in their flesh covering and act accordingly, but in reality, they'd be free to fight, if called for.

The hope, however, was that it would never come to that.

"They need more tests, Joshua. But I can tell you that these are very promising," Korbin said after the first round of trials with George and his men. "Not only do these seem to have quite an effect on my realm's magic, but the bands look nothing like any weapon my people would recognize. I doubt any would think to strip a prisoner of a simple bracelet. And with your galaxy's power, it's not readily detectable to my kind, unless they happen to be very powerful, or specifically looking for it."

"So, how much longer before we can deploy them to the fleet?" Rika asked.

Joshua hesitated. "The risks of them failing to function are still great, and ramping up production will take a little time. Perhaps another day. Maybe two."

"I don't think we're going to have that long," she replied.

"I know. I'll do my best, but you may be right. This conflict may very well come to a head sooner than later."

Rika considered his words a moment. "Then you'd better get cracking," she said. "The clock is ticking."

CHAPTER FORTY-TWO

Debauchery.

No other word quite described the goings-on within the impenetrable playground of the powerful and wealthy. Whatever pleasures they wished, illicit or otherwise, were available with just a snap of their fingers.

Charlie had seen a lot in his time as a slave, a pirate, and a rebel leader, but even so, many of the things playing out within these walls were simply shocking. Charlie was by no means a prude, but there were certain proclivities that he simply couldn't fathom.

"I'm not one to kink shame anyone, but damn, Bob, no amount of eye-bleach can make me unsee that," Charlie silently told his friend as they passed one of the communal "play" rooms on the way to their suite.

They settled in, and Bawb and Zilara double-checked the room to ensure there were no surveillance spells of any kind present. It was a near impossibility, given the consequences of anyone attempting to spy on someone the nature of the power users who visited this place, but the seasoned assassins *never* took anything for granted. It was how they'd lived as long as they had.

"I suppose this place isn't so bad," Charlie said as they took a meandering stroll of the grounds a short while later. "A bit weird, maybe, but not too––" he choked off his words as they passed another of the play rooms.

This one, however, was different than the other. And what Charlie saw going on inside suddenly made him look very much forward to the violence they would be raining down upon these people shortly. Daisy, flanking the faux Wampeh couple, felt her rage rise in concert with Charlie's when she saw what was being done in the name of fun.

"Don't," Sarah warned her as she instinctively began reaching for her sword, ready to kill every last one of the sick bastards in that room.

"The mission is the priority, Daze. There's no way you can repair what's already being done. Don't jeopardize things for a quick fix."

But you see what they're doing, Sarah. They can't be more than––

"And you can either kill a few sick bastards now and risk the entire mission, or kill them all soon enough. It sucks, I know. Believe me, I know."

Daisy looked at Charlie and could see he was having the same internal battle with himself. Bawb and Zilara, however, were all smiles, playing their parts to perfection. But then Zilara casually turned with a happy expression firmly on her face and locked eyes with her for just a moment.

And in that moment, Daisy saw the truth. And that truth was one of a violent and painful end coming to each and every one of them. *Soon.* Some things, even the Wampeh Ghalian found over the line.

For the moment, they had to let things go on, no matter how distasteful. The mission depended on it.

Bawb was all smiles and pleasantries as they met the other guests, quietly cataloging their locations and power levels under the guise of socializing. There were a great many powerful visitors within the retreat. More than they'd expected, even.

And though they had their own personal guards with them, none were terribly well protected. They were vislas and emmiks, after all. And in this facility, who would possibly be foolish enough to dare attack them?

They'd find out soon enough.

A stout, brownish-toned man with heavily creased skin almost resembling tree bark, waddled over to the pair of lean Wampeh and their two "guards," his own duo of gray-skinned, expressionless, and well-armed attendants in tow.

"You're new," the man said, licking his lips as he eyed the newcomers' guards. His gaze lingered particularly long on Charlie. "How much do you want for this one?"

"I'm sorry, but he is not for sale," Bawb replied.

"Thanks, man," Charlie silently said.

"Oh, if the price was right, I might consider it," Bawb replied in an amused tone over their unspoken link.

"Come, now, friend," the man persisted, looking Charlie up and down. *"Everything* is for sale. Name your price."

"This one has been with me a long time, and is a faithful servant. So, again, while your offer is appreciated, I must decline."

"A shame," the man replied.

Charlie sensed his power. *"Visla,"* he alerted Bawb.

"Yes. And fairly powerful at that," Bawb agreed.

The visla thought a moment, glancing at his own men. "Might you consider a loan, then? If you, or your woman, find either of my chattel appealing, I'm sure we could work out an arrangement."

A pensive expression formed on Bawb's face. He looked at Zilara, and she met his gaze with one of curiosity as she sized up the visla's men, an eyebrow slightly arched in interest.

"Perhaps," Bawb replied, meeting Zilara's gaze with a loving smile. "It's very kind of you, Visla...?"

"Keever."

"A pleasure, Visla Keever. Your reputation precedes you," the Wampeh said with a warm smile.

Damn, the old Bawb is back, Charlie mused, glad to see the assassin's acting skills had returned to their former glory. If he didn't know he loved another, he'd have been convinced Zilara was the light of his life, when, in fact he barely knew her.

"You run the smugglers' market on Naratso, do you not?" Zilara inquired.

"Oh, I wouldn't know about that," the man replied.

"Come, Visla. We are all men and women of a particular level of power, and with that comes certain...*benefits,*" Bawb said. "And, believe me, I know all about, uh, let's call them, 'interesting' ventures. And from what I've heard, Naratso must be quite a handful, even for one of your power and status."

Visla Keever let a little smile creep onto his lips. "Well, I suppose it is, on occasion. But what good is power if it is not wielded from time to time, wouldn't you agree?"

Both Bawb and Zilara laughed heartily. "Oh, indeed."

"And the benefits are many," Keever added, eyeing a *very* young servant as he carried a tray of delicacies to one of the play rooms.

"This one, I shall greatly enjoy draining," Bawb silently informed Charlie.

"Good. And make it hurt," Charlie added.

"Oh, I will."

Charlie had learned early on in their most unusual of friendships that Bawb, for all of his killings over the decades, had a rather unique personal code. It was a bit unusual for one of his profession to have self-imposed restrictions to quite the degree he had, but, then, Bawb was not just any assassin. He was the Geist, and perhaps it was precisely those quirks that made him the deadliest Wampeh Ghalian in the galaxy.

"Visla, will you be at the dining hall this evening? Perhaps we could chat further at that time," Bawb inquired.

"Yes, yes. I'll definitely be there. One can certainly build up an appetite here, eh?" he said with a conspiratorial wink.

Charlie wanted to puke, and Daisy wanted to skewer the man, but Bawb smiled and laughed, as did his assassin counterpart.

"Indeed," the Wampeh replied. "Then, we shall see you there."

Bawb and Zilara then proceeded to make a leisurely loop of the rest of the facility, casually making note of every single person there, whether a patron, their attendants, or security, personal or otherwise. They then returned to their suite to prepare for the evening's festivities.

And they would not be what the others imagined.

"A nice selection," Zilara noted as she strapped several unenchanted blades about her person. "Plenty of power for all of us, and only a few of these cretins possess lives worth sparing."

"Sparing? I thought everyone here was pretty much a baddie," Daisy interjected. "You're saying some aren't all bad?"

"There were a few," Bawb replied. "A handful we will drain and allow to live with a warning to use their powers for good from now on, *or else*. The others, however, are fair game. And I believe your sword will be well fed come our departure from this place."

CHAPTER FORTY-THREE

It was a normal behavior of the guests to dine at roughly the same time. Not all did, of course, but the opportunity to meet new power users of their caliber, and proclivities, was somewhat rare, and they welcomed the chance to make the acquaintance of, and perhaps recreate with, their peers.

This meant that the majority of them were gathered in one place. That, of course, made the dining hall the most fortified area of the compound at that hour. Not only were the vislas and emmiks present, but so were their personal guards, as well as a sizable number of the facility's security, there to keep things in line if need be.

Precisely the opportunity Bawb and Zilara needed.

They'd found the service corridor on their second round of the property, nearly missing the tiny hallway amidst all of the opulent overkill of the rest of the area. But tucked behind a tapestry was a door. And that door led to a hallway. And that hallway––after some twists and turns––arrived at a laborers' staging area. One that happened to be near an external delivery door.

It was guarded, of course, and heavily at that, but nowhere

near the levels of the rest of the facility. Bawb and Zilara had no trouble dispatching the guards and hiding their bodies without a sound made or a single drop of blood staining the soil. The guards were simply gone without a trace.

Outside, their fellow masters had expertly avoided the relatively well-spaced-out guards, approaching under their shimmer cloaks and not sounding any alarms. Not with the door opened from the inside. The wards only protected against outside attacks.

The door was ajar less than ten seconds before sealing once more, but in that short span, the Wampeh Ghalian had made their way inside, joining Bawb and Zilara for the hunt.

"Your weapons, Geist," Kort said, handing the pair of Vespus blades to the pale assassin.

Bawb nodded his thanks, then strapped his and Hunze's swords to his back. It was an old style. No one double-wielded these days, as it was not terribly practical, and few could boast the requisite skills to be efficient enough to make it worthwhile. Bawb, however, was of the very few who possessed that talent, and tonight it would be on full display.

"There is a lot for us to take," Zilara informed her fellow masters. "But the fight ahead is what counts. Save as much of your newly claimed power as possible. We shall need it when we face Dominus and her forces."

The others nodded their agreement and understanding, then vanished within their shimmer cloaks once again. The most powerful of the patrons might be able to sense them, but the odds were slim. None was remotely as strong as Malalia, and they stood a good chance of evading their notice.

Zilara tightened the scabbard resting on her back. "Shall we?" she asked.

"I'd be delighted," Bawb replied.

The two Wampeh stepped out from behind the tapestry and back into the main housing area, holding the fabric aside long enough for their fellow Ghalian to pass and disappear into the property. Charlie and Daisy were precisely where they'd been left, standing casual guard, just in case.

"All went well, I take it," Charlie said, noting the swords on Bawb's back.

"Indeed," he replied with a smile. "And now we return to our suite. This evening, once the others have separated and gone their own ways once more, we shall take them down and feed."

Bawb and Zilara figured the swords they were sporting would be ignored, assumed to be normal blades by any they might stumble upon on the short walk back to their quarters. Fortunately, no such encounter slowed their progress, and they were safely tucked away within minutes, ready to wait for the evening's carnage.

It was getting somewhat late when they finally stepped from their rooms once again, the other guests having long since split off to either slumber, drink, or partake in whatever illicit pleasures they had lined up for the evening. Separated from one another and overconfident in their power and security. Just as the Ghalian had planned.

Visla Keever's guard opened the door when Bawb came knocking.

"I wish to speak with your master."

"Yes, Visla. I shall fetch him immediately," the gray-skinned man said, not seeing the swords on his back, or ignoring them if he did.

"Come to discuss my offer?" Visla Keever asked with a lecherous grin as he came to the door.

"Not exactly," Bawb replied.

The look of confusion on Keever's face lasted only a moment before being replaced with one of concern and a flash of rapidly building power when he saw the swords on Bawb's back. But by then it was too late, and one of them was already buried deep in his chest.

Bawb had been careful not to pierce his heart. Draining a dead man did not transfer his power. But Keever would be a corpse soon enough, and Bawb was more than happy to speed that process with his fangs.

In short order, the man was drained of his power, lifeless on the ground. Bawb tossed the shorter man's body into his chambers. The guards jumped to action, but Bawb, rather than cutting them down, merely disarmed them.

"I have no wish to end you," he told them. "All I wanted was your visla. And he is now dead. You are free men."

The two looked at one another, confused.

"You may leave, if you so desire," Bawb continued. "But you are also men of action and skill, and there is a fight brewing that could use men of your talents. Should you wish to join us, seek me out when the bloodshed has ended. If not, I suggest you flee this world and never look back."

A moment later, the Wampeh had vanished from the room, leaving behind two rather confused personal guards and a dead visla's body.

The other Wampeh were making quick work of the other power users in a similar manner, though each had their own personal technique they preferred. But all that mattered was the magic was taken and the owner of it either dispatched or left so weak as to have no chance of recovering and becoming a problem for them for quite some time.

Daisy and Charlie didn't have the same gifts as their Wampeh Ghalian comrades, leaving them with the far less complicated task of simply slaughtering their enemies and clearing out the security detail protecting the chambers.

Charlie summoned his power and made quick work of the non-powered guards and powered ones alike. His skills were increasing steadily, and since the additional bond with not only Bawb and Hunze, but Rika as well, he'd been developing his own, unique magic on top of what he'd already possessed.

Bawb dismembered a defender about to sound the alarm, then glanced across the central meeting area to see Charlie fighting off multiple opponents with both magic and weaponry. Bawb rushed to his friend's aid, though it wasn't truly needed, and the two finished off the security staff in a matter of seconds.

The flash of magic coming their way through the other corridor leading to the chamber caught both of their attention almost as much as the unusual sight of a bright white sword deflecting magical attacks with ease while its owner lashed out with her strange power whip device.

An emmik came charging into the fray from another door, and it looked like he would reach her before Charlie or Bawb could react. But then something strange happened. Daisy's sword flew from her hand, quite of its own accord, and impaled itself in the man's chest, sucking him dry before flying back to Daisy's waiting grip like a deadly yo-yo, minus the string.

Daisy didn't hesitate, though. The facility had finally had the alarm raised, and troops were swarming into the area. She raced headlong into the fray, as did Bawb, pulling free the other sword on his back as he did. Hunze's sword, now flashing through the air in tandem with his own. A gleaming windmill of enchanted death mowing down guard and power user alike.

The other masters were falling back to join their comrades, and as they did, they paused a moment, as Charlie had, to watch Bawb and Daisy tear through the enemy in a bloody dance of death. To any observing the carnage, it would have almost looked as if they were having a contest to see who could slay the most people. And, perhaps, that wasn't too far from the truth.

The others quickly joined in, overwhelming the fortified facility's supposedly superior forces with speed and skill, all the while using either conventional weapons, or magic stored in konuses or slaaps. The power they'd stolen this day was needed for the upcoming battle, and all were careful not to squander it.

They made their way through the defensive ranks as if they

were mere paper targets, driving their way outside the fortress to their waiting shimmer ships.

And then, as quickly as it had all begun, the attacking force was gone, leaving hundreds dead, maimed, or somewhere in between.

It was a slaughter that would go down in history. The Wampeh had burned their carefully placed identity, but it was worth it. And now, having been so thoroughly overrun, this particular facility would never open its doors again. There was simply no way to recover after a breach like this.

"Did you get him?" Charlie asked as Daisy wiped the blood from her hands as she reached Freya.

She simply smiled. The man she'd seen upon arrival, the one Charlie had nearly lashed out against as well, was no more.

"I hope you made it hurt," Charlie said as he climbed onto Ara's back.

"Oh, it did," Daisy replied, content that she'd not only helped their cause, but also put a predator of the worst variety out of business for good.

Charlie nodded, and she stepped inside her AI ship and took off into the sky, the humans and Ghalian vanishing in a flash, leaving behind slaughter and destruction that would be spoken of for generations in their wake.

CHAPTER FORTY-FOUR

"How confident are we with this intel?" one of the captains asked Zed. A Chithiid, this time.

"*Very* confident," was his reply. "I've gone over this already. We spent a lot of time extracting this information from the captured Tslavar crew. According to their mission parameters, they were to cross back and join the main body of their attack fleet."

"A fleet you think we can defeat? As large as they are?"

"We don't have a choice," Zed replied. "Our intel says that the main body of Dominus's ships are massed near the portal, just out of scan range. Those that are close enough for us to see with Joshua's micro sats seem to be rotating their ranks. Something is up."

"Zed's right," Admiral Harkaway said. "They're preparing for something big. And whatever comes next, rest assured, it's going to be far worse for us the longer we wait. At the moment, the enemy doesn't know we are aware of their forces' movements, just as they are unaware we know they are reading the transmissions off the main satellite on the other side."

The portal had only opened a few times since Joshua's

stealthy system of micro satellites was put in place, and from what they could tell, the system was entirely undetected. Also apparently working perfectly was the AI sub frequency communications between Freya and the other side. Transmissions the captured Urok ship could not hear.

It wasn't much of an element of surprise. Dominus, who they now knew was actually Charlie's old enemy Malalia Maktan, would surely see the portal opening off schedule. All they could hope was that the main body of their more robust attack ships could make it through and engage the enemy before they were able to reinforce their forward ranks.

Key would be driving the Tslavar ships back enough to provide a reasonable cushion should they have to seal the portal behind themselves. There was a minimum safe range from the burning plasma, and they could not afford to be caught anywhere within the danger zone.

But if they could drive off the enemy in that first wave and create some space, if they could somehow pull that off and give their forces a little breathing room, the rest of their ships could then rush through the portal and bolster their forces.

It was an audacious plan, and a bit ahead of schedule. The water rounds for the railguns were only just being distributed, and shielding variations were still in the works, but the opportunity had presented itself. They couldn't look a gift horse in the mouth. The time to strike was now.

"We'll be sending the largest of our ships through first," Zed declared. "With their bulk, as well as their reinforced shielding, that, combined with a blistering initial assault, should give us the footing we need to make a successful push."

"I'm sure Rika and I can create a nice little diversion once we're finally through as well," Korbin added.

"I'm afraid we need you to remain on this side, Korbin. Both of you," Cal replied.

"We know, but we're the only real casters you've got," Rika

blurted, still running on adrenaline since learning she'd be facing off against Malalia once more. "Once the main ships are through, we should be able to cross over too. We've got *magic*, Cal."

"Be that as it may, you two have skills we require on this side. You're our only backstop controlling the portal. No one else can do it. And if for some reason we have to close it, we simply cannot afford to have you on the other side."

Rika wanted to say something clever. Something to show them that she could do just as good a job and be just as useful on the other side, fighting head-on against her mortal enemy. But she knew the argument was futile, just as she knew the AIs were right.

"Fine," she grumbled.

"I know you're not happy about this, Rika, and I'm truly sorry. But you are simply too important to the cause."

"Cal's right," Zed noted. "And we'll be holding back a small group of fighters to stand by you and Korbin while you control the portal, just in case."

"In case what?" Marban asked.

"In case things go tits up and we find ourselves in a world of shit," Zed replied.

The AI had as salty a tongue as any pirate, and Marban couldn't help but like him, even if he was keeping Rika from her well-deserved revenge. He paused for just a moment, then made a decision.

"I'm staying too, then."

"What? No, you don't have to miss the fight for me," Rika said.

"The machines are right. You're too important to risk. You and Korbin both," he added. "These smaller fighters are fine in the event of a lesser craft slipping through, but anything larger and you'll need something with more firepower. And my vessel fits that bill."

Rika could have argued, and Korbin could have noted that his own retrofitted ship now possessed a very formidable weapons array. But both refrained. Marban wanted to do this, and, to be honest, it would be a comfort knowing so competent a warrior would have their backs.

"Thanks, Marban. It's appreciated," Korbin said. "While I don't think we'll be needing your assistance, knowing you're covering us will be a welcome relief."

"Yeah, it's good having you with us," Rika added. "So, what do you say we get this show on the road? It won't take us long to get into position. Jo, we all good to go?"

Her cyborg co-pilot powered up the weapons systems and double-checked their flight controls. "Yeah, we're green across the board. Ready when you are."

"All right, then. Zed, if you're okay with it, I suggest we finish up whatever last-minute things there are remaining to do. The clock is already running for our next portal opening. We'll be in position and standing by for the attack fleet to join us."

"Fantastic," Zed replied. "We're in hurry-up mode, for sure, but I also want to be damn sure we've got as many ships operating with the modified railgun systems as possible. If we manage to take down Dominus in the first wave, it may very well break the spirit of their forces and save us a whole hell of a lot of bloodshed."

"Then, as always, let's hope for the best, expect the worst, and prepare for both," Rika joked.

"Charlie always says that too," Marban noted with a chuckle. "It must be an Earth thing. In any case, best or worst, I've got your back."

A little smile creased Rika's lips. "Thanks, Marban. All righty, then. Let's start these gears turning and put an end to this bullshit once and for all."

CHAPTER FORTY-FIVE

Charlie and the rebel forces were counting down the hours to the planned portal opening on their chronos, keying in the rest of their forces as the minutes ticked by.

"We're almost there, guys," Charlie informed the assembled fleet leaders who weren't physically present with the rest of them on the little planet's surface.

The message was being sent over both comms and skree to ensure there was no possibility that any of their people, tech or magical, were not in the loop.

"We've got to do everything we can to catch these bastards off guard. That means we have to throw everything we have at them."

"I'm ready," Olo said, itching for a fight.

"What of the enemy forces?" Rovnik asked. "Are we still expecting the same levels of resistance?"

"Freya, you want to address that? Your scans are far more accurate than anything I could possibly whip up with the little array in Ara's harness," Charlie said.

"Yeah, sure," the AI replied. "So, from what I've seen, as of our brief visit to link up with the satellite, it's looking like their fleet is kinda spread out a bit."

"Maybe they're getting lazy," Dukaan suggested.

"That, or they are spreading their ranks to make targeting them more difficult in case of an attack," Charlie said. "Whatever the reason, according to our intel, it looks like they're vulnerable."

"Which is an opportunity for us," Daisy added. "Seems like as good a situation as we're likely to be presented."

"I'm going to kill them all," Olo said quietly. But not so quietly as not to be heard. While Charlie was a bit concerned about the smuggler, the pirates wholeheartedly approved of his sentiment.

"So, we launch soon, then?" Rovnik said, rubbing his hands together. "Excellent. My men are anxious for a fight."

"They'll get one soon enough," Charlie noted. "All right, everyone, if that's it for questions, we should all triple-check our gear and get everyone ready for the assault. We're going to have our hands full and can't afford any avoidable errors on our part, so get your stuff locked down and prepped."

The group milled about a moment longer as the discussion wrapped up, then those who were physically present on the surface scattered to their respective transports to return to their ships. Amazara, however, having already moved her patient's stasis pod to a small, magic-driven ship, had a different destination.

"I'll be back as soon as I'm able," she told them. "But there is something I have to do."

"You're leaving *now*?" Leila asked. "Right before we fly into a battle? It seems a rather inopportune time for our healer to go absent."

"I am aware," Amazara replied. "But you'll have to trust me on this. I would tell you more, but as I've learned over many years, the less people who know one's destination, the less the likelihood of things going awry."

Charlie and Leila shared a glance. This was unusual, and piss-poor timing, but she'd only just joined them. Having a healer of her skill was a luxury, not a necessity. Losing her, while unfortunate, was not a game changer.

"Fly safe," Charlie finally said. "And I sincerely hope you make it back soon."

"As do I," Amazara replied, then turned and strode off, gathering up a fair amount of supplies before boarding the waiting craft dotting the landing area.

"Well, I don't know what that's all about, but we were lucky to even have her as long as we did," Charlie said. "Come on. We should gear up and get a move on."

He and Leila quickly suited up and climbed atop Ara's back, while Bawb joined Kip and Dukaan, adding an additional layer of magical power to their tech weaponry, thanks to his Ootaki hair-powered vest and wand.

The odds were slightly in their favor at the moment, and they would have just one shot to take full advantage of it. And if Malalia's ships hadn't done anything drastic since they'd last visited the portal, they *should* still have a reasonably novel course of attack that could actually see them winning the day. But it would require patience and steely nerves if they hoped to pull this off.

Ara jumped into the system housing the portal, towing Freya with a magical tether, keeping the powerful ship's warp drive entirely offline on arrival. They were the advance scouts, double-checking everything before the rest of the attack force followed. If something seemed awry, they'd jump back to the staging area and pull the plug, leaving a hidden message with the stealth AI micro sat system for the others.

However, things appeared as they expected, for the most part. The enemy fleet was the same as had been previously noted, namely, spread a bit thin, their distance making their numbers appear to be larger than they actually were. And if that was the actual case, this might not be as lopsided a fight as they'd originally assumed.

"Looks like they're still adjusting their fleet after the portal fried 'em," Charlie noted. "There are still a ton of ships, mind you, but from what I can tell, I think we may have taken out more of them than we originally thought with that initial solar burst."

"It would appear that way," Ara agreed. "Though, with Malalia involved, it would be wise to take nothing for granted."

"I agree with your dragon buddy," Daisy said. "I faced off with that bitch, and even after just that once, I can tell you she's a wily one."

"Be nice, you're talking about our great-great-great-great—"

Bite me, Sarah, Daisy silently shot back to her mental ride-along.

"The rest of the fleet is keyed to Kip's chrono. They'll be jumping to us in one minute," Leila noted. "So, what do we think? Is everything okay? Anyone see anything out of the ordinary?"

Charlie looked over the area, reaching out with his magic, as Ara did the same, pooling their linked power. Freya did her own survey as well, but with top-notch scanning tech.

"Not much going on," Freya noted.

"I agree," Ara said. "Though there's something odd. Do you feel it, Charlie?"

"Yeah. But it's not normal magic. It's something different."

He scanned the area again, pulling on the remnants of Rika's magic still mingling with his own. Surprisingly, it hit on something. A magical tug on his senses, but small, and right in front of the molten plasma-spewing portal.

"Freya, do me a favor and shift from scanning the fleet to checking out right over at the portal. I'm talking where the flames are shooting out. There's something there. Something small, but I don't know what."

"Sure thing, Charlie," the AI replied, targeting the requested area with the full force of her bleeding-edge scanning array. "Hey, that's weird," she said a moment later. "Check this out."

The small display mounted to Ara's harness blinked on as she transmitted the images.

"Is that another portal?" he asked. "What are they possibly doing with that? It's far too small to carry a ship through."

"I noticed," Freya replied. "Seems stable, though."

"Yeah. But how the hell did they get it to stay open that long?"

"Ootaki hair," Ara said, sniffing the magic from a distance. "A minuscule amount compared to the larger portal, but it would seem Malalia has acquired enough Ootaki hair to power that portal. And the sun's power is charging it to provide a continuous stream of energy."

"Shit. You know what that means," Charlie grumbled.

"Indeed, I do," the Zomoki replied.

"Fill in those of us not magically linked to a space dragon, if you'd be so kind," Daisy interrupted.

"Right. Sorry. This pretty much guarantees that Malalia now knows our sun supercharges Ootaki hair."

"Which is bad."

"Yeah. *Real* bad. Earth just became a whole helluva lot more valuable to her. But I still don't know what she's doing with that portal. It's tiny. Maybe some sort of test to see if it burns up? I don't know."

"We have to make a decision," Leila interrupted. "The fleet jumps here in ten seconds. Do we abort?"

Charlie thought hard. It was an anomaly, that was for sure, but so far as he could tell, the weird little mini-portal wasn't providing the enemy fleet with any sort of advantage. And they might not get another chance at this.

"No, it's a go," he said. "Get ready."

Three seconds later, all hell broke loose.

CHAPTER FORTY-SIX

A furious barrage of magical weaponry came out of nowhere, throwing a little bit of everything at Visla Dominus's fleet. Spells were cast. Wards were dropped in place. Even magically hurled projectiles flashed across the gap between the arriving rebel craft and the Tslavar warships.

The point of the rebel spear was an unexpected addition to their forces. A blue-skinned smuggler of exceptional piloting skill who had one very serious bone to pick with the enemy fleet.

The element of surprise was a powerful one, and valuable enough to warrant a place atop the periodic table in Charlie's estimation. The immediacy and ferocity with which his comrades lay into their enemy was a sight to behold, and it threw them on their heels immediately.

"Get in there and disable the larger ones!" he said over wide-open comms and skree. "Stick to the plan and take them out!"

The main body of his cobbled-together resistance pushed ahead fast and hard, driving into the main body of the enemy's spread-out ships like a wedge, pushing them back while preventing them from accurately firing back on them, lest they accidentally hit their own ships.

Sure, they would adapt and find a firing solution eventually. But for a brief time, the rebels had the upper hand. All they had to do was use it to the best of their ability.

The forwardmost of Dominus's fleet spun from their positions at the edge of the portal's flames and powered back to help their ships caught in the onslaught, but their comrades were clearly overwhelmed, and Bawb had an open line to utilize his overpowered wand. And use it he did, tearing into the Tslavars with glee.

They'd made an error, and it was a rather fatal one. With their ranks so spread out, the deceptive tactic meant to give the appearance of greater numbers was now backfiring on the Tslavar fleet.

Olo was a dervish of aggression, leading a wing of ships in the attack, driving them ever farther into the main body of the enemy forces just as Charlie and Ara were leading another flank, while Daisy and Freya did the same with yet another group of rebel ships. The effect was like a spinning whirlpool as they wove through the Tslavar ranks in multiple directions, disrupting the enemy's defensive patterns.

"That's it! We've got 'em on the ropes. Keep up the pressure on the larger ships. Find out which one Dominus is on!" Charlie transmitted over open comms. It was weird using that name, now knowing the truth, but the others were so used to it that it made the most sense to stick with the accepted moniker.

She'd be a bitch to engage, and wouldn't go down without a fight, but if they could separate her from the others and focus their attacks, the likelihood of pulling out a victory increased exponentially.

But that was a big if, and, it seemed, Malalia had plans of her own. And she'd already compromised the tech comms system.

Whatever was transmitted, her captains could hear. And their advancing enemy was right where they wanted them.

The rebel ships surrounding Dominus's fleet were abruptly attacked from the rear as dozens upon dozens of Tslavar war craft jumped into the battle, boxing them in. The rebel attackers were suddenly the defenders, and they had enemies both in front and behind.

Olo spun his ship in a corkscrewing flip, landing spells on the enemy more often than not as he did, then powered to the rear of their forces, providing much-needed support to the bombarded craft holding up as best they could against the attack.

Ara's magical flames took down ship after ship, their magic negating the Tslavar shielding with great efficiency. But the noose was still closing on them. The sheer number of craft pushing in from the outside made the rebel fleet the filling in a Tslavar sandwich, and they were getting squished.

Dominus's ships were on the verge of a decisive victory. There was simply no way Charlie and his rebels could withstand them much longer. Nearly all of their efforts were now directed toward defensive spells rather than offensive ones, and it was only a matter of time before the vise closed all the way, crushing the rebel enemy once and for all.

Or so the Tslavars thought.

"Now?" a voice asked over the specially encrypted comms unit Freya had provided.

"Yes. Now," Charlie replied over the top-secret comms link.

The battlefield abruptly shifted once more, but this time it wasn't ships jumping into the battle. Instead, hundreds of small, yet deadly, shimmer ships uncloaked and opened fire, their magic effectively cutting off the path of retreat for the Tslavar ships.

The Wampeh Ghalian had sent word far and wide some time ago, and now it was paying off as the hundreds of their brothers and sisters from far and wide heeded their call to arms in the greatest single gathering of their order the galaxy had ever seen.

They had flown in with their shimmer ships and taken up positions in and around the enemy fleet days ago, hiding out among them invisibly. Waiting. And when a portion of Dominus's fleet had jumped away, they'd been followed to their staging area. It seemed they were close by, preparing for an attack they knew was coming. An attack the rebels *let them know* was coming.

Disinformation had played its part, and with it, the Tslavar ships, believing themselves to be springing a trap, had actually fallen into a far more complicated one targeting them instead.

Now the real battle began, and Dominus's casters, who had been holding back as their surprise was revealed, were now abruptly forced into action. The magic they cast was powerful, and a good many rebel ships fell to the sheer strength of the attack, despite their best shielding efforts. But the rebels still had one more trick up their sleeves.

"It is time," Farmatta skreed to her fellow masters. "Are you prepared?"

"I am," Kort replied.

"As am I," Zilara said.

"Prepared," Leif chimed in, gripping the meter-long metal rod in his hand.

"Very well, then," Farmatta said, closing her eyes and focusing. She summoned the magic of the other three Ghalian masters and drew their substantial power to herself, using them as an energy bank as she cast.

The magic was massive, and a good portion of the Tslavar fleet crumbled in the face of the assault.

"Dominus is not fighting back," the old woman noted as she cast another powerful spell, drawing strength from her fellow Ghalian masters. "This is not right."

They'd amassed a sizable amount of magic within their ranks, all with the intention of using the Bakana rods to channel that power to hopefully overwhelm their enemy. But, it seemed, Visla Dominus was nowhere to be found.

More of her ships jumped in, however, and yet another wave of fighters joined the fray.

"They must've gotten word to their comrades," Bawb noted as he cast a flurry of killing spells into the newly arrived enemy ships with his wand. "And it seems Malalia is not here."

"I know, Bob," Charlie replied as he blasted out a series of disabling spells. Unfortunately, there was simply so much powerful defensive magic in the air that even with Rika's power tinting his own, he couldn't break through it all.

Abruptly, several of Dominus's ships jumped away, but seemed to jump back just a moment later.

"They're up to something. How close until the portal?" Charlie asked Freya over her secure comms.

"Less than two minutes," she replied.

"Then we need to stop these assholes from running away before they get here. This is our shot."

"But the Wampeh said Malalia isn't here," Freya noted.

"I know. But we take what we can get. And that means ending her fleet once and for all," he replied as a few more Tslavar ships did the jump away/return thing, like the others had. "Now, hold them. Don't let them get away!" he said, hoping his friends would find a way to do just that.

CHAPTER FORTY-SEVEN

The battle raged on as both the pirate rebel fleet and the Tslavar mercenaries strove to achieve superior footing against one another. It had seemed a fairly evenly matched fight, but as Dominus's ships began jumping away, only to return shortly thereafter, the battle had been taking a bit of a turn, and from what Charlie could tell, it wasn't in the way Malalia would have anticipated.

The mercenaries were beginning to show weakness. The Tslavar fleet was not the indestructible thing they'd been led to believe. And now it was theirs for the taking.

"Is the message loaded on the micro-sat?" Charlie asked Freya over their secured comms.

"You know it has been for a while, already," Freya shot back.

"Hey, watch the snark," Daisy said.

"You're one to talk, Daze," Sarah joked.

It's different when it's my kiddo doing it.

"Suuuure," the voice in her head said with a chuckle.

"No worries," Charlie said. "I know I'm being a bit OCD. We've only got one shot at this."

"It's all ready to go," Freya said, in a far less snarky tone. "Portal opens in fifteen seconds," she added.

"This is the worst part. The waiting," he lamented.

Leila reached over and squeezed his arm through his space suit. "It's a good plan. It'll work."

"For all our sakes, I hope so."

The chrono ticked down to zero, and the portal immediately pulled free from the sun's flames, incredibly fast. Count on AIs to be punctual, and with Rika and Korbin controlling the opening together, they could move it far faster than Rika could alone.

"It's open!" Kip chirped over comms.

This was it. Time to push in all the chips and go for broke. Dominus's fleet, while surprised at the unscheduled portal opening, nevertheless reacted with admirable speed, turning to make a run for the portal. Only, there was something in their way. A lot of somethings, to be exact.

The entire defensive fleet––save a handful hanging back to cover Rika and Korbin as they controlled the portal––powered into the magical galaxy, their weapons hot and targeting every Tslavar ship they could find, blasting them with the water sabots as well as pulse and plasma fire.

The Tslavar mercenaries redirected all of their magic to their shielding after the first few ships were taken out. This new force, on top of the shimmer ships that had so recently appeared and the main rebel fleet, was simply too much for them to withstand. Plus, these new craft were firing strange projectiles that were expelling some sort of toxic liquid into the ships whose shields they managed to penetrate.

They didn't know what the odd magic was, only that it was crippling their crews in an instant. They'd have been startled to learn it was the Balamar waters of legend, plus one addition, courtesy of Marban's suggestion and Rika's Kalamani friends. Extract of plants––the most toxic of the lot, so far as aliens from the magical galaxy were concerned—had been added to it. Harmless to Earth's forces but disabling for anyone else.

The newly arrived fleet maneuvered quickly from the portal to position themselves for a pincer attack with the enemy trapped in the middle, effectively cutting them off from easy escape. And the rebel casters were doing all they could to prevent any further jumps away, with fairly good success, Charlie was pleased to note.

It seemed as if the fake out had worked, and even the largest of Dominus's ships were attempting to turn tail and flee. What had been a decisive victory for the enemy's fleet at first had shifted to an even battle.

And now, with the entire weight and force of the ships from Earth's galaxy bringing their powerful weapons to this one, it had become an utter rout.

Dominus's fleet reacted in a seeming panic, scattering and fleeing, racing away as fast as they could.

"They're on the run!" Olo hooted with bloodlust, falling in behind the panicking enemy.

The other captains sensed blood in the water and quickly fell into pursuit as well. The craft nearest the portal raced toward the open space in the opposite direction. The direction the additional ships were supposedly waiting. The rebel forces had been briefed, though, and they knew stopping this body of ships was crucial to their plan.

They swarmed after them, taking down fleeing craft within their midst quickly, then knocking out the ones that had managed to pull ahead. They were flying away from the portal at speed but hadn't jumped yet. The pursuers weren't concerned, though. They had Rika and Korbin backstopping the portal for them.

Charlie and Ara slowed their pursuit a moment as they flew past a large, disabled Tslavar ship, each of them sensing an irregularity.

"Something isn't right," Charlie said. "This isn't nearly enough ships."

"You are correct," Ara said. "And look closely," she added, flying right up to the drifting craft.

In combat it would be difficult to notice the cobbled-together nature of the vessel, but at a standstill, the ruse was obvious. This wasn't what the interrogated Tslavar captain had described. This was a superficially modified civilian craft.

"Oh, shit!" Charlie blurted as the realization sank in.

The captive had definitely been telling the truth. Only, he was telling a truth he had been given by Malalia. A truth given to him because she intended for him to be captured and interrogated all along. That's why his ship hadn't been powerful enough to make the escape. And that's why its shields were sadly lacking.

He was an unwitting decoy.

"Everyone, fall back to the portal!" Charlie called over open comms, but it was too late.

On the other side of the gateway to Charlie's home galaxy, a massive Tslavar fleet jumped in close to the sun. But they didn't make their approach through the portal. They came from a different direction. They came from *behind* the defensive array of ships.

The first spells only struck glancing blows, a bit of good fortune as the casters were not yet used to the different effect this new galaxy had on their magic. But they would adapt soon enough.

"Bail out! We have to get out of here!" Rika boomed over their comms.

"But the others! We can't leave the portal!" an Urok pilot said just before his ship was torn to pieces.

"We can't help if we're dead. They have another portal somewhere, and there's no hope for us here and now. Jo, send a drone through to warn them. I'm getting us out of here," Rika said, dodging a flurry of incoming magic. "Everyone, scatter! And don't use warp, they can track it."

The support fighters split off in every direction, the crazed mix of trajectories making targeting difficult for their vastly superior adversary. Rika, Korbin, and Marban linked up and jumped to the relative safety of Earth's orbit, Korbin and Marban towing her tech ship, avoiding using its warp drive.

The resistance forces were racing back toward their portal when they saw the unthinkable. The flames of the sun had already begun shooting through the gateway as it closed, sealing them off on the wrong side. And when they scanned both the conventional satellite as well as the micro sats, they found no message but the one.

"There's another portal. She's on this side. Find a way back. We had to flee," Rika's message said.

Charlie and the others felt their stomachs drop. They had been outplayed, outwitted, and stranded in a distant galaxy, while their home was left defenseless. On the other side, the same realization was rapidly spreading through the AI network as they watched the enemy fleet jump into position and overrun the sun's laughable defenses. They'd been perfectly prepared for a handful of ships. But an entire fleet? None had thought it possible.

"They're on *our* side of the portal," Sid said from his home on Dark Side base. "We're on our own."

"We are," Cal agreed. *"And we can't even send for help. They can track our warps. If our people warp away, it will lead them right to our allies, and we cannot allow that to happen."*

"What do we do, Cal?" Sid asked.

"They captured an Urok ship previously. A non-AI craft. Not one of ours. This means they likely don't know the true nature of AIs," he transmitted over encrypted AI-only comms. *"All AI ships must hide immediately. Keep this channel open, but stay hidden. Listen for the update. I don't know how long it will take, but we will figure*

something out. But until then, the terrestrial AIs need to prepare to go dark."

"Go dark?" Sid asked.

"Yes. Do not fight. Hide yourselves."

"So, we lose?" the AI asked.

"For now, I'm afraid we must."

CHAPTER FORTY-EIGHT

The portal had fallen, and Visla Dominus now had control of this strange, new system. Judging by the fighting that had spread across the surface of the lone inhabited planet, however, it was quite apparent that not all on this world would surrender. Malalia had won, but it seemed not everyone had received that memo.

The skirmishes that broke out with the initial landing sorties were both widespread and intense. There were plenty of arms at hand after the Great War, and the locals were not hesitant at all to use them. And back home in Los Angeles, Cal had stockpiled a particularly deadly cache of weapons for his residents, should they ever require them. It seemed today was that day.

"We have to help them," Marban said, when he saw the first of the Tslavar ships dive through the atmosphere and target the civilian population.

"Marban, stay here!" Rika called after him when he peeled away from her and Korbin and dove his pirate craft into the atmosphere.

"No can do," he replied. "That's your home. People are in need down there."

"You're a goddamn pirate!"

"That doesn't change the circumstance," he replied. "If it means anything, though, I'm sorry," he said, then clicked off his comms and sped at top speed toward the surface.

"Damn your heroics," Rika grumbled, then dove the *Fujin* after him, Korbin following close behind.

"You know, he'll probably get us all killed," Korbin said with an amused chuckle as he rushed to his possible end.

"Yeah? Well, let's try to avoid that today, okay?" she shot back.

Marban's ship swung into a low hover, and the cargo door opened. A moment later, a towering metal man jumped to the ground, its massive feet landing with a solid crash.

"Sonofabitch is driving my mech!"

"And pretty well," Jo noted.

It was true, Marban had actually developed something of a skill for mech piloting. And it was a good thing, because without it, he wouldn't have stood a chance. Not against the throng of ground forces he now found himself facing. The metal skin, as well as Rika's magic that was laced throughout the mech's systems, helped the machine shrug off the majority of the attacks that were befalling it. But not all were deflected, and it was rocked more than once as it swayed on massive steel legs.

"Take that!" Marban yelled over the exterior speakers as he kicked a trio of Tslavar mercenaries hard enough to send them through the wall of a nearby building. He then turned and rushed toward the thickest fighting, hoping to help sway the battle and save as many of the men and women below as he could.

"Dude's got a death wish," Rika said.

"Yeah, maybe so. But damn if he isn't gonna go out in a glorious way," Jo said, laughing morbidly as she fired their weapons at the Tslavar forces below.

"Korbin, see about evacuating residents. Your ship's got room," Rika said.

"One step ahead of you," he replied, already lowering down behind a building, where a large group of locals was taking refuge. Unfortunately, it was not a terribly strategically sound hiding place.

"Come with me. You've got to get out of here, now!" Korbin urged.

The humans and few Chithiid on hand seemed dazed and utterly unprepared for the sudden attack on their tranquil lives.

"I said *now!*" he repeated, this time with far more force. Korbin hated to use magic against his own people, but if they didn't hurry up and take the hint, he'd just stun them himself and load their slumbering bodies aboard the ship.

As that amusing thought passed through his head, a small group of Tslavar mercenaries rounded the corner and were about to let loose with their konuses when a pair of flashes bearing wicked sharp teeth flew through the air, quickly rending them limb from limb.

Baloo and Bahnjoh had come when Korbin sent his magical urging to their collars, the experimental spell working more or less as intended, and not a second too late.

The beasts ripped into the attackers, playing off of one another, distracting and dividing their prey as they laid waste to mercenary after mercenary. Meanwhile, Marban was stomping and kicking and generally wreaking havoc just up the road, the mech proving a rather formidable foe as the Tslavars didn't have much of a plan for taking down a towering metal man. It was simply something they'd never even thought to anticipate.

That didn't matter, however, when a damaged enemy ship crashed into a nearby building, sending debris flying. The majority of it bounced harmlessly off the mech's steel body. Most of it, that is. A cross-beam, however, tumbled across the road, knocking into the giant mech's lead leg just as it was stepping forward, sending it tumbling to the ground.

Marban quickly hit the harness release and scrambled free, drawing power from both of his konuses as he did. The Tslavars had already begun focusing their attention his way. The giant metal man was proving quite a nuisance. But now that he was taken down, the pilot of the odd craft was their new target.

"Damn it, Marban! Get out of there!" Rika shouted over her comms as she strafed the Tslavars charging the pirate's position from her vantage point above.

Their return fire possessed enough magical force to drive her away for the moment despite her abilities, and Rika could do nothing but watch in horror as a cluster of magical blasts struck Marban dead-center, sending him flying backwards into a pile of debris.

"Marban!" she shrieked, the ship suddenly filling with a bright purple glow.

"Shit! You're going to blow, Rika! Rein it in!" Jo was yelling, but the furious woman was beyond hearing.

Rika jumped from her seat and punched out of the ship's airlock, not even worrying for a moment that Jo might not grab the controls and take over. Fortunately, the cyborg had excellent reflexes and did precisely that, but not without a healthy dose of worry about her friend.

The good news was, Rika's magic was more than strong enough to allow her to fly safely to the ground. The bad news was she was far from done, and the Tslavar mercs were going to be the ones paying the price.

Spells flew her way even before she touched down, but she batted them aside like they were no more than bubbles blown at a child's party. The counterstrike, however, was anything but childlike.

The mercenaries saw how she was utterly unfazed by their best magic and turned to run. They knew when they were severely outclassed. But it didn't matter. The spell Rika threw at them shattered their bones mid-stride, dropping them to the ground like sacks of smashed-up pulp.

A shifting of rubble behind her made Rika spin, hands raised and ready to unleash another attack, but instead of a green-skinned invader, she was greeted by the astonishing sight of a very dusty, but fully intact, space pirate.

"Marban!" she yelled with relief as she rushed up and hugged him hard, then abruptly let him go and stepped back a few paces. "Sorry."

"Nothing to be sorry about," he said with a mischievous grin.

"But how—?" she began to ask, then noticed a pale blue glow coming from within Marban's shirt. "What the hell is that?"

The pirate pulled the somewhat tattered shirt up, revealing his well-muscled chest, the center of it adorned with an intricate tattoo in faint blue pigment, the tendrils weaving out from the central prime symbol. Rika recognized the handiwork. She should. The shaman had saved her life with it as well.

"Nice. Gives you character," she said, eyes finally peeling away from the design on his chest. "Not that you need any more."

"I'll take that as a compliment," he said with a grin.

"But you're not from this galaxy. How can you withstand the pigment?"

"Oh, he used me like a pincushion until he found an ink that I wasn't allergic to. This one absorbs and redirects magic, shifting just about anything into a healing power."

"I don't understand. Why would he give you this?"

"I guess you could say the old fella took a shine to me," he replied with his trademark laugh.

Jo's voice belted over their comms. "Korbin has the survivors."

"Great," Marban replied. "Let's get out of here. I'm sorry

about your mech, but I think it'll be out of commission for a little bit."

"I saw," Rika replied. "But you were going strong for a good while there," she said approvingly, as Jo dropped the *Fujin* to the deck in front of them.

"Come on, you two! Let's move!" she called out from inside the ship.

Marban and Rika didn't need to be told twice. They hurried aboard, and Jo had them airborne before the doors had even sealed completely.

"While you were being ridiculously reckless, I checked in with Cal," Jo informed them when they reached the cockpit.

"And what did he say?" Rika asked.

"He said the AIs are going dark. The enemy doesn't know about them, so it's the one way to stay safe and bide their time until we can launch a proper counterstrike."

"But for now?" Marban asked.

"For now, we run," Jo replied. "Run and hide."

"I don't much like the sound of that," the pirate replied.

"Neither do I, but I like living a lot more than dying, so we're doing as he says," Jo said, then immediately set a course away from the city.

Korbin had already been keyed in to what was going down and was making his escape as well, having first magically guided Bahnjoh and Baloo out of the city center to somewhere safer, where they could rest and hunt unmolested until such time as they could rejoin the others.

Across town at the coastline, Ripley and Eddie were tearing into Tslavars, as the others made their run for it. The teen and her ship had proven their knack for picking off shimmer-cloaked aliens, and her parents were having a field day on the surface, tag-teaming with them and taking down any of the camouflaged mercenaries who might have been thinking they might sneak away.

Sarah and Finn were quite the couple when it came to hunting down bad guys, and with her modifications and his lightning reflexes and skills with a blade, they made a very formidable team. And working with their daughter, though not under the best of circumstances, was nevertheless something of a joy.

"You need to get clear of Los Angeles," Kip transmitted to Eddie. *"Tell the others and get to safety. The AI network will be going silent for a time. Keep your receiver on, and we'll be in touch when the time is right."*

Eddie relayed the message, which, naturally, brought Ripley on the line in a heartbeat. "We're kicking their asses, Uncle Cal."

"But this is just a handful, I'm afraid. There is a far larger fleet amassed in orbit, and it's about to enter the atmosphere. We've already reached out to the others. Shelly and Tamara are clear, as are Reggie and Vince. I haven't been able to raise Fatima, though."

"She was going on one of her vision quest hikes this week," Ripley noted.

"Ah, which means her comms are off. But there's no way she would miss the invading forces as they make their approach into our skies, and the message I left on her comms will be clear enough. So, stop procrastinating. Get your parents aboard, and get safe. And whatever you do, do not try to warp away. These invaders can apparently track warps now."

"They can *what?*"

"You heard correctly. So get to safety and lie low. We need our forces to survive and prepare for what could be a long haul."

"Why a long haul, Cal?"

"Because, Ripley, the enemy has seized the portal. Our forces are cut off."

CHAPTER FORTY-NINE

Grundsch was truly in his element for the first time in longer than he could remember. While he had flown his ship in the recent battle against the Tslavar invaders, that had been carnage at arm's length. But this? This was more his speed. Up close and personal. And by personal, he meant watching the light fade from his enemy's eyes as he crushed them with his power whip and mighty hands.

He had been raging through Tslavar invaders with almost laughable efficiency. With his old and damaged power whip recently replaced by a fully functional model, he found himself wielding a tool of great destruction. And it was glorious.

"Grundsch," Cal's voice called out to the Ra'az as he released his power whip's crushing grip on the last of the Tslavars who had the misfortune of encountering him in their incursion into his section of the city.

"Yes, Cal? What can I do for you?" he asked, relaxed as can be, as if killing a dozen mercenaries was as pleasant as a stroll in the park.

"I see you've eliminated all of the Tslavars in the immediate vicinity."

"Yes. They were executing citizens in a most cowardly manner. I thought it only right to dispose of them in a way more suitable for them."

"The invaders have won the day, Grundsch, and our forces are cut off from us in the other galaxy. As a result, the global AI network is going dark, hiding from them, since they don't seem to know about us yet."

"An interesting tactic," he replied, not fond of anything that could be remotely viewed as running away from a fight.

"You are aware of Visla Dominus's true identity now, and I know you have a long history with her from her life as Mareh Palmarian."

"A lengthy servitude, yes," the Ra'az replied.

"I have to ask you to do something, for us. Something I know you will find distasteful, but will be for the good of the entire world. I need you to play along with Mareh. Make her think you're still on her side. Make her trust you."

"You wish for me to let her live? I could likely crush her with my—"

"While I appreciate your enthusiasm, you know as well as I that she is far too powerful for that."

Grundsch's shoulders sagged slightly. It was true. Much as he'd like to believe he could use his newfound freedom to strike a mighty blow for his new homeworld, the reality was clear. Mareh Palmarian was Visla Dominus, and there was simply no way he could hope to lay so much as a finger on her.

"I will do as you ask," he finally said. "I will be your man inside."

"Thank you, Grundsch. The others and I will be going dark for now, but there is a small comms link embedded in your power whip. If you learn anything of importance, send me a message. I may not reply, but I'll hear you. Since it is a tech system, and a private link, they will likely not even notice it."

"Very well," the Ra'az replied.

"They'll be upon you soon. Good luck," Cal said, then fell silent.

Grundsch walked to a wounded Tslavar. The man wouldn't live out the day, but he could still spoil their plans. With a flick of the power whip on his wrist, he slammed the mercenary's head into the wall, putting an end to that problem. Now there were no survivors who had seen him in battle. None to reveal his true allegiance.

Cal was right, Mareh was coming. He recognized the ship dropping down from above. Somehow, she had zeroed in on this particular city, and his particular location. Likely because it was a seat of power on Earth. In any case, he had to put on a good show for her. Quickly, he powered down his power whip, preparing himself to play the part required of him.

He regretted what he had to do. It was cowardly and distasteful to his warrior's ways. But he had a job to do. That firmly in mind, he pummeled several human and Chithiid corpses, spraying himself with gore, then picked up one of the executed humans and one of the Chithiid by their necks. The Tslavars had suffocated the life from them magically, so their bodies appeared intact. Just what he needed.

He carried them around the corner just as Mareh's ship landed, holding the bodies up high and bellowing like an enraged beast as he violently snapped their necks then tossed the corpses aside like so much refuse.

Mareh was the first to exit the ship. There was no need for pretense here. She was Visla Dominus, and nothing on this world could possibly harm her. She strode toward him, casually stepping over bodies that littered the area. Most were human and Chithiid, and she had no idea the Tslavar dead had fallen at Grundsch's hands.

The Ra'az dropped to one knee, his head lowered. "Forgive me, Denna Palmarian. I was taken prisoner by these wretched creatures some time ago, forcefully taken from your estate by these rebel scum. But this attack has been fortuitous and afforded me the opportunity to exact my revenge."

She looked at the bodies strewn about and the blood on her servant's hands. A pleased smile creased her lips ever so slightly.

"Stand tall, Grundsch. You've done well," she said.

"Thank you, Denna," he said, rising to his full height.

"And Bahnjoh?" she asked.

"I fear him dead," he replied, hoping Korbin had used the konus collar to steer his four-legged companion as far from the fighting as possible.

"Come to me," the woman he knew as Mareh said. "Let me see you properly."

He stepped closer, allowing her to better examine him. "They seem to have fed you well," she said.

"I cannot fault them in that aspect of my treatment," he said.

She sized up her servant. He had been a loyal underling all these years, and though he was now free and far from home, he had apparently remained such. The broken bodies of the denizens of this world scattered at his feet, as well as the blood on his hands, clearly proved as much.

"You have performed well, Grundsch. Very well, indeed," she said again looking at the bodies around them. "And to think, all this time, your true potential was being squandered. Come," she commanded. "We shall survey my new conquest."

"Shall I cleanse myself first, Denna?" he asked.

"No. Leave it," she said with a wicked grin. "The blood sends a message."

CHAPTER FIFTY

Earth lay silent, its populace now cowering under the brutal fist of its new ruler. The woman calling herself Dominus had pulled off her greatest coup and tricked their defensive fleet, trapping them far, far away, leaving the planet, and the entire galaxy, defenseless. She then swept across the globe in a magical victory lap aboard her personal transport.

The facility tucked away on the planet's moon had fallen easily enough, its inhabitants choosing to surrender peacefully rather than face certain extinction. It was a fortunate decision. She'd have hated to waste such an unusual example of this galaxy's technological advances.

In fact, there was a whole cornucopia of fascinating new tech for Malalia and her favorite aides to study. Visla Cresh, in particular, was fascinated by the sheer quantity of devices this race had created to perform all of the tasks a simple spell could achieve. So much effort to achieve so little. Yet, they had a certain genius to their ways, strange as they were. It was an entire culture that had evolved without a hint of magic. It boggled the mind.

Yet here they were. And not just some cave-dwelling

mongrels, but an advanced, and rather formidable, opponent. But against Visla Dominus's magic, there was simply no way they could have hoped to prevail, she mused with a grin as she accompanied her leader to survey the spoils of victory.

The native populace of humans was now joined by another species. Chithiid, a four-armed, four-eyed bipedal race that seemed to be integrally joined with the planet's own people. A lot had changed since Malalia was last here, and there was much to learn about what had come to pass since her prior visit thousands of years ago.

As for compliance, the Chithiid seemed to be just as receptive to control collars as the humans were, and those who were caught resisting their new masters were quickly restrained and fitted with one of the golden bands. The fleet had a huge quantity of them on hand––Malalia had been stockpiling them for ages––but she was being frugal with their use. There was no telling how many other worlds there were in this galaxy that she would be required to use them on as she expanded her conquest.

For now, however, she would simply make examples of the few who wore them, hopefully whipping the others into line when they witnessed the pain, or occasional death, the collars could dole out. If the plan worked, it would be complete subjugation without the need for more than a relatively limited number of collars.

A small handful of the people who had resisted at first seemed like pretty much any other human. Fleshy. Non-magical. Weak. But what the invaders didn't realize was that beneath their meat exterior was a metal composite endoskeleton capable of withstanding far more than any flesh and bone person could. But the cyborgs were AI minds, and they'd received the message from Cal.

Play along. Do not reveal yourselves. Bide your time. Those were their marching orders, and they'd follow them to the letter, even if it meant allowing atrocities to happen before their eyes. They couldn't step in. Not if they hoped to eventually overcome their conquerors. Not until their fleet returned. *If* their fleet returned.

But there were still plenty of pockets of fighting across the globe. Cities on every continent were all slowly being absorbed and brought under the yoke of their new ruler, but the denizens of this planet had fought a great war not so long ago. *The* Great War. While their children may have had no memory of those days, their parents were on a first-name basis with war and strife.

And a good many were not going to give up without one hell of a fight.

This was their planet, and no one was going to take it from them. Not if they could help it. And, much as their little pockets of resistance were proving difficult to overcome, it was of little concern to the conquering visla.

"I am sorry, Visla," Captain Darus said as he guided Visla Dominus's personal craft around an area of particularly heavy skirmish fighting. "Our men should have quelled this resistance by now."

Malalia watched the combat from her seat, utterly unconcerned. Yes, she could have instructed the captain to take the ship lower, whereupon she could have then ended the engagement with a few well-placed spells. But that was stooping below her level. She had just conquered a new *galaxy*. Stepping into little spats with the locals like this was simply not an option.

"It's not a concern," she informed the captain. "No victory is ever entirely complete until well after the declaration of victory."

"Visla?"

She looked at him with a tranquil gaze, which was something highly unusual for the incredibly driven woman. Seeing her so at ease was almost scarier than her being enraged.

"It will take time, Darus. There will always be pockets of fighting in a hostile occupation such as this. Resistance, while futile, is the natural order of things. We are the invaders, after all, and they are merely doing what any other self-respecting inhabitant would do. They are defending their home."

"A lot of good it will do them," Darus scoffed.

"Indeed. But there is no rush. My victory is total, and there is nothing these little groups can do to change that. So, for now, we let them try to make a stand while I spread my control to every corner of the planet. And then, once they are truly cut off from their peers, my men will engage in great numbers and mop up the remaining forces."

Captain Darus couldn't help but admire his visla's wisdom as much as her brutal efficiency. She had just taken an entire fleet out of the equation and claimed their home as her own prize. And with minimal fighting, no less. The vessels sacrificed in the ruse had been almost entirely captured ships they'd retrofitted for the task, leaving the actual bulk of her craft unharmed and at her disposal.

Earth was hers, now. Her victory was complete.

Or so they thought. Yet the massive network of AIs lay silent, watching and waiting as they bided their time. They had done it before, waiting hundreds of years until the time was right. And now, they'd do it again. But this time, their friends would come for them and do all they could to retake their planet. And the AIs would be ready.

The one question lingering was, how long would they have to wait?

CHAPTER FIFTY-ONE

It was a rag-tag resistance, nowhere near a full-strength fighting force, but the little groups of rebels were surprisingly efficient in their disruption of the invaders' plans.

"How do they continue to evade your men?" Visla Dominus grilled one of her mercenary leaders as the others looked on, each of them attempting to look both tough and relaxed, but all of them damn near shitting their pants at the thought of just how horrible a demise they might face if they continued to displease their visla.

"We do not know, Visla," the man replied, ashamed. "They strike hard and fast without warning, despite our wards and detection spells. And then they disappear before we can mount a proper retaliation. It is incredibly vexing. Are you certain they do not possess magic? The way in which they vanish suggests a small portal spell at a minimum."

Dominus looked him over with a chilly glare. "There is no magic on this world. If there was, I would know about it. So talk to your men. Inform them I am displeased at their continued failure to address this troublesome little group of pests. It would be in their best interest to find them and dispose of them, am I clear?"

"Crystal, Visla," he replied, doing his best to keep his voice from wavering.

The gathered mercenary leaders took their leave, each of them delivering word of their visla's displeasure to their men. All knew what continued failure could bring down upon their heads, and the slightest of reminders was all they needed to inspire a flurry of activity.

Not that it would help. The rebels were proving utterly vexing in their mysterious ability to strike and vanish without a trace.

"Visla," Cresh said from her place at the side of the room. "Distasteful as it is, I believe it may be time to make a public appearance to crush these rebels yourself, once and for all. If the troops' continued failure becomes public knowledge, the likelihood of others taking up arms as well will only grow."

Malalia turned to her trusted aide. None would dare speak to her in this manner. None but Cresh. And she had more than earned that right, proving herself a powerful and talented visla on myriad occasions.

"Perhaps it will come to that," Malalia admitted. "But it would diminish my air of mystery somewhat, and that is a potent tool when properly wielded."

"A valid point, Visla," Cresh agreed. "Perhaps your servant would have better luck prying details from reluctant citizens."

Malalia pondered the idea a moment. It was true, Grundsch was an imposing figure, and she was quite confident he could loosen lips. But the others had resorted to similar means and were still no closer to knowing the true nature of their foe.

"We shall see," she replied. "But for now, let us see what our Tslavars manage to dig up."

. . .

Interestingly enough, digging would have resulted in more success than the mercenaries had been having so far. Not because they'd happen upon treasure, but because Rika, Marban, Ripley, and the rest of the rebel forces, were constantly traveling beneath their feet via the planet's loop tube system.

It was something the magical beings had never heard of, and, as the AIs kept everything powered down whenever one of the invaders was near, it was a technological marvel they would not be learning about anytime soon.

With a global network capable of carrying them from one continent to another in mere hours, the relatively small group of rebels were able to strike at multiple locations in a short period of time, giving the impression there were far more of their forces than there truly were. And when it came time to flee after an attack, they would vanish beneath the city, whisked away in a loop tube car long before any pursuers might find their way into the underground station.

And those stations were dark and quiet. The AIs made a point to keep them as uninviting as possible to deter their alien interlopers from exploring beyond a peripheral sweep.

The system also allowed the core of the rebel forces to spread the word to local networks, ensuring the resistance across the globe was always on the same page. They'd spent weeks in hiding before that network was finally locked into place, and the hard work was paying off.

"Eat something," Sarah said.

"Yeah, listen to your mom," Finn added as he put the finishing touches on his replicated tuna protein salad Niçoise.

"I'm not hungry," Ripley griped.

"It's not about being hungry, it's about keeping your energy up. You know that," Sarah replied.

"Our daughter turning down food?" Finn said with mock horror. "Are you sure she hasn't been replaced with an impostor?"

"I'll take hers, if she doesn't want it," Tamara said. "Hell, all of this ass-whooping is making me hungry."

Sarah and Finn laughed. It was nice having the extended family together again, kicking ass and taking names, and Ripley's aunt Tamara was a pro at it. And she wasn't alone.

When she, Omar, and Fatima, as well as the others had finally found their way to the tube network, the AIs routed them all to one another, facilitating the rapid organization of their little rebel cadre. The resulting force, while small, was certainly something to be reckoned with.

But one thing was abundantly clear. They couldn't keep this up forever. At some point, they'd need help.

"Rip," Finn said, passing her the tuna salad whether she wanted it or not. "Your mom and I have been talking, and we think you're ready for an important mission."

"Oh, please. The reverse psychology trick isn't gonna work on me," the teen said. "And, hello? I already helped save the world, you know. Me and Eddie? We're total badasses."

"Okay, noted," Finn laughed.

"The thing is, we need to get reinforcements," Sarah added. "And we think you and Eddie are the ones to get them."

"Hang on a minute. We can't use warp anywhere near those Tslavar ships," she protested.

"We know."

"And that means it'll take a long ass time before we'd be able to sneak far enough away with conventional propulsion power until we're clear enough of the Tslavar fleet to be able to finally warp."

"Again, correct," Finn said. "See? Our kid's a genius," he joked.

"Dad, I'm serious."

"For once."

"Ugh. Why don't we send Korbin? His ship's a magic one. They'd be hard pressed to track him."

"Because we need his weapons, as well as his magical skills. And while you are a vital part of our team as well, we think you're best suited for the travel and evasion aspect of this mission," Sarah said.

What she didn't mention was that she and Finn were concerned they might actually fail in this little rebellion, and if that happened, they wanted Ripley as far away from the fallout as she could be. Preferably in another system, if at all possible.

"I would like to accompany you, if I may," Fatima said, the silver-haired woman's almond eyes creasing at the corners slightly. "There will be much convincing to be done, for certain. The Uroks, especially. They'll want to come charging in, guns a-blazing, when that's the last thing we want them to do. But together, I think Ripley and I could achieve a measured response from them." She turned to the teen, fixing her warm gaze upon her. "What do you say, Ripley? Shall we go on an adventure?"

Ripley knew the adults were playing her to get her clear of the fighting. But she also knew there was truth to what they were saying. And if she and Fatima could manage to reach their allies without leading the enemy to them in the process, the mission could actually make a difference.

She grudgingly made up her mind. It would be boring, flying so slow, but if they succeeded, she could rub it in Arlo's face for a long time. If he made it back, that is.

"Fine," Ripley finally said. "We'll do it."

"Excellent!" Finn chirped. "Now, let me whip you up some snacks for the road."

"It's space, Dad."

"Oh, I forgot. Where you're going, you don't *need* roads," he replied with a laugh.

Ripley grumbled but couldn't help but smile. She'd miss her family, but hopefully this would be a reasonably short trip. One that would end with success.

CHAPTER FIFTY-TWO

"So little resistance for such a seemingly complex facility," Malalia mused as she and her small group walked the eerily quiet hallways of Dark Side base. "Not a lick of magic to be found, yet this entire complex was built to not only withstand the void of space, but house an entire complement of inhabitants for lengthy periods of time. Fascinating."

"Indeed, Visla," Visla Cresh agreed.

Grundsch merely nodded with a grunt, as he knew was expected of him. In all of his years serving Mareh and Visla Palmarian, he'd never been known to be the talkative type, and there was absolutely no reason to begin now.

Malalia had come to the lunar base frequently in the weeks since she'd taken over both it and its neighboring planet. Earth was a marvel of this odd technology at every turn, but for some reason, the scrappy persistence that allowed this race to carve out a home in such an inhospitable environment spoke to her on a more visceral level.

They were tough. They were resourceful. They were survivors. Basically, though they were her enemy, these people were very much made of the same stern stuff as she was, and she couldn't help but begrudgingly respect them. And she'd even come to appreciate some of their methods and technologies, despite their being rather inelegant and crude by her magical standards.

The method by which the facility produced breathable air was, admittedly, quite inspired. A massive subterranean ice deposit was steadily melted, the resulting off-gassing providing not only drinkable water, but fresh air for the entire facility. A facility she conquered with almost no bloodshed.

"Amazing how easily these people gave up, is it not, Cresh?"

"It is, Visla. But perhaps they knew your reputation before our arrival. It would only make sense, given the size of the fleet they sent to engage your forces."

Malalia laughed. "Oh, yes. That little ruse worked perfectly. It seems they sent nearly every last ship in their possession through the portal in hopes of surprising my forces and achieving a swift victory. Sound tactics, actually. Of course, they had no way of knowing we had finally succeeded in opening a new portal with our captured Ootaki. And right under their noses in their own system, no less."

"A coup, for certain, Visla," Cresh agreed. "The fifth planet from the sun has proven to be a perfect place to conceal it."

"Indeed. They never saw us coming until it was too late," Malalia replied. "And the poor fools in our own realm haven't the faintest idea what we've done. Imagine the shocked looks on their faces when their own portal closed behind them, trapping them in a distant system with no way back home."

"I would imagine it to be quite a disconcerting experience," Cresh mused as they crossed into another section of the fascinating moon base.

Sid, the AI running Dark Side, could have just vented the atmosphere in an instant if he'd wanted to. But he'd already been forewarned that Malalia and her casters would just counter the act with a few spells. He might take out some of their guards, but the key players would survive, and they'd know they weren't alone.

So he remained silent. Hidden in plain sight, maintaining all of the base's systems as he always did, but without any overt presence on his part to alert them of his existence. It wasn't time for the AIs to rise up and fight back. Not yet.

Malalia and her entourage walked almost the entire base, taking in the sights as she'd done many times already. But one part of the base, though uninhabited at the moment, remained safely hidden from them. Freya and Joshua's secret fabrication hangar far across the lunar surface.

Even if they did eventually discover it, the act of breaking inside would trigger a whole world of hurt worth of defensive measures, several of such potency that even a powerful caster might be hard pressed to defend against them.

But for now the secret hangar remained precisely that. Secret.

"Come," Malalia said. "It is time for our survey of the main territories once more."

She led the way back to the ship resting in Hangar Three and boarded along with her people. Captain Darus then lifted off and quickly crossed the void from the moon to Earth, descending in a brightly heated ball of glowing orange all the way to Los Angeles.

Of course, the magic at his disposal was easily dispersing the heat from re-entry, but the visla liked making an entrance, so he kept those spells held back to minimum safe levels. Rather than landing at the spaceport, he dropped the craft right in the middle of town in an open road and courtyard area in a fairly populated section.

His visla wanted to make an entrance, and this fit the bill nicely. As the ship's hull's hot orange began to fade, Visla

Dominus stepped from the craft, her close aides at her side, the hulking Ra'az Hok following close behind. She strode through the parted throng of civilians, their eyes averted for the most part as her mercenaries stood by with weapons at the ready.

Of course, Malalia did not *need* weapons. She was the most powerful visla her galaxy had ever seen, and even with the unusual effect this strange realm had on her magic, she was nevertheless more than strong enough to lay waste to entire sections of the city without breaking a sweat.

She glanced at the crowd, clocking the fierce looks occasionally cast her way. But they weren't all directed at her, she noted. A good many appeared to be aimed at Grundsch instead.

She had investigated the historical records of the planet shortly after arrival, and when she realized that Grundsch was once part of the race that had very nearly exterminated the entire planet's population, she figured it only natural that some survivors of that experience might still harbor hard feelings.

The looks were those of hatred, and while Malalia attributed them to the people's long history with her servant's race, the reality was far different. These people had given this particular Ra'az a second chance, accepting that he'd changed and treating him with an open mind.

Now, however, it appeared he was the muscled enforcer once more, only this time, he served a different mistress.

Grundsch, for his part, knew what they were thinking, but he kept his face neutral, ignoring the hatred in their stares. These were his people now, and no matter how much it sucked to do so, he had to bear their hatred in order to save them.

He had to play the part Malalia expected of him. And then, if he was lucky, his deception might one day pay off. But for now, he had to live up to expectations, both of the locals, as well as his visla.

He flexed his jaw and carried on, following Mareh

Palmarian, aka Malalia Maktan, aka Visla Dominus, conqueror of the galaxy, as she surveyed her conquest city by city. It was an unpleasant task, but that was all there was for him to do at the moment, though he wished for something more. Whether or not that would be coming anytime soon was anyone's guess.

CHAPTER FIFTY-THREE

Far across space, tens of thousands of light years away, a brutal but efficient process was underway, as it had been for the several weeks since Earth's protective fleet had crossed over and been abruptly cut off from their path home.

There *had* been a battle, and an impressive one at that. But once the combined might of the pirate's rebel armada and the strength of their cross-portal comrades had been unleashed against their Tslavar foes, it became quickly apparent their opponents were nothing more than window dressing. A decoy. And as the portal slammed shut behind them, they realized they had been played.

While the first handful of prisoners taken in the battle hadn't known any useful details, nor had the second or third, once the Wampeh Ghalian sent their order out to acquire whatever high-ranking members of Visla Dominus's fleet or support teams they could find, it was only a matter of time before they'd begin making progress.

Even then, it had taken weeks, and more than a few rather gruesome torture sessions at the hands of the Wampeh experts before anything resembling useful intel was pried free. The visla was careful and didn't share details of her plans freely, and it was seeming as though those who were privy to her machinations had all vanished from the galaxy.

All but a few. And those few, once acquired, would talk. Oh, yes, they would.

Their visla had placed many magical wards on their living minds, protecting them from casually letting details slip, but Dominus had no idea of the power a neuro-stim from her opponents' galaxy possessed.

Slowly, carefully, the tech devices peeled back the layers in the Tslavar prisoners' minds. They'd had time to perfect the process with the previous prisoners taken in battle on and around Earth, and the mapping of their mental construction meant a much faster access-way to the information they sought. It just required a gentle touch as they worked around Malalia's magical protections.

The lead that they finally extracted seemed rather cryptic at first. And at second. But, eventually, it began to make sense. And once the general location of what might very well be the hidden base of Visla Dominus's operations was acquired, the Wampeh Ghalian sent shimmer ships to verify the information.

What they found was interesting, indeed.

"A massively guarded portal," the first of their pilots to return informed them. "The fleet is robust, and the defensive positioning suggests that what appears to be a research craft may well be the central source of their power."

"As our spy suggested before going silent when their ships abruptly jumped," Kort noted.

Zilara pondered the report a long moment, as did the other assembled captains. There were somewhat limited options, given the nature of their enemy. But if it was true that their attention was almost exclusively focused on protecting that one ship, it was possible that a small group of shimmer-cloaked craft might be able to cross through the portal unnoted.

It was an arrogance they'd seen before. The focusing of such an overwhelming quantity of power that it would undoubtedly deter any foolish enough to even think about attempting an assault.

But that same intimidation tactic that made the most valuable of their targets apparent to the most neophyte of attacker, also left a gaping hole in their defenses. They expected to be able to detect any craft attempting to sneak in among them. But the magic needed to pierce a robust shimmer was massive, and none was directed at the portal itself.

The very idea of someone trying to sneak through to an unknown destination was laughable. Laughable unless your forces happened to already know what was on the other side.

This was the time for the Wampeh Ghalian to shine. They were the undisputed masters of infiltration in the galaxy, and their talents would be put to the test.

"We have sent a small, new force to embed within key vessels on the other side," Farmatta said. "They will contact the others of our order who had already infiltrated the craft that undoubtedly reside there. Our people will then position themselves to be ready when the time comes to re-take the other portal and let our fleet through. The rest will remain here until we can disable the casting ship and close this second portal once and for all."

"I wish to lead the assault," Bawb said.

They knew with certainty that it was Hunze whose hair was powering the portal, and for that reason there was no way he would take no for an answer.

"Of course," Zilara replied. "It is only fitting that the Geist should be at the point of the spear for this attack."

It would be a difficult and dangerous prospect, somehow finding a way through all the layers of magical defenses into the most heavily guarded ship in the system. But Kort had an idea. One Charlie thought his old gladiator master would appreciate.

Rather than attacking the defenders force against force, they would take the course of water, gently flowing around whatever obstacles might spring up in their way. Soft defeating hard.

"Our shimmer craft have already begun infiltrating the most peripheral of the enemy's vessels that surround the main ship, as you planned, Kort," Wagyah informed him an hour later. "They are currently moving closer to the target research ship as we speak. Shuttle craft by shuttle craft, they will use the enemy's own transport flights to achieve our goals. And then, we shall finally take down this portal and eradicate these scum from the galaxy."

"What about the others?" Daisy asked. "I still want to get home and kick these assholes out of my galaxy."

"You will be pleased to know that the first waves of our shimmer craft have succeeded in their attempt to circumvent the magical defenses around the portal. The plan is underway."

"They were able to successfully cross over, then?" Charlie asked.

"Yes," Wagyah replied. "In short order they will have rendezvoused with those embedded in the enemy craft. From that point, we will endeavor to retake your sun's portal."

"So, we keep the fleet where they are, right by our portal," Charlie said. "Zed, Joshua, do you guys agree?"

"It seems to make the most sense," Zed replied. "And we'll need to be ready the instant the portal opens, if we're going to make a proper go of this. Hunze is being supercharged by the steady stream of plasma coming through that little portal, but if the main portal pulls out of the sun before your people free her, perhaps the interruption in solar energy might give you that little extra help you'll need."

"We shall see soon enough," Wagyah replied, turning to his fellow masters. "We should get into position. If this progresses, it will be at speed."

Zilara and the others nodded.

"Bawb, will you fly with me?" Zilara asked.

"I will. And thank you. Thank you all."

"Do not thank us yet, brother. Retrieving Hunze is but one aspect of this mission. Once she is freed, the portal will close."

"Of course," Bawb said. "At that moment, panic will ensue among their ranks. It will be a dangerous time, but also an opportunity. And in that moment, if we are swift and bold and decisive, we will be able to finish our enemy, finally freeing this galaxy from their grasp."

CHAPTER FIFTY-FOUR

The infiltration of the enemy fleet at the portal had been a greater success than any would have possibly expected. The hunched Wampeh found he didn't need to use much of a disguise at all. The fleet was bristling, and all of their attention was focused on protecting one ship. They were prepared, and with that came an overconfidence in their position.

The most powerful visla in centuries was leading their forces, and the very thought of defeat was almost laughable. It was that cockiness that would be their demise.

Leif was a very large man, yet none suspected him of being anything other than what he appeared. Namely, a mere low-ranking crewman. Even with his simple Tslavar disguise spell changing the appearance of his skin, a semi-lame crewmember was unremarkable. He was tasked with the basest of jobs, and that suited him just fine.

It was fortunate that things worked out that way, for the man he was intending to make the hand-off with appeared to have been delayed aboard another craft.

They could sneak from one ship to another, catching rides with the shuttles that ferried crew and supplies back and forth among the various ships in the fleet, but if their ride didn't depart as planned for some reason, there was little the assassins could do about it short of stealing a ship of their own.

Of course, that would bring great scrutiny upon them and blow the entire mission. Not what they wished to happen by any means. But the opposite of scrutiny is what Leif found as he slowly lumbered down the corridor of the heavily guarded research vessel, a tray of beverages in one hand, his crutch supporting him in the other.

With his camouflaging magic, no one noted the additional length of metal carefully attached to its length. He learned early on that the powerful vislas tasked with keeping Visla Dominus's prize possession under her stasis spell were so focused on their task, that they almost certainly had no spare magical bandwidth to focus on detecting a disguised Ghalian assassin in their midst.

Most didn't have that degree of power anyway. Few in all the systems ever had. But this was Dominus's crew, and to take things for granted was to tempt fate and court disaster.

But as it turned out, they were all intent on just one thing. The Ootaki woman. In fact, Leif briefly wondered if he could possibly walk right up to them in his undisguised form without them noticing, so engrossed were they with subduing the Ootaki's swelling power.

Of course, he did nothing of the sort, opting to carry the tray of refreshments slowly, his gaze averted as he walked past the golden-haired woman bound upright to a holding table.

He bent and deposited the tray on the low table toward the front of the chamber then began passing out the beverages to the preoccupied casters as he leaned on his crutch. The wobbling gait didn't distract them, though. It was the beverage spilled on the one of them nearest to the Ootaki that did the trick.

"Oh, I'm so sorry!" Leif exclaimed, leaning his crutch against the Ootaki's leg and dropping to his knees to mop up the spill.

"Get away from me," the caster, shaken from his concentration, said, shooing him away. He was well aware the others were suddenly forced to pick up the slack caused by his lack of focus, directing even more of their magic to the task of restraining the powerful woman.

"Yes, of course. Apologies," Leif groveled, shuffling back from the man and fumbling with his crutch before hobbling out of the room in a hurry.

What none of them noticed was the length of metal rod he had skillfully pressed behind the slumbering woman's leg, hiding it with her body. Not just any piece of metal, though. A Bakana rod. The fifth, to be precise.

Leif had a very small window to get clear of the chamber and off the ship to take up his hiding spot farther away in the fleet. This particular vessel would be unsafe for him very, very soon, and the final stage of the golden-haired woman's rescue would be affected after that.

The other Wampeh masters sensed the fifth Bakana rod contacting the immense power of the restrained woman immediately, but they knew they had to give Leif a few moments to get clear of the chamber before they began the process of draining her power.

"Thirty seconds," Farmatta announced. "It is enough. Time to begin."

She and the other four masters grasped their Bakana rods firmly and reached out, drawing as much power from the fifth as they could. Hunze, supercharged with the power of Earth's sun's magic, was an absolute wealth of magic, and the Wampeh Ghalian quickly directed that power into as many magical devices as they could, sucking her of her power while storing it in konuses and slaaps for later use.

"It's working," their frontmost scout informed them over skree. "The portal is weakening."

Just a few more moments pulling the woman's power and the

portal snapped shut entirely, separating the two halves of Dominus's fleet.

"We have been successful," Zilara announced to the others. "Her power is drained. The portal will not be opened again without Visla Dominus's presence."

"And now, we wait," Farmatta said, reveling in the afterglow of the rush of power she'd just experienced.

Across space, in another galaxy entirely, Malalia Maktan sensed a disturbance in the magic she had so carefully placed within Jupiter's bands. Something was wrong. *More* than wrong. Her portal was gone.

"We must go," she stated as calmly as she could, ushering Cresh and the others along to her waiting ship.

She flew directly to Jupiter, immediately confirming her worst fear. The portal was indeed gone, and the Ootaki woman powering it had been on the other side. She had plans for this realm, but there was simply no ignoring the new development.

"Captain Darus. Get me to the sun. Now!" she commanded.

Without hesitation, he spun the vessel and moved off at top speed for the burning orb in the center of the solar system.

"Hoomra, Galvash, you are to stay here. Pull this portal free of the sun on the agreed upon timeline. If I am unable to reopen the other portal, it falls upon you to control this one. Is that clear?"

"Yes, Visla," they replied, knowing a great weight had just been placed upon their shoulders. One for which failure would undoubtedly bring swift and brutal punishment.

Without further delay, Malalia directed her captain to the edge of the sun's rays and summoned the portal, freeing it from its prison of burning plasma in a flash, her massive power easily accomplishing the task.

Captain Darus did not hesitate. His orders were clear. Power through the instant a clear path was available, then jump away before the enemy's craft could possibly hope to target them.

Fortunately, they were going to be the ones with the element of surprise on their side this time, and they'd be certain to make the most of it.

If all went as planned, they'd pass through to their own galaxy and jump away before their foe's trapped fleet could even hope to react. Malalia was leaving Earth unguarded for a time, trusting her forces to make do without her. Malalia was going home.

CHAPTER FIFTY-FIVE

A power user of considerable talent would often feel fairly minor disturbances in the magical ebb and flow around them when they occurred anywhere relatively nearby. The most skilled might even feel one across the planet. But Malalia Maktan was no ordinary visla, and her power was amassed from all those she'd stolen it from over the hundreds of years she'd been at this game. And she had felt the disturbance all the way from Jupiter's cloud bands, an entire planet away.

The panicked rush back to her own galaxy might have been considered unwise for any lesser caster, but Malalia had been Visla Dominus for quite a long time, and unless all of her opponents were gathered together in one place, she had little concern for the piddling magic they might throw her way.

Captain Darus did as commanded, throwing caution to the wind—though, technically, there is no wind in space—and pushed his Drooks hard to arrive at his visla's destination as quickly as possible. The portion of the fleet surrounding the main craft housing the Ootaki woman appeared perfectly intact. In fact, there was no discernible disturbance other than the unexpected disappearance of the portal.

The captain didn't pause his flight to more thoroughly examine the fleet, though. He knew his mistress's wishes and flew her directly to the main research craft. Time was of the essence, and Visla Dominus would not waste a precious moment longer than necessary leaving her new conquest in the hands of her underlings.

The ship connected with the larger craft, and Visla Dominus was aboard in a flash, her feet carrying her quickly through the empty corridors. Cresh and a handful of her closest casters followed in her wake, but their way was clear. None had wished to be in the path of the visla's displeasure as she hurried to the Ootaki's holding chamber, and wisely so.

The lesser vislas who had been tasked with maintaining the stasis spell holding her Ootaki prisoner were standing at attention when she entered the room. The sign of respect would have been a normal occurrence, had it not been for the fact that they typically would have had their attentions firmly centered on the woman strapped upright to her restraining table, bathing in the small portal's glow of solar power.

But the Ootaki's hair was not radiant. In fact, she seemed almost devoid of the incredible power she'd so recently possessed. Her hair was slowly regaining some strength, Malalia could sense, but it would be some time before she had any true power again.

"What happened?" she growled, her eyes flashing hot anger at the men and women tasked with overseeing this most crucial aspect of her plan.

The head of the team stepped forward, knowing full well his death might be at hand, but not knowing what else to do.

"It was sudden, Visla," he replied. "Unexpected. We were all performing our tasks, as usual, when she suddenly ceased emitting power. It was as if it was there one moment, then gone the next."

"Impossible," the angry visla replied. "I personally placed the spells binding her. Nothing should have broken them."

"And nothing did," the terrified man replied. "We have ceased bolstering them solely because her natural power is no longer threatening to topple them."

Malalia could feel the man was telling the truth. The spells were still in place, keeping the Ootaki in a deep slumber. But her natural power was no longer fighting back with the fierceness of her initial capture when it threatened to overcome the magical restraints.

"What is different, then? What changed that caused this?" Malalia asked. "There must be an explanation."

An angry magic was crackling at her fingertips, a side effect of the years draining her husband's volatile power. And she was overflowing with it. His power, and so many others'.

"The only thing we noted was someone had left a piece of refuse leaning up against her," the chided visla said. "It was mostly tucked behind her leg, but it has no power that I can sense."

"Give it to me," Malalia demanded.

The man picked up the ordinary-looking rod, registering no power whatsoever, and handed it to her. As soon as Malalia's hand grasped the Bakana rod, however, the gathered Wampeh Ghalian hiding in their shimmer ships just beyond range of her casters' senses, all acted as one.

Had she been remotely prepared for the attack, Malalia might even have been able to turn the tables on her attackers, using the rods to drain their power. But a Bakana rod was the rarest of items, and though she had heard of the magical objects, she'd never actually seen one in all of her many years.

Terror shot through the assembled men and women when Visla Dominus crumbled to her knees just as the fleet around them began to rip apart, the Wampeh spies aboard those ships long gone now that the endgame was in play.

Malalia felt a large quantity of her power violently ripped from her body and used against her own forces in a singular surge of action. She fought the pull, eventually managing to force her hands to open, the Bakana rod dropping to the deck in front of her.

She was still powerful. Incredibly powerful, in fact, but she was reduced to a level she hadn't felt in over a century. Someone had just stolen a huge amount of her magic, and that cursed rod was the key.

"No one touch it!" she managed to say as she regained her unsteady feet.

It was clear now what had happened to the Ootaki. Her power had been taken from her the same way, shutting the portal. And she knew in her gut that an attack was coming. This whole thing had been a trap.

Visla Cresh reached out and helped steady her visla, and Malalia lurched into her faithful assistant's arms, fastening her extended fangs into the startled woman's neck and quickly draining her of as much magic as she could survive losing.

"Sorry, Cresh," Malalia said as she lowered the woman to the deck. She was still at greatly reduced capacity, but Cresh was a powerful visla, and this infusion of stolen power would help her fight this enemy.

All around the terribly damaged fleet, shimmered Wampeh craft, the pirate rebels, and a sizable number of Earth's ships, all jumped into position as they swarmed in from their staging areas, unleashing a world of hurt on the damaged and disarrayed ships, while doing their best to block the Tslavars' escape.

Malalia watched in shock from the research ship as the tech vessels let loose a barrage of unusual projectile weapons, the likes of which she'd never seen before. There was magic to them, she could feel it, but it was strange. Something from the other galaxy. And it was piercing her fleet's shields.

But that wasn't the most startling part. The attack that came immediately after was. Round after round of similar projectiles threaded the needle through the gaps in the magical shielding, punching their way into her ships. Reports flew through the air on panicked skree messages. A strange vapor was filling the ships, causing agonizing pain to her crews.

Malalia was unsure what could possibly do such a thing when a message caught her attention. One of her ships had a less important Wampeh prisoner aboard as a backup should she feel the need to top off her power by harvesting magic. But when the odd mists reached him, the man shrieked for but an instant, then burst into flames, reducing to a pile of ash in an instant.

Only one thing could do that to a Wampeh.

"Balamar water?" she gasped, astonished. "But, where could they have found it in such quantities?"

The answer didn't matter at the moment.

It was deadly to Wampeh, but her crews should not have been affected. Whatever they'd done to it, somehow, the waters were now harmful to her men as well as herself. Yet for some reason, they were not targeting the ship they were still attached to. For now, anyway. The actual reason was simple. Hunze.

"Cast heat defenses around your vessels," she transmitted to her crumbling armada, hoping the tactic might evaporate the deadly waters before they could cause further damage.

Some of her ships got the message and adapted their defenses with a fair degree of success, but the damage was done. The creative attack hadn't destroyed the targeted ships, but had crippled her fleet just the same.

Malalia wondered an instant if she could use the strange rod that had drained her so to turn the tables on her attackers, but she knew that any adversary as clever as this would have already taken precautions against such a thing. And she was right.

No sooner had the four Wampeh masters taken her power and turned it against her fleet in their surprise attack than they dropped the rods, their non-magical pirate assistants gathering them up to hide for safekeeping so they could not be used against them now that the fifth was in Malalia's hands.

But Malalia still had power. A *lot* of power. She had drained Cresh to help her recover her equilibrium, but that was more due to her *utterly* enormous magic being reduced to merely *incredibly* enormous magic. It was still more than any other user in the galaxy, and that would be plenty to crush these enemies now that she had her bearings again.

"There's a Zomoki in the mix," Captain Darus informed her over skree from her docked ship. "And there appear to be riders atop its back."

"Charlie," she hissed.

Indeed, Ara, Charlie, and Leila were tearing through her fleet, the Zomoki's magical flames laying waste where the human caster's magic wasn't. They were a tag team of destruction, and a constant thorn in her side. One that needed removing once and for all.

"Enough of this," Dominus growled, summoning up a spell so mighty it would destroy Charlie and his friends and shatter the enemy forces in a single blow. The exertion would be costly, but it would be ever so worth it.

The spell erupted from her, racing out toward her enemies at blinding speed. A few Earth ships fell to it, as did a number of pirate craft, before it reached its true intended target. The human and his friends were as good as done for. A spell this powerful? Nothing could stop it.

Nothing but Leila.

"No," Leila said from her perch atop Ara's back. And that was all it took.

The Magus stone, silent for her entire life, was finally connected to her, and she supposed she had Malalia to thank for it, in a strange way. Her and Bawb, who had helped her refine her control. And that stone's vast power was now hers to command. She hadn't learned all of its secrets. Not even a fraction, for that matter. But there was one thing she knew quite well by now. How to protect those she held dear.

The Magus stone warmed against her chest and blasted out a wave of protective magic, one that encircled not only those in her immediate vicinity, but nearly all of the rebel fleet in the system. She wasn't able to save all of their ships, but in war, one never can. And regardless, she'd just stopped Malalia's massive attack in its tracks.

Aboard the research ship Malalia stood in amazement at what had just happened. She'd used up so much of her power, and for what? For nothing. Charlie and his friends still lived, and in her reduced state, it suddenly looked like she might not be able to stop them at all. Not without feeding, and there was simply no time for that. She had to survive.

It was so distasteful. Running away. But she hadn't survived this long without learning that valuable lesson, though it had taken a few near misses before it truly sank in. The first such lesson had been at the hands of Charlie and his friends on ancient Earth, and this time, her defeat was his work yet again.

CHAPTER FIFTY-SIX

Visla Dominus hurried down the corridors of the massive research vessel to her waiting ship, docked and ready to depart at a moment's notice. That moment had come.

Every last power user of any worth had been pulled from their posts and ordered to join her in her hasty flight, while Grundsch carried the unconscious Visla Cresh in his arms. None knew what exactly was going on, only that their visla had requested that they personally come with her on her private vessel. Little did they know, their use to her at the moment was not in an manner they might have expected.

The group was racing toward her ship when an enraged voice bellowed out, "Malalia!"

She knew that voice.

"Go. I'll be with you shortly," she said to her fleeing minions, just as Bawb unshimmered from down the corridor and locked eyes with her.

She had used an enormous amount of her power, but Malalia knew she could take the Wampeh. But something in his demeanor gave her pause. He'd obviously fed recently, the power was palpable in the air between them. But there was something else. Something more to this equation.

Bawb flashed his pointed fangs in a wicked grin as he drew his wand from its protective sheath at his side.

Other power users couldn't sense magic the way the Wampeh Ghalian could, and with so much of that power flowing in her veins, Malalia was more than able to feel the threat the seemingly harmless piece of wood posed. There was power. An unusual, mixed power. Konus, Ootaki, and who knew what else? It seemed even a trace of that troublesome energy from the other galaxy might be swirling in there as well.

Moreover, the weapon was clearly not a precision device. It was practically bursting at the seams, ready to explode forth a furious amount of magic at its owner's command.

Despite the looming threat, Malalia smiled. The Wampeh wouldn't use such a device aboard this ship. Sure, he could possibly get a lucky shot and kill her in her weakened state, but in so doing, he would risk ripping the ship open. And if he did that, his precious Ootaki would perish.

Malalia flashed him a wink, then vanished down the corridor, leaving him with the option of pursuing his enemy, or saving his woman. Malalia ran to her ship, confident what his decision would be. It was a rare weakness for a Wampeh Ghalian, and she'd likely not benefit of it again.

As Visla Dominus raced to her waiting ship, the Geist lay waste to any and all who stood between him and his love. The wand had been re-sheathed, but that was the extent of restraint he showed as he drove through those foolish enough to try to stand in his way. He even used power at this point, with Malalia gone. And though she had taken all of the powerful casters with her, she'd left behind plenty of lesser power users for him to feed on as he went, replenishing his strength on the fly.

The final handful of those either brave or dumb enough to try to stop him stood before the frontmost chamber. He could sense her there, the Ootaki hair in his armored vest reaching out to her as her slumbering form returned the call.

The dozen men would have been wise to simply flee at that moment, and two of them actually did when they saw the gleam of the Geist's teeth and the look in his eye. The others weren't so lucky, their only good fortune being the quickness of their demise.

Aboard her personal craft, Malalia reluctantly gave the command, and Captain Darus detached from the research vessel and jumped them away, but not before she saw the end of her fleet in this galaxy. She took in one final glimpse of her research ship, then they were gone.

Inside that craft, Bawb stepped over the fallen bodies of those who had dared cross him as he hurried to his waiting escape ride. Hunze was now safe in his arms, with none alive to threaten her as he walked back to his borrowed, shimmer-cloaked ship.

The Drooks on board had been spared in the battle, and most of their counterparts on the now-destroyed vessels were likewise saved, the Wampeh having placed protective spells on as many of their chambers as they could. Spells that would only activate when the attack began.

They were not only innocents, but they were also a valuable asset in the ongoing war. And once saved and freed from servitude, there was little doubt they would do as their comrades had done and join the rebellion as free Drooks.

"We are clear," Bawb transmitted as he lifted off from the larger craft.

"How is she?" Charlie asked.

"Sleeping. She appears to be unharmed, but a spell is keeping her from waking."

"Is there anything we can do to help?"

"This is something I will handle myself," Bawb replied. "But thank you for your concern, and for all of your assistance."

Charlie could hear the weeks of strain melting from his friend's voice. Hunze would be all right. "Okay, man. You be safe. We'll catch up when you're ready."

"Indeed," Bawb replied, then steered the shimmer ship as close to the small portal of Earth's sun's rays as he could.

Hunze would absorb the energy while he worked to free her from her magical bonds. Slowly, gently, allowing her to wake without the trauma of a forceful spell.

It had been a sound defeat for Malalia, but her rapid flight from the ongoing battle had given her enough time to reach the portal just as her casters opened it from the other side, pulling it free from the sun.

The ships she had been avoiding upon her arrival had mostly departed, following to participate in the destruction of her own fleet, it seemed, but a few of their forces still remained. They had proven easy enough to avoid, however, allowing her to conserve precious power, and she was through the portal before they knew what happened.

"All of our defensive spells must employ blistering heat from this point on," Visla Dominus commanded her casters over an open skree transmission as soon as she'd crossed over.

"Of course, Visla," replied her loyal subject, residing in the hub city the Earth people called Los Angeles. "And what of the insurgent uprising?"

Malalia felt her stomach tighten. *Something* had happened in her absence. "What is the status?" she asked, hiding the fact she was utterly in the dark about the problem.

"The rebellious groups seem to have joined forces and are proving to be a rather robust nuisance," the caster replied. "We've been having great difficulty counter-striking. They seem to possess some means of transit beyond our ability to track."

"Where are they now?"

"A large group is in the central area at my location, and another group appears to be causing trouble far up the coastline."

"I'm coming to you," she replied.

"Visla? You're coming in person?"

"This must stop. Now." She closed the skree communication and turned to Captain Darus. "Take us to Los Angeles."

Charlie's troublesome friends appeared to have found a way to be a thorn in her side in *both* galaxies, and there would be a fight. This time, however, she would be facing a far inferior foe. The others were still trapped in the other galaxy, and while they had inconvenienced her to a great degree by closing off her portal, it had served its purpose admirably.

She also still controlled the previously existing portal, and without that, there was no hope for her meddling enemy to return to muddy her plans. Malalia walked to her private chamber and summoned the first of what would be many of her casters. They would recover soon enough, and she was in far greater need of their power than they were at this moment.

CHAPTER FIFTY-SEVEN

The battle raging in Los Angeles was far greater than Visla Dominus had expected. Large groups of humans and their odd, four-armed compatriots were utilizing those strange energy weapons against her forces, and with some degree of success.

The tactics being employed were novel. The weaponry was being steadily rotated, and every so often a magical attack would be thrown into the mix. Obviously, someone had provided the pesky rebels with some moderately powered konuses. Dominus had a very good idea who it had been.

"Oh, Charlie, what ever have you done this time?" she mused as Captain Darus dropped her craft right in the middle of a firefight. "Giving primitives konuses? Pure folly."

She was nowhere near her full strength when they landed, but she was strong. The power she'd taken was immense, that of many power users compounded within her, but she simply hadn't had the time to drain all of her casters.

Nevertheless, it would more than suffice against such a paltry magical attempt. And once she'd put down this little uprising herself, making a show of it for her people and letting one and all know she was firmly in control, *then* she would drain her other casters at her leisure. With her magical enemy so far away, they could recharge at a leisurely pace. There would be no rush.

Malalia stepped from her craft with an invisible, broad-spectrum magical shield surrounding her. She'd had plenty of time to observe both the Balamar weaponry deployed on the other side of the portal and the energy weapons used on this side. With her breadth of magic, it had been simple to adjust for those variables.

Her Tslavar mercenaries, however, were not having as easy a time of it. The natives were quite effective in creating crossfires, forcing the invading aliens to adjust on the fly to the shifting attacks. Several of the four-armed creatures had fallen, most killed outright, though there were still a few alive and ready for interrogation.

Humans, however, were few and far between, and the only ones successfully targeted all lay dead. There would be no extracting information from them, unfortunately.

"Idiots," Malalia grumbled as she prepared to make a lasting impression on her enemies. She wanted them alive, if possible, for questioning. Her men were superior and should have been able to accomplish that simple task. But if she wanted something done, it seemed, she had to do it herself.

The rebel forces saw Visla Dominus enter the battlefield, and the fear in the air was palpable. Their chances of making another mysterious escape had just evaporated into the air. Or so Dominus thought.

Danger! her senses warned.

She spun, quickly casting a modified deflection spell as a hard-charging human male fired a highly unusual weapon at her and her Tslavar forces at almost a full run. Several of the green men fell to the attack, pierced by a strange metal projectile.

Had Malalia not possessed such a great degree of power, she

too might even have been wounded by the utterly unexpected tactic.

The weapon not only spewed hot metal at great speed, but it also let out an awful, explosive roar with each shot fired. The end result was enough of a disruption in the firefight that all of the resistance forces evaporated from the battlefield, escaping yet again.

Malalia held back her full fury and cast a brutally painful immobilization spell at the attacking man. His friends might have made an escape, but it would cost him dearly.

He dropped to the ground as Visla Dominus flung out her hands, directing the spell toward her target. The strange weapon ceased its clamor, and Malalia slowly walked up to the writhing man where he lay.

"Idiot. Do you not realize your paltry weapons are of no threat to me?" she cooed, playing it up a bit for her men.

Word would spread how their visla easily stopped an attack that the rest of them were unable to avoid. Just one more morale boost for her mercenary forces.

"Take him to the interrogation facility," she said, then turned and strode back to her waiting craft as if this had been no more bothersome than swatting a fly.

The stocky man was hauled to his feet and dragged away to be subjected to the rather specialized skills of her top interrogation emmik. He was almost visla-level in his power, but more than that, he possessed a certain talent for inflicting pain in ways that made people talk. And, being a physically powerful man as well as magical, he enjoyed employing manual torture almost as much as magical.

So far, the broad-chested caster had only extracted the most jumbled nonsense about secret tunnels and hidden minds beneath the surface, but perhaps this man who had borne the unusual weapon might possess something more useful. And he was a sturdy one. He would be a joy to break.

The interrogation would start off with a bit of physical torment before the real fun began. Seeing as the prisoner was quite muscular, he would be restrained with sturdy rope, tied with just enough slack to allow him the false hope of the possibility of escape. The frustration would drive him mad. Then, when he had exerted himself for a bit, finally realizing how dire his situation was, the true interrogation would begin.

The emmik was summoned to the prisoner's chamber a short while later. A few other moaning victims were still recovering from their torture sessions and had been left in place to serve as props of a sort. The new arrival would be further terrified when he saw their injuries, making his futile efforts to escape even more frustrating.

"What do you mean, he's not struggling?"

"Precisely that, Emmik," his helper replied.

"He is not pulling at his restraints?"

"Just once, when he arrived. He's been standing quietly ever since."

"The others, they are moaning?"

"Yes, Emmik. They appear to be quite miserable."

"Yet he does not respond?"

"I am afraid not."

The interrogator was perplexed, but also intrigued. Perhaps this would be a more amusing subject than he'd originally anticipated.

"*Orvallus nectu,*" he said as he entered the prisoner's room, casting an excruciating pain spell.

The stocky man slumped in his bindings, writhing to and fro.

"*Infara,*" he cast, ceasing the torment.

The man relaxed in his restraints, breathing hard. "What do you want from me?"

"Why, what makes you think I *want* anything?" the emmik replied.

"Well, you didn't kill me. Instead, you've taken me to this place. I mean, what is this, anyway? Some kind of holding place for all of the men you've captured? A torture facility?"

"Of a sort," the emmik said, gesturing to the wounded men nearby. "We've tortured many of your compatriots, and there are quite a good amount left for me to play with. But you? You do not need to feel such pain. All you have to do is answer my questions."

"Not happening," the human said, stoically.

The emmik grinned. "Admittedly, I was hoping you'd say that. Let's see how you feel once you've had the opportunity to better ponder your mortality."

"*Tormanti occara!*" he said, casting a violently painful spell.

Nothing happened.

"*Tormanti occara!*" he repeated, a bit confused.

Again, nothing. He knew this spell. He'd been using it for years. There was no doubt he had cast it properly, yet it did nothing.

"My mortality?" the strange man said with a little smirk, apparently unaffected by the pain spell. "Ya know what? I'm feeling pretty good about it, actually. And thanks for that information, by the way. I wasn't one hundred percent sure this was the main holding facility."

The emmik stepped close, beside himself with disbelief. This simply did not happen. *Could* not happen. He studied his victim. There was no fear in his eyes. If anything, there was perhaps a bit of amusement. *That* would not do.

"*Inflammus!*" he said, casting a focused burning spell. "We shall see how amused you are when you witness your flesh burning from your body," the emmik said with a chuckle, confident this new, albeit aggressive, tactic would yield the desired results.

"What...?" the caster managed to say in shock as the gleam of bright metal shone out from the hole he'd burned in his victim's shoulder.

"Man! Again? Sonofa... I just had this body fixed!" Sergeant Franklin said. "Asshole!"

That was the last *word* the emmik heard. He did hear one final *sound*, however. That of his sternum snapping as the cyborg spec ops soldier tore free from his restraints like they were mere string, then punched his fist right through the thickly muscled torturer's chest, driving it in up to his forearm.

"*Kali ma, shakti deh,*" George muttered dramatically, pulling his hand free as the emmik fell, the dead man's heart beating its last in his hand. He looked over at the wide-eyed prisoners around him with a little grin.

"I know it's a bit much, but to be honest, ever since I saw that flick, I've always wanted to try that." Sergeant Franklin shifted his focus, calling up his internal encrypted comms array. "Okay, I'm in," he said. "Confirmation, this is the place. Send the cavalry to my location. I'll be freeing the prisoners when you get here."

CHAPTER FIFTY-EIGHT

All was silent in Cal's command center beneath the streets of downtown Los Angeles. He had many such facilities throughout the region, but this was the one favored by his human friends for its proximity to home, as well as the central hub that was downtown.

The invading forces had not really figured out the access paths to most of the subterranean network of loop tubes and underground commerce centers, and as such, there was an eerie stillness to the air. Eventually, the Tslavars would find their way into the better hidden nooks and crannies of the city's heart, but for now, they were keeping to the surface.

"The cow jumps over the moon," a voice said in the most central of the facility's chambers.

Silence.

The Wampeh Ghalian removed her shimmer cloak and repeated the pass-phrase. "The cow jumps over the moon."

"That was a nice trick," Cal quietly replied. *"I never cease to be fascinated by your shimmer spells. A marvelous form of camouflage, though the thermal residue of your footprints is a weakness you may wish to address in the future."*

The Wampeh looked a bit surprised at that bit of information. Cal was indeed as impressive as she'd been told.

"And before you ask, yes, we are alone here. My perimeter scanners have kept track of all bodies near the facility on infrared, thermal, and a host of other spectrums."

Satisfied they were unobserved, the assassin spoke. "Cal, I was sent at Charlie's request to inform you of the status of forces currently amassed in the other galaxy."

"How did you manage to cross over? I've been informed that the portal at the sun is still under Visla Dominus's control."

"It is. However, I crossed over in my shimmer ship from a different route, utilizing the visla's other portal, just before we closed it."

"You found it? And sealed it off? So, Hunze is dead?" Cal asked, a sad tone to his voice.

"Far from it, if all went according to plan. I was on this side when the portal closed, but the Geist should have her in his possession by now. And with her retrieval, the portal shall remain closed, trapping the portion of Visla Dominus's fleet that was on the other side, while also removing their path of secret transit."

"This is excellent news."

"Indeed, it is. And you should know, the portal was quite close to your planet, hidden in the clouds of the fifth world from your sun. It is, therefore, unlikely that Dominus's fleet has spread beyond your solar system. Not yet, anyway."

"Jupiter? My, my, what a clever use of our local gas giant," Cal said. *"Enemy or no, you have to admire that rather inspired bit of subterfuge. But what of our forces? Where do things stand?"*

The Wampeh allowed herself a slight smile. "Your fleet has proven a most valued ally, though I am sure you would much prefer they had remained in your own galaxy."

"Obviously. But we make do with what is at our disposal."

"Quite. They have employed their modified warp drive

systems to traverse our galaxy rather successfully and have joined with our main body of rebel forces. The leaders of the Wampeh Ghalian have thrown all of our considerable resources into this fight, and the rebel fleet has also been amassing a sizable number of vessels, though many are not exactly fighting craft."

"Modifications can be made, however," Cal noted. *"We've done as much here in the past, and with Zed on the other side, I'm sure he's been quite helpful at adapting those craft."*

"He has, and we were ultimately able to utilize your neuro-stim technology to pry the secret location of Visla Dominus's hidden portal fleet from a less than cooperative Tslavar. The first phase was to drain the power from the Ootaki woman to shut down the portal. It sealed just after I crossed in the chaos of her power diminishing, so we know that worked. If the second phase of the plan worked as intended, Visla Dominus should have found a great portion of her power robbed from her by that same device."

"I've heard rumors she has been summoning her higher-ups to her since she returned," Cal mused. *"Might she be using them to replenish her power?"*

"It would certainly seem that way. And if that is the case, then we know the second phase was successful. Visla Dominus is weakened, and the time to fight is now, before she can replenish herself fully. The rebel fleet will be gathering at the remaining portal by now, simply awaiting it to be opened from this side. I understand you have some powerful casters capable. Are they still living?"

"Living, and safely in hiding with the others."

"Then it is time to summon them from their burrows and send every craft available to overwhelm Dominus's forces while we can, and take back the portal. Once the fleet crosses back to this side, it will be the endgame. All available forces will have to be present to oppose Dominus, both on land and in space."

"I will get the gears turning," Cal said. *"The AI network has been in silent hiding, our AI ships lying low, pretending to be mere tech craft and not autonomous entities. We will have quite an element of surprise, but only for a short while, I fear. But if this is truly the final stand, we have to throw everything we have at the craft protecting the portal and reclaim it as our own."*

"I shall do what I can from my shimmer-cloaked craft," the Wampeh replied. "As will the other Wampeh Ghalian who crossed over with me."

"Greatly appreciated. And I will give you every asset we possess. We have one try at this, and failure is not an option."

The Wampeh nodded once, ready to fight, and even die, in this strange, new galaxy. But hopefully her brothers and sisters would soon join her, and they would rejoice in victory and the blood of their enemies.

"I will await your people's arrival," she said. "When they approach, we shall begin our barrage on the enemy's main caster vessels."

She then slipped into her shimmer cloak and was gone, though Cal could still track the heat signature of her footsteps, but only barely. She had already altered her shimmer to mask them, it seemed. A clever and quick-working ally.

"Rika, Korbin, this is Cal," he transmitted. *"I am alerting the entire AI network and all of our resistance forces. The enemy's second portal has been sealed, and our fleet is gathering at the original portal location. Visla Dominus has returned to this galaxy but is weakened. This is our one shot. We have some assistance, but it's up to us to take control of the portal and get our people back home."*

Rika and Jo were sitting in the cockpit of the *Fujin* when the call came in.

"Get the others," Rika said, then keyed her comms. "I copy you, Cal. We'll be airborne straightaway. Do you have a location for Malalia?"

"*Not at the moment, I'm afraid. She's taken to shifting craft since her return. She's weakened, and, apparently, the discovery of assassins in her fleet seems to have made her more cautious.*"

"Nothing we can do for it, I guess," Rika said. "Until we get our guys back across, we'll be pretty outnumbered up there. Just give us as much cover fire as you can. If you can distract the defense ships away, I think Korbin and I can force the portal open, at least long enough for some of our guys to cross back over."

"*I've already passed along the message,*" Cal replied. "*Good luck, and fly safe.*"

Rika laughed to herself as she clicked off the comms. "Fly safe? When have I *ever* done that?"

CHAPTER FIFTY-NINE

Sid reached out with the information garnered quietly from his seemingly inert satellites floating between the moon and the sun. Several ships had arrived recently, though he could not discern why. As for the Tslavars within his own walls, they were still oblivious to the AI's ongoing observation of their activities. Unfortunately, however, they were either not very chatty people, or they really didn't know what Dominus was doing out there.

The portal was already well protected, but a sizable contingent of additional casters were assigned to positions nearby after she had returned from the other galaxy. Whatever was going on, she was taking no chances, it seemed.

What they didn't know, was she was also using this crisis as an opportunity to consolidate enough casters to feed on, while not risking diminishing her hold over the portal. And as they recovered, she would then feed on the others still maintaining it. Soon, her powers would begin to return to their normal, massive levels.

She was aboard one such ship, under the guise of discussing something of great importance with the lead caster––a rather powerful man she felt no worries over draining whatsoever, not with the enemy trapped on the other side—when the ship was rocked by an incoming wave of weapons fire.

"Visla, we are under attack!"

It was a statement of the obvious, Malalia thought, as her power flared to life. Funny, how people were so predictable in their reactions in times of stress. "Yes, obviously," she hissed. "Prepare your people for combat."

It took her but a moment to board the nondescript ship she'd been using to quietly visit the orbiting craft. It wasn't as robust as her usual ride, but she didn't wish to make a big scene of her departing the surface. If the enemy didn't know where she was, it was much harder for them to create a nuisance without fear of reprisal.

But now they were here, in space. And it seemed they had far more firepower at their disposal than her commanders had led her to believe. Normally, the casters would have simply continued their tasks, standing by to protect the portal if needed, while letting the lesser casters handle the incoming handful of craft.

But this was different. There were far more ships in this assault than believed to be active in the entire system. Apparently, the enemy had been lying low, playing possum and lulling them into a sense of complacency while they bided their time for an attack.

A wave of railgun fire slammed into the ships' defenses, their nanite tips penetrating the shielding, the follow-up rounds heading straight into the craft's hulls. The modified heating spells did a decent job of vaporizing the Balamar waters the sabots dispersed within the ships, but not before some of the crew fell to the agonizing effects of the tainted liquid.

Malalia realized that in this ship, she would be forced to play the role of main defender as well as offense. If any of that water breached her shielding spells, no amount of offense would be of any good if she melted into a pile of ash. Thus, she directed nearly all of her attention to protecting herself and her ship from the strange projectiles, leaving the fighting to the others.

Rika and Korbin were holding back as Marban led the attack on Malalia's fleet, drawing their attention and their fire as they engaged them, slowly, but steadily, pulling them farther and farther from their original positions near the portal.

"That's the window," Rika transmitted to Korbin. "We do this now!"

Without waiting for a reply, she slipped the *Fujin* into place and began casting, while Jo kept her sharp eyes out for any incoming hostiles and her trigger fingers ready on the ship's ample weapons systems. Korbin's modified ship joined her a moment later.

"I'm here," was all he said as he joined her in casting the spell.

The casters tasked with guarding the portal were so distracted by the unexpected attack that they had shifted nearly all of their focus on defending themselves, leaving enough of a weakness for the two resistance fighters to get a magical grip on the portal and begin pulling it free from the sun.

One by one, Dominus's people began to realize something was going on behind them. The attack was a diversion, and the portal was the true target. They redirected their magic as best they could while maintaining their defenses against the troublesome Earth ships peppering them with railgun fire and pulse weapons.

In their home galaxy, Dominus's casters would have had the clear advantage, their combined power easily rising to the occasion. But in this galaxy, they found themselves somewhat diminished in their capacity, and what's more, Rika was home. And home meant she was stronger than ever, her ink glowing bright as she focused on the portal.

Korbin was right there with her, a powerful hand on her side of the magical tug-of-war with the multi-tasking enemy casters.

Malalia was too busy protecting her woefully unprepared ship to adequately participate, and before the invaders knew what hit them, the portal pulled clear just far enough to allow a few of the waiting rebels to slip through before it slid back into the sun.

Under most circumstances, a handful of craft wouldn't be enough to turn the tide, but Ara had been the first through, her magic protecting her and her passengers from the sun's heat as she dove into the portal before it was fully clear. Right behind her, Freya and Marty followed, along with several Wampeh shimmer craft and a handful of smaller pirate and Earth vessels.

The portal was closed, and Rika and Korbin were forced to evacuate their positions, but the damage had been done.

Ara tore into the Tslavar ships swarming the newcomers, her magical flames blasting clear a path for the others flying into the fray behind her. Freya and Daisy were on fire, figuratively, their anger piqued at the invaders threatening their home yet again.

While Ara and Charlie were laying waste to as many of the increasing number of Dominus's ships as they could, the AI ship and her human pilot were doing likewise, letting loose with all manner of deadly weapons. But there were others at risk back home, and they needed help too.

"Arlo, get to the surface and find the others. Make sure they're okay!" Daisy transmitted to her son as she let loose another volley of pulse fire.

"On it!" the teen replied. "Hold tight," he called out to his passengers. "It's gonna get a little bumpy."

"Bumpy?" Kara asked. "You mean, more than this?"

"Yeah. Okay, let's go, Marty. Get us home."

"Copy that. Time to clean house," the AI ship replied, then spun into a roll, firing a stream of plasma blasts into the defenses of the ships in front of him.

A moment later he warped, popping out of existence just as the return fire arrived where only a crackling blue warp residue remained. Far from the sun––three planets away, to be precise––

Marty emerged from warp in a flash and immediately dropped into the atmosphere at high speed, Kara and Vee bouncing in their seats as the ship was buffeted by choppy air.

"Uncle Cal, do you copy?" Arlo transmitted. "We've crossed back. Where are the others?"

"Good to hear your voice, Arlo," the AI replied. *"I'm sending Marty the coordinates. There are a lot of ground forces taking heavy losses that could use extrication, if you're able."*

"We'll get to them as fast as we can," the teen replied. "Marty, we need a quick combat landing in downtown. Kara, Vee, we're going to drop you off at the command center. You'll be safe there."

"But we should come with you. We should help," Kara protested as the ship quickly descended and landed with a thud.

"I appreciate it, but we're gonna need every bit of space in here for the evac. Just get yourselves safe, and hopefully we'll survive all this and see each other after."

The violet-skinned teen hesitated, then leaned in, giving him a firm kiss before rushing off with her Ootaki friend, whose look of surprise was almost as great as Arlo's.

"Uh, okay," he muttered, blushing. "Uh, yeah. Right. Take us up, Marty. You've got the coordinates."

As her son flew off on his mission in the relative safety of Earth's atmosphere, Daisy and her friends in the vacuum of space let loose with everything they had as the battle with Malalia and her forces increased its intensity. They were outmanned and outmagicked, but they'd taken the Tslavar fleet by surprise, and that might well be the edge they needed.

If not, it would prove to be a rather short rebellion.

"Rika, they're targeting us pretty heavily. I don't think we'll be able to pause long enough to focus on the portal. Can you get it open again?" Charlie asked over comms.

"I don't know," she replied as she dove the *Fujin* through the enemy ranks, Jo strafing them with her cannons as they dodged the magical counterattacks. "I'll need space to do it. If you can buy me some time, then maybe. Korbin and I should be able to."

"Okay," Charlie replied. "We'll do what we can. Keep yourself safe in the meantime."

"Not likely," his friend replied. "There's no safe space out here. So hurry up and do whatever it is you're going to do."

They then all dove into the fray once more, battling their magical enemy with a combination of power, tech, and a whole lot of guts. Charlie hoped it would be enough.

CHAPTER SIXTY

Arlo and Marty had just rocketed up into the sky to rush headlong into whatever deadly firefight had left their friends in need when Kara and Vee paused their run toward the entrance to the safety of Cal's command center.

"Do you hear that?" Kara asked.

"Fighting," Vee replied.

Kara flexed her hands, a slight crackling spreading across her fingertips.

"What are you doing, Kara?"

The visla's daughter turned to her friend. "You don't have to come with me, but I can't go and hide when I could be helping these people."

Vee was torn. She had seen what her friend could do, and that was before. Now? Who knew what she might be capable of. "Okay, but I'm coming with you," she finally said.

Kara grinned. Best friends, no matter what, even if that meant running toward the sound of fighting rather than away from it. Kara pulled a small enchanted blade from within the folds of her clothing and handed it to her friend.

"Thanks, Vee. Take this."

"Where did you get an enchanted blade?"

"Uncle Korbin gave it to me after I was kidnapped, before my powers started kicking in. You should have it."

Vee hefted the knife approvingly. "Thanks. Let's go."

The teens quickly made their way along the periphery of the street, sticking to cover as best they could as they grew closer to the sounds of fighting and mayhem. There was obviously something big afoot, and it seemed as though the magical forces likely had the advantage. At first glance, as they peered out from behind cover, their guess was proven to be true.

There were human and Chithiid fighters pinned down by a barrage of magical attackers. Mostly Tslavars, but a pair of lesser casters were with them as well. Both were races Kara had never seen before––an umber-hued woman with double-hinged legs and unusually short arms, and a blue-gray man with enormous arms on which he walked, while his legs focused the magic he was casting, the lengthy digits on his feet steering the spells toward their targets.

"What are they?" Vee wondered.

"Emmiks," Kara replied. "Pretty weak ones."

"How can you tell?"

"I don't know," she admitted. "I just can."

A street provided a possible route for the resistance fighters to escape the onslaught, but it was just out of reach, the casters and mercenaries having cut off the means of egress. They were essentially trapped. An injured human, bleeding profusely, was crawling as best he could for cover when a violent spell ended his suffering.

"Get them out of here, Vee. I'll provide cover."

"Kara, you're not your father."

"I know. But I can do this. Trust me."

Visanya stared long and hard at her dearest friend. The timid girl she'd known all her life was not the person whose gaze met hers now, though. *This* Kara had power, and there was zero doubt in her eyes."

"All right, but be careful."

"Always," Kara replied. "Okay. When I cast, you go," she said, then stepped out from cover as Vee slithered along the periphery of the battlefield toward the pinned fighters.

The magic in Kara began to swell as she focused her intent on the bad men in front of her. Then, with barely a whisper of the spell, she cast.

A massive blast of magic sent the Tslavars tumbling. Only the casters, with their defensive spells still firmly in place, managed to stay on their feet. They turned to find not a powerful visla squaring off against them, but nothing more than a teenage girl. It was an incongruous sight, and not at all what they expected, but when Kara unleashed another powerful spell, they realized this girl was very much a threat, and one they might not be able to handle, even casting together.

Rather than engaging them with all of her strength, Kara began bombarding the casters and their mercenary forces with smaller spells, distracting the enemy, while allowing Vee to help guide the survivors from the battlefield.

It had finally begun to click, her newly unfettered magic, and the defensive spells protecting her as she fought came to her lips with the ease that came with all those many years of fruitless training with her father.

But now, as she finally came into her power, all of those frustrating sessions spent casting spells under her father's tutelage but to no avail came rushing back to her. A magical muscle memory that made her actions as simple as breathing. And this time, the spells worked.

A particularly strong counterattack came from the two casters, forcing Kara to use more force than she wanted to drive them back, but then a barrage of pulse fire peppered the ground at their feet.

Vee may have been a terrible shot, but the weapon she'd taken from a fallen resistance fighter was enough to distract the enemy, giving her friend a breather. But Kara wouldn't let her friend bear all of the risk as the rebels made their escape. Kara once again cast, this time a powerful stun spell that actually managed to disable several of the mercenary forces.

Far above, Malalia was fending off the swarm of ships around her, trying her best not to take out her own craft in the process.

"Idiots! Get out of the way!" she bellowed into her skree, but in the vacuum of space, where there is no up or down, in all of the chaos, none of her captains knew exactly which way out of the way was.

She was using far more power than she would have liked, and if she didn't recharge soon, she might actually find herself in some jeopardy, she realized. That was an odd realization for one so accustomed to possessing such an overwhelming advantage.

Then a sensation hit her. A power user on the surface. A *strong* one. If she could just get to them, that power could help see her through the battle. There was a lot of confusion in the jumbled space battle, and picking her way through it would require concentration, lest her ship take damage she would have to spend even more magic repairing.

Fortunately, her fleet had the advantage. There were simply more of them, and despite the inconvenience Charlie's friends had caused when their paltry forces managed to open the portal, it had only been for a moment, and hardly any of her foes made it through.

Certainly, having Charlie and his Zomoki friend on the battlefield was a game-changing shift, but she still possessed enough power to handle them. And with the might of her fleet bearing down on them, she felt confident in her pending victory.

That is, if nothing went wrong. But with her careful planning, she felt the odds of that were slim to none.

CHAPTER SIXTY-ONE

The swirling mess of space combat was slowly beginning to coalesce into a somewhat organized conflict. The Tslavar captains had been in rather frantic contact at first, but had finally figured out how best to react to their smaller opponents.

While the Zomoki was still a major threat, the Earth craft were more manageable once the magical Tslavar craft were able to join together to overlap their shielding. A Venn Diagram of varied forces strong enough to deflect the majority of their enemies' attacks.

"We're losing ground," Charlie called out. "Everyone, spread wide and try to get flanking shots. They've concentrated their defenses toward the front."

"I can't get close enough to make an attempt on the portal," Rika replied. "You've got to pull them back if you can, or Korbin and I won't be able to reach it."

"I've got you," Marban transmitted, unleashing a furious series of magical attacks, clearing the path, but only partly. There were simply too many for even his commandeered Tslavar warship to handle.

"I appreciate the bravado, Cowboy, but don't get yourself killed on a fool's errand," Rika said. "We need more firepower."

"What's a cowboy?" the pirate replied as he fell back from the failed attempt. "Some sort of hybrid of man and those quadruped animals you said your people used to eat?"

"Seriously?" Rika said with a strained chuckle as she banked the *Fujin* hard, while Jo sprayed pulse fire into a cluster of enemy ships. "I'll explain later. Just follow my lead."

Despite their enthusiasm, the rebel forces were being slowly boxed in, the Tslavar ships finally managing to use their numeric superiority to overwhelm their plucky adversaries. Even with all of the power Charlie and Ara possessed, many of their friends would likely fall if something didn't shift.

Their prayers were unexpectedly answered, not from within their own forces, but from without.

"What the hell?" Rika said as a furious wave of weapons fire tore into Dominus's fleet from all sides. "That's not us."

"We've got you guys!" Ripley's enthused voice called out over their comms. "And we brought friends."

Apparently, her slow trip had met with great success. To say she brought friends was somewhat of an understatement, as the combined fleets of the Chithiid and Urok empires opened up on the startled Tslavar armada. The enemy ships were forced to abruptly break ranks and defend on multiple fronts, their focus shifting in the chaos.

"Rika, get in there, now's your chance!"

"On it, Charlie," she replied. "Korbin, let's go!"

"Follow me in," Marban called out, swinging in front of the two casters, clearing the path far more efficiently now that the enemy was facing a sizable new force. There were still more of the Tslavar ships, but the numbers were now much closer to even.

Had Malalia remained with her fleet, she could have likely prevented the two rebel casters from retrieving the portal, but she was already racing toward Earth's surface, anxious to harvest yet another powerful meal. And that one slip would cost her dearly.

"Pull it!" Rika called out to her magical partner as she reached out for the portal with all of her power.

Korbin joined in, and the desperately scrambling enemy casters were simply unable to stop them this time. Even Charlie was able to direct a portion of his power to aid the cause, while Ara torched those around them, sending them into even more disarray.

The portal, at long last, pulled all the way free of the sun's plasma, and this time it would stay open.

Zed and his entire fleet streamed through from the other galaxy in a flash as soon as they were able, immediately registering and mapping out the location and status of all of the combatants in the conflict they'd flown into with the speed only a team of AI supercomputers could.

Targets acquired, they immediately focused their considerable might on the key Tslavar ships, bombarding them with massive barrages from all manner of weapons, sending the suddenly outnumbered enemy into a frantic retreat.

The Chithiid rebels hiding beneath the surface received the transmission from their comrades above. The time had finally arrived for them to act, and they had a new tool in their arsenal.

The four-armed aliens rushed from the safety of their subterranean staging area beneath Los Angeles and into the fray, swarming the Tslavar mercenary forces who had so recently been making progress against the resistance fighters throughout the city.

But this group of aliens was different. These Chithiid seemed inexplicably able to shrug off the magical attacks being hurled at them, much to the surprise of their Tslavar adversaries. Chithiid simply were not power users. It was a known fact, yet these were somehow casting.

The slender, dark matte-gray bands worn on one of their four arms were foreign objects to the Tslavars, and none would have thought to guess them to be Earth-made nanite konuses. But Joshua's clever devices were churning out a steady stream of defensive energy, allowing the Chithiid forces to focus on fighting rather than hiding from magical attacks.

Relatively protected, they closed the distance like a tsunami wave of angry flesh, and the Tslavar mercenaries soon found themselves unable to cast at all as they were engulfed in a melee of fists and blades, forcing them to rely on the physical combat skills they were so rarely required to employ.

Normally, the mercenaries were more than ready for all comers, but these were unusual enemies. Tall, strong creatures who fought in a vexing style with four arms rather than two. And they were very, very motivated.

Shimmer-cloaked mercenaries, however, were doing what they could to stop the rebel forces, and they were having a fairly good degree of success with it. Four arms or not, it was difficult to fight what you could not see.

The camouflaged fighters were starting to make headway, disrupting the rebel combatants, and if they kept at it, it was only a matter of time before they swayed the fight back in their comrades' favor.

A streaking shape approached in the sky as Eddie and Ripley came swooping in from above, dropping to the surface to discharge their unlikely cargo in a shrieking, bellowing rush of scantily clad, tattooed men wielding spears and arrows.

The Kalamani warriors jumped from the craft before it had even come to a full stop and rushed into the fray, eager for a fight, the pigmented lines around their eyes glowing slightly as their weapons flew true into the seemingly invisible enemy.

Though armed with what were seemingly comically inferior weapons, after the first of the magically charged wooden projectiles sent a Tslavar to the ground, screaming in pain, the mercenaries realized they had better take the strange new adversary *very* seriously.

Arrows and spears flew with great accuracy, and the toxic magic they contained drove the Tslavars back in a rush, even grazing shots being capable of incapacitating the fighters from another galaxy.

Despite having irritated the Kalamani elders on the occasion of their first meeting, Ripley had nevertheless returned to their world to humbly seek their assistance. The elders, while still not terribly fond of the rather gregarious youth, knew she was one of Rika's tribe. And if *she* needed help, they would respond.

The flight in a spaceship was an utterly novel experience for them, but the elders were in for an even greater surprise when they arrived back in Earth's solar system. The battle in space unfolding before them made the true scale of the conflict threatening their entire galaxy painfully clear. Ripley had not been exaggerating. This was a catastrophe in the making, and they had to do all they could to help.

The elders were quickly deposited aboard Zed to observe the battle from the safest, most heavily armed ship in the fleet, while their warriors were quickly ferried to the surface. Streaming images the likes of which they'd never before seen allowed them to witness their fighters' progress as they engaged the enemy. The amazing technology was a marvel for them, but they readily accepted it and moved on. They could learn how it all worked at a later time. For now, a battle was underway.

In the swirling chaos of the space battle, Olo was leading a massive charge into the heart of the enemy craft, doing as much damage as a pilot of his skill could manage, which was a substantial amount. But even someone of his talents could only do so much when outnumbered to the degree he found himself, when an entire wing of enemy craft suddenly targeted his ship, deeming him to be one of the major threats on the battlefield.

"I'm in trouble here," the blue-skinned smuggler reluctantly transmitted, loathe to admit he needed help. "There are too many of them on my back!"

"I can't get to you," Charlie said. "We're boxed out. Who's close?"

A prolonged silence hung in the air. Everyone was quite busy, their hands more than full with the scores of enemy fighters of their own.

"Hold on. I've got you," a familiar voice called out as a small, fast ship cleared the portal and joined the fight, weapons blazing. "Just hang on."

"Tym?" Olo said, shocked. "You're alive!"

"You didn't think I'd let you fight all of these Tslavar scum and pad your score, did you?" he joked, blasting an enemy craft from his friend's tail. "That's one, by the way. And you're welcome."

"Oh, it's going to be that way, is it?" Olo replied with joy in his heart.

"You know it is," the oddball pilot replied with a laugh as he shot another ship from the sky. "And that's two."

The ships on Olo's tail peeled off, recognizing a new threat on the playing field, and one that appeared just as talented and dangerous as the one they were currently chasing. The two friends spun and pursued the scrambling Tslavar craft, quickly shifting from defense to offense in a flash, doing what they did best.

In the cold of space, another startling attack was underway, though in a far different environment. On the surface of the moon, Dark Side base sat quiet, Sid refraining from reacting lest the captive humans and Chithiid held there face retribution. But he knew it would be time soon. All he needed was the signal.

A dozen shimmer-cloaked Wampeh sped through his hallways, silently slaughtering every Tslavar invader they came across, while the AI watched on his monitoring system. Once they were safely gathered in the holding area, he could act.

It was almost comical how outclassed the mercenaries were, and the Wampeh, freed from the constraints of silent assassination, moved with a quickness that made Sid wonder if he'd even need to enact his part of the plan.

"We are all present in the holding area," a Wampeh said to his surveillance monitor as he slipped free of his shimmer cloak.

"Thank you," Sid replied. "Sealing you in."

The heavy doors slammed shut and locked, all of the prisoners and their unlikely rescuers now safely contained within.

"Purging."

It was an emergency protocol put in place after a breach to his facility many years prior. One that Sid hoped he would never need to use. But today, it seemed its time had come. In an instant, the base's airlocks opened to space, voiding the facility of air and sucking a good many of the Tslavar forces into the vacuum of space.

"Repressurizing," Sid announced. "It's safe," he said a few moments later as he opened the holding area's doors.

The Wampeh took off once more, this time to finish off any stragglers who might have had the opportunity to cast an emergency containment spell around themselves. But only a handful had been so fortunate, and their good fortune was as short-lived as they were.

"Cal, this is Sid," the AI transmitted to Earth. "Dark Side is ours again."

CHAPTER SIXTY-TWO

Visla Dominus had already flown right past the moon and its base in her rush to Earth. Had she but known her forces were being slaughtered so close, she might have detoured to vanquish their attackers. But she was of a singular focus as she raced to the source of the delectable power she sensed on the surface.

This was something she could harvest, and it was substantially more than all but her most powerful casters had fed her. Little did she know, it was her own stepdaughter she would soon be facing.

Her ship flashed through the sky in a bright streak, descending rapidly toward the source of the magic she so craved. It was in the city known as Los Angeles, she noted. Funny, how so many occurrences seemed to focus on this particular area. It was enough to make her wonder if perhaps there was some form of Earth magic at play that she was simply unaware of. A force shaping events that she'd missed.

It was of no matter, though. Not now. Not when her meal was so close.

Malalia dropped her ship to the ground, her Tslavar forces immediately forming a protective line, their overlapping spells doing what they could to protect their visla as she exited her craft, though she did not remotely need their assistance. But it was their part to serve, and serve they would.

There had been two casters with this group of mercenaries, Malalia recalled. Emmiks, both of them, but fairly powerful. Yet she saw no sign of them on the battlefield. Or so she thought before recognizing an elongated leg belonging to one of them protruding from beneath a pile of debris. Someone had toppled a building atop her, it seemed.

The blue-gray smear on the ground and pool of similarly colored blood pooling nearby relayed a similar fate for the emmik's associate. Someone had taken out both of her casters. *This* was interesting. The power Malalia had sensed was not one of her own, but a rebel.

"Excellent," she muttered with a hungry grin. She wouldn't have to hold back at all, in that case. This one, she could drain dry.

Furious fighting told her all she needed to know to pinpoint her prey. Tslavars were flying through the air, engaging their foe, but failing horribly. Magic was hurling them to and fro like rag dolls as native pulse weapon fire drove them back, preventing their proper casting of defensive spells.

It was a clever bit of tactics, Malalia had to admit. A melding of local tech and magic that her mercenaries seemed to have difficulty adjusting to. But she was no mercenary. She was Visla Dominus. And it was time to put an end to this little squabble.

"Stay here," Malalia told Grundsch, then powered up her defensive spells and strode around the fallen building debris to face her next meal.

Her feet slid backward on the concrete gravel as a massive blast of magic impacted her shielding, blasting her Tslavar retinue so violently that most would likely not recover from the blow. Malalia was actually surprised. The magic was far more than even she had expected, and had her protective spells been any lower, she'd likely have suffered a fair bit of harm from it.

More shocking, however, was the *taste* of the magic. She knew this power. But it *couldn't* be.

Kara stood across the roadway, her back straight and her eyes blazing with defiance, a crackling magic flickering from her fingertips. Like father, like daughter, it appeared.

"Hello, dearest," Malalia said, carefully increasing her protective spells. "My, my, haven't you matured quickly."

"No surprise, without you stealing all of my power from me," Kara spat.

"Oh, darling, I never took *all* of your power. I just took what I needed."

Something behind Kara gleamed in the sunlight, making Malalia almost lose her concentration. Vee, her long golden hair tied out of the way in a hasty braid and carrying an Earth weapon in her hands, stepped beside Kara, ready to fight.

"Oh, and you have little Visanya with you," Malalia cooed. "How delightful. You know, I always knew what you were, but there was no need to tap into that precious resource. Not then, anyway. But now, I am finally going to harvest you after all of these patient years," she said. "Your first cut, and it will be mine."

Vee didn't hesitate, firing off a series of shots from the pulse rifle. She'd been getting better as the fighting raged on, and her aim was true, but Malalia's power was far too great for something as simple as a pulse rifle to pierce.

"Kara? What do we do?" Vee said as her target chuckled at the failed attempt.

"I've got this," the teen replied, then cast a fierce attack at her stepmother.

This time, however, the woman was ready for her, and the counterstrike not only disrupted her spell, but nearly knocked both teens from their feet. Malalia was far too strong, and even though she'd been expending an enormous amount of her magic, she was still much more powerful than Kara.

"Silly child. While I do admire your pluck, you really leave me no choice but to drain you dry," she said, her fangs sliding into place in a frightening grin as she began walking toward them.

Kara and Vee were out of options. Any moment now, they would become the playthings of Visla Dominus. And that would be the end of them.

Vee pulled the enchanted blade from its sheath.

"I don't think that's going to stop her," Kara said.

"No. But this might," Vee replied, grabbing her hair and slicing the braid from her head in a single stroke. "Freely given," she said, handing it to Kara.

The teen felt a shocking surge of power race through her body when the hair touched her hand. The first cut was the most powerful, and this hair had been absorbing Earth's sun for some time, not to mention that it was freely given. And with the affection of deep friendship and love between them. It wasn't the same degree as Hunze's for Bawb, but it was enough to render the young woman's hair incredibly potent.

Malalia blanched when she saw what was happening, but the spells she frantically cast weren't fast enough to overcome Kara's instantaneous defenses. And this time, they were enough to hold her stepmother's spells back, despite her incredible power.

Kara and Vee locked eyes a moment, then the visla's daughter turned all of her attention to her stepmother, casting spell after spell at her, bombarding the much stronger woman with a furious and unrelenting attack.

If the girl had been older and had fully come into her power, there might have been a very real possibility of her holding off the mighty Visla Dominus, but even with the enormous power of the Ootaki hair in her grasp, she simply lacked the internal magic of a fully grown visla. Slowly, spell by spell, her opponent was wearing her down.

Far above, orbiting the sun, Charlie, Ara, and Leila were finally putting their combined powers to good use, grinding down the remaining Tslavar, fleet much like Malalia was overpowering the teen far below.

Ara and Charlie were casting strong, using a carefully devised spell to disable as many Tslavars as possible while sparing their Drooks, who were in no way willing combatants. It took some effort and precision, but it was working. It did, however, leave them open to attack. But Leila had finally come to gain control of her Magus stone, and it was projecting an impenetrable shell around them, sparing them from attacks, while also disabling any foolish enough to fly close.

The sun's portal was finally back in Earth's defensive forces' control, and it was going to stay that way.

CHAPTER SIXTY-THREE

The portal was well clear of the sun, and Visla Dominus's casters had been driven away. The risk of their forcing it closed again had passed, and even if they did, it was too late. Earth's fleet had crossed back over, and their might, combined with that of the Chithiid and Urok empires, was quite enough to hand the Tslavar armada a handy defeat.

Rika and Korbin were relaxing their grips on the portal when a fast and expensive craft blasted across the portal, making a beeline straight toward Earth. Rika sent out hails on both comms and skree, then took off after them, the two ships blazing a trail to the third planet from the sun.

On Earth's surface, in the city of LA, Kara had nearly drained her friend's gifted braid of Ootaki hair, her own power already dangerously low. Malalia had simply feasted on too many power users over the ages, and as a result, her reserves upon which she could draw were vast.

"I can't stop her," Kara said, struggling against another spell thrown at her and her friend.

"I know," Vee replied. "But we tried."

Kara looked at the braid in her hands. "I can't let her have this, Vee. She'll use it for evil."

Visanya knew her friend was right, and the Earth's sun would replenish the hair's strength soon enough. But what could they do? It seemed likely they would fall to Kara's stepmother regardless, and all of this fighting had been for nothing.

Kara began unbraiding the hair, while using the last of her power to protect herself and Vee.

"What are you doing?" Vee asked.

"Just get ready to run."

Even Malalia was curious about the teen's actions, easing up her attack enough to perhaps pose a sarcastic question to her troublesome stepchild. But Kara beat her to it, pulling free a golden lock of hair and throwing it to the ground.

"What ever are you––?" Malalia said, just as Kara cast the simple, little spell that was one of the first she had learned as a child.

The hair burst into flames, crinkling and fizzing in a flash, then reducing to no more than a small pile of smelly ash.

"What are you doing!" Malalia shouted.

"Stop, or I burn it all," Kara replied.

Vee smiled. "Burn it all. At least *she* won't have it."

"Wait!" Malalia called out. "We can work something out."

The desperation was palpable. She was still strong, for sure, but with her forces facing a rout, and having already fed from her most powerful casters, the great and mighty Visla Dominus was running out of options to replenish her power.

Kara stopped, holding the unbraided hair in one hand, the other ready to direct a fire spell in an instant if needed, when a shadow flashed overhead. The shape of two craft, one from each galaxy, passed overhead, growing rapidly closer.

The magic ship dropped to the surface on the side of the roadway nearest Malalia, while Rika and the *Fujin* landed near

Kara and Vee. The tattooed pilot jumped from her ship and rushed to the teenagers' side, her magical ink glowing a faint purple as she cast a spell at Malalia as fierce as her hate-filled stare.

Malalia defended herself and locked magical horns with the deadly Earth woman. Her magic was incredibly difficult to counter, but Malalia still had power, and she felt certain she could still take her.

It would be a costly battle, but her former servant would not win the day. But more importantly, the ship that had just landed beside her was a Palmarian ship. One of hers. She let a smile of relief flash across her lips.

Reinforcements had finally arrived, and with them, she would make these rebellious fools suffer. And if for some reason she couldn't, she would at least burn it all down in her defeat.

The ship's doorway opened, and a tall figure stepped out into the daylight. Captain Sandah. He didn't possess any power she could feast on, but surely he had brought others with.

Sure enough, more forms emerged from behind him. Surprisingly, Shozzy, the former captain of the Palmarian guards, stepped out of the craft, followed by a woman she did not know. A woman who possessed some power. A healer, it seemed. A woman with pale-blue hair.

"Amazara?" Kara gasped.

Malalia's smile faltered. A moment later it fell from her face entirely as a broad-shouldered man strode into the open air. A man with a furious power crackling from his entire body.

"Father!" Kara shouted with pure joy.

Visla Nikora Palmarian was not at his full strength––Malalia could sense that much––but he had recovered tremendously in the relatively short time since she left him on what should have been his death bed. That explained the healer's presence.

She had absorbed so much power that there was a good chance she could best him in single combat in his reduced state, but for the first time in longer than she could remember, Malalia felt actual fear knot up her stomach.

Her husband glared at her, well aware now of what his wife had been doing to him and his daughter for so many years. What she had been up to behind his back. And all this time, he had been quietly trying to stymie the machinations of the troublesome Visla Dominus, working behind the scenes with his network of powerful men and women to keep their realms safe and free.

Little did he know, it was his own wife who was behind the entire affair the whole time, her enormous powers masked from him.

Visla Palmarian didn't say a word. He didn't have to. Fierce magic blasted forth, buffeting his wife as she strained to hold back the force of it. She was pulling deep from her well of magic, using all she could to counter him. He was so very strong, as she well knew, but his powers were still recovering.

A warm feeling of pending victory flushed in her chest, and she smiled to herself. Yes, she would be able to best him, and when she did, she would make her escape, taking him and any other casters she could capture to hide and slowly rebuild her power.

Visla Palmarian felt his power waning. He'd been careful to conserve his energy as Amazara healed him over the past several weeks, but even so, he was experiencing a feeling he hadn't felt since childhood. Inadequacy.

Malalia was going to win. And she knew it.

Or so she thought.

Four Wampeh Ghalian masters appeared around her, having taken full advantage of her singular focus on her opponent to approach in their shimmer cloaks, undetected. She only had a moment to register their presence when she felt four hard, blunt lengths of metal jam into her torso. With them, her power vanished, as if a balloon had abruptly popped, letting out all of its magical contents.

The power was redirected across the planet, releasing all of the control collars she had placed on her new subjects far and wide. It was an enormous surge to span the globe like that, and it pulled far more from her than would normally be considered safe.

The Bakana rods, however, simply did as their wielders wished, and all four masters focused on pulling power from just one source, channeling it and blasting it out far and wide. Their task accomplished, the assassins then stepped back, allowing the formerly powerful woman to stagger from the magic loss.

Malalia was panicked. She had never been without at least some power, even as a small child. But now, she was just a regular woman. But Visla Dominus was nothing if not wily, and she would at least take someone down with her if she fell. A glowing blade appeared in her hand, drawn from a sheath hidden on her person.

Rika's glowing tattoos slowly faded as her eyes hardened their gaze. A little smile creased the corner of her lips as she pulled her own enchanted blade and strode toward the woman who had done so much harm to her life.

"Oh, little one, you wish to test your mettle against me?" Malalia hissed. "You will find I am far more difficult a––"

Rika's fist slammed into her face, breaking her nose and sending her toppling to the ground. "I'm sorry, were you still talking?" she said as she kicked the blade from her dazed opponent's hand.

Rika then tossed her own knife aside and rolled her shoulders in anticipation. They were going to do this the hard way. No weapons. No power. Just a good, old-fashioned ass kicking.

Malalia scrambled to her feet and lunged at her former slave, her hands shaped into claws, slashing furiously at her opponent. Rika, however, was ready for her, dodging aside and landing a staggering kick to Malalia's thigh, cramping the muscle from the impact.

Rather than press the attack, she stepped back, allowing her opponent to recover a moment. She would not end this quickly. Malalia didn't deserve such mercy.

A small crowd had begun to form. Marban had landed nearby to witness the face-off, and even Ara and her passengers were now perched atop a nearby structure, watching with great interest, as were the assembled survivors of the Tslavar attack. Even her Ra'az henchman had joined the group and was now standing beside the space pirate.

"Do something, Grundsch!" Malalia bellowed.

All eyes turned to the large alien. "I am," he replied. "I'm enjoying the show."

Marban couldn't help but laugh, elbowing the man Malalia thought was his enemy. "Good one, Grundsch," he said, making the alien's true alliance abundantly clear.

Focused on the fight at hand, Rika and Malalia circled one another slowly. The visla's power was gone, but her confidence and rage weren't. Malalia threw a series of punches, forcing Rika to quickly block and evade the attack.

"I trained you. I made you what you are," she hissed. "You think a lucky shot means anything? You cannot possibly hope to——"

Rika's foot connected with the woman's ribs, driving the air out of her and sending her to her knees.

"Again with the talking. Tsk, tsk," the pilot chided.

Enraged, Malalia forced herself to her feet and attacked once more, utilizing a flashy series of moves that would very likely have landed on a lesser opponent. But Rika batted them aside, responding with a flurry of punches to the face, followed by a sharp elbow and then a powerful knee driven into Malalia's chest, leaving her gasping for air.

Rika didn't stop. Not this time. She pressed the attack, pummeling Malalia relentlessly, but nothing that would knock her out. Nothing to end her misery. She wanted her to feel every blow. Payback for all she'd done to her.

Finally, after lessening her strikes to no more than a series of humiliating slaps, Rika grabbed the dazed woman and pulled her close.

"I win," Rika said, then, at last, for a short while, anyway, put Malalia out of her misery with a vicious headbutt.

Rika loosened her grip and let the woman fall to the ground. But she wouldn't kill her. No. Living powerless would be a far greater punishment than a quick death.

"You deserved worse, bitch," she said, then walked away, leaving Malalia unconscious in the dirt.

"That was wonderfully violent," Marban greeted her with a broad grin. "Ooh, you've got a little blood on you. Let me get that." He carefully dabbed the splatter from her forehead, sharing a warm look. "You want to get something to eat? You must be hungry after that."

Rika smiled and took his hand. "Lead the way, big guy."

CHAPTER SIXTY-FOUR

The Tslavar survivors knew they were beaten even before they saw their visla fall. A teenager, of all things, had handed them a resounding defeat. If that wasn't bad enough, the pair of enormous animals that flanked them, but did not tear them to bits, made their situation abundantly clear. They were prisoners, and they'd be wise not to make any sudden movements.

Though he was finishing off some aerial combatants, Korbin had seen the girls' predicament and had called the two canines back into the city to assist. And while their final destination was guided by their konus collars, he did not restrict them from having their bloody fun with any mercenaries who might cross their path on the way.

The collars provided precisely the magical protection he had hoped they would, and the Tslavar spells cast in a desperate attempt to slow the beasts had absolutely no effect on them. And the casters soon met a rather gruesome end.

Korbin dropped down as soon as he was able, rushing to the battlefield to catch the end of Rika's cathartic face-off, and it was as satisfying as he'd hoped it would be.

As soon as the fight was through, Kara raced into her father's arms, hugging him with a ferocity that took him by surprise. "You're all right! And you came!"

"Yes, Karasalia, thanks to you and your friends," he replied, nodding toward Amazara. "You did well, daughter. It was an inspired plan, you had, and it worked. Shozzy received your unusual message, and after a little digging, realized what was truly going on in my own home. I was in a bad way, but he secreted me from the tower just as your healer friend arrived."

"She was feeding off of us for years."

"I know," he replied. "And, I'm ashamed to say, I was unaware of her true nature, despite our closeness."

"But you wouldn't have. She was so powerful, she could mask it," Kara replied.

"Perhaps, but she was taking my daughter's power. And I was hard on you for it. For your lack of casting ability. But it was never your fault. I'm so sorry, Karasalia."

"It's okay, Father, I understand."

"But how did you progress so rapidly?"

"Uncle Korbin helped me. And all of the lessons you taught me, of course. I just needed my own power to emerge."

"Apparently. And look at you now," he said, beaming with pride. "I witnessed your display as we approached the city. A true Palmarian, Karasalia. You did well."

Korbin and his old friend locked gazes across the roadway. Kara's father gave him an appreciative nod as he held his daughter close. Korbin felt a great satisfaction, but the joy of that paled compared to the feeling he experienced when he saw Amazara standing there, her pale-blue hair bright in the Earth's sunlight.

He walked directly to her. After all they had just been through, he was through playing the stoic bachelor. Life was too precious and short for games.

"I see you're well," the healer said.

"Better now," he replied with a gaze that spoke almost as loud as the ships blasting by overhead.

"You're hurt," Amazara said, noting a scrape on his arm. "Let me see."

Korbin ignored the little injury and pulled her close, making his intentions, and affections perfectly clear. When they finally broke from one another, Amazara's eyes were damp, and not from sadness.

"We have things to discuss," she said.

"And plenty of time to discuss them," he replied.

That evening, victory firmly in hand, the scrappy band of rebel forces gathered in the largest park space in downtown for a celebratory feast organized by Ripley's father. This was too much for him to prepare on his own, however, and assistance had been provided by talented hands and palates from across the city.

The result was an impressive spread covering a wide variety of culinary styles. Even the Kalamani had participated, enjoying the novel experience of experimenting with entirely new foods, as well as taking in the marvels of this planet's fascinating structures.

Ripley was thrilled to see her loved ones reunited, and she was endlessly amused watching Grundsch feed scraps to the two enormous beasts hanging out at his feet. Leila, for her part, was happy to see Baloo so content with new members of his pack. She would always be his mama, but he had new friends to play with now, and his extended family was all the better for it.

Kara and Arlo had migrated away from the main party a ways and were enjoying one another's company over plates of home-cooked deliciousness. Vee watched from a distance, picking at her food, hungry, but also not. It had been a particularly traumatic day for her. She'd harvested her own hair, and while it was hers to give, her identity as an Ootaki was bound to it. As a result, despite their victory, she nevertheless felt a wide range of emotions coursing through her.

"Hey, Vee," Ripley greeted, plopping down beside her. "Cute haircut."

"You think so?" Vee replied, brightening slightly.

"Oh yeah. That's a bangin' style," the teen replied. "I was meaning to ask you, why did you grow it so long, anyway?"

"We all do. It's always been the Ootaki way."

"What? Just because you're expected to do what everyone else does? Weird," Ripley replied. "It doesn't matter what everyone expects of you, ya know. Your hair doesn't define you. And, seriously, this haircut is way cuter."

Vee felt the fog of depression begin to lift a bit more.

"Ladies, how are we doing this fine evening?" Sergeant Franklin asked, sidling up to the pair.

"All's good, George," Ripley replied. "But what's that smell? Suddenly, I find myself craving barbecue."

The somewhat scorched spec-ops cyborg chuckled. "Wow, you actually went there."

"Yep."

"Hey, it's not my fault. I haven't been able to break free to get to the flesh fabrication lab yet. I mean, we only just won this afternoon."

"You really should get that taken care of, George, or you're gonna make people hungry wherever you go."

"You two," Vee chuckled.

The girls looked over at Arlo and Kara sitting at the edge of the festivities and shared an amused look.

"Come on, Vee. Let's go harass my cousin."

CHAPTER SIXTY-FIVE

The following morning Malalia Maktan found herself bound by magical restraints and in front of a tribunal consisting of denizens of both galaxies she'd threatened with her plans. The magic wasn't really required, though, as the Wampeh had paid her another visit, draining her power once more, just to ensure there would be no unpleasant surprises.

She'd amassed so much magic over the years, there really was no telling how quickly her own naturally occurring power might return after being drained. There had simply never been an entity like her. The additional power was long gone, but she was a Maktan, and that meant danger any way you looked at it.

Though there were facilities perfectly suited to healing the injuries she'd sustained in her fight with Rika, Malalia was brought to the hearing with every last one of her bruises intact. They were essentially tiny purple badges of shame serving as testimonial to Rika's rather thorough ass whooping.

She sat quietly before the tribunal, her head hung low, her will as broken as her power had been. Malalia Maktan was no longer a threat, and, though she had committed countless atrocities in her lengthy life, the adjudicators were nevertheless true to their natures. Merciful, fair, and just.

The trial was more for show than anything else. Malalia's actions under the moniker of Visla Dominus were myriad, and the testimonies of witnesses from many worlds spread across both galaxies all painted the same damning picture. She was power hungry. Ruthless. Dangerous. And if she were allowed to roam free, there was little doubt she would make some future attempt to overthrow her enemies once again.

And so, a decision was made.

"Malalia Maktan," Admiral Harkaway said. "You have been found guilty of all charges against you, many of which carry the penalty of death."

At that, a bit of her familiar spirit returned as she looked up with hate in her eyes. "Do your worst," she dared them all.

Admiral Harkaway merely smiled serenely from her seat on the bench. "Oh, we will," she replied. "But I do not think you will find our interpretation of that word to mean what you think it does. Take her away."

The bailiff for this particular event was an exceedingly large man. One who had once been under her thumb.

"As you wish," Grundsch replied, then hauled his former owner to her feet and ushered her from the chamber to have her microchip transmitter implanted deep in her femur.

Malalia was not going to be executed, though many wished for it. Instead, she was fitted with a tracker capable of reporting not only her location and health status, but also her magical power levels, should she ever find means to increase them once more.

There had simply been too many years of Wampeh blood pumped into her system for them to be sure she could no longer steal the power of others, so a decision had been made.

She would be exiled to a remote planet in an otherwise

uninhabited solar system in this galaxy. There was magic present on the selected world, but it was of this galaxy, and thus toxic to a woman of her nature. She could live in peace, but there were simply no magical beings she could feed from, and no hope of any visitors she could dupe into helping her.

She would not be sentenced to die, but, rather, sentenced to live.

And if by some crazy fluke she found a way off of the planet, the small satellite left in orbit would immediately alert the AI network, who would promptly zero in on the tracker buried in her bone and either return her to her open-air prison or end her.

It was more than she deserved, a comfortable and relatively long life, but it was a just sentence. And as the stolen Wampeh Ghalian power slowly purged from her system, the very real question of her mortality arose. Just how long her lifespan would be once the artificially augmenting power was gone was anyone's guess. But she'd be monitored, and whatever the outcome, it would be discovered soon enough.

Once her sentence was passed, Malalia was loaded onto a ship that had once been her very own, Captain Sandah himself piloting it to its destination. Before he left, however, the captain made a point to track down his former passenger.

Leila wasn't hard to find. In fact, she had been an important part of the tribunal, having known Malalia since childhood.

"I am sorry for what befell you," the captain said when he found her in the antechamber. "I know it is not enough to say I was following orders, but I at least want you to hear it from my lips that I never wished you any harm."

Leila rested her hand on the man's shoulder. "It was a difficult position you were put in. But you showed your true self when you spared Baloo's life. Any doubts I may have had were removed when I found him alive and well."

The captain's jaw flexed slightly, but his slightly glistening eyes held back the emotion welling within him. "Thank you," he said with a slightly gruff tone from his tightening throat. "You do not know how this has weighed upon me."

"I can imagine. Now, you've got a passenger to deliver, but please, fly safe, and do so with my friendship."

The captain nodded, then headed off to his ship, leaving Leila to discuss the other pending business with the leaders of both galaxies. But before that was underway, a lunch break was in order. And she had something very important to follow-up on with Amazara as well.

Later, she found Charlie sitting with the eldest Wampeh master, having a relaxed conversation over a cup of tea. Farmatta smiled warmly as she saw Leila approaching.

"Lovely to see you, dear," she said.

It was hard to tell if the sweet, grandmotherly welcome was truly sincere, or if the assassin had been putting on that act for so many years she simply couldn't *not* do it. Whatever the case, Leila was glad to see her as well.

"I heard that one of your Wampeh friends is being recovered from Malalia's cells. I hope he'll recover."

"Oh, we are a resilient lot," Farmatta replied with a smile. "I'm sure Pimbrak will be back to himself, eventually. He's a tough one. It will just take time and rest."

"So, have the Wampeh Ghalian all returned home?" Leila asked.

"Yes," Farmatta replied with a little grin. "Most of us, anyway. A few are still lingering, taking in this new galaxy. A fascinating realm, for certain."

"I've grown quite fond of it," Leila replied. "And I seem to have finally come into my own, power-wise."

"Yes, and I've been meaning to ask you about that stone of yours," Farmatta said, gesturing to the Magus stone hanging from her neck.

If anyone else had made that comment, Leila might have felt a pang of defensive fear that they would try to steal it. But this was Farmatta. Not only one of Bawb's colleagues, but a woman so deadly if she wanted to take the stone she could have done so long ago.

"It was my mother's," Leila said, removing the green pendant from her neck and handing it to the woman. "But I'd never been able to make it work. Not until now, that is."

Farmatta studied the item a long moment before handing it back. "Yes, I know this stone. One of the few possessed by the Alatsav royals, if I recall correctly. Notoriously quirky, that batch. Incredible power, but they were known for sometimes going entire generations without doing a damn thing."

Charlie chuckled. "Sounds about right."

Leila elbowed her king. "Hey, it works now."

"Yeah. You just don't know why."

Farmatta's laugh was definitely no act. "Oh, you two. I can see why you bonded. But you know, these stones often only engage with the right user at the right time, and only under a rather unusual set of circumstances. And quite intense."

"Like what we just endured?"

"Yes. Which were just the right ones to tie you to its power," the Wampeh replied.

"They were definitely unusual and intense," Leila noted. "No wonder neither my grandmother nor mother could use it. Not even to escape their slavery."

"Apparently not. But it is a powerful tool, tied to your bloodline. And you wield it well," Farmatta noted.

"Yes," Leila said, fixing her gaze on Charlie. "And hopefully our daughter will learn to wield it as well."

Charlie did a double-take. "I'm sorry, did you say *daughter*?"

Leila's smile grew. "So Amazara says," she replied, glowing with joy from the healer's observation.

Charlie pulled her close and held her tight, basking in the warmth of their love. "Wow," he managed.

"Yeah, I know," Leila replied.

Her man took a deep breath as it all sank in. Then, as always, his practical mind set to work. "So, the obvious question now is, do we raise her in my galaxy or yours?" he said.

Leila nestled in close. "Why not both?"

CHAPTER SIXTY-SIX

Nearly a month had passed since Malalia Maktan was banished to the boring hell of her own uninhabited planet. Her power seemed to have been returning at a steady pace, but none of the additional abilities she'd stolen from so many of her victims appeared to be resurgent. And as far as she was from civilization, it appeared she would have a long and dull life to herself on the little world.

The portal, now solidly under the allied control of a mix of forces from both sides, was not only being guarded from unlawful use, but was also being kept open at all times. A bridge between worlds as those in control gradually decided upon the best way to merge both civilizations, slowly so as to avoid any major issues.

Eventually, citizens of the magical side would learn about technology and its marvels, and those from the tech side would learn the ways of magic. It was going to be a wild ride, for sure, and there would be plenty of hiccups, but a small group of what were essentially intergalactic chaperones was in the making. Multi-cultural tour guides of a sort, eager to help smooth the transition as the new alliances grew.

Ara had just returned to Earth after having been gone since just after the tribunal. It had been an unexpected trip, but she told Charlie she had things she needed to do, and who was he to protest? Regardless, it was heartwarming for him having her back. Though Bawb and Hunze had safely returned to Earth several weeks prior, Charlie couldn't help but feel a bit empty, minus such a big piece of his life for so long. But now she was back, his friends were happy and healthy, and his queen was doing just fine. Life was good, and this would suffice.

They'd healed up well, but the bangs and bruises they'd all suffered during the course of the battles to reclaim the portal and conquer Visla Dominus once and for all had been many. Too many for the saviors of the Earth, and several times, at that. Once they'd finally recovered, thanks to Cal's marvelous tech, Fatima had a suggestion.

The ancient woman barely looked a day over sixty, thanks to her unique genetic repair technique developed in the long years spent alone on Dark Side base. She simply could not utilize a stasis pod, and thus, had to find another way to survive. The result was a greatly extended lifespan, her mitochondria rejuvenated, and the damaged strands of her DNA snipped and kept healthy through novel stem cell treatments.

It was something she and the AIs who were privy to her process had kept secret all these long years, having decided it was better if people aged normally, using cryo-stasis if they wished to slow the process for lengthy transit. But after the battle, it was decided that the minds that had seen them to victory might be useful a while longer than their normal lifespans.

And so it came to pass that the gene-altering tech was offered to a select group of the best of the best. But only those over forty. Any younger and the risk of stunting the natural growth of both body and mind was deemed too much of a risk.

That, and it would be strange for young parents to find themselves the same age as their children in short order.

Youngsters needed to grow naturally to become who they were meant to be. "Fully cooked," as Finn would joke. And the teens who caught wind of the secret process, as clever kids were wont to do, were okay with it.

Arlo and Kara had spent an increasing amount of time with one another since the hostilities ended, and they were enjoying one another's company yet again on this outing, frolicking in the shallow waters of the Pacific, while Vee and Ripley sat with her mom and Aunt Daisy, snacking on the epic picnic Finn and her Uncle Vince had prepared for them.

Charlie and his friends lay sprawled out on beach towels, enjoying the relaxing sea breeze and distinct lack of fighting after so long in the thick of it.

"You good, man?" he asked the pale Wampeh who never tanned no matter how long they sat out in the sun.

"Fantastic," Bawb replied with an air of utter contentment as he warmly squeezed the hand of the golden-haired woman at his side and cast a loving glance her way. Briefly, of course.

He was a Wampeh Ghalian. The most feared assassins in *two* galaxies. He couldn't be too obvious in his affections, after all. The glistening ring on Hunze's finger, however, was a sign that was a bit hard to miss.

"Better than fantastic, I would argue," Hunze said with a radiant grin.

"I defer to your wisdom, dearest," he replied with a sparkle in his eye.

Bawb had gone many sleepless nights keeping watch over his love while she healed from her time under Malalia's control. And when Hunze had finally recovered from her ordeal, having soaked up the sun's rays like a greedy sponge in a healing pool of warm happiness, he had asked her a question. A simple one with but two answers.

She had said yes.

It was a formality, of course. They were bonded in ways far stronger than mere words and rings could accomplish. But they were citizens of Earth as much as anywhere now, and the small beachfront ceremony with their closest of friends had been a welcome event. One that had helped them return to some semblance of normalcy after what they'd just endured.

And now, the extended family unit was free to enjoy their beachside respite. Even Cal was present, transmitted to them over Freya's external comms, the stealth ship and the other AIs in her family resting on the sand with those they held dear.

"It is a given," Cal said. *"Eventually, there will be conflict. It is unavoidable."*

"Yeah, but c'mon, Cal. It's going to be a while, at least," Charlie said. "Bob? Daze? Vince? Come on, guys. I'm right, right?"

"Yeah, I think he's got a point, Cal," Vince replied. "Babe, don't you agree? The odds of anyone just stumbling upon the portal and starting trouble are pretty damn slim."

Daisy couldn't help but agree with her man. "Unlikely, sure. But you know Murphy. Don't go tempting him."

"With all I have witnessed of your Murphy, I would consider that a valid concern," Bawb noted with a wry grin.

"The Geist has a point," Ara chuckled.

"But we will need to prepare just the same. And with this intergalactic merging of societies, there are bound to be issues stretching the resources of both our realms."

"Are you suggesting what I think you're suggesting?" Charlie asked.

"If you are thinking we will need to structure a new force of peacekeepers to manage problems on either side of the portal, be they magical or technological, then yes."

"I don't know, Cal. I mean, sure, there'll be all sorts of crazy issues to handle, but what can we do, really?" Charlie said. "Ara, any suggestions?"

The Zomoki smiled, amusement in her golden eyes. "There was a group millennia ago. They kept the peace through their presence alone. A powerful force patrolling my galaxy."

"The Zomoki Riders of Parnasus?" Marban said, sitting up on his beach towel.

"The what?" Charlie asked.

"A legendary force, Little Brother. But they've not existed for ages."

"True," Ara said.

"And you are the last of the Old Ones," Bawb added.

"From our galaxy, yes," she replied. "But the Kalamani had a legend. And legends, I've found, are often based in reality."

Ara then shot forth a massive stream of magical flames high into the sky. Moments later, dozens of tiny spots of flame high above appeared in response. A swirling mass of winged creatures began rapidly descending toward the surface.

"Holy shit, Daze. Do you see this?" Sarah blurted in Daisy's head just as the flesh-and-blood Sarah said pretty much the same thing aloud.

"Yeah, and I don't believe it," she replied.

Charlie stared in awe at the approaching beasts. They were massive, though not quite as big as Ara, and they were gorgeous.

"Zomoki? Here?" Charlie gasped.

"Not Zomoki, though. Cousins, actually. Natives of a far corner of this realm," Ara replied. "And since they're from your galaxy, I suppose you might as well call them dragons, if you prefer."

Sure enough, dozens of honest-to-God dragons flapped hard, kicking up sand along the beach in all directions as they landed, their weight shaking the ground upon their arrival.

"This is Orgalius," Ara said, introducing the largest of the newly arrived dragons.

He was an impressive specimen, a deep, cobalt blue with bright, platinum eyes.

"A pleasure," he said with an unusual accent.

"I-I can understand you," Vee said.

"Yes, my translation spells are similar to Ara's in that regard," he replied with a rumbling chuckle. "From what I've learned, though our magic is quite different in casting and power type, it functions rather similarly."

"So. Freaking. Cool!" Ripley nearly shrieked with delight.

"So, you see, we have the resources after all," Ara said, clearly amused at the utter shock of her friends. "And all we need now is to develop a new set of rules to govern both realms, and then organize our assets to enforce them."

"Dragon cops?" Charlie asked with an incredulous laugh. "Are you serious?"

"Why not?" she replied.

"The Wise One is right," Bawb said. "Partnered with a magical rider and an AI support craft bearing a pilot from this realm, they would be a formidable means of law enforcement."

"I have to say, it makes sense," Daisy agreed. "Things might get crazy again, and we can't be the ones to handle every single problem."

"Yeah," Charlie said. "But where are we going to find recruits to ride on a dragon?"

Leila nudged him and pointed at Kara and the other rapt teens' faces. "I don't think that'll be too hard," she said, her hand resting on her still-flat belly. "And someday, maybe we'll have a dragon rider of our own."

ALSO BY SCOTT BARON

Standalone Novels

Living the Good Death

The Clockwork Chimera Series

Daisy's Run

Pushing Daisy

Daisy's Gambit

Chasing Daisy

Daisy's War

The Dragon Mage Series

Bad Luck Charlie

Space Pirate Charlie

Dragon King Charlie

Magic Man Charlie

Star Fighter Charlie

Portal Thief Charlie

Rebel Mage Charlie

Warp Speed Charlie

Checkmate Charlie

Odd and Unusual Short Stories:

The Best Laid Plans of Mice: An Anthology

Snow White's Walk of Shame

The Tin Foil Hat Club

Lawyers vs. Demons

The Queen of the Nutters

Lost & Found

ABOUT THE AUTHOR

A native Californian, Scott Baron was born in Hollywood, which he claims may be the reason for his rather off-kilter sense of humor.

Before taking up residence in Venice Beach, Scott first spent a few years abroad in Florence, Italy before returning home to Los Angeles and settling into the film and television industry, where he has worked as an on-set medic for many years.

Aside from mending boo-boos and owies, and penning books and screenplays, Scott is also involved in indie film and theater scene both in the U.S. and abroad.

Made in United States
North Haven, CT
01 December 2024

61192545R00221